Praise for Stephanie Rowe's paranormal novels

"Rowe is a paranormal star!"
—J.R. Ward, #1 *New York Times* bestselling author of *Lover Mine*

"A hilarious underworld romp filled with mayhem, sass, and romance to die for."
—Katie MacAlister, *New York Times* bestselling author of *Love in the Time of Dragons*

"Stephanie Rowe has penned just what the paranormal genre needs—zany romantic comedy with a twist."
—Lori Handeland, *New York Times* bestselling author of *Chaos Bites*

"Rowe carves out her very own niche—call it paranormal romance adventure comedy."
—*Publishers Weekly*

"Snappy patter, goofy good humor and enormous imagination... [a] genre-twister that will make readers... rabid for more."
—*Publishers Weekly*

"Hilarious... blissfully bizarre."
—*Booklist* (starred review)

KISS AT YOUR OWN RISK

STEPHANIE ROWE

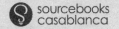

sourcebooks
casablanca

Published by Sourcebooks Casablanca, an imprint of Sourcebooks, Inc.
P.O. Box 4410, Naperville, Illinois 60567-4410
(630) 961-3900
FAX: (630) 961-2168
www.sourcebooks.com

Printed and bound in the United States of America.
QW 10 9 8 7 6 5 4 3 2 1

*For Ariana, my best friend, my joy,
my laughter, and my heart.*

Chapter 1

WHEN THE BLACK SKULL AND CROSSBONES CARVED into Alexander Blaine Underhill III's left pec began to smoke, he knew tonight wasn't the night he was going to get his newest cross-stitching tapestry finished. His escape from the Den of Womanly Pursuits, the hellhole he'd been imprisoned in by a black witch for the last hundred and fifty years, was about to get complicated. "Look pretty, boys, we're going to be entertaining."

"Shaved two days ago. Good enough?" Nigel Aquarian was sprinting beside Blaine, his shitkickers thudding on the stainless steel floor of the Hall of Embroidery. He was wearing only dark leather pants and a pale pink rose tattooed on his left cheek. His palms had turned to blackened charcoal, and burning embers were sloughing off onto the floor. "Forgot the cologne, though. Never remember to smell nice after I party with starving piranhas." He held up the pinkie finger he'd had time to grow back only halfway. "I hate fish."

Blaine leapt over a breeding pit for vipers that was blocking his path. "Spiders are worse."

Nigel grimaced. "Bet the witch is good with spiders."

Blaine refused to revisit that particular hell in his mind. "Toughened me up. It was fun."

Nigel shot him a knowing look. "Yeah, I bet it was."

One hundred and fifty years at the non-existent mercy of Death's grandma, Angelica, had given new meaning to the definition of hell. The black witch was diabolical in her quest to become the most powerful practitioner in history, and she wasn't exactly the nurturing type when it came to her experiments. Ruthless evil bitch from hell was probably a better way to describe her. But after a century of planning their escape, it was finally *hasta la vista* time for Blaine and his boys.

Blaine flipped a grin at one of the security cameras he'd disabled only moments before. "Hope you miss us." He was so jonesing for a little *mano a mano* to make her pay for all she'd done, but his brain was the one thing she hadn't managed to mess with, so he was hitting the road instead of gunning for a battle he couldn't win. Embarrassing as hell that one grandma could kick the shit out of four badass warriors. Not going to be posting that on his online dating profile when he got out.

Green and pink disco lights began to flash, and the screams of men being tortured filled the air.

"The fire alarm? Come on, guys. Can't you two keep the smoke in your pants for five minutes?" Jarvis Swain sprinted up beside them. A checkered headband was keeping his light brown hair off his face, and he was streaked with sweat and blood from the spar he'd been winning when Blaine had pulled the trigger on the escape. For Jarvis, a practice session ended only when his opponent was on the bleeding edge of death. He was clenching his samurai sword in his fist.

"Nice pants." Nigel nodded at the yellow tulip cross-stitched on the hip of Jarvis's badass martial arts outfit. He raised an eyebrow at Blaine. "Is that your delicate touch, Trio?" His question smacked with friendly insult.

Blaine ignored Nigel's sarcastic reference to his pedigree. Far as he was concerned, everyone he was related to could go to hell. Hoped they already had, in fact.

He looked over his shoulder to check on the progress of the most important member of their team, Christian Slayer, but the Hall of Embroidery was empty. "Where's lover boy?"

"He detoured for his girlfriend when we passed through Flower Appreciation." Jarvis hurled his sword at a small black box tacked onto the seventeen-foot high ceiling. "He caught her scent, said she was nearby, and took off to get her." The blade hit cleanly, sparks exploded, and the alarm went silent.

Without breaking stride, Blaine leapt up and grabbed the sword. "We're in the middle of a daring escape from our own personal torture chamber, and he's taking time to get a girl?"

"That's what he claimed," Nigel said. "He can't lie worth shit, so I tend to believe him."

They continued to haul ass toward the door at the end of the hallway. Freedom was less than fifty yards away. "Well, damn." Blaine hurled the sword blade-first at Jarvis's heart. "That's really sweet of him."

Jarvis snatched the sword out of the air easily, his hand unerringly finding the handle. "You think?"

"Sure. It's not every man who will strand his team in a war zone so he can go rescue a girl." Still running hard, Blaine pulled out a pair of small blue balls from a sack strapped to his hip. "Of course, I'm going to have to kick the hell out of him for doing it, and there's no way he's going on future missions with us, but I admire that kind of choice."

The three men he'd handpicked to escape with were the only residents of the Den of Womanly Pursuits he'd trust with his life. He didn't take loyalty lightly, and neither did his team. Yeah, Christian's detour showed that honor could be a liability, but Blaine was down with that kind of cost. Anyone who refused to leave someone behind had his vote, no matter what the repercussions were.

He heard the muted pitter-patter of little feet skittering around the corner behind them, and he swung around to face their pursuers, spinning the blue balls in his hand. Instinctively, one hand went to the long tube he'd strapped to his hip. Just checking to make sure the one cross-stitching project he was taking with him was still secure.

It was.

"Personally, I think he's lost his sense of perspective." Nigel planted himself at Blaine's right shoulder and extended the burning embers of his hands toward their oncoming pursuer. "Getting laid has completely compromised his ability to think clearly. I'm thinking celibacy is the way to go. You boys in?"

Blaine snorted. "Sex can be good for the brain. Depends on the situation." Blaine's blue balls caught fire, and he swiveled them in his palm. He wanted to toss those suckers at the bastards on their tail, but he'd blow Christian to hell if he were in the middle of the pack. Where was the slacker?

"How would you know whether a man's brain gets fried when he gets laid?" Jarvis asked. "When was the last time you got some, Trio?"

"A real man doesn't discuss his conquests." Blaine caught the faint scent of kibble and he stiffened, hoping he was wrong about what was after them. Yeah, a good battle was fantastic for achieving inner peace, but some things really were the stuff of nightmares.

Jarvis barked with laughter. "A real man keeps a journal and reads it to his sex-deprived buddies. Last action we got was the stick figures Nigel painted on the bathroom wall with toothpaste."

They'd all agreed long ago that the forced intimacy with Angelica didn't count as sex. Some things had to stay sacred.

Nigel shot Jarvis an annoyed look. "Don't knock my artistic talents. You're just jealous because you can't knit your way out of a weekend of torture with the witch."

"I choose to suck at knitting. Being subjected to another of her experiments makes me tougher." Jarvis began to whip his sword over his head in a circle. The air crackled with the energy he was generating. "You're the pansy, choosing to make beautiful pictures so she's happy with you and lets you skip out on the torture."

"I like to paint." Nigel's unapologetic tone was a truth that Blaine knew they all felt. Anything they could do to get through another hour, another day, under the blonde despot's reign was a victory. Nigel was lucky she'd chosen painting for him, because the lightweight actually dug it.

Counted cross-stitch hadn't exactly been a mental haven for Blaine.

His team was comprised of the only four men left from the batch of thirty boys kidnapped and brought to her realm that night a hundred and fifty years ago. Most had died. A few had been rescued. Jarvis and Nigel had hoped to be saved for a while, but Blaine had never bothered.

Even as a four-year-old, he'd known no one would come for him. He'd heard his own parents make the deal with the sorceress. Still remembered sitting there at the top of the stairs, clutching the wolf he'd just finished carving for his mom's birthday. The clunk of the animal hitting the wood floor, the snap of its leg breaking off, as he'd sat there in stunned silence, listening to his own mother hand his soul over to the devil.

He'd been no match for Angelica when she'd come to get him, and the thick scar down the length of his forearm was proof. He rubbed his hand over the mark, the last injury he'd gotten before he became her plaything and developed the ability to heal from anything.

That scar was his reminder never to trust a soul with anything that mattered to him. The day she'd dropped him on his ass in that cellar was the day he'd decided to save himself. There were times when his thirst for freedom had been the only thing keeping him going. Lying there, his life bleeding out, the witch standing over him... his refusal to die a prisoner had often been the only thing strong enough to pull him back from the edge of death.

His resilience had made him one of Angelica's favorite playthings.

And now he got to win. Rock on.

"I hate knitting. My hands are too damn big for all those little knit/purl things." Jarvis flexed his fingers as he moved beside Blaine. Shoulder to shoulder to shoulder, in strict formation. The witch tried to emasculate them with womanly pursuits so she could control them, but she'd also wanted her warriors to be tough as hell. She had no idea how far they'd taken it.

Today was her lucky day. She was about to find out.

"Knitting is about finesse, not the size of your hands." Thick black smoke flowed out of Nigel's palms. "It seems to me that you have a mental block about it."

"Nigel does have a point, Jarvis." Blaine focused his energy into his chest. The skull and crossbones mark burst into flames, and he opened himself to the pain. *Bring it on.* "I've seen you do some good detail work with the knitting needles when you're in the zone." The flames licking at his chest were orange. Not hot enough. He thought of the last time he'd been alone with Angelica, and what she'd done to him. Fury rose hard, and the flame turned blue-white. Now that's what he was talking about.

Then their assailant arrived. The first of the schnoodles rounded the corner, teeth bared, ears pinned. Blaine tensed as it erupted into frantic yapping. *Dammit.* He'd wanted to be wrong.

It could have been the demons.

It could have been the pit vipers.

But no. She'd sent the schnoodles.

Their odds of making it to freedom had just gone to hell.

———— ⁓ ————

"Seven days until you're murder free!"

"Nothing like jinxing me to add to the challenge," Trinity Harpswell teased (okay, maybe there was a little bit of seriousness, aka panic, there as well as teasing). She raised her water and clinked it against the wineglass of her best friend, Reina Fleming. It felt a trifle premature to be celebrating breaking the black widow curse, but she was down with trying to stay positive. She'd made it this far, right? It was all about having the faith. "I can make it a week, don't you think?"

Trinity was wearing flip-flops and a black pencil skirt so narrow that she was reduced to a penguin waddle when wearing it. An outfit chosen specifically to make it difficult to sprint after unsuspecting prey if the curse decided to have its merry way with her morals, ethics, and basic human values.

She was so not loving that feeling of spiraling out of control. That moment when the lights got too bright, when her heart started to race, when her mind was screaming at her not to do it, and somehow, someway, she couldn't stop herself yet again. The black widow curse was decidedly ruthless in its drive to get her to fall in love and force her to send the guy gallivanting off to the Afterlife. Not the stuff teenage dreams are made of, for sure. Or the dreams of twenty-nine-year-old single gals either, actually.

"Of course you're going to make it." Reina was wearing a sparkly red cocktail dress and strappy sandals. Her auburn hair was in an updo, and her eyes were dancing with the thrill of life, as they always were. Her positive, uplifting spirit had buoyed Trinity so many times, and she treasured her friend. "You've made it almost five years. What's another week?"

"I don't think the curse is going to let me go without a fight. Something's coming. I can feel it." Trinity leaned back in her chair, not quite able to keep the worried tone out of her voice. "I had this dream last night that I was walking through the Boston Common, and this marching band of really nice guys came by and they wanted to buy me dinner and then I killed them all." Her stomach churned at the memory. "And they were all dads. And now their kids have no dad and their wives are all single moms and—"

"Stop!" Reina tossed a roll at her. "For heaven's sake, girl, you need to get a grip. You aren't going to orphan any kids or take out an entire fleet of guys. You're not that bad!"

"You don't live in my body. I can feel this darkness pulsing inside me. All the time. It's freaky." A flirty giggle caught Trinity's attention, and she glanced over at the table beside them.

A twenty-something couple was just arriving. The woman was wearing a beautiful off-white dress, and the man flashed dimples at her as he pulled out her chair. The gal beamed up at him as he guided her into the seat, his hand light on her back with the tenderest of touches. They both smiled, and then he bent and brushed his lips over her cheek.

Trinity propped her elbow on the table, chin in her palm, and sighed. "Okay, that's the sweetest—"

"Hey!" Reina grabbed Trinity's arm.

Trinity tensed and looked at her friend. "I did it again, didn't I?"

"You have *got* to stop noticing nice guys." Reina pointed at herself with her first two fingers. "Focus on me, killer girl. You know it's no good for you to be looking at love. It gets you all worked up, and then I have to sit on you to keep you from killing the poor guy."

Trinity almost laughed. "Somehow I don't think you sitting on me would stop me if I was really caught in the thrall."

"I know. You're crazy girl when you fall in love." Reina twirled her goblet between the tips of her fingers. "You know, I have to say I'm completely impressed you've gone this long without killing. You've done good, girl."

The words released some of her tension, and Trinity felt a sudden thickness in her throat. "Thanks. I appreciate it."

Reina sat back in her chair and faked a sigh of exasperation. "You do realize, however, that if I ever thought you'd make it this long without knocking anyone off, I'd never have decided to become your friend."

Trinity grinned. As one of Death's most promising young talents, Reina spent her time around all things dead, which is why she'd been so attracted to Trinity when they'd first met. "Yeah, well, I'm glad you misjudged me."

Reina winked. "Me too. Your angelic ways might not be helping my career, but you still rock."

"Amen to that, sister." Trinity might have baggage, but carting people off to the Afterlife didn't exactly make Reina one of the most popular girls on the block either. Most human and Otherworld beings could sense her aura of death, and they naturally shied away from her, some without even understanding why they were doing it.

Admittedly, Trinity had been a little wigged by Reina when the feisty stranger had shown up at her apartment door armed with a chocolate cake and an offer to be friends, but in the end, it had been too much to resist bonding with someone who knew what she was like and still dug her, even if Reina did have a vested interest in capitalizing on Trinity's mistakes.

A perfect, enduring friendship between a couple of freaks.

Reina leaned forward. "So, your black widow curse expires Sunday night at seven fifteen, right?"

"Assuming I don't kill anyone between now and then, yep." Trinity had etched that date in her mind five years ago, when she'd forced herself to visit her last true love in the morgue, her ice cream cone still lodged in his carotid. She'd stood over his mint chocolate chip scented body and vowed to him that she would break the cycle, that no one else would fall victim to the blackness coursing through her veins. The black widow curse was a fickle creature, and if Trinity could go five years without killing, the curse would leave her.

She had no clue how she'd been lucky enough to acquire the curse. No one did. She'd been kidnapped as a baby for six months, and when the police had found her in a pet store snuggling in a pile of puppies, no one had known what had happened to her.

Until she'd turned sixteen and fallen in love for the first time. It hadn't taken Trinity and her parents long to figure out what had happened, and the Internet was rife with all the info she needed to find out exactly what was wrong with her and how to break it.

Diagnosis: Evil killer bitch. (Sigh.)

Treatment: Abstain. (Yeah, so easy. Not. Way harder than giving up caffeine and chocolate. You don't believe? Pick your worst habit and try to break it. Not so easy, eh? And you're not even compelled to do it by some wicked, supernatural force.)

Worst-Case Prognosis: Forever a murderer if she killed five times. (Up to four now. The first couple of years had been tough...)

Best-Case Prognosis: Forever free if she could go five years without killing anyone. (One week left.)

She was down to d-day, and she knew her curse wasn't going to let her go easily.

"So, not that I don't fully support killing, you know, as Death's assistant, but as your friend, I really want you to succeed." Reina twirled her wineglass between her thumb and finger. "I talked to Death and got him to offer up his cabin in Minnesota. We could take a girl's week and watch bad movies and avoid men."

"Oh, wow." Relief rippled through Trinity at the thought of escaping. "That sounds so good."

"Fantastic." Reina grabbed her iPhone and started dialing. "I'll just call him and let him know. Don't want any of his harem girls hanging around when we get there—"

Trinity set her hand over the phone. "I can't duck out on this, Reina."

Reina pried Trinity's fingers off her mobile device. "Why not? Running away is a basic human reaction when pure, unadulterated hell comes looking for you. People try to flee from me all the time. "

Trinity raised her brows. "And does it work when they hide from you?"

Reina shrugged. "Well, no, but I'm really persistent."

"And the curse isn't?"

"Mmm… true. But this is different. I mean—"

"No." Trinity leaned forward. "I need to prove to myself that I'm stronger than the curse." If she could resist temptation while under the dictates of the curse, she would be able to believe in herself, to know there was something worthy in her soul. "I need to know I'm not some evil killer who uses the curse as an excuse to do bad things."

It scared the daylights out of her whenever she got caught in the thrall and watched herself do horrible things to good people. Her family and Reina all gave the curse full credit for her actions, but she couldn't help but think that if she was good enough, strong enough, that she should be able to stop herself. She had to know what the truth was. Had to know that somewhere inside her was a person worth liking.

Reina studied her, clicking her tongue quietly. "You have no idea what a good soul you have, do you? You should see some of the scumbags I go after. *Those* are bad people—"

"Trinity? Trinity Harpswell?"

Trinity glanced up to see two women standing beside her table. They were both wearing suits and looked like consummate professional types. Probably had careers that took them into close proximity with men every day, unlike Trinity's job at a company that helped divorced women turn their lives around. Had these women been to one of the support groups? Is that how they knew her? "I'm sorry, I don't recognize you—"

"It *is* you." One of the women grabbed Trinity's hand and shook it vigorously. "I'm so happy to meet you."

Trinity shot a look at Reina, who shrugged. "Um, I think you may have me confused with—"

"You aren't the woman who singlehandedly murdered the Boston Bedtime Strangler in your own bed?"

Ohh… Trinity pulled her hand free. "His name was Barry Baldini, and he was a good man—"

"Yes, that's her," Reina interrupted. "But it's still very traumatic for her. If you don't mind—"

"Oh, of course." The woman ducked her head in

acknowledgement. "I just wanted to say that you are such an inspiration for me. The way you were able to stand up against a man who had oppressed so many women, when the cops had no clue how to stop him. You're total girl power." She gave a sheepish grin and did a little "hoot hoot" fist waving thing. "You're the reason I went to law school, and I'm now the assistant district attorney, and I put away scumbags like the Strangler every day—"

Trinity's fist clenched in her lap. "He wasn't a scum—"

"Thank you," Reina interrupted, kicking Trinity under the table. "Have a nice day."

Trinity glared at Reina as the women hurried away. "Barry wasn't a scumbag, and I don't deserve accolades for killing him. It was murder—"

"Drink, girl. You need to chill." Reina pushed her wineglass across the table. "He strangled two dozen women. The females of Boston are lucky you fell in love with him and killed him. Give yourself a break. The whole reason you started to date him is because he was such a misogynist pig that you knew there was no way you could fall in love with him. He wasn't that good of a guy, even aside from the serial killer thing."

Trinity's heart tightened at the thought of their last night together, when Barry had made dinner for her, presented her with champagne and roses, and told her she had showed him how to love himself for the first time in his life. In that moment, she had lost her heart to him, and an hour later, he'd lost his life to her. "Yes, I know he had bad traits, but beneath all that, he was a really caring and sensitive guy. I had no clue he was the Strangler when I killed him. I offed him because he was a good guy—"

"And if the rest of the world thinks you killed him because he snuck into your room to torture and strangle you, then you need to let it stay that way." Reina rolled her eyes. "You have to stop defending him. I mean, he deserved to die. He killed all those people—"

"So, anyone who kills innocent people deserves to die? Like me?"

Reina's eyes flared. "Oh, come on, don't start with that. You know you're different. You're being compelled."

"So was he. Yeah, it wasn't a curse, but it was still a compulsion. What makes me so much better?" Her parents had always told her that she wasn't a bad person, that it wasn't her fault, but how did they know? She was the only one who felt that satisfaction pulse through her when she stood over the body of a man she loved. Yeah, she was usually crying and felt like throwing up, but deep inside, there was always this feeling of pride. Maybe it was the curse. Maybe it was her true inner being.

She had to find out which it was.

"You're a good person!" Reina argued. "You—"

"Don't you understand how scared I am that I'm like Barry? That I should be killed to save everyone else from me?" Trinity fingered the heart bracelet on her wrist. The one that had "believe" engraved on each charm. "I need to know I'm different. I have to know that I'm more. The only way I'm going to prove it to myself is if I can face the curse and have enough good-ness in my soul to trump my need to kill. "

Reina sighed. "I hate it when you manage to make the insane sound logical."

Trinity let out her breath. "So, you'll help me get through this week? I'm not going to hide. I have to face it."

Reina shook her head in resignation. "Fine. I'll help you, but I still think we should take a girl's retreat at the cabin. Why risk being damned for all eternity just because you need to prove something to yourself?"

"It's complicated."

"I know. And I'll support you, but I'm going to try to keep talking you out of it." Reina took her wineglass back from Trinity, who hadn't even considered touching it.

As if she was going to lower her inhibitions with alcohol right now. Seriously.

Reina took a sip of her wine, then set the glass down on the table. "Okay, well, I was going to surprise you with this, but I feel like maybe you need some inspiration. A proverbial light at the end of the tunnel. A kick in the pants to stop you from feeling all weepy and morose about what a bad person you are."

"I'm not weepy. I'm realistic. There's a difference." Trinity picked up a roll and pulled it apart. Steam rose from it, and she inhaled the scent of fresh bread. Reina had insisted on the nicest restaurant in Boston, and it was worth it for the rolls. "And your surprises scare me. You remember when you invited Death to be a stripper at my twenty-first birthday, and my mom thought he'd come to take me?" She rolled her eyes. "I had no idea my mom could throw a baseball that hard. She actually knocked him out."

Reina winced. "Okay, so that wasn't my best effort, but this surprise is a good one." She held up her iPhone, showing a silhouette of a man leaning against a telephone pole. The photo was dark, and Trinity couldn't even make out his face in the shadows. "Assuming that you do manage to keep your hands off the jugulars of the opposite sex for the next week, I have a guy for you to meet." Mischief twinkled in Reina's pale blue eyes. "I already arranged a date with him, starting one minute after your curse expires. No time to waste, girlfriend. You deserve to live again."

"A date?" Instinctively, Trinity tensed up. Dates were such bad news. Even dating a misanthropic serial killer hadn't been enough to keep her hands clean. Seemed like the bigger jerks they were, the more she saw herself in them and felt empathy. "I can't—"

"But you *can*. That's the point. Come Sunday, you can date again." Reina grinned. "For real."

For real. Trinity took a deep breath and tried to unclench her fingers. "It feels so weird to think I could actually let myself like someone." The only dates she'd had for years had been guys intentionally picked for their degree of heinousness. The curse was ruthless in its quest for her to find true love, and she'd had to figure out how to satisfy the urges it created in her while somehow avoiding finding Mr. Right. Reina had been extremely helpful in tracking down the more scum-laden eligible bachelors for the occasional date. "How many tentacles does he have?"

"None! And no horrific stench emanating from various body parts." Reina wiggled her eyebrows. "I think he's just right for you. He's tall, really muscular, and can crush buildings simply by thinking about it."

"I don't know. I'm not sure I'm ready for that yet." Trinity took a sip of her tap water and rolled the cool liquid around in her mouth. A little ripple of hope quivered in her heart that maybe, just maybe, on Sunday she would really be in a position to date again. To trust herself. To believe she deserved the chance to be happy.

"And the best part is that he was in prison for homicide for twelve years," Reina continued. "So he won't judge you for the four boyfriends you've already killed."

"No." Trinity set her glass down. "I'm not dating a murderer."

Reina raised her brows. "That's a little hypocritical, don't you think? I mean, you did fall in love with the Boston Bedtime Strangler, plus you've left a trail of corpses behind you."

Trinity bit her lip. "If I make it to Sunday, I want to start over. Leave it behind. Begin a new life. No more deaths. Of any kind. By anyone."

Reina patted Trinity's hand. "Sweetie, I love you, and I think you're a wonderful person, but you've murdered four men. You can't suddenly become someone new. For heaven's sake, you smell like death. I can get a high off you when you're a hundred yards away. That will never change."

"It has to." Trinity began to drum her fingers on the table. "Sunday isn't only about leaving the curse behind. It's about starting over and—"

"Trin!"

She looked up at the frantic shout. Her dad, Elijah Harpswell, was running toward her, dodging the tables set with fine china. He leapt over a distinguished patron in a tux and nearly took out the man's beautifully adorned date. Elijah was wearing jeans, an old T-shirt, rainbow flip-flops, and he had wet clay splotches on his clothes.

His artist attire.

He never allowed *anything* to interrupt a sculpting session.

"Dad!" She leapt to her feet, all too aware nothing short of death would drag her dad away from work. Was it her mom? Her stomach congealed and she gripped the edge of the table. "*What's wrong?*"

Chapter 2

JARVIS LET THE SWORD DROP TO HIS SIDE AS THE schnoodle neared them. "Is she serious? A little tiny dog?" He held out his boot. "Come on, Cujo. I dare you to try to get those little teeth through my hide."

"It's not a dog." Blaine had been one of the test subjects when the witch was perfecting this particular creation. The first time, it had ripped half the skin from his body.

The second time, he'd blown it up.

And then she'd sicced forty of those puppies on him at once. That day had seriously challenged his love for four-legged creatures of any kind.

"It only *looks* like a dog." Blaine forced the fire to spread over his body. Burned like the acid the spiders had dripped on him last week. He hated arachnids.

The schnoodle launched itself into the air from a good thirty yards away, aiming straight for Jarvis.

Jarvis snorted with amusement. "Bring it on, killer." He rested the tip of his sword on the floor and leaned on the handle. "Yeah, so scary."

Blaine folded his arms and leaned against the wall. He raised his brows at Nigel. "Just watch. This'll be good."

"You'd think the karate kid would've learned not to underestimate her by now." Nigel lifted his palms, and smoking black blades slid out of his fingertips. Fiery hot branding irons that cauterized as they cut. Handy for surgery. Not so fun to have one fishing around inside your belly. And Blaine knew that for a fact because the witch often forced them to torture each other. Her primary goal had been to test their offensive and defensive talents, but she'd also wanted them to hate each other. But there was nothing like stabbing your buddy in the heart to make guys bond. Women never got that.

Jarvis sheathed his sword. "It's a freaking Chihuahua, guys. You've been watching too many horror movies—" The pooch's head suddenly elongated, its tail exploded with spikes, and barbed wings burst out of its back. Its eyes turned rose red and acid dripped from the tips of its claws. Curly fur gave way to scales, and its little pearly whites were replaced with glistening jaws of salivating saber teeth. And then it exploded forward, like a bat out of hell, right at Jarvis's throat. Jarvis dove out of the way, avoiding decapitation by about a millimeter. "What the hell's that?"

"Nice reaction time. Didn't realize you could move that fast." Blaine tracked the assault weapon screeching through the air. "Designer monster. Cross-breed a schnoodle with a shapeshifting dragon and a demon runt, and you get the perfect weapon for invading receptions at megamansions and spying on the blueblood families who prefer their dogs to be one of a kind." The schnoodemgon rose up high, hovering in midair above the men. It was too close for Blaine to use a blue ball. Even he wouldn't survive its blast.

The beat of its wings was so loud it sounded like an oncoming locust invasion, and the wind made Nigel's locks flutter. The damn things came halfway down his ass. Hauling those chick magnets around all day was half the reason the man was built like a linebacker.

"It's part hummingbird too. Look at the sucker hover." Jarvis was holding his sword in an offensive position, but not striking for first blood. Like the rest of them, Jarvis was too seasoned to launch a premature attack at an unfamiliar assailant before they knew what it was capable of. "What's it doing?"

"Trying to decide who to eat first." The mutt was getting larger, its wingspan almost up to ten feet already. Blaine's lungs tightened, and he coughed to try to clear his chest. Then his flames began to flicker, and he realized what was happening. "It's feeding off the oxygen in the air." Last time he'd had the pleasure of meeting the creature, it hadn't had that talent. Clearly, their warden had tweaked it with the goal of taking on Blaine.

For a psychotic bitch, she was impressive as hell.

Tweety Bird let out a sudden shriek and dove straight for Blaine.

He grinned. About time he could fight without having some overly controlling chick pulling his strings.

He waited. And waited. And waited. The instant his assailant entered his auric field, he triggered his flames. The explosion was instant, deafening. The creature shrieked, and the detonation catapulted it into the wall. It exploded into a pile of black dirt instantly upon impact.

"Well, I think it's safe to say that wasn't a schnoodle." Jarvis's sword was on fire from absorbing the energy from Blaine's explosion, but Jarvis and Nigel were intact. Blaine's team was well-versed in self-defense when around one of Blaine's ignitions, and they'd been quick to position themselves behind Jarvis's sword and its handy ability to absorb energy blasts. "Nice shot."

The scrabble of more feet filled the air, like thousands of fingernails on a blackboard.

Jarvis jerked his sword up. "That sounds like a lot. You think that's a lot?"

"Nah." Blaine's fingers closed around his flaming balls. One sphere would take out a large chunk of their assailants, but he didn't dare use it until he knew where Christian was. It grated at him to be rendered weaponless, and he was going to shove one of the damn balls down Christian's throat when he finally showed up. "Maybe just a few million of them. Nothing we can't handle." As a unit, they began moving toward the exit.

"Christian." It wasn't a question by Nigel. It was a statement.

"I know." Once they went through the doorway and sealed it, Christian would be left behind. He'd face the witch's wrath on his own, and she'd be more than a little cranky after losing her three favorite toys. Christian was Blaine's number one. They'd arrived the same night and bonded instantly against the brutality of the world they'd been thrust into. "Come on, Christian," he whispered. "Get over here."

"He ordered us to go without him if he didn't show." Jarvis moved toward the stone arch, Nigel on his heels.

"We wait." Blaine faced the hallway, not bothering to see if his team obeyed him. If they bailed, they bailed. He was prepared to go it alone. He always was. Yeah, he trusted them, but when the stakes were high enough, promises meant nothing. The only one he'd really trust was Christian, and the softie was off chasing skirts.

Because Christian would never leave anyone behind. And damn if Blaine would let him die for that.

The sound of toenails shifted into the beat of hundreds of wings. Shadows darkened the hallway, and Nigel swore under his breath. "It sounds like quite the celebration. You think we're invited?"

"I've always wanted to party with schnoodles." Blaine set himself on fire again, and this time he spread it to his whole body. He walked several yards into the hall.

Nigel was right behind him. "I've got your back."

"I'm in," Jarvis said.

Blaine couldn't stop from shooting them a surprised look when they came up beside him. "No shit?"

Nigel rolled his eyes. "Clean it up, Trio. At some point you've got to ditch the 'everyone abandons me' shtick and accept that we're not your mama."

Blaine shot a fireball at Jarvis's face. "I figured you'd be too scared to stand up to the bad guys."

"Hah." Jarvis snorted and flicked the sparkler away with his sword. "I just chugged a quadruple espresso. I gotta fight something. Might as well be the vicious hellion who's tortured us for the last couple of centuries."

Blaine grinned. "You need to ditch the addiction, buddy. Bad for your complexion."

Jarvis rubbed his hand over his leathery jaw. "Like a baby's bottom. The chicks dig it."

"Well, then, let's get out of here and find some to fondle you." Blaine extended his flames up to the ceiling and out to the walls and down to the floor, creating an impenetrable wall of white-hot fire. "Sure hope you boys have been practicing your battle skills."

Thousands of monsters exploded out of the darkness

before anyone could reply. Blaine reinforced his shield as the first winged fangbanger crashed into it. It shrieked and disintegrated on impact. Another came right after it. Then two more.

"Well, damn." Nigel shook the schnoodemgon ashes out of his hair as he let Blaine take the hits. "You're like one of those mosquito zappers. You should rent yourself out for garden weddings."

"I'll think about it. There's something really appealing about the idea of becoming a lawn ornament." Blaine's muscles began to tremble, and he knew the schnoodemgons were draining the air of oxygen. Since he was fifty percent fire, he'd be more sensitive to oxygen deprivation than the normal human-turned-mutant. He'd never felt weak before. Good to find out he didn't particularly like it. "So, yeah, I'm thinking Angelica bred these creatures specially to attack us."

"She figured we were going to make a break." Using Blaine as a shield, Nigel tied a bandana around his hair to get it out of his way, as he always did when he was about to get serious. "You have been a little moody and distracted lately. Not your usual chipper self. Dead giveaway, if you ask me."

Blaine grinned when he saw Nigel had painted an artistic rendition of the witch's death on the bandana. "Nice accessory."

Nigel flipped the ends out of his face. "It inspires me. Not sure why."

"Might be the rosy tint to her blood? It's kind of a cheerful color."

Jarvis peered at it. "Maybe it's the way the blood spatters look like smiley faces. Sets a friendly tone."

Nigel brushed his smoking palm over the headband, leaving behind glowing embers. "I think it's the fabric. I've always been partial to the feel of silk against my skin."

More poor bastards hit his shield in a three-pronged attack, and Blaine gritted his teeth as his defenses faltered for a fraction of a second. "You boys better suit up. Not sure how much longer I can—"

And then he sensed Christian's presence. A faint metallic taste in his mouth told him Christian was in trouble. "Christian!" He shielded his eyes against the incoming assault, searching the crowds for the one man he couldn't leave behind.

And then he saw Christian. He was down on the ground, hunched over like he'd just been disemboweled.

"Damn." Jarvis moved up beside him. "That's not good."

"Christian!" Blaine yelled. "Come on!"

"You're still here? Thought you guys would have been on the beach by now." Christian's voice was strained as he lurched to his feet. "You guys sure take your time getting the hell out of Dodge," he shouted over the roar of the wings and bug zapping.

Relief made Blaine's fire surge. "About damn time!" he yelled back. "Get your ass over here!"

To protect himself from the assault, Christian had already shifted his human skin into millions of metal scales, so his body was encased in chain-link armor, like the dive suits that shark wrestlers liked to wear. The only nonmetallic parts of him were the glowing blue orbs of his eyes. Christian's body armor was poison to anything that brushed against it. Nylon was the only protection against him, which made Blaine damned curious what other unholy attributes nylon might have. He was already planning an assortment of experiments when he got out.

The schnoodemgons were attacking Christian, and each time they touched his armor, they'd shriek and turn into a noxious red gas. The air was thick and crimson above Christian's head. He squatted and scooped a mound off the ground, and Blaine realized it was a large bundle wrapped in a nylon blanket to protect it against his scales.

Nice. "He got his girlfriend." Damn, he respected that.

A team of schnoodemgons body-slammed Christian into the ground, taking advantage of the one weakness of Christian's armor: its inability to protect him against sheer, crushing force. The buggers disintegrated upon impact, but on their heels was another crew, descending with enough speed to finish the job.

"No fair picking on pretty boy." Nigel flicked his wrist, and a dozen burning blades cut through the air, taking out the crowd milliseconds before they turned Christian into roadkill. "Step it up," he shouted. "We don't have time to save your ass."

Christian flipped him off and lowered his shoulder to shove his way through the masses of beating wings. The wind was fierce, and Blaine had to brace himself to keep from being blown over. Like lemmings, they kept at him, hundreds of them crashing and burning as they hit his field. Hello? What kind of suicidal strategy was that? Almost made him feel bad for the scaly meatheads.

Well, almost. The fact they were on the fast track to killing his team sort of balanced out the love. They were relentless and the supply endless, and he knew they'd come until they broke him. Nigel maintained his assault against the ones trying to crush Christian, and Jarvis was using his sword to absorb Blaine's energy so he didn't incinerate either Jarvis or Nigel, but this happy moment wasn't going to last forever. "How about a little hustle, lover boy?"

Christian was less than thirty yards away and moving fast when the first of the red gas from the dead schnoodemgons hit Blaine. His lungs burned, then searing pain assaulted his muscles.

"What the hell?" Nigel went down behind him, his muscles contorting visibly beneath his skin. "Yeah, I was just thinking this was getting boring, but—" His word cut off as another convulsion twisted his body.

Jarvis was still standing. "Talk to me, Trio." They all had different vulnerabilities and talents, and they discovered new ones every day. None of them knew exactly what they were capable of anymore, or what their weaknesses were. Jarvis was apparently getting away unscathed with this one. Point for him.

"Poison gas attacking muscle tissue." Blaine redirected his fire and sent it racing through his cells. He ground his jaw as the heat blistered his body, but the flames burned up the toxin... only to have it replaced immediately with his next breath. He sent another wave of cleansing through his body. "Get Nigel out of here."

"On it." Jarvis swung the twitching warrior over his shoulder and sprinted toward the door.

Christian was less than twenty feet away, and he was staggering now that Nigel wasn't there to protect against the body slams. Bright purple blood seeped out from his scales. "I think I'm going to be a cat person after this."

"Cats aren't manly." Blaine's body was shaking now with the effort of holding up the shield while using half his fire for soap duty to keep the toxins out.

"Neither is flower arranging, but I find it soothing." Christian reached Blaine. "What's the magic word?"

Blaine grinned. "Freedom." They were inches from it. Once they made it through that door, they were home free.

Christian's eyes flashed with hope. "Freedom," he repeated, his voice almost reverent.

"Let's do it." Blaine raised his arm and allowed a small window to form in the flames.

Christian dove through it, and then Blaine filled it in.

Taking advantage of Blaine's distraction and his weakening shield, another schnoodemgon hit hard, and his claws raked across Blaine's chest before it turned to toast. The gashes burned with cold, and Blaine looked down. The slashes had turned ice blue, and water was dripping from the wound. How about that, huh? It hadn't been acid oozing from their claws. It had been *water*.

Fire didn't play well with Poland Spring's finest, and neither did Blaine. An enema of ice water in his veins was freaking brilliant. Damn the bitch for being such a visionary killer.

His fire shield flickered, and then it was out.

Chapter 3

"GET DOWN!" ELIJAH REACHED THE TABLE, GRABBED Trinity by the back of the neck, and flung her under the table so hard she crashed into the center table leg and split it with a loud crack. She rolled onto her side, biting her lip against the pain shooting through her shoulder. Oy. Shouldn't at least some of her dad's strength be dissipating now that he was almost three hundred years old?

Reina's head popped down beneath the table. Her eyes danced with delight. "I smell death! Someone's going to die!"

"Really?" Oh, *man*. Trinity scrambled to her knees. Possible shoulder dislocation was so trumped by dead people.

"We need to get her out of here," Elijah said. "Reina! Get up here!"

"Oh…" Reina's smile faded. "I *really* hope it's not you that's going to kill someone." She disappeared from view, leaving only knobby knees and a short hemline behind.

"Thanks for that support." Trinity threw the linen tablecloth out of her way and crawled out.

Her six foot six father was standing on her chair, spinning in circles as he scanned the restaurant.

Trinity rubbed her shoulder and tested her range of motion. Definite *Ow!* factor, but full mobility was a good thing. "What are you looking for?"

"Martin Lockfeed."

Trinity froze mid-rotation. "*What?*"

Reina grabbed Trinity's uninjured arm and pulled her to her feet. "Who's Martin Lockfeed?"

"My first kiss." Her first love. Only the fact that he'd moved away right after the smooch, before she'd realized she'd loved him, had kept him alive. At age fifteen, it took a bit to discern the difference between thinking a boy had cooties and being in love. But once he'd left… she'd sure figured out her feelings for him. She'd spent more than a few hours on the Internet trying to find him, and she'd never forgotten him.

Elijah wiped a clump of gray clay on his jeans. "Martin's here."

"What?" Trinity's mouth went dry. "How do you know?"

Her dad shot her an impatient glance. "I drank his blood so I could track him. What do you think?"

Trinity blinked. "But drinking human blood is illegal."

"So is murder." Her dad went back to surveying the room. "Your mom and I spent a lot of money to get his family relocated so quickly, but I didn't trust the boy, so I tapped a vein before he left. Just in case."

"Excuse me, sir." A tuxedo-clad *maitre d'* lightly brushed Elijah's arm. "I'm afraid you'll have to leave."

"There!" Her dad pointed across the room, and Trinity whirled around.

She saw Martin right away. Nearly bald, he was wearing a black suit and a red bow tie. No wedding ring, but he was dining with an attractive woman in a dress that matched his crimson pocket handkerchief.

Pressure began to build in Trinity's heart instantly. She closed her eyes and imagined a purifying glow filling her chest cavity.

"What are you doing?" Reina's voice was right next to Trinity's ear.

"Meditating." But she couldn't concentrate. All she could think about was Martin, less than a room away. Of his kiss. Of the way he'd come to her cheerleading try-outs and taken her out for ice cream after she'd crashed into the captain and been banned from ever setting foot on the field again. He'd been so sweet that day.

Okay. That was *not* the smartest memory to be having right now.

She tried to clear her mind. Empty it of anything but a white light. This was her opportunity to prove she could withstand the curse. To show herself she wasn't the monster she was so afraid she was.

"Trinity!" Her dad yanked her so hard she had to grab a chair to keep from falling over. "Let's go. We'll head out the back entrance."

"Yes, sir, that would be a good idea." The *maitre d'* was hovering, and Trinity felt the heat from his presence.

Uh, oh. She shouldn't be sensing him when he was still several feet away. Warily, Trinity opened her eyes. The room seemed so bright. The lights were glaring. Hypersensitivity to heat and light meant one thing: the curse was coming to the party.

Her body was tingling like there were thousands of beetles racing across her skin. She clenched her jaw. "I can do it—"

"Trin!" Reina was in front of her now, her face pinched with concern. "You have seven days! Don't blow it now!"

"Losing the curse means nothing if I can't prove I'm stronger than it." Trinity twisted out of her father's grasp and faced Martin. She allowed the fullness of his being to flow over her. Embraced her feelings of affection for him. Let his worth settle deep in her heart. "He's a good man. He deserves to live. He's a good man—"

A rainbow prism appeared over his heart. It was sparkling as if the sun was shining on it.

"Oh, man." That was a really bad sign.

She stepped back, unable to rip her gaze away from the glittery diamond that was her guide. Her unerring map on how to kill him.

As she watched, a holographic image formed in front of Martin. The semi-transparent glittering prism took human form but it was amorphous, with neither a gender nor an identity. The 3-D figure slammed its palm onto Martin's heart. A holographic Martin clutched his chest and fell to the ground. Dead.

Again and again it killed him, repeating the move like an endless loop of murder.

It was showing her exactly how to kill him. Martin had a weak heart. If she hit his chest with enough force, it would stop his heart. Instant death.

Her muscles began to contract, little convulsions as they flexed, preparing themselves for the assault. Thirty more seconds and it would be over for her. The black widow would be in residence.

She'd failed to contain it.

Tears filled her eyes and she lunged for her purse. She tore it open and yanked out her new present that she'd bought for herself yesterday. Her heart sank when she saw the black gun sitting beside her wallet. How had she fallen this low? But she had. There was no way to deny it.

The curse was building fast and strong, faster than she'd ever felt before. Another few seconds and she'd be gone. She gritted her teeth and pulled her last resort out of her handbag.

"A stun gun? Are you kidding?" Reina gaped at the small black weapon.

Trinity's body was shaking now, and her ears were humming. She hit the power button and—

"No!" Reina ripped it out of her hand. "Do you have any idea what that will do to your childbearing capacity?"

"I can't stop myself from killing him." Trinity grabbed it back and aimed it at her leg. Then she hesitated, her finger frozen over the trigger. It felt so wrong to make this choice. To admit this kind of failure. To give up. But she could feel her blood burning in her veins, and she knew she was lost. She had no choice, not if she wanted Martin to live. She forced her fingers to close over the trigger—

"No!" Reina grabbed it and threw it across the room. "You're not some crazed beast that has to be brought down by electric shock!"

"That was *such* a bad idea." Trinity stared with horror as the gun skidded across the floor and slipped under a table at the far end of the room. On the other side of Martin. She'd have to walk right past him to get it. Her gaze flicked to Martin, and her heart began to thud. Like it was getting bigger and bigger. Oozing out between her ribs. "Martin," she whispered. She took a step toward him. Then another. And ano—

"Trinity!" Elijah grabbed her shoulders. "Your eyes are sparkling. You're seeing how to kill him, aren't you?" He moved in front of her, cutting off her view of

Martin and breaking the curse's hold on her enough for her to realize what she was doing.

"A blow to the chest," she whispered numbly. "He has a weak heart."

Elijah swore.

"Get me out of here." She hadn't gotten any stronger than last time; she was just a puppet for murder. Five years of shoring herself up, and she'd accomplished nothing. She'd failed.

"Okay." Elijah was all business now. "Reina, get her purse."

"I'm on it." Reina lunged for Trinity's bag as Elijah turned her toward the back door. His grip was tight on her arm, but Trinity twisted around to take one last look at Martin.

He was staring right at her.

They locked gazes, and she saw the flash of recognition in his face.

And then he smiled.

Her body began to tremble, and her skin was burning as if it were on fire. She strained against her dad, trying to get closer to Martin. "Dad." Her voice was strained, edged with violence. "I'm losing it."

Martin stood up and waved. "Trinity! Trinity Harpswell!"

"Oh, hell." Elijah pulled her toward the exit. "Reina! Help! The curse is making her too strong for me."

Reina grabbed Trinity's other arm.

Trinity gazed down at the hands trying to hold her. They blurred out of focus, and then her gaze sharpened. She could see every hair, every pore. She could smell the blueberry muffin her dad had had for breakfast. She could hear the blood rushing beneath their skin.

She smiled. The black widow was back. And it felt good.

Trinity pursed her lips and blew lightly on her dad's fingers. Elijah flew backwards with a shout of protest and smashed into an eight-person table against the back wall.

Reina stared at her, her grip tight. "Don't do it, Trinity. You need me."

"I know." And then she blew in Reina's face.

Reina shrieked and went careening through the air. She landed on the table Elijah had hit. It collapsed and went down under a pile of screams and bodies and shattering china.

The crash of crystal and shouts made something deep inside Trinity pulse with satisfaction, and her cringe of horror was a mere shadow at the edges of her soul. She laughed softly, amused by her spineless aversion to doing what she wanted to do. The tenderhearted side of her would soon be gone. She would be free.

And Martin would be the one to liberate her. She turned toward him. "Martin," she whispered. His smile was gone, his face shocked as he gazed at the carnage of the five-star restaurant. The horror in his expression touched something inside her, and a tenuous thought whispered through her mind. *I'm so sorry, Martin.*

And then she launched herself at him.

The first wave of schnoodemgons hit Blaine so hard he felt like his body had been ripped apart. Teeth sank into his wrists and ankles, and then his assailants began to pull in four different directions. The air echoed with a high-pitched cackling that sounded suspiciously like the witch when she'd had too much champagne.

His joints began to stretch, and he realized they were going to pull until they literally ripped his limbs from his body. And since that wouldn't kill him, that would kinda suck. Cross-stitching would be extremely difficult.

"On a scale of one to ten, how would you rate the pain you're feeling right now?" Jarvis's sword flashed past Blaine's wrist, and four schnoodemgon heads went flying.

"Not even on the charts. Below zero." Blaine was already stumbling to his feet by the time he hit the ground. His legs weren't working particularly well, and water was still oozing from his pores.

Jarvis took out three more nasties with one sweep of his sword. "You're leaking all over my new boots."

"I needed a shower. I like to smell fresh and pretty for the girls." Blaine sloshed toward the door and swore as more claws raked into him. "Go!"

As one, Jarvis and Blaine drove through the opening, and Nigel and Christian slammed the door shut. Blaine rolled onto his side as another beast attacked. For a moment, all four men went into battle mode to take out the dozens of creatures that had made it through the gate with them.

But three minutes of party time left five people and no mutant canines alive.

The hard edges of Christian's scales began to melt into each other. For a split second, his body appeared to be a single piece of smooth, molten metal, and then in a rapid flash of movement too quick to decipher, the shiny material morphed into human flesh. Naked and bare, it took less than another three seconds for body hair to appear, leaving Christian with two days' worth of stubble and dark hair perfectly coiffed. No matter what state Christian was in when he went scaly, he always returned the same: whiskers and gelled hair. Just how the witch liked her men. Christian immediately shoved his hand through his hair and messed it up. "Well, damn. I'm going to miss that kind of fun."

"Almost makes me feel a little teary to be leaving." Blaine touched his hip to make sure his cardboard carrier was still intact as he glanced around the room they'd never accessed before. Just as they'd reconned, it was a foyer, and stainless steel webbing laced through the glass window of the door. Blaine limped over and looked out.

Nothing to see but gray mist. Beyond the swirling clouds lay freedom. He wanted to slam his fist through the glass and get the hell out, but he couldn't risk touching the metal. Now wasn't the time to be getting handicapped by the allergic reaction to stainless steel that the witch had spliced into all the men. Blaine and his team had spent decades learning to work with it in secret. They'd taught themselves to tolerate it, but it was Christian who had developed the strongest talent for manipulating it. It was his skills they were banking on to break through the window.

"You sure there's life out there?" Nigel was flexing his arms, trying to work the poison gas out of his muscles. "I'll be pissed if we get out there and it's just mist."

"It's a portal," Blaine said. "The smoke hides her lair from others so no one can see it." Once they left, they wouldn't be able to find their way back, even if they wanted to.

Odds of that? Not so high.

Christian squatted beside his cargo and untied the bag. It fell away, revealing his girlfriend, Mari Hansen. Her brown hair was matted, her face was pale, and she was trembling. She grabbed for Christian and they hugged tightly for a moment. Blaine still didn't get what Christian saw in her. The gal was too weak and fragile, and Blaine had a bad feeling she'd never survive on the outside.

But she'd won Christian's heart when the witch had assigned her to monitor his demise after a lethal experiment. The minute Mari had walked in to start documenting his decay, something in Christian had woken up. He'd recovered fully, and for that, Blaine would always be grateful to Mari, even if she didn't set quite right with him.

Maybe it was simply the fact she was the witch's apprentice and she'd been present for far too many of his torture sessions. Yeah, she was a prisoner like the rest of them, but she didn't look as uncomfortable as he'd have liked when she was documenting Nigel shoving hot pokers through Blaine's heart.

Not that it mattered now. They were getting out. Christian could deal with the reality of his new relationship without being under the auspices of the witch.

Blaine passed his hand over the stainless steel window standing between him and freedom. "Christian. Now."

"You got it." Christian started to stand.

Mari grabbed his arm. "Wait, Christian, my leg—"

"We'll have to fix it later, my love." Christian gave her a quick kiss that turned carnal.

"Christian," Blaine snapped. "Later!"

"Right. Sorry." Christian wrenched himself out of Mari's grasp and jogged over to the window.

What the hell was Mari offering that could get Christian to suck face when freedom was inches away? Made no sense. Blaine eyed the chit as she struggled to her feet. Her ankle was swollen and turning purple. She must have been bitten through the bag. "Christian!" She set her hands on her hips. "I need help."

Did she really think her ankle mattered right now? "Hey." Blaine caught her arm and turned her toward him. "Not now." He gestured at the door. The pounding of schnoodemgon bodies against it was deafening, and the door was bulging from the impact. Trickles of the noxious red smoke were leaking through cracks. "Right now is not about you."

Mari paled. "How long until that breaks?"

Nigel and Jarvis were weapons out, facing the archway. "Two minutes," Nigel said. "Max."

Mari made a small noise of distress, and she looked up toward the ceiling.

Blaine followed her gaze and saw there was a twenty-four-inch vent above his head, plenty big enough for any assortment of mutant predators to fit through. "Christian?"

"Five seconds." Christian placed his hands on the glass. His palms began to smoke, but he kept them there. He closed his eyes and leaned his head back.

Jarvis began whipping the sword over his head, faster and faster, until the air crackled with a loud humming. Energy filled the room, and Blaine's skin prickled. Metal ridges appeared on Christian's shoulders, and they began to vibrate in time with Jarvis's humming. Christian was channeling both his own energy and Jarvis's into his palms so he could generate enough force to break the stainless steel webbing.

Still keeping one eye on the ceiling vent, Blaine edged up next to Christian. He'd never seen Christian absorb energy at this intensity, but they'd decided that it had to be done if he had any chance of breaking through the stainless steel quickly enough. The witch controlled the metal, and it was like a living creature bending to her will.

Christian's shoulder ridges thickened, and the glass began to vibrate beneath his smoking palms. Blaine could feel the pressure building on the other side of the door. His team was so weakened that they wouldn't survive a full-scale attack if the schnoodemgons broke through.

It was now or never.

Blaine did an internal scan and felt sparks flickering in his body. He was drying up and the flames were returning. "Can you take it if I add my power?"

Christian was sweating now. "Do it."

Blaine set his hand on Christian's shoulder and thrust his own energy into the other man.

Christian gagged and his body convulsed, and then the window exploded.

The glass was still tinkling to the floor when Nigel vaulted through the opening. He was first, as they'd planned. He'd use his knives to take down any assailants. Jarvis was on his heels and the two men disappeared into the mist. Into freedom.

Blaine and Christian looked at each other, and something shifted between them. "You first," Blaine said.

Christian shoved himself to his feet, ignoring the muscle twitches making his head vibrate back and forth. "No." Christian walked over to Mari. "I need to go last. Mari's energy will close the portal. She has to be at the end, and I'm going to go with her."

Like the men, Mari had been kidnapped by the witch as a child, but that was where the similarity ended. Mari had been gifted with the witch's tender loving care, and she'd been groomed as her assistant. The witch regularly sent Mari and the other women into the mortal world to retrieve new children or items for her, confident that they were so tied to her they would always come back. The energy signatures of the women had been manipulated to trigger the closure of the portal after they went through it. It always stayed shut for seventy-two hours, a precaution to keep others from following in their path as they went back and forth.

Blaine didn't like leaving Christian behind, but there was no other option. If Mari went first, she would strand them. He slammed his hand down on Christian's shoulder. "I'll see you on the outside."

"On the outside," Christian agreed as he put his arm around Mari. She was looking up at the ceiling vent again. Blaine narrowed his eyes and then he passed his hand between the woman and the vent. His hand sparked.

"She's sending energy up there." His skull and crossbones mark began to smoke. "She's betraying us." His fist caught fire.

"No!" Christian shoved her behind him. "Don't kill her. She's knocking out anything that tries to come down there after us."

Mari was backing away from Christian, and she was staring intently at the vent. Her mouth was moving quickly as she whispered something. Now that she wasn't trying to hide her energy, Blaine could see a pale green light filtering up, almost like dust in the sunlight. "Stop," he snarled. "Now."

"There's something up there," she said. "I'm holding it off."

Blaine swore. "Christian—"

"Go. We'll be right behind you." Christian met his gaze. "You really think I'd screw up my chance for freedom? I know I can trust her."

A loud crash made them both turn toward the interior door. A two-inch crack had opened, and claws were sticking though, trying to rip it apart.

"I hope you're right. I'll be watching her once we get out." Blaine turned and sprinted toward freedom. He hoisted himself up through the window and shoved his feet through first, making sure the tube with his cross-stitching project didn't catch on the frame.

His skin went numb when it hit the mist, and a prickling sensation crawled up his legs, to his hips. The smoky tendrils began to pull him away from the door. "It's working."

Christian grinned. "I can't wait—"

A loud shriek ripped through the air and Christian swung around as a pair of shapely legs appeared in the vent. *The witch.*

"Hurry, Angelica!" Mari shrieked. "They're getting away."

Christian's face went cold with betrayal at her words. Blaine felt something in his own gut rip apart for the anguish on his friend's face. Mari had been using him all along.

The witch dropped through the vent. She was wearing Seven for All Mankind jeans that hugged her tight ass and a silver tank top that showed off assets that had been the product of many, many experiments. She set her hand gently on Mari's shoulder, tenderness she had never showed the men. Her blond hair was tossed around her shoulders, her eyes were frigid green, and she had a ruthless smile on her face that made Blaine's other fist ignite. Ready to defend himself.

"You boys did well," she said. "I'm impressed."

"Christian!" Blaine lunged to get back to the window, fighting against the mist that was tugging him away from the building. He grabbed the frame and hung on. "Come on!"

His friend bolted for the window and he leapt for the opening. Blaine reached through the window, and he caught his buddy's wrist. Christian's hand clamped around his, and Blaine stopped fighting the grip of the mist. It sucked him back, and he began pulling Christian through the window with him.

"No!" The witch held up her hands and flicked both of them at the warriors. Noxious goop exploded from her skull and then dozens of tentacles laced with poison spikes shot forth and wrapped themselves around Christian's torso.

Christian's face paled and he looked at Blaine. "Too late," he gasped. "We're too late."

"No! Dammit! Hold on!"

Christian's grip went slack as the strength drained from his body, and his skin turned ashen. Blaine fought to keep his hold on his friend, but the mist was relentless and the tentacles were too powerful. His flingers began to slide off Christian's wrist. "Hang on, dammit!"

Christian willed his head up and he met Blaine's gaze. "Live for me," he whispered.

And then the mist ripped them apart.

Chapter 4

IT HAD BEEN FIFTEEN YEARS SINCE TRINITY HAD SEEN Martin Lockfeed, and all she could think about was how much she had loved him.

Which meant it was time for him to die. Irony at its finest.

Trinity tore across the five-star dining room toward him, and smiled as she saw his eyes widen. Something inside her screamed at her to stop, but it was lost in the sound of the wind as she rushed across the luxurious wood floor. Like a slow-motion horror show, she neared him, closing in on him, on death.

She had to stop. Had to find a way. But her body kept going. Driven by a force stronger than her own willpower (willpower? self-restraint? what's that?). Less than two yards away, she raised her hand to pound it against his chest and—

Her dad tackled Martin from the side and shoved him out of her path. The two men tumbled across a private table for two, and Trinity slammed her hand down into the empty space where Martin had been. The momentum catapulted her past his table and she crashed into the wall.

Stunned, she staggered backward, dry bits of plaster caking her mouth like a stale rice cake. She had to find Martin. Where had he gone? She spun around, but the restaurant had erupted into screams and chaos. People everywhere.

"Trin!" Reina grabbed her arm. "What have you done?"

"Nothing, yet. Where is he?" Her body was shaking with the need to finish what she had started. It was like this craving, crawling down her spine, into her cells.

"Look!" Reina jerked her through the crowd and pointed.

At first, all Trinity could see was her dad sprawled on the floor, blood oozing from a head wound. "Dad!"

He wiggled his pinkie in response, and she let out a shuddering breath. Of course he would be fine. It was incredibly difficult to hurt him. "He's good. It's okay."

"It's not okay. Look to his right."

That's when she saw Martin.

He was flat on his back, several feet from her dad, and a pair of dinner forks were protruding from his chest. "Oh, wow. That can't be comfortable—"

She realized suddenly that her skin had stopped burning and there was no longer a prism over Martin's heart. The chandeliers had dimmed back to an atmospheric romantic tone. The black widow had hit the road... for good?

Hah. The odds of that? Not so high. But if Spider Woman had taken off for a facial and pedicure, then that made no sense. She'd never left when there was prey ripe for the munching. Oh, man... did that mean there was no one left to kill? "Reina."

Her friend glanced over. "Yeah?"

Reina's eyes were gold with black pearlized rims, as they always were when Reina was present at a death. *So not a good sign right now!* Trinity whirled around to look more closely at Martin. This time, she saw the bleak gray tinge coating his skin, creeping up his arms toward his face. The death mites were already bringing out the champagne. Martin was dead.

Her dad had become a murderer to save her soul.

Stunned, she gripped the edge of an overturned chair to keep herself upright. Could she be any more of a failure? Almost thirty years old, and so weak she couldn't even handle her own issues without her dad turning into an assassin to protect her from herself?

She'd wanted to kill Martin. There had been no hesitation. She could still feel the anticipatory rush of taking his life. All her meditation, all her belief in herself... nothing but delusions.

Despite all her efforts, she would have killed Martin. No one could have stopped her, and in her depraved state, she'd loved that feeling of power. She'd thought it was fantastic to shove the two people she loved most against that table.

Yeah, the motivational speaker she'd listened to on her iPhone this morning had been all into appreciating yourself as step one in overcoming addictions, but who in God's name could be feeling the self-love right now? *Hi, I'm a murderer, and I think it's the coolest thing ever that I can't stop myself from killing people I love. Group hug, everyone?*

Numbly, she watched Martin's date kneel beside him.

"I'm so sorry, Martin," Trinity whispered. She hadn't gotten better. She'd gotten *worse*.

She forced herself to watch as his date leaned close. Made herself listen to the words of anguish. As if maybe, just maybe, something in the woman's grief would touch a chord inside Trinity and awaken the humanity she was beginning to doubt existed within her.

"Martin, my love." His date laid her hand on his shoulder and lowered her mouth to his ear. "This serves you right, you cheating bastard. I hope the fires of hell feel good on your lying ass."

Trinity blinked as his date slipped her hand into his lapel jacket, filched his wallet, then marched out of the room, not a tear in sight.

Reina started laughing beside her. "Oh, man, you have such the knack for falling in love with winners. Did you see that? That's a true quality relationship right there."

Trinity scowled at her. "It's not funny. It doesn't change the fact that I'm a freaking murderer."

"Yeah, but you have to admit, it's a little humorous, you know, given the whole Barry the Serial Killer thing—"

A lady in a black cocktail dress and a look-at-me-now diamond necklace pointed at Elijah who was still sprawled on the ground. "Someone call the police! That man murdered him!"

The shouts of the onlookers sliced through Trinity's damning self-assessment. She couldn't let her dad pay the price of the death that should have been her responsibility. "Dad!" She jumped up and raced over to him. "Grab our stuff, Reina."

Reina held up Trinity's purse. "Still have it from the last escape attempt. Efficiency is always handy when death and destruction are involved."

"Excellent." Trinity hooked her dad under the arms and dragged him across the floor. Without the curse in its active state, she wasn't much stronger than an average five foot four human female. "Wake up. You're heavy as hell." Damn his six and a half foot sugar-addicted hide. People were swarming now, shouting at her not to take him outside.

"I've got him." Reina tossed Trinity her purse and then hoisted him up on her shoulder. "Call your mom."

Reina had been around for Trinity's last assassination five years ago, and she knew the drill. How pathetic was that? That her best friend knew the family's process for covering up a murder and moving to a new location? They actually had a process, for God's sake!

But times like this, she was glad they did. Trinity fished her phone out of her purse and ran after Reina, who was clearing a path with strategically placed laser-like shots of death powder. People were sneezing and turning ashen with indeterminate fear as they stumbled back from the nightmare they couldn't quite put their finger on.

Her mom answered on the first ring. "Tell me he got there in time!"

"We need a relocation. Now."

"Oh, Trinity!" Olivia sounded heartbroken. "You didn't kill someone, did you?"

"I didn't. Dad did."

"Dad?" Her mom's voice was incredulous. "How in the world did he manage that?"

"Mom!"

"Right, for later. Well, thank God it was your father who did the killing today. I'll be there in three minutes. Find a patch of grass, and I'll come get you. Bye, hon." Trinity's mom had an intimate relationship with Mother Nature, and using plants to travel was one of the more handy benefits. Unfortunately, Trinity hadn't inherited it. Hadn't inherited Olivia's ability to refrain from murdering either. Oh-for-two.

Reina tossed her an amused grin as they hurried down

the hall past the screaming patrons. "Your family is too cool. I just love them."

Trinity grabbed Reina's arm. "I won't risk anyone anymore. Call your boss. Tell him we're going to the cabin in Minnesota. No more deaths."

Reina let out a sigh of relief. "Good call, girlfriend. That's the smartest choice. You're doing the right thing."

"I know." But it felt so awful. It was an admission that she was a failure, but she wouldn't risk any more lives just so she could love herself. Today had been too close, and even if Martin was a lying, thieving bastard, it wasn't her role to decide when he got his permanent tropical vacation. "Call him."

"As soon as I get your dad outside—"

Elijah suddenly lifted his head and slid out of Reina's grip. "I don't need to be carried." He landed without a whisper of sound on his feet, then stumbled.

Trinity caught him as he tried to right himself, frowning at his weakness. "That was foolish for you to kill for me. You know how badly that affects you." It would take him several years to heal even the small scratch on his forehead. Even accidentally stepping on a bug depleted him severely. Taking a person's life? It would take him at least six months to be able to walk normally again. And his pottery... she shuddered. He'd be sculpting some seriously scary things for a while.

Elijah laid his hand on her cheek. "Oh, Trinity, if you had any idea what your mother and I owe you. I'd kill a thousand times to keep you from doing it."

The heavy guilt in his tone made her stiffen. "What are you talking about? What do you mean, you owe me?" She was the one who owed them. Her parents had put their lives on hold to help her beat the curse. She owed them so much, and they were part of the reason she'd had to test herself.

She had to be worthy of what they'd sacrificed for her.

And apparently she wasn't. And that felt really, really good. Not.

Elijah glanced at Reina, as if debating whether to speak in front of her. "There's something you should know about your curse."

Trinity stopped walking. "What else could there possibly be?" Things were even worse than she'd thought? Hallelujah. Just when she'd thought life was boring, nothing like a little unexpected bomb to juice things up. "What have you not told me?"

Elijah winced. "When you were a baby—"

The front door burst open and in walked a wizened man with cinnamon-colored skin. He was wearing faded jeans, a battered T-shirt, and an ancient fedora. His beard was ratty and gray against his dark complexion, and he was so hunched he could barely lift his head enough to make eye contact.

And he smelled like overripe banana.

Reina stopped. "Did you catch a whiff of that?"

"Oh, yeah." Trinity averted her gaze, praying for him to walk past them into the dining room in search of someone else.

But he didn't.

He looked right at Elijah, and then smiled.

"This is really bad," Reina whispered. "Welcome to hell."

—∿—

On one level, it was kind of cool to meet a man whose trail of dead bodies numbered well into the seven figures. It was the first time Trinity had ever been around someone who made her feel somewhat angelic. And it felt good, so amazingly good, to have a brief "I'm okay" moment.

But on a more immediate level, having this particular man come in search of you was not a good thing. Really. Even if he was coming for tea, crumpets, and a friendly warning. He wasn't exactly known as a first-choice dining companion.

More like your last choice, and your last one. Ever.

He called himself Augustus.

To the rest of the world, he was better known as, "Oh, shit, it's Augustus."

He smiled.

They all flinched.

He doffed his tattered fedora and bowed low, showing a tear in the seat of his crusted jeans and an unsettling rash on the back of his head. "My name is Augustus." His voice was the cultured refinement of a blueblood born with a plaid blazer, a penchant for fine cigars, and membership at the most exclusive of golf clubs. "So lovely to meet you."

Okay, so his voice made him even creepier. Shouldn't he sound like a chain-smoking mafia underling who spent his days stalking the fish pier with a baseball bat and an attitude?

Augustus returned his hat to his head, and then held out his hand. "Elijah Harpswell. It is time."

"What?" Before her brain had registered the insanity of her action, Trinity jumped in front of her dad. "You can't have him!"

Augustus blinked, as if startled that someone would stand up to him. "No?"

Trinity noticed her dad was edging back toward the door. *You go, Dad!* "No."

"Very well. Please give me a moment." Augustus flashed his brown teeth and pulled out an iPhone. He tapped the screen a couple of times, then nodded. "Ah, yes. Did or did not Elijah Harpswell snuff the life from an innocent human with a pair of dinner forks at approximately nine thirty-one tonight?"

Trinity stared at him. "That's why you're here?"

Augustus nodded. "It is."

Okay, that made no sense at all. Augustus was for serial killers, people who tortured fairies and gnomes, and for anyone stupid enough to try to kill a member of the Triumvirate (the ruling body of arrogant, over-sexed men and women who got to make up rules and ruin lives just because they happened to elect themselves to the board in charge of all things Otherworld). When Augustus came to pick someone up, it meant the trial had already occurred, the verdict was guilty, and the execution was less than a week away. No due process for Otherworld nasties who could take down the Triumvirate during an extensive trial process. "But you're at the top of the assassin food chain. Why would you be sent to deal with the accidental death of one mortal?"

August smiled again. "Thank you for the kind words. I always appreciate compliments. I take my work very seriously." He cocked his head. "Not many people appreciate my skills, but you do, don't you?"

Oh, she was so not going there. "I'm sure there's been a mistake. Elijah isn't a danger to—"

Augustus reached into his pocket and pulled out a small, pink star with barbed points.

"Uh, oh." She stepped back, and Elijah broke for the door.

Reina leaned forward to peer at it. "Huh. That's so much smaller than I thought it would be—"

Augustus chucked the star at Elijah's face.

"Don't catch it!" Trinity yelled.

But it was too late. Her dad instinctively nabbed the star with his left hand to protect his face. He screamed immediately, and his hand disintegrated into pink dust.

"Drop it!" Trinity leapt across the floor and tried to pry the star out of his hand... but his hand was already gone.

His arm turned pink and then disintegrated into dust, and then the rosy assault raced up his shoulder. He looked aghast as he watched himself turn pink. "This really hurts," he said. "I had no idea."

"Dad!" Trinity caught his upper body just as his legs went powdery.

"Trin." Elijah turned his head toward her as his torso began to fall apart. "I love you, and I will never regret my choice. Tell your mom I love her."

"You tell her yourself when you get out! We'll come get you—"

"No one gets out after they've been dusted."

Trinity's heart dropped at the words she knew were true, and then her dad's head turned pink. For a moment, the only things in the air were his eyes, staring at her, and then they poofed into a cloud of pink dust and were gone.

"Oh, wow." Reina brushed her hand through the air where Elijah's head had been. "I've never seen that happen in real life before. That's pretty creepy."

Augustus began to sweep up the pink dust strewn across the floor.

Trinity fought back the urge to tackle Augustus and demand the return of her father. Getting dusted herself would not help her dad. "How can I get him back?"

Augustus raised his brows. "No one comes back after I take them."

Trinity's legs began to tremble. "Please, there has to be something I can do. We both know he didn't do anything to warrant being pinked."

At that moment, Augustus's phone broke out into the tune of "If You're Going Through Hell." He didn't even bother to answer it. He simply handed it to Trinity. "For you."

"Me?" She grabbed the phone and eyed the pile of her dad while Augustus knelt down with his broom and dustpan. "Hello?"

Reina pressed her ear up next to Trinity's so she could listen.

"Trinity Harpswell?" It was a deep male voice with an edge that sounded like fingernails being scraped over a blackboard.

Reina winced, and goose bumps popped up over Trinity's body. "Yes. Who is this?"

"Press the blue icon, please. We have a deal for you."

Was he delusional? There was no way Trinity was going to get tangled up with anything having to do with Augustus or his phone. People died around him. Constantly. "No way—"

Reina caught her arm. "Your dad is bubble gum right now," she said. "What have you got to lose?"

Augustus was sealing her father in a transparent bag. He nodded and tucked her dad in his pocket. "Have a lovely day, ladies." Then he walked out the door with her dad in a Ziploc.

Trinity pressed the blue icon.

Chapter 5

BLAINE SLAMMED THE FOURTH BOTTLE OF SAM ADAMS Boston Lager down in the middle of his dining room table. "For Christian."

Nigel and Jarvis raised their beers. "For Christian."

Blaine took a long drink of the local brew, but it tasted like sand, and not the good kind. Which aggravated the hell out of him, because he loved that beer. Stolen moments with the boys and Sam A. had been some of the few good memories he had of the Den. And now that he was out? Too pissed off to even enjoy it. He tossed the bottle back onto the table next to Christian's untouched beer.

Once the mist had dumped his team in the middle of the Boston Common, they'd spent hours searching for the portal, but it was gone. Just tourists, too many damn Red Sox hats, and a bunch of ducks.

It was as if the witch's lair simply didn't exist, which, of course, was her goal. They'd finally decided to regroup and figure out a plan that actually involved strategy and some likelihood of success, so they'd secured some new digs and holed up. Cash talked, even money stolen from a psychotic witch who had created the stuff out of the ashes of dead test subjects. Blood money took on a whole new meaning with Angelica.

Blaine's new place was a top floor condo with a view of the harbor, floor-to-ceiling windows, and an expansive deck. Granite counters, stainless steel appliances, everything the realtor had said was top-of-the-line.

After a century and a half of deprivation, Blaine was going to settle for nothing but the best, and Nigel and Jarvis had bought places in the same building.

And it felt desolate without Christian there to share it.

No one had said it, but they were all thinking it. There was no plan to make, no rescue to attempt. The tentacles were bad shit. Christian was dead.

Blaine shoved his chair back. "I'm getting some more pizza."

He strode across the hardwood floor into the kitchen, but when he got there, he ignored the food. He fisted the back of a chair, leaned on it, and dropped his head. His fingers dug into the black metal, and he felt the material give beneath his grasp. "Fuck," he whispered. "I'm sorry, Christian."

"Blaine." Angelica's singsong voice danced through the kitchen.

He spun around, flames exploding from him in violent aggression. Sparks singed the wall and the floors and the cabinets, but there was no witch to kill. There was nothing in the kitchen but what was supposed to be there.

Jarvis and Nigel tore into the room, both of them fully armed. "Where is she?" Jarvis demanded.

Blaine shook his head, turning slowly around. "She never leaves the Den."

"I heard her too." Nigel's blades were out and he was ready.

"Oh, Blaine, dear."

He finally saw that the stainless steel fridge was sparkling. "There!" He hurled a fireball at the appliance and all he got was her amused chuckle.

"My delightful Blaine, you should know by now you can't hurt me."

Blaine swore and he let his flames subside to a simmer. Nigel and Jarvis had moved up behind him, facing the fridge. She was right. They'd tried hundreds of times to kill her, and they'd never so much as singed one of her artificially blond tresses. Escape had been the second choice.

The cooling unit shimmered again, and Angelica's smug visage appeared as a faint shadow in the metal. Blaine's upper lip curled in disgust and he turned his back and walked out of the kitchen without another word. The overbearing girl-power freak had no control over him anymore.

Nigel and Jarvis followed him, and they silently sat down at the table.

They all drained their beers.

"She's going to stalk us," Nigel finally said.

"Blaine!" She sounded pissed now.

He did a quick scan of the living room. There was no stainless steel for her to possess. He leaned back in his chair. "I'm thinking of remodeling the kitchen," he said loudly. "I find the stainless steel a bit austere for my tastes."

Nigel grinned. "I was thinking the same thing about my place."

"Blaine!" she yelled. "Christian's not dead!"

His hand clenched around the bottle, and his teammates went still. No one said a word.

"But he's suffering horribly," she shouted.

The bottle shattered beneath Blaine's grip, and glass sliced his palm. The witch knew suffering.

"If you bring your team in, I'll give Christian back to you," she called out. "Nigel can heal him."

Blaine shoved back from the table and walked over to the window. The sun was setting, and the city was beautiful. Miles and miles of world for him to explore, whenever he wanted. Total freedom. The witch was lying to get him back. Christian was dead. He'd failed him. No more to discuss.

"Fine. Talk to him yourself," she snapped. "I just don't understand why you refuse to trust me. When have I ever lied to you? How come men constantly confuse torture and lying?" she muttered. "They're just not the same thing."

Blaine deliberately turned around. He could see into the kitchen from this angle, and the witch's high cheekbones and long eyelashes were clearly visible. She looked aggravated, and the veins on her neck were popping out as she struggled with something.

Jarvis and Nigel edged their seats over so they could see the show.

The estrogenized dictator made a grunting sound that made Jarvis wince, and suddenly, Christian's face was next to hers in the fridge. He was ashen and fuzzy, his eyes closed and swollen. "See?" she said. "This poor sweet boy is going to pay for your escape until you three get back here." She patted Christian's cheek. "Tell them, my child. Tell them to come save you."

Christian's eyes flickered open. He was alive! Blaine sprinted into the kitchen and crouched in front of the fridge. "Hey, man, how are you doing?"

The sky-blue eyes were hazy, and he looked past Blaine. "Nice digs," he mumbled.

"The best." Blaine set his hand on the fridge, then swore when it seared his palm. It hadn't burnt him when he'd used it before. The witch had twisted the stainless steel to her control already. "You'd like it. Got a sixty-five-inch flat screen."

Christian nodded. "You keep my room open. I'll be there soon."

"Hello? There will be no off-site visitation." The witch dug her fingernails into the side of Christian's neck, and the warrior's eyes rolled back in his head. "Tell them to come home, darling. You know you all belong to me."

"Trio, if you come back for me, I'll kick your ass for all eternity." Christian opened his eyes, and his gaze was unfocused. "You'd never let me give up my freedom for you, and the same rules apply." He raised his hand, and Blaine set his palm against Christian's. The stainless was cool, and he knew Christian was easing the sting of the steel between them.

Which told him it wasn't a delusion.

Christian was really alive, and he was in Angelica's clutches.

Blaine didn't give a shit what Christian wanted him to do. He was going find a way to bring him home, no matter what the cost. He didn't care that it was an impossible task. He'd find a way.

Unlike his parents, Blaine didn't leave people behind. Ever.

-∞-

The moment Trinity's finger touched the blue icon on Augustus's iPhone, the restaurant disappeared into a world of blinding white. No contrast, no color, just a juiced up blizzard of nothingness.

Reina's fingers dug into her wrist. "This looks like heaven. I feel like I'm going to throw up."

"Augustus is involved, so there's no chance of pearly gates." But what was it? Trinity had no clue, but it was kind of unnerving her, given the close proximity of the whole bubble gum dust and murdering incidents and all. "I'm thinking this was a bad choice." She hit the blue icon again, in case that would, oh, you know, reverse the process and spit them out into a spa or something equally delightful.

No such luck, as there was a sudden din of large bells, and then they were in a cold, dank cave. It was so dark, they could barely see beyond the outline of rocks and the sound of rushing water.

"I agree. Not heaven." Reina relaxed her grip. "Gateway to Hell? River Styx, maybe?"

Trinity's stomach tightened. "Not funny, Rei. I'm a little sensitive about Hell these days."

"I wasn't making a joke, sweetie."

"Oh—" A dim light filled the cave, and Trinity quickly looked around. Stalactites hung down from the ceiling, and water dripped into a small pool of shimmering aquamarine water. Exotic pink, yellow, and blue flowers surrounded the pool, and an inviting stone bench sat beneath a palm tree on a patch of tempting white sand. A rainbow colored fish did a double flip before disappearing into the sparkly depths. The sound of bubbling water filled the air, soothing and quiet.

Or not so much. "Oh, man," Trinity said. "It's the lobby of the Triumvirate's headquarters."

"How fantastic!" Reina pulled out a digital camera shaped like a dagger and began snapping pictures. "What a great opportunity. Death will be so interested in this report. He's never been invited here." She walked closer to the sandy oasis. "I could definitely get some points for reporting this—"

"Ms. Harpswell." A tall, elegant woman in a gold gown stepped out of the wall (um, hello? Solid stone, anyone?). She was wearing black stilettos, a diamond necklace large enough to put her in the next weight class, and her platinum hair was coiffed in a perfect bun.

Trinity had no idea who the woman was, but Reina instantly did a fan-girl squeal. "It's Felicia Maguire," she whispered. "The greatest assassin ever to walk the planet. She's been so good for business. She comes for dinner all the time, but I've never been permitted to meet her."

Okay, yeah, so that was not looking like a good sign that Oh, Shit, It's Augustus had taken her dad and then sent her off to meet with a premiere assassin.

Reina held out her hand. "Hi, I'm Reina. I'm one of Death's assistants. It's really a great pleasure to meet you, Ms. Maguire."

Felicia gave Reina her fingertips. "Lovely to meet you, my dear."

Reina took a picture of Felicia. "Can you drop me a hint about your next assignment? I'd love to be there to see you in action. I can turn into vapor, so no one would know if I was observing."

A soft chuckle escaped Felicia. "My dear, I'm afraid

that's classified material." She winked. "If I told you, I'd have to kill you."

"Done." Reina bared her neck and gestured to her throat. "It would be a huge honor to have you kill me."

Felicia raised her brow. "You're immortal," she said dryly.

Reina waved her hand. "Semantics. I'll pretend to die."

Felicia's smile warmed. "I like your attitude. Maybe another time." Then her smile faded and she turned to Trinity. "Today is about you."

Trinity winced. "Yeah, I'm not really surprised to hear that."

Felicia strode powerfully across the cave, ditching the elegant walk she'd sauntered in with. She vaulted over a pile of stones, then plunked herself down on the bench. She leaned forward, resting her elbows on her splayed knees. If her dress wasn't so long, she'd be exposing all her girly parts for viewing. Interesting pose. "Here's the deal, Trinity. There's a beast running around Boston getting his jollies out of killing too many people. We've all tried to take him out. No success."

Trinity eased down onto a rock. "Um, okay."

Felicia grabbed the collar of her dress and pulled it down. There was a chunk of flesh several inches long missing. "It thought I was sexy and this was its way of asking me on a date." She paused to smile for Reina's camera. "Took me three days to recover, and it wasn't even trying to kill me." She let the neckline return to its place. "No one can figure out how to stop it, or even what it is. It changes form and none of us have seen the same image."

"Oh…" Trinity had a bad feeling where this was

heading. One of the gifts of the black widow was the ability to know how to kill any living creature, not simply the ones she was in love with. Of course, the only ones she *had* to kill were the ones she loved. Such a lovely twist. "My dad wasn't taken by accident, was he?" Had the Triumvirate set up the entire situation so they could force Trinity to help them? If so, that was damned impressive. A little creepy and Big Brotherish as well, but impressive nonetheless.

Felicia smiled. "My, what a smart girl." She handed Trinity a black kitchen timer set for six days, twenty-two hours, five minutes, and eight seconds. "Your dad's execution is scheduled for seven o'clock on Sunday night. This clock tracks the official countdown."

Trinity reluctantly accepted the timer and set it beside her. Her dad's death was scheduled for three minutes before her curse would expire, assuming she managed not to kill anyone else, of course.

"If you kill our resident psychopath," Felicia said, "Elijah will be pardoned."

Reina sank down next to Trinity. "Tough call, girlfriend. That would totally cut into our girls' retreat in Minnesota."

Trinity's throat tightened. "I can't kill again."

"Then Daddy dies." Felicia handed Trinity a sheaf of papers. "Here is the limited information we have on the creature, as well as a contract for your services. Payment for the kill is your dad's freedom." She held out a pen. "Here you go."

Trinity scanned the papers. *I, Trinity Harpswell, do hereby swear that I am a black widow, and I will use my black widow talents to kill the target*—Her stomach lurched and she looked up. "I can't do it."

"Isn't there another option?" Reina asked. "I mean—"

"These were the terms we decided on when we sent Augustus after Elijah. You trade the heart of one beast for your father. Nothing less will do." Her voice became reverent. "Augustus is extremely inflexible in the administration of his duties. Once he's set into motion, he simply can't be stopped. He's as formidable as he is handsome."

"Handsome?" Reina echoed. "Hunchbacks and rashes are hot? He smells like rotting bananas."

Felicia laughed. "Oh, my dear, you have so much to learn." She fluttered her hand over her chest as if trying to dissipate sudden heat. "Well, Trinity. Are you going to sign it?"

Reina put her arm around Trinity's shoulder and squeezed. "You don't have to do this," she said. "Your dad would understand."

"He'd be furious if I kill someone to save him." Trinity could already hear him yelling that if she loved him, she would let him die and take her freedom as his gift to her. But she couldn't let her dad die, not on her behalf. If she allowed others to suffer for her weakness, what was the point of living? She was more than that. She knew she was. There had to be a way, and she had seven days to find it.

Martin hadn't been the real test.

The real test was now, and her dad's life and her own soul were at stake.

"Trin?"

She took the pen and signed the contract.

The kitchen fell silent as the fridge went blank.

Blaine was stunned. Christian was alive. And he was being tortured by a gal with quite the penchant for it. If they hightailed it back there, he'd be free.

No. Not free. Spared.

Big difference.

Nigel spoke first. "If we return, she'll hand him over to us, but all that shit will start right back up." He held up his hand. "Granted, I appreciate the man I've become as a result of life's little challenges, but I'm really done with the prisoner/torture/emasculation crap."

Blaine swore and stood up. "No way are we turning ourselves in."

"I can't believe you guys don't want to go back and party with a psychotic she-demon with questionable ethics. You two are a couple of pansies." Jarvis yanked open the fridge to get another beer, using a pot holder to grab the steel handle. "You know she's fixed all the weaknesses in her system. We go in, and we're not getting out. Ever."

"No. Not acceptable." The skull and crossbones on Blaine's pec was burning. "But we're not leaving Christian there."

Jarvis retrieved a beer, then scowled at it. "Warm. The bitch heated it up." He tossed the beer back in the fridge and slammed it shut. "How is it that women are so damn good at knowing exactly what little things annoy men? Is it in their genes? Do they teach it in little study groups? A cold beer. That's all I want, and she knew it."

"She has to die." Nigel wove a paintbrush between his fingers, a thoughtful look on his face. "It's the only way for this to end."

"Yeah, and good luck with that." Jarvis pulled open a cabinet and grabbed a bag of beef jerky. Even the simple act of eating whenever they wanted was a gift. "Because she's such a delicate little thing."

"There's a way to kill everything," Nigel said. "We just need to figure out what it is."

"Hell, it'd be my biggest wet dream to end her existence. I'm game." Jarvis tore open the plastic and pulled out a large hunk of dried beef. "I'm not going back in there on her invite, though. We take one step inside, and it's curling irons and mani/pedis again. Been there, done that. Had enough." He took a bite of the smoked cow and rolled his eyes. "This is incredible. So much better than arugula and beet salad, light on the dressing. I can feel my chest hair growing already."

"So we lure her out. Take her that way." Nigel picked up another brush and began weaving it through the fingers on his other hand.

"And kill her how?" Jarvis ripped another hunk off. "Don't think I was listening when you mentioned that part of the plan."

"We're standing here, aren't we? Free? There's always a way." Nigel held up his hands. The brushes were moving so quickly it was a blur, the frosted handle nothing but a glittery prism of light flashing between his fingers. "It's like art. Opening your mind to the great possibilities. Releasing resistance."

Jarvis snorted. "I think you got out too late, dude. There's no recovery for you. Your one-eyed-snake is gonna fall off if you don't find some testosterone soon."

"See the magic," Nigel said, holding up the fluttering brushes so they caught the light. "See the beauty."

Blaine narrowed his eyes, focusing on the prism. Watched it flicker faster and faster until it seemed alive. A person. Running through Nigel's fingertips. Fleeing. Running. Like a hologram of a real person. Prisms. "Wait." He stared more closely at the brushes. "Nigel's onto something."

"Yeah, insanity."

"No. It's the light refraction—" It finally clicked in the back of Blaine's mind and he slammed his fist into his palm. "Son of a bitch. A black widow would know how to kill her."

The paintbrushes stilled. "Nice, Trio. You're right. She would."

Jarvis froze, a large chunk of jerky halfway to his mouth. His eyes were glittering in anticipation. "Hot damn," he whispered. "That would do it." He tossed the bag on the counter, grabbed a linen napkin, then scowled at it. He tossed it on the floor and wiped his hands on his jeans instead. "I'm in. Where do we find one?"

"Her files." Blaine was already striding toward his computer. Before he'd left Angelica's lair, he'd set up a back door in her system so he could access her notes. They'd been hoping for a way to figure out how to destroy the Den of Womanly Pursuits, or get an idea of when she was scheduling new kidnappings, but he hadn't found that information yet. "I remember seeing something about a black widow in here..." He logged onto her files, and then followed the path he'd searched before. "Here." He went six layers deep in a set of folders. "These are all the creatures she's unleashed on the mortal world—" He clicked on a folder called Girl Power and opened the first file.

It was a photo of a young woman with raven black hair, green eyes, and a smile that would make any mortal man's heart stop.

"Look at those emerald beauties." Nigel peered at the screen. "I'd love to paint her. I've never seen such innocence juxtaposed with the hardness of death. It's as if there are two different people looking out from those eyes."

"Her eyes?" Jarvis snorted. "How about her—"

"Trinity Harpswell," Blaine read from the file. "Honored guest from age four months to ten months." He felt a flash of regret for the baby who'd been victimized by the delusional blonde tyrant. At least he'd been four by the time he'd arrived. "Infected by the black widow curse seventeen times." He snapped his fingers. "Bingo. We found her."

"Created by the great inventor herself." Jarvis grinned. "Poetic justice. I love it."

Blaine shoved the chair back from the desk. "I'll go check it out. You guys keep looking through her files and see if you can find anything else. I want all our options open."

"On it." Jarvis took over the seat.

Nigel propped himself up against the desk and folded his arms. "Yo, Trio, watch yourself. If this chick really is a black widow, it'll be a piece of cake for her to finish you off." He raised his brows. "And you are quite the looker. If she falls in love with you, you're toast, big guy."

"Love? Keeping dreaming, artist boy." Blaine snorted. "Besides, if I was that easy to kill, I'd be dead already." He let a single flame dance at the end of his index finger. Just a reminder of exactly what he was: a fire warrior (okay, yeah, he'd self-titled, but he figured it was better than cross-stitching girly man). "I'm really not worried about some almost human chick who's been out in the mortal world her whole life—"

"Uh, fellas?" Jarvis raised his hand. "We've got a slight complication."

Blaine and Nigel turned to Jarvis, who was still studying the computer screen. "Spill," Blaine demanded.

Jarvis pointed to the top right corner. "Her file's been flagged with a yellow tulip."

Blaine extinguished his flame. "Shit." The flower meant only one thing. "She's the Chosen. If we kill the witch, her soul will jump into Trinity's body and keep on trucking."

"Hell," Nigel muttered. "Any woman whose eyes contain such passionate depth deserves more than to be the witch's safety net. Do you guys realize the extent of the paradox in her eyes between good and evil? So rare. A gift to paint."

Jarvis stared at Nigel in disgust. "You got out of the Den, Nigel. Do yourself a favor, ditch the dreamy creative shit and get manly. She's not some angelic muse to spawn your next inspiration. She's the Chosen." He leaned back in the chair with a sigh of bitter resignation. "And you know what that means."

"Yeah." Blaine scowled. "It means that after I finish with Trinity Harpswell, she has to die." Son of a bitch, that pissed him off. After watching too many innocents suffer at the hands of the witch, and having his own powers be harnessed to kill and torture others, the last thing he could stomach was the harming of more innocents.

No matter.

He'd do what needed to be done. There was no point in killing Angelica if they were going to sit back and let her soul leach into her Chosen's physical body. That soul-sucking estrogen predator was one female who wasn't going to get a chance for a second life under a new identity.

It was rare for a witch to have a Chosen. Yeah, they all wanted one, but it was a damned tricky spell to set up. After carefully tracking Angelica's files and women for a century and a half, they'd finally concluded she'd been unable to make it happen.

Wrong.

A hell of a mistake to make.

"Well, at least we know." Jarvis rubbed his jaw. "I can't even tell you how pissed I'd have been if we'd finally knocked her off, only to have her jump ship. At least we can take the Chosen out now."

Nigel and Blaine looked at each other, and he knew Nigel was thinking the same thing: Trinity Harpswell was an innocent, and they were going to use her to murder Angelica, and then he was going to have to kill her. "Life can be a real bitch sometimes," Blaine said quietly.

"It's the only way to save others from the same fate." Nigel's voice was grim.

"And Christian," Jarvis said. "He's what matters right now."

"I know." Blaine ground his jaw. "I'll do it." But he would be merciful. It was the least he could do. Leaving Trinity Harpswell alive so her soul would be taken over by the witch was even crueler than sending her to the Afterlife.

Sometimes death was the best choice.

Chapter 6

IT WAS NEARLY TWENTY HOURS AFTER THE MEETING
with Felicia by the time Trinity was able to sink down
in the lavender scented bubble bath and focus on the
enormity of the problem she was facing.

It had taken several hours to finish all the paperwork
involved in the deal, and then Trinity's mom had been
waiting when she stumbled up the front steps at dawn.
After spending most of the day at Pop's Corner Deli
arguing with her mom, Trinity had finally ditched her.
It was almost five in the afternoon by the time Trinity
was finally back in her Boston condo, which showed the
mind-numbing effects of the top New York City feng
shui designer she'd hired to promote inner peace and
encourage abstinence.

She'd spent money and time she didn't have redeco-
rating it, hoping it would calm her itchy trigger finger,
or at least lessen her "love him, kill him" addiction.
Apparently not so successful. And, as an added bonus,
the place was so dead of life and love and energy, it
kinda made her want to torch it instead of bask in it.

Instead of tranquility, she saw a living space devoid
of color, drained of spirit, deprived of joy. Which meant
that whenever she walked inside, resentment sort of fes-
tered inside her, like the boil on Noah Schmergal's neck
right before it had exploded. (Okay, yeah, so she'd been
the one to poke it with a number two pencil during the

GMATs and cause its fatal explosion. But it had really been his fault for insisting that true love meant sitting right next to each other during standardized tests. Even she knew that her defenses would be down in that kind of stressful situation. The fact she'd later found out he'd sat next to her so he could cheat off her paper? Okay, yeah, that had eased the guilt a bit. She had studied a lot for that thing.)

But boils aside, she was desperate for a place with vibrant colors, passionate décor, and a huge, decadent bed with a mattress that would consume her (and anyone who happened to be with her—ahem) for hours. Not this acrid den of sterility that reminded her of being stranded on the Sahara desert without sunscreen or adequate hydration.

The only plus of her condo was that she had big windows that let in copious amounts of sunshine. She craved the warmth on her face, but she never felt it in her heart. It was as if the sun was bouncing off her skin, never making it inside past all the evil caked within her.

And yes, she'd spent hours coming up with that analogy, thank you very much, and she was quite proud of it. If she was going to be big-time messed up, she might as well be poetic about it, right?

Her cell rang, and she dried her hand on her wheat-colored towel before grabbing the phone from the edge of the tub. "Hi, Reina."

"So? Did you look at the file on your target yet?"

"No." The sheaf of papers was perched on a nearby bamboo stool. She'd thought maybe she'd be able to handle it better if she was relaxed and riding high from the scent of lavender, but she was already shriveled like a prune, and still not feeling any particular inclination to pick that sucker up and start reading. "I just got my mom out of here an hour ago."

"Oh, wow. What did Olivia have to say?"

Trinity poked a mauve toenail up through the bubbles and swirled the water. "She told me I would be doing a disservice to my dad if I took the deal and killed someone. If I was a good daughter, I would let my dad die and all that. She was pretty upset I wouldn't go to Death's cabin in Minnesota, and she left in a huff."

"Don't let her give you the guilt trip. If you want to murder someone in order to save your dad's life, you should be able to do it without your mom giving you grief. She needs to let you be your own person."

"Yeah, I feel bad though." Trinity picked up the bottle of lavender bubble bath, then frowned when she caught its floral scent. She was so tired of surrounding herself with objects meant to strip her of passion and fire. "I really upset her when I said I didn't want to let Dad die." She put the bottle back down and leaned out of the tub. She flicked the cabinet door open and retrieved a small, black case from behind the muted off-white towels.

"Well, you know how moms are. Always thinking they know what's best for their kids." Reina paused. "You know, Trin, I've been thinking."

"I'm sure you have." Trinity unlocked the case and unzipped it. Her heart did a little flip when she saw the neon pink plastic bottle of Passion Fire Bubble Bath tucked inside. Never opened. She'd been saving it for Sunday at seven. She traced her finger over the label and a shiver ran up her arm. How she wanted to know what it felt like to engage her passions, to drop her shields, to embrace life the way she'd always wanted to, with her whole heart and her entire soul.

"See, I think maybe this whole hired-assassin-twist is a sign that black widowhood is your true calling. Maybe it's time for you to embrace your destiny and the fact you're going to spend a lifetime killing men. There are worse fates."

"No." Trinity slammed the case shut. "I'll find a solution." She jammed the lock shut and threw the bag back into the cabinet. "I refuse to accept that that's my only choice."

"Well, maybe you should. We could have a lot of fun together—"

"Good-bye, Reina." She ended the call over her friend's protests, then tossed the phone across the room. It landed with a clatter on the beige tile floor that was so miserably cold.

She glared at the phone and thought about Reina's suggestion. It rankled her, and she sat up.

All right. It was time to step up and take action. She wasn't accepting her fate. She was going to own it, whatever it was. She eyed the files and flexed her fingers, preparing to pick it up.

It was time for some creative strategizing. She was smart. She could handle this. Yeah, she had a willpower problem, and an apparent inability to value human life, but she had gotten five online masters degrees while hiding out from men. Surely one of those money pits would pay off here, right?

Amen, sistah. She was all over this. She reached out and grabbed the files—

The front door opened with a bang, and she jumped. Her mom again? She sighed. Of course Olivia wouldn't have given up so easily. "Mom! I'm in the bath!" She shoved the papers behind the toilet. No need to make her mother feel worse.

Footsteps thudded down the hall, and Trinity winced and shrank back under the fading bubbles. Olivia must be on a serious rampage to be making that much noise. Yes, even at five foot three she was generally a lead foot, courtesy of a heritage involving disenfranchised giants, but she was ultra sensitive about her large feet and prided herself on moving quietly. But right now, it sounded like there was a herd of cattle thudding right toward her—

The door flew open, and in walked a man who was most definitely not her mother.

And if the handcuffs, leg shackles, and gag in his hands were any indication, he wasn't there to offer his services for a spa-style mani/pedi.

He was there to kidnap her.

—⁓⁓⁓—

Her kidnapper had greenish mottled skin, a weird hump in his left shoulder, and the noxious odor of sulfur gas filled the room. Were those beetles crawling in his hair? A flatulating troll. Excellent.

Yeah, not so hard to figure out what had happened: Thank you, Mom, for arranging a kidnapping by such a nasty man that even a black widow queen couldn't find him attractive.

Appreciate the thought and the love. Not so high on the interference. She was naked and in the middle of trying to figure out how to assassinate someone without actually doing it. Not exactly overwhelmed with time to thwart an attempted kidnapping by Thor the Nasty.

Did moms ever let go of the apron strings or what?

Thor raised the handcuffs. "We going to make it easy or hard?"

Trinity rolled her eyes. "Come on. Couldn't you at least try to be original? Clichés are a sign of mental laziness." She lunged for the gun she had stored in her medicine cabinet (like a woman with a one-track mind for murder would be capable of not having guns around? She'd thrown out nearly a hundred of them, but couldn't stop from buying new ones. Generally, a completely sucky habit, but right now? So feeling the love for always being prepared).

Her fingers brushed over the barrel, but the hulk of a man grabbed her before she could secure it. His warty palms slipped over her oil-slicked body, and her stomach turned at the feel of his hands on her.

That was good at least. No visits from the black widow tonight. Rah, rah, sis boom bah.

She slammed her elbow into his gut, and he let out his breath in a gush. His grip loosened, and she scrambled free and bolted for the door. "I'll pay you more than she's paying you," she shouted.

"Now, that's a cliché line." He launched himself after her and tackled her at the top of the short staircase leading to her foyer. Trinity shrieked as they tumbled down the stairs, and she gasped when they slammed into the front door.

She was too stunned to move, her breath knocked out by the force of the hit. He hoisted her numb body onto his

shoulder, and headed into the living room. Not the front
door? She twisted around to see where he was headed. A
patch of sod was plunked down on her straw rug.

Grass. Olivia must have stashed it on her earlier
visit when Trinity wasn't looking. What a twisted little
mind she had! Being all weepy while planning her own
daughter's abduction. Trinity would have no shot at getting away once they hit the sod.

She twisted frantically, but her captor had her anchored too tightly. "Mom! Don't!" She had no idea if
her mom was listening through the grass. Her mom had
nailed her more than once by lurking among the green-
ery on a spiritual level. "Let me go! I swear—"

There was a sudden burst of heat over her body, and
then the entire south wall of her apartment blew up in a
flash of white fire. She and her captor were blown backwards, and they crashed into the six-foot stone fountain
her last designer had ordered her to set up. The stones
sliced her back and she landed in the water.

She tried to scramble to her feet, but her captor
grabbed her ankle and dragged her back. He flung her
over his shoulder and sprinted for the sod. "Stop!" She
ground her knee into his throat, but he shoved her out
of his way and kept running, straight into the blinding
flames. "Not the sod!" she shouted. "Don't touch it—"

Heat rippled suddenly over her bare skin, and she had
a fraction of a second to think that it felt suspiciously
like her captor had grown a second set of hands, and
then she was yanked right out of his grip and into the
arms of the sexiest warrior she'd ever had the misfortune
of laying eyes on, let alone had her naked body crushed
up against.

Her rescuer tucked her under his arm and thrust his palm toward her abductor. White-hot flames sprayed from his hand and it swept the green beast off his feet and carried him right out the window on a magic carpet ride of fire.

The last sound she heard was his scream mixing with the crackle of flames, and then he was gone.

And she was alone with a man who was very, very bad news for her soul.

Blaine had about two seconds to register that the woman tucked under his arm was... well... the first naked chick who'd been pressed up against him in a good half-century or so. Saying it felt nice was kinda like saying it felt nice to wake up after a torture session and realize he was still alive. Yeah, that freaking fantastic.

Then that same blow-his-mind feel-good sensation jammed her elbow in his kidney.

"Shit!" The pain knifed through his lower back as she squiggled out of his distracted grasp. Good to know that a female in the buff made him forget to protect himself so completely that a mortal's elbow thrust could make him stumble.

The boys would be laughing their asses off at him right now.

Trinity raced down the hall, and Blaine swore as she disappeared around the corner. He sprinted after her, putting more effort into his run than he'd done in centuries. A little late to realize he had no clue how mortal she actually was. The witch could have done anything to her in those six months. For all he knew, she was turning into a bat and flying the hell out of his life right about now.

Damn. He'd be impressed if she did that.

Pissed, but impressed.

He skidded around the corner and crashed face-first through a closed door before he had a chance to stop. Again with the lack of focus? Nice not to notice a sheer wall of wood blocking his path.

Women were no good for battle acumen. Maybe Nigel's celibacy idea had merit after all.

The splintered door thundered into the walls, and he careened to a stop in the middle of a small bathroom. He promptly found himself eyeball to barrel with a handgun.

And damn if the chit wasn't still naked.

Just like a woman to use her breasts as a weapon by distracting him with them. How irritating to know it worked. But at the same time, it was always good to add info to his strategic recon arsenal. Women's nipples were now in his "high risk" category, especially ones that were pert with a slightly rose tinge... Crap! He jerked his eyes off her chest and glared at her. "Put some clothes on."

She snorted. "And have you attack me when I put the gun down to grab them? Fat chance of that. The answer's no."

"No?" Where was his manly, make-them-cower side? He glowered at her and folded his arms across his chest. At least his target was still in the room and hadn't sprouted wings yet. "You do realize you could put that bullet in my head and I'd be dancing the rumba within about a minute? Guns don't stop me."

She blinked. "You can rumba?"

He scowled. "I just said a bullet to the brain wouldn't hurt me, and you're impressed that I can dance?"

She raised her brows. "I'm quaking in fear. Can't you tell?"

He studied her. Her eyes were a brilliant green, tendrils of dark hair had escaped from her bun and were plastered to the side of her neck. Her chin was thrust out, and her grip on the gun was solid. Didn't see a lot of fear there. "You're mocking me." A century and a half with Angelica and her girls had pretty much cured him of any love for female ridicule.

A small smile quirked at the corner of her mouth. "I'm not mocking you. It's just that you're the one who should be quaking in fear, especially now that I know you can rumba. I've always wanted to learn how to ballroom dance, and a scarred warrior who can also rumba is way too tempting. So, yeah, you should run, hot stuff." She raised the gun higher, which made her breasts lift as well. Perky little things—

"Ah…" He jerked his gaze off her body and stared at the wall behind her head, trying to think about war instead of how her breasts were just the right size for his mouth. "I like the wheat grass designs in the tile. Soothing. Makes me feel like I'm standing in Kansas."

"Wheat grass?" She sounded disbelieving. "Didn't you hear me tell you to leave? I really mean it. It's not a good idea for you to be here. I'm far more dangerous than you are."

He eyed the ocean vista above the toilet. "You're worried about the black widow thing?" Damn, he could use five minutes alone with his new wild butterfly pattern right now to pull himself together—

Shit. Had he really just thought that?

Damn, he needed five minutes with a punching bag and brass knuckles to pull himself together.

Yeah, better. No way was he letting that witch stalk him now that he was free. He was a man, not some artiste like Nigel.

The gun clicked as Trinity cocked it. "What do you know about the black widow thing?"

He eyed her. Checked out the flexed triceps, the battle stance, and then his gaze settled on the small, yellow tulip tattooed on her collarbone. Same pattern the witch had emblazoned above her bed. And on the ceiling of the Cavern of Hellish Moments.

Adrenaline flooded his body, and his skull and crossbones began to tingle. Yeah, no problem thinking of Trinity as a threat and not a woman when he looked at that damn flower. Heat pulsed beneath his skin, and his muscles thickened, preparing him for battle. Much better. Screw the cross-stitching softie. Try murderous gladiator.

Trinity's eyes widened. "Did you just get taller?"

"Probably." He walked across the small bathroom until the gun was pressed against his heart. Against his tattoo.

Trinity stiffened. "You even try to kiss me, I'll shoot you."

He growled. "No chance in hell is there going to be any lip-locking between us. Trust me, that's one thing you don't need to worry about." Lovemaking with a yellow tulip was not gonna happen. Not by a long shot.

She blinked. "I don't?"

He almost laughed at the surprise on her face. Typical witch progeny: so used to being a man magnet that they didn't get it when a man failed to respond. He wrapped his hand around the barrel of the gun and turned it away from his heart. "You forgot to shoot me."

She stared down at the gun that was now pointed at the mirror. "Dammit," she muttered. "I have no will-power whatsoever." She sighed and released the gun. "Someday I'm going to have the strength to shoot a man as good looking as you who comes here to abduct me."

He took the gun and tossed it into the still-full bath-tub. "I need your help."

"Hah." She turned away and grabbed a black thong from a small pile of clothes on a bamboo stool in the corner. She bent over to pull it on—

Shit and hellfire. That was one nice ass. Muscular, but curvy at the same time. The woman clearly worked out, but hadn't lost that soft side that made her all female—

Then he thought of her flower and smiled when he felt fire burn in his cells. Yeah, who needed a cold shower? A yellow tulip was the best mood killer around. "You're going to come with me and use your black widow talents to kill someone."

She yanked the thong over her hips and turned to face him. "You have *got* to be kidding."

He was about to deny it when he saw the fire in her eyes.

And then he remembered lesson #76.5 from Man Decorum 101: Never tell a smart, pissed-off female what to do. Ask her. Nicely. Preferably with roses in hand.

He stared at her.

She glared back.

Ask her to kill someone for him?

Trinity rolled her eyes and grabbed a black bra from the chair and fastened it around her ribs. "At least the fact you demanded such an asinine thing makes it slightly less dangerous for you. It must be your lucky day to be smart enough to behave like a thoughtless beast around me." Her gaze slipped to his chest. "But you still need to go away. Fast."

Like, *ask* her?

Screw that. The witch was the one who'd given the lessons. She was a man hater, and everything she'd ever forced on them was solely for the purpose of humiliating them.

He was a warrior. Not a counted cross-stitch uber talent.

Trinity pulled the straps over her shoulders, and those perfect breasts disappeared from view.

Which put him in a worse mood. He'd liked them and had already gotten used to having them blink cheerfully at him. Didn't appreciate having them taken away. He narrowed his eyes. "You have three seconds to get dressed, and then we're going on a witch hunt. I find her. You kill her. Got it?"

Trinity stared at him, then she grinned. "On the one hand, that's completely fantastic that you're being such a boor. Even your yummy shoulders and huge biceps aren't going to win me over if you keep making those kinds of demands of me."

"I—" He stopped. Couldn't remember anything she'd said after "huge biceps." When was the last time any female had made any comment about him that wasn't about how much pain he could take? Kinda liked it.

"However, the part about needing me to kill someone is a little scary, especially since you might be big enough to make me do it." She smiled even wider, and there was no missing the intense relief in her voice. "But now that I know that you're unkillable, you have totally freed me up to defend myself. And for that, I really appreciate you."

He blinked at her visible honesty, at the earnestness on her face, and something inside him turned, knowing that he was the one responsible for the release of her tension. He'd made her feel better without even trying. What a guy.

Then she reached into the tub, grabbed the gun, and shot him in the heart.

Chapter 7

OKAY, SO HE HADN'T BEEN READY FOR HER TO *SHOOT* HIM.

Blaine was still falling to the tile in a pool of blood when Trinity ducked past him and ran for the door. The pain in his chest was eerily reminiscent of when his deranged jailer had decided to test his resilience to Jarvis's sword. Nice memories of his dear friend.

But as he watched Trinity sprint away, his amusement vanished.

Turning into a bat would have been impressive.

Shooting him in the heart?

Not really feeling the love for that.

The pain might have been all warm and fuzzy, but the actual act of a woman shooting him reminded him too much of the females he'd spent the last century and a half with. Estrogen junkies who tortured him, and then laughed. Not his favorite type of girl to get naked with.

Yeah, maybe he wasn't going to feel quite as bad when he had to off Trinity Harpswell.

He hit the floor and rolled onto his back, concentrating on sending fire to his chest to seal the wound. She had about thirty seconds before he'd be up on his feet again, and this time he was ditching the nice guy shtick. Christian's life was at stake, and now that he knew Trinity Harpswell was like every other woman he'd known, there'd be no mercy. She deserved to wear the badge of the witch on her collarbone—

Then she stopped in the hallway and looked back at him. Her gaze went to the blood on his chest, and she got a stricken look on her face. "Oh, God. Look at you."

He felt his heart begin to knit back together, and he prepared to launch himself at her. Ten more seconds and she was his—

"Dammit!" She raced back into the bathroom and grabbed a towel off the rack.

He was just reaching out to grab her ankle when she knelt beside him and pressed the towel to his bleeding chest. Her face was pale, and her hand was shaking. "Damn you for bleeding and looking hurt! You weren't supposed to do that!" Her voice was trembling, and she sounded near tears. "You're such a bastard!"

He stared at her. "What are you doing?"

"Baking a cake, what does it look like?" She pressed harder on his wound. "I can't believe you're bleeding this much! What, do you have like an ocean of blood in you or something? That was completely cruel to make me think I could shoot you and not hurt you! I have issues with hurting living creatures. You could have warned me!" She glared at him. "I don't like you."

"You don't—" Blaine finally comprehended that she was wrecked over the fact she'd shot him. That he'd bled. Hell, the woman had been halfway to freedom (or at least, she thought she had been. In reality? He'd been hot on her tail) but she'd ditched the escape and come back to help him.

Women didn't do that. No one did that. They just didn't. No one came back to help him.

But she had.

He looked up into her teary eyes, and he stiffened. Yeah, it just seemed that way. She had black veins. No way had she come back just for him. She had a reason, and he'd find out what it was. And in the meantime, he was going to make sure she helped him get Christian home.

He grabbed her ankle, and she jumped. She looked down, and her lips pressed together when she saw his hand fisting her leg. "Please. I can't kill for you. Don't ask me to do it."

That "ask" word again.

Didn't anyone get he wasn't going to ask? Christian's life was on the table, and he wasn't going to be polite about saving him—

She laid her hand over his, and he tensed, waiting for whatever trick she was going to try to pull on him. Waiting for the pain. For the poison dart she'd try to shoot into his skin.

But nothing happened. Her hand was gentle where it sat on his. "If you have any mercy at all in you as a warrior, you will walk away and leave me alone."

He was still waiting for the attack. "Mercy was tortured out of me a long time ago."

She looked up and met his gaze. "I can't deal with you right now. I just can't."

He saw the truth in her eyes. She might be wearing a yellow tulip, and she'd shot him in the heart, but she was out of reserves.

And she was touching him. Softly. Her hand was warm. Her skin soft. And it felt incredible. No one had ever touched him with tenderness. Even if she was going to stab him in another minute, right now, in this second, he had the happiest damn hand on the planet.

And she'd come back for him, at risk to herself.

Yeah, she shot him, but *she'd come back for him*.

Hellfire and damnation. He didn't want to do it. He wasn't going to do it.

But she'd come back for him and that was… well… that was something he couldn't overlook.

Ah, hell. He was going to do it, wasn't he?

He was going to be nice.

———⁓———

Trinity tensed when the warrior's face got all twisted, like he was in pain. Or dying? She grabbed his wrist. "Are you okay?" Oy! What had she been thinking, shooting him? She was a black widow, for heaven's sake! What kind of risk had that been to shoot a man in the heart? She was much too good at killing men to engage in that sort of activity!

He laid his hand on her face, and she stiffened. But his hand was warm. It felt wonderful.

"Trinity."

"Yes?" Her voice was too throaty, too soft, but she couldn't help it. It felt so good to be touched.

"I'm asking you for your help," he said quietly. "Please."

Trinity blinked at the roughness of his tone. At his urgency. And his politeness? "I—"

"There's a man who will die if I can't kill the woman who's torturing him. I need to bring him home." His palm was becoming hotter, almost too hot, as if he were on the verge of catching fire again.

There was anguish in his eyes, and she realized that he'd bared his truth to her, asked her for help with a task of monumental importance to him. Saving someone he loved. Her heart swelled—

Ack! She couldn't afford to feel empathy for him! That was the first step down a very dangerous path! "Don't be likable," she snapped, scrambling out of his reach. "I don't want to hear about anyone nice getting killed."

She whirled away and grabbed her jeans. Her heart was pounding, and she couldn't get those dark eyes out of her mind. He knew hell. She could see it. She hated that. Couldn't deal with someone who'd suffered like she had. The urge she was feeling to hug him right now was just so, so, *so* dangerous.

"Trinity." His voice was low in her ear, and she went rigid at the feel of his breath on her neck.

The towering boor was right behind her! "Go. Away."

"I—"

"No!" She whirled around and slammed her hands into his chest to get him to back off.

He didn't move.

"You don't get it! I can't afford to kill anyone right now! My own dad's going to die if I can't figure out how to assassinate some monster without actually wielding the blade, and you want to add more to my list? Are you kidding? I—"

"That's easy." A sudden grin broke out over his face, a look of pleased relief. "I'll take care of it for you."

"And furthermore—" She stopped suddenly. "What did you say?"

He shrugged. "I can kill anything. It's no biggie. I'll kill your monster and you kill mine."

The room started to spin and she had to sit down on the edge of her tub. Her chest was tight. It couldn't really be this easy, could it? "You'll just waltz in here and kill something for me?"

He plucked her shirt off the chair and crouched in front of her. "Here's the deal." He picked up her hand and shoved the shirt into her grasp. "I can kill anything except the woman who has Christian. She's unkillable."

Trinity laughed softly. "Nothing is unkillable. Not by me." Not by the monster within.

He grinned, a smug look on his face. "That's why I need you."

Oh, nice work, Trin. She sighed. "I walked right into that one, didn't I?"

He shrugged. "Yeah, but you looked good while doing it."

"And looking good so matters to me right now." In another lifetime she might have laughed at his inappropriate and cavalier remark. Right now, it felt more fitting to lay down the welcome mat for the devil himself. But there was also something so appealing about flirting back, about pretending this great nightmare wasn't pressing down on her from all sides. "In fact," she quipped, "right before you got here, I was inspecting my closet and trying to decide what outfit would show off my breasts to the best advantage."

He raised his brows. "And you went with the shirtless look? I'd say that was the right choice, you know, for that goal."

She couldn't stop the small laugh that bubbled out. "Shut up. This isn't funny." She found her way back to her cranky state and took the shirt from his hand.

He leaned forward, his gaze so intent it made her uncomfortable. "Christian needs help, and I'm the only one to do it. The witch has to die, and you're the only one who can cover that. I'll kill your monster, you kill mine. Fair trade."

"I can't." She pulled the shirt over her head. "I'll be cursed for life." She sat up, feeling stronger now that she had a top on. "I can't deal with a life of murder."

He didn't say anything. He just studied her face. Then he reached toward her throat. She jerked back, but all he did was brush his thumb over her collarbone, over the flower-shaped birthmark she hated. "The black widow curse," he said quietly. "You're down to your last kill?"

She pulled free and walked over to get the jeans she'd dropped in her moment of panic when he'd done the hot-seduction-breath-on-her-neck move. "I have less than seven days. If I can make it that long, then I'm free. I've come this far. I can't blow it. I—"

"Killing's no big deal," he said.

"Yes, it is! And being forced to do it…" She yanked her jeans over her hips. "I hate not being in control of my actions. I'm sure a badass like you has no clue what it's like to be condemned to a life that chafes at your very soul, but trust me, it sucks."

He swore under his breath. "Oh, I get it."

She scowled. "How can you possibly understand what's it like not to be master of your domain? You're like this uber warrior. Who could possibly bully you?"

He went silent, staring at her, but there was intense turmoil in his eyes. Finally, he simply said, "Fine."

She zipped her jeans. "Fine, what?"

"You get one reprieve for coming back."

"Coming back from where?"

But he was already walking toward the door. He was leaving? "Where are you going?"

"Don't push it, Harpswell. I'm not this nice of a guy, and if I don't find another black widow, I'm coming back for you." The boards cracked under his feet, and he disappeared into the hall.

She stared after him. It was good he was leaving. She couldn't afford a man right now, especially one who believed in killing. He wasn't like Barry, who had been compelled. Granted, Barry had been directed by little voices in his head, but it had still been a compulsion like Trinity.

But this warrior killed because it was no big deal. Because he could, and because it was an easy answer to his problems. A chill ran through her. Was that what she'd become after she killed enough? A monster who didn't even care about the trail of corpses? Would she stomp ants and laugh?

She didn't want to be around a man like that, someone who represented her greatest nightmare of what she was becoming.

She heard his boots thudding down the hall. Were there other black widows alive to help him? There had to be. He wouldn't be back.

Then she looked down at the sheaf of papers on her chair. The details on the monster she had to kill. He could take care of it for her. She took a step toward the door to call him back, then stopped herself.

The cost was too high. If she killed the witch for him (like she could hurt a defenseless female, but that was so not the point at the moment), then she would still be in the same situation, cursed for life. Her dad's sacrifice in vain. It was all her fault her dad was dust right now. If only she hadn't told him what her vision had shown her, he never would have known how to kill Martin—

Oh! That was it!

"Wait! Wait!" She raced out into the hallway, desperate to catch the warrior before he disappeared forever. "Don't leave!"

She ran around the corner as he was yanking open the door to her apartment.

He didn't even turn. "Don't push me—"

"What if I told you how to kill her? What if I saw it, and then you did it?" Her stomach rolled at the idea of orchestrating someone's death, but at least it wouldn't trigger the curse. Her own soul was a different matter.

He paused and turned toward her. "That works?"

She nodded, numbly, her soul recoiling at the offer to help him murder someone, even as the words tumbled out of her mouth. "When I see a death, it's not me in the hologram. Anyone can kill them using the method I see. I could tell you how to do it." Her stomach roiled again, and she forced herself to take a breath. "And will you help me with... the other one?" She couldn't even say it. Couldn't believe she was asking a man to murder twice for her, just to save her soul.

The fact killing didn't bother him was of no help. She cared. But what other way was there? Her dad's life was at stake, and he mattered more than anything else.

The warrior shut the door and walked toward her. The closer he got, the larger he seemed, this dark shadow of death closing in on her. Her soul, her spirit, and her fate were all tied up in his hands.

What was she thinking? She couldn't do this. There had to be another solution. But even as she thought it, she knew she was lying to herself. There was no other way to rescue her dad. The terms had been agreed upon with the Triumvirate, and Otherworld magic had sealed the deal.

The beast's heart for her dad. No other option.

The warrior stopped directly in front of her, and she had to crane her neck to look up at him. His face was shadowed, his eyes dark and weary, and angry. Dear Lord, he was angry. At her? At the world? Didn't matter. She could see death in his eyes, a killing machine, everything she was so terrified of becoming. A darkness rumbled inside her, and she went rigid at the sensation of the spider girl stirring

Okay, like the situation wasn't crappy enough without the eight-legged freak coming to life in recognition of a kindred spirit. The widow was waking up because this man reflected the truth deep inside Trinity's being, the one she'd been fighting for so long.

Was the delight in killing contagious? If he sneezed on her, would she suddenly be infected with the need to celebrate life's little victories by snuffing out another life? She didn't want to be around him. Not when she could hear the little miss digging on him. "Nevermind. It was a stupid idea—"

"I agree."

She froze. "What?"

"You tell me how to kill her, and I'll do the deed." He got a highly satisfied look on his face. "I never thought that would be an option for me, but to have the chance to do it myself…" He grinned. "Hot damn. I'd trade a century of torture for that chance."

"Torture?" He was into torture *and* murder? Spending time with him while the deadly night-shade was in residence inside her was like asking a

Labrador retriever to work in a dog food factory. "I don't think—"

"And I'll take out your monster too. It's done." He held out his hand. "My name is Blaine Underhill, and I'm your new partner."

Every instinct screamed at her to run from this man who was everything she was so terrified of being. But she couldn't let her dad die. Not for her. Blaine Underhill might threaten her, but he also gave her a chance. This man could save her father's life, without cursing her to eternity. If she made it to Sunday, and the curse was gone, all she'd have left to contend with would be her soul.

The rest would be up to her. She could do it. She knew she could.

He raised one eyebrow.

Slowly, she set her hand in his, and he clasped it instantly, his grip hard and unyielding. He smiled. "Welcome to hell, Trinity Harpswell."

Chapter 8

Angelica used to be fast enough.

But when the stockinged foot with the red pedicure caught her under the chin, she knew she was slipping. Or, more like flying across the room with a bruised jaw and a swollen lip. Yay, her. She braced herself, but that was sort of like the *Titanic* trying to slow down when it hit the iceberg: not a lot of mileage coming from that move.

She smashed into the light blue padded wall of the Girl Power room, and slumped down to the floor. Covered the whimper of pain with a snarky snort of derision that didn't sound authentic enough to satisfy her. Note to self: Get thicker padding. Addendum: It was not empowering to think about how much pain she was in.

Or how much she really wanted to cry. Talk about a major pain factor. What the hell was that cushion stuffed with? Steel with a backing of concrete?

"Oh, Angelica, I'm so sorry!" Mari rushed across the room toward her. "Are you okay?"

"It was a perfect hit." Ow. Pain. Ow. Need help. She managed a plucky smile as she waved off help from the assistant who was just too young and impressionable to ever be allowed to know how much she had just hurt her mentor. "Nice job." Oops. Her voice was a little too high-pitched. Nothing like a heel plant to the solar plexus to make a three-hundred-year-old grandma realize she was definitely no longer in her second century.

Mari was biting her lower lip, and her mascara had run down her cheeks. Her eyes were red and puffy, and her face was pale. Her navy sweats were hanging off her hips, and the girl looked like she'd lost about thirty pounds in the last six hours. "I didn't mean to hurt you."

"Hah. You didn't hurt me." Angelica hopped to her feet and let out a shout of pain that she quickly morphed into a Sheena Warrior Princess call of victory. Me, feel no pain. Me, tough. Go me. "I was just showing you how a mortal man will react to that kind of hit. You can't damage *me*."

Which was true. No one could touch her. So, why now? Why today? She didn't feel pain anymore. Not like this. It looked like it was time for a little spa treatment to update all the spells protecting her from this, that, and the other thing. Last time she'd felt pain like this was when—

Nope. Not going there. Bad memories were specifically banned from her brain. Especially when they had to do with a certain six foot four black witch who had shown a young maiden all there was to know about love, sex, and magic.

Until she'd figured out all the stuff he'd lied to her about, of course.

Unlike Mari, who wouldn't hit the century mark without knowing everything she needed to know about all three, because she was lucky enough to be under Angelica's brilliant and devoted tutelage. Angelica eyed the gal who was on the fast track to becoming her number one apprentice. "What's wrong with you, dearie? You're awfully pale today."

Mari walked over and retrieved a pale yellow towel from the stack carefully folded next to the silver tea set. Angelica noted a smudge on the sugar bowl and tried to remember which warrior had been in charge of tea today. Right. It had been the junior one. Pascal. So promising, but such a stubborn beast sometimes. She had been planning to assign him to Blaine when…

She smiled. Blaine would be back. He was doing so well. She was so proud of him. Another century and he'd be almost a good guy. He already had the manly warrior thing down, and he was turning into a halfway decent human being. She had such hope that he'd be the tender, loving considerate mate within the next hundred years. Her first real success. She was so proud of herself. And him, of course.

Mari wiped the sweat off her brow before turning to face her. "I'm upset about Christian."

Angelica had to stifle a sigh. Of course the droopy bottom lip was about Christian. "Listen, my dear—"

Mari sniffled. "He's dying, isn't he?"

Oh, for the love of all that was well-muscled and manly! "Of course he is." Hats off to her for keeping the impatience out of her voice. She would never talk to any of her charges the way she'd once been derided. The Den of Womanly Pursuits was all about the love. "But it's just part of his character development. If the boys step up, Christian will survive." Hopefully. The tentacles were dragging him down a little bit more aggressively than she'd expected. And since she couldn't try to save him until Blaine showed up… well… she was hoping Christian found an inner strength and fast.

Mari put her hands on her hips. "You promised he'd be okay if I turned them in. You said he wouldn't die."

"He's not dead, yet." Ye gods. Could her girls be any softer? "Haven't you learned anything? Christian still needs work to be worthy of you. Didn't you say you hadn't had a single multiple orgasm with him?"

Mari's cheeks reddened. "Well, yes, but he said that most women can't—"

"See?" Angelica set her hands on her hips, her jaw flexing with aggravation. How many years had she bought into that old shtick that it was her fault she'd never had the big "O"? It wasn't until she'd tried out the Rose Bud Rocket Booster of Love that she'd learned exactly who had been at fault during her marriage. Yeah, uh, it ain't been the girl. "That's what unskilled men do to hide their inadequacies: They try to delude us that it's our fault so we accept less than we deserve. I'm trying to make these guys worthy of you, but you have *got* to be strong enough to stand up for yourself." She gently clasped Mari's shoulders. "Know your worth, my dear. It's the greatest gift you can give yourself."

Mari gave her a skeptical look. "So I can be three hundred years old and the only sex I get is from men I have to torture into touching me?"

Angelica blinked. Ow. Direct blow to the gut. Two in less than a minute? Not a good start to the day. She immediately thought of the visioning exercise she'd done less than ten minutes ago, imagining the dark warrior of her fantasies tenderly caressing her. The feel of his hand on her body. Gentle. Of his own free will. Wanting to be with her—

"I'm starting to think that maybe your plan isn't all that good." Mari scowled. "I'm tired of hurting Christian. Despite all I've done to him and his friends, he still likes me. In fact, I think he might be falling in love with me."

"Love?" The four-letter word jerked Angelica back into the present. For a split second, she couldn't remember what they'd been talking about. Her brain was still leaking the residue of man-hands on her naked body. Then she saw Mari's pout, and she remembered. That's right. Mutiny discussion underway. "For heaven's sake, Mari, this is for your own good. Love is the ultimate disempowerment tool, at least until everything is set up correctly."

"You're just bitter because—"

"Hey!" Time to drop the BFF act, apparently. She always felt so bad being sharp with her girls. Hated it when they made her give the tough love. "I'm not bitter. I'm smart. I believe in love, but with the right guy who's adequately trained to be good to you. Trust me when I say you don't want to fall in love with a man before he's properly cultivated. Men have too much power over us, and once they win our love, they can abuse us and we come running back for more—"

"Christian's already nice to me. He doesn't deserve to suffer any more." Mari grabbed her sweatshirt. "I'm going to go visit him, and I'm not going to hurt him."

Angelica sighed as she watched her most promising protégé march out of her Girl Power room. Did no one appreciate what she was doing for them? If she didn't get her love vaccine up to snuff soon, all her girls were going to be wrecked. Her chest tightened at the thought of her sweet babies falling in love. Too soon, too soon. The minute Trinity Harpswell was ripe for harvesting, Angelica was going to give her girls the greatest gift a mother could give her darlings, and they would so appreciate it when they were no longer vulnerable to the men they fell in love with.

"Gram, you have got to give it up. I mean it."

"Prentiss!" Angelica beamed as she turned toward the south wall in time to see her favorite (well, her only) grandson shimmer through the padding. As always, he was wearing a D&G suit, and the diamond in his left ear was even bigger than the last time she'd seen him. She hurried across the room to give him a hug. He towered above her now, taller even than his dad had been.

He crushed her in a hug that made her smile.

"Always the show-off, aren't you?" she teased. But the muscles were impressive. "You've been working out?"

He winked at her as he released her. "It's a guy thing. We need to flex."

She rolled her eyes. "Oh, I know all about the male need to strut." She touched the glittery bowling ball in his left ear. "What are you up to now, Prentiss? Eighteen carats?"

Her grandson, man of fame, power, and money, groaned like a little boy. "Gram! You have got to quit calling me Prentiss. I bought out the Grim Reaper's contract almost a hundred and fifty years ago. The name's Death now."

"Oh, please." She flicked the earring, making him wince. "Prentiss is a name that denotes intelligence and sensitivity. Death is… well… it sounds like you're a seventeen-year-old Goth drug addict who lives in a blacked out van smoking crack and hanging out with sixteen-year-old prostitutes."

Her unrepentant grandson grinned. "Ah, the youth I failed to have. I like the sound of that. I think I'll go buy a van."

"Prentiss! No decent girl is going to like a man named Death."

"Fortunately, I don't need to be liked. I'm rich and powerful. It pretty much does the job with the ladies." He sauntered across the room, his glistening shoes soundless across the gym mats. "And the stone is forty-one carats, by the way. It's a blue diamond, originally given by Ivan the Terrible to his first wife, Anastasia, on their wedding day, among other illustrious owners. You like?"

Sweet Hail Mary. What she would give to get her hands on her arrogant progeny for a year. Even a couple of months in the Den would clean him up a bit. What chance did he have of ever being worthy of a decent girl who could love him? Yes, he was a lowland filth project when it came to women, but she knew he had a beautiful heart. Or at least he used to. She was so worried about him. "Wearing a diamond as big as a golf ball makes you look arrogant."

"I am arrogant." He walked over to the row of photographs on the wall, all her girls who had gotten a fifth degree black belt or higher. He pointed at the third one, a picture of Mari. "What's her name? She's new."

"No." Angelica plucked Mari's picture off the wall. She'd known those golden locks were a bad move as soon as Mari had decided to wear her hair down around the men. "You don't get my girls. You aren't nearly nice enough."

"My girls think I'm nice." Prentiss flipped her a grin that was so cheeky it reminded her of the happy youth she'd raised. Before he'd become overly aggressive, dominating, and entirely unapologetic, of course. But she knew the good man was in there somewhere, even if he'd done his best to kill him off.

She hid Mari's picture under the vase of white roses. "Your girls tolerate your insensitive and demeaning treatment of them because you pay them large sums of money to allow you to behave badly."

Prentiss walked along the line of photos, dismissing each woman he looked at. "I know. It's a racket. They'll put up with anything for a chance at my money and the fact that I'm singlehandedly responsible for the fate of their souls." He turned and gave a long look at the photo she'd hidden beneath the flowers. "It works."

Angelica moved in front of the vase, blocking his view of Mari's photo with her body. What lascivious thoughts could a man possibly have when confronted with a grandma? "I love you, my boy, but when my black widow inoculation is ready—"

He snorted. "It won't work on my girls. There's no love."

She cocked her head, surprised by his comment. Her orphaned grandson had never uttered that word in her presence. Not since he'd stood there as a five-year-old and watched his parents turn to ash when one of his grandpa's experiments went awry. "Doesn't that bother you? That none of your women love you?"

"Of course not." Prentiss ambled over to the weapons table and picked up a pocket dagger she'd magically enhanced to unerringly find the target that its wielder was picturing in her mind. She'd created the spell for her younger girls, who didn't have the skills to protect themselves yet.

He ran the blade along his finger until it drew a trickle of blood. "I'm the most powerful man in the universe. Nothing bothers me, least of all the fact that the two hundred women living in my palace don't love me."

He closed his eyes for a moment. Then he opened them and hurled the dagger straight at the wall in front of him. The dagger spun in mid-air, so fast it was a blur, then it shot in the other direction and embedded itself in a landscape on the west wall. "Huh."

Angelica grinned. "You were thinking of the painting, so that's what it hit. I just finished the spell yesterday."

"Impressive as hell, Gram. I'll take a dozen. It'll come in handy for some of my lower-skilled apprentices to take out the reluctant souls." He walked over and plucked the dagger out of the wall. "It's not good for business to let beings get away after I've taken money to ensure their demise."

Angelica raised her brows. "You so need some time at my school."

"Thanks, but I have too much to do. The privatization of the Death business into a for-profit corporation has been an incredible time sink."

"Ah, life is so tough." Angelica removed the knife from his hand. "This is for my girls. I didn't create it to make money."

"We need to talk, Gram." Her grandson's amusement faded, and he got his "I'm going to lecture you" face on. She almost laughed when she saw it. It reminded her so much of the eight-year-old walking into her office and telling her that she needed to double the number of chocolate chips in her cookies.

But the man her co-chef had become folded his arms across his mighty chest and shot a dominating tone in her direction. "The word's getting out that you're going a little crazy over here with the matchmaking scheme. I've actually had to assign a full-time ward to watch this facility because you have so many beings so close to death all the time."

Angelica mimicked his pose and lifted her chin. The days when a man could talk down to her were so over. "Okay, I've had enough grief today on my tactics. I'm helping my girls defend themselves against the kind of emotional devastation only a man can wreak, and I'm doing my best to turn my men into decent guys. It's not my fault if they act like a bunch of resistant teenagers and get themselves killed!"

"Hey, I'm all for offing as many as possible, but you need a new business plan." He gestured at the peeling paint hanging down from the ceiling. "You do realize that you've been operating in the red for almost three hundred years now, and the only thing keeping the creditors from burning up the place and taking your intestines hostage is the fact that I keep killing off their head enforcers."

His comment made her pause. "You're doing charity work for me?" Was that so sweet? Granted, protecting her from assassins was the role of a lover and husband, but still. It felt lovely to have a man looking out for her. Not that she needed it anymore, but wow…

She felt her throat tighten. It felt good. And that was

just an embarrassment. If her girls ever found out that she couldn't deliver the "I don't need a man" attitude she demanded of them, they'd laugh her out of the place.

"Hey, don't be trying to diss my reputation by making it sound like I do anything for free." Her grandson grinned. "Most of these guys have enemies, so I'm running a healthy profit off protecting you, but still, you're brilliant. You're sitting on a major cash cow here. Torturing can go for a lot these days. Governments are desperate for some experts."

"This facility isn't about torturing. It's about creating lasting and meaningful unions between men and women. I don't torture for fun!"

"Well, no, for profit, of course. Doing things for fun is a waste of time."

Angelica sighed. "And to think I once thought you had a chance to be a decent man."

Death grinned. "You know you love me, Gram." His smile faded. "But I think we need to get you financially solid here."

How tired was she of hearing that from him? Did no man think a woman was capable of a decent business plan? "For your information, everything is coming together nicely. Trinity Harpswell will be fully ripened within the week—"

Prentiss snorted. "The black widow thing again? You've been working on that for centuries. Each girl ends up falling in love with someone more powerful than she is, and she gets axed when she tries to kill him. It's not a viable business model, Gram."

She stiffened at his derisive tone. "Trinity is different. She's stronger, and once the curse sets, I'm going to harvest her and make a fortune off the curse. Every woman who has ever been in love with a jerk but couldn't summon the willpower to get him out of her life will need it. And there are billions of women in that situation! It's brilliant!" She couldn't keep the excitement out of her voice. After all her work, everything was coming to fruition. It was time. Her vision was finally coming to life.

But Prentiss was shaking his well-coiffed head, and she could tell he wasn't even listening to her. "Gramps isn't going to be happy when he finds out you've wasted all his resources. You're going to empty the last of his reserves by the end of the month."

"Gramps?" Angelica felt like someone had sucker punched her in the belly at the mention of Napoleon, the black witch who had been her first love. Her husband. The father of the wonderful daughter who hadn't survived his reckless experiments. The grandfather of the man standing before her, the boy she'd barely rescued from his clutches.

Angelica had spent almost a week crying on the shower floor after Napoleon had walked out on her three hundred and twenty-seven years ago, then it had taken her another twelve hours to crawl across that tile floor to the towel rack. Only the realization that her darling grandson was counting on her had gotten her off that cold tile and trying to rebuild her life.

She could still remember the day perfectly. She'd been sitting at the kitchen table, so proud that she'd made her first batch of cookies without ever moving from the chair or touching a single item from the kitchen. And they were good! Napoleon's favorite kind, apple cinnamon raisin, and now he could have them whenever he wanted, even when she was working. How happy she'd been when he'd taken a bite and declared them the best he'd ever had. His smile. The warmth in his eyes. His pride for how he'd taken her from a 99 percent mortal seventeen-year-old into a powerful apprentice who could whip up a batch of cookies with nothing more than magic sparkles.

And then he'd set that cookie down on the midnight blue granite counter. Shoved his hands in the pockets of those faded jeans that hugged his lean hips so nicely. Given her that "I've been a bad little boy look," and then announced that his black magic contracting business had gotten too big, and he wasn't interested in the domestic lifestyle anymore. He was done with pretending to be the nice husband, the good guy, the mentor, and he was checking out.

And then he'd turned and walked out. Just like that.

Sweet saint of agony, that moment when she'd pulled herself out of her stupor and raced after him. Stopped in the doorway of their castle just in time to see two women with long legs, too much makeup, and magically enhanced breasts climb into his new Lamborghini. They'd both hunkered down out of sight in the region of his lap, and then he'd driven off with a screech of tires.

The smoke rising from the asphalt was the last thing she'd seen of her no-good, son-of-a-bitch true love.

The smell of burned rubber still made her nauseous.

Napoleon was her inspiration, in every way, for the gift she was bringing to the young men and women in her care. He was the reason she'd become the pillar of strength, a beacon of love and nurturing, and the self-love goddess that she'd become. Anything to give the lucky women and men in the Den of Womanly Pursuits a chance to avoid what had happened to her.

So, yeah, three cheers and bottoms up to the bastard.

But the fact that he was the driving force behind her empire didn't mean she actually wanted to *think* about him, let alone hear his name spoken.

And her very astute grandson was well aware of that. She eyed him. "Why on earth would you bring him up?"

Prentiss raised his eyebrows. "You haven't heard?"

Angelica gripped the edge of the weapons table at the sudden caution in his voice. "Heard *what?*"

"That I'm back, my dear." Napoleon's deep voice filled the room

Angelica's whole body shuddered. The room started to spin, and her skin got hot, prickly. She was going to pass out—

No! She was stronger than this! He couldn't affect her anymore. For heaven's sake, it had been three centuries! *I am a goddess. I am a beautiful, sexy woman. I love myself.*

Prentiss's brow furrowed, and she saw the concern on his face. "Gram—"

That did it. No way would she take pity from the man who now owned the soul of every being in existence, a man who had once been a boy who slept in her bed every night because he was too scared to sleep alone once his grandpa had left him.

She raised her chin, took a breath, and turned to face the misogynistic liar with great hair who had nearly destroyed her on every level of being a human, a woman, and a witch.

Chapter 9

AS HE AND TRINITY SHOOK HANDS TO SEAL THE BARGAIN, Blaine was not pleased to note that her skin was still as soft as it had been when she'd tried to stop him from pre-empting her ankle. Well, it was actually the fact he still liked the feel of it that was decidedly inconvenient.

Never thought he'd have to worry about getting all brain-drained over a woman, let alone one linked to the she-devil who'd spawned an entire generation of well-trained female pain-inflictors. But damned if he didn't just want to keep on holding that cute little hand of hers.

Verdict in: His mental acuity had apparently not survived the Den intact. He was officially insane, because he still hadn't let go.

"So." Trinity plucked her hand out of his, and he released it.

Self-discipline of steel. He was such a man.

Trinity turned toward the bathroom sink, grabbed a bottle, and began to spritz the contents on her wet hair, something a completely ordinary woman would do. Weird. He never thought of women as… women.

She glanced at him. "Tell me why this woman who has your friend needs to… die."

"Angelica? Maybe because she's a hellacious bitch from hell who gets her jollies out of kidnapping children and then torturing them for centuries, assuming they live that long." He leaned forward and sniffed. Whatever

Trinity was spraying smelled good. "Is that lavender? With a hint of mint and a dash of apricot?"

Trinity paused mid-spray and eyed him in the mirror. "Are you serious?"

"I'm always serious." What kind of question was that? "Angelica's not going to be winning any social justice awards, despite what she may think."

"No. I meant about the apricot. How could you possibly smell that?" She held up the bottle. "I love apricot, but even I can't distinguish it in this spray."

"What?" Had he said the apricot thing aloud? He replayed his words in his head and realized he had. What kind of warrior talked about lavender and freaking apricot? For hell's sake, he'd been out from Brainwashing Central for almost ten hours now. Toughen up, man! "I can kill a man with an apricot from a thousand yards away." Yeah, that sounded better.

Trinity raised her eyebrows. "And you think that's cool?"

He shrugged, folded his arms over his chest, and propped himself up against the wall. "It comes in handy." He made his voice nice and deep.

She set the bottle down and turned to face him, her gaze searching his face. "You really don't mind taking lives?"

He frowned at her tone. "Why would it bother me?"

She sighed. "Yeah, that's what I thought." She pulled open a drawer and grabbed a pale blue comb. "I guess it's good."

He watched her pick up a lock of her hair and run the comb through the ends. "What's good?" He had no clue what they were talking about. Couldn't concentrate on anything except that comb sliding through her hair.

"That you're the way you are. It's safer for you that you scare the living daylights out of me."

He was fascinated by the way she worked through the tangles. The witch and her progeny cleaned themselves up with a flick of their hands. He'd never seen a woman comb her hair before. It was... sensual... yeah... the way her fingers drifted over her hair... the way she tugged so gently at the knots.

"Blaine."

"Mmm." Her fingernails were a pale pink, barely shimmering in the dim light of the bathroom. None of the bright, daring colors he was used to seeing. Her hands were small. Delicate. He was used to thinking of women's hands as weapons. Hers seemed different. He reached out and brushed the back of her hand with his fingers.

She froze. "What are you doing?"

"Touching you." He turned her hand over so he could inspect it.

Trinity went very still. "What are you looking for?"

"Not sure." He traced the lines on her palm, felt the softness of her skin. There was no tingle of black magic. Just skin. That was the difference. She wasn't tainted. He sandwiched her hand between his. "Your hand is warm."

She swallowed. "I always run hot."

"I like it. I'm used to cold hands." He pressed her palm to his throat. She didn't try to strangle him. Didn't try to hurt him. Damn, it felt good.

Her green eyes were wide and wary as she allowed him to play with her fingers. There was no nefarious plotting in her expression. Just uncertainty with a faint blush to her cheeks. She looked like a woman, not an enemy.

Her comb slipped out of her hair and caught the neck of her shirt, pulling it away from her collarbone. Exposing the witch's mark.

He tensed at the sight of that yellow flower. At the reminder that she was the Chosen, that she'd been spliced with the witch's DNA to make her a receptive vessel. Getting smitten over her hands just because they didn't make his skin crawl? Not a great plan.

"Now you look mean. I don't like mean." She smiled, relief flickering in her eyes. "So keep it up." Trinity pulled free and turned away, but her cheeks were flushed.

He scowled as he watched her finish her hair. He'd be a fool to buy into the blushing thing. He'd seen women fake girly blushes and then unleash a herd of starving wolverines on him. The minute he let his guard down, Trinity would come after him. Didn't even matter if she didn't want to. It had been bred into her with magic, evil, and probably a little bit of torture.

His tattoo began to burn at the thought of Trinity getting tortured. Yeah, not a smart choice to like her, but getting pissed on her behalf sure felt good. Another item to add to the list of reasons why Angie-Babe needed to be shipped off to the world of eternal night.

Trinity set the comb down and grabbed a ponytail holder. "Okay, they're calling this thing I need to kill the Chameleon. So, the first thing we have to do is find it—"

Unacceptable. "No. Witch first." Feeling empathy for a sexy green-eyed victim wasn't the same thing as being stupid enough to actually trust her to uphold her end of the deal once she'd gotten what she wanted.

Yeah, he still had his shit together. It was all good.

Trinity shoved her hair up in a ponytail and turned to face him. "Here's the deal, Blaine. You can't kill this witch without me, but I can kill my target without you. So you need me, and I don't need you. So we do mine first, because I won't help you until my dad is free."

He narrowed his eyes. Huh. She had it right. How the hell had she twisted it like that? On the other hand... "You won't kill it." He was bluffing, but he was pretty sure he was right. She was talking smack, and she didn't want to kill Chammie-Boy.

She sighed and pressed her lips together. "I don't know if I could do it," she admitted.

Hah. Bingo. High five, anyone?

Her gaze went to his. "But I do have the capability to accomplish my goal. Can you say that about yours?"

Well, that was handy. They both knew the answer was a negative. How about them apples? Somehow, he'd been so distracted by her hair, or her breasts or whatever, that he'd forgotten to watch his babbling and he'd spooned her too much info. And now she was using it again him?

Nice work, Trio.

Aggravating, but still, he liked it. The chick was smart, using her brain instead of black magic branding irons, and he respected that. Almost made him want to kick back and spar with her for a bit. War with words. Hadn't been much of that in his life. Unfortunately, not really the time. "Listen, I could make you do it the way I want, of course, but we don't have time. So, here's the deal. We'll find the Chameleon, have a tea party for two with Angelica, and then I'll do the double down and take them both out at the same time. That make you happy?"

Not that he wanted to make her happy, of course. He folded his arms over his chest. "That's the plan and you can take it or walk," he added. Yeah, that was better.

A small smile played at the corner of her mouth, like she knew she'd won. "That'll work." She fished a folder out from behind the toilet. "Here's the information on the Chameleon." She set it in his hands. "I don't even know where to start. Any ideas?"

Blaine started to leaf through it. "Changes form," he read. "Different one each time. Kills in random areas." He felt the wheels in his brain begin to turn. He looked at a map of the assassinations and saw a pattern. Had a good idea where it would hit next. It felt good to go to battle against a foe he could defeat.

But as he studied the file, he couldn't help but slant an occasional glance at Trinity as she finished getting ready. He wasn't used to seeing a female get dressed, put on makeup, dry her hair. He liked it. Made her seem softer. Less like an instrument of torture and more like a female. Less perfect. More touchable.

He wasn't used to looking at women as… well… accessible, and as he watched her pull on a pair of sneakers, he felt something stirring in him. Something that made him want to throw her over his shoulder and protect her from the witch, like he was trying to do with Christian.

Yeah, like that could happen. Doing that would blow all his plans to shit and leave Christian dying in hell. He shut the file. "I'm going to take you back to my place. You can stay there while I take my team out after this shapeshifter."

"I have to go with you. It's part of my contract. I have to bring the…" she stumbled over her words. "Heart."

"I'm going alone." No way did he want to spend more than a minute with her. She tempted him and he was just not down with that. Didn't make him weak to admit it. Made him strong. Any good warrior knew exactly where his limits were and made sure to take care of them.

She frowned at him. "I—"

He took a gamble. "You want to be there to see that thing die? To see me rip out its heart?"

She paled and slowly shook her head. "No," she whispered. Her face was stricken.

Shit, now he felt like an ass for putting that expression on her face. But that was okay, because now he was in control. Of her. Of the situation. He liked it. It was how it should be. But he couldn't help rubbing her shoulder to ease her stress. "It'll be okay. You won't have to see it."

She nodded. "Yeah, that's probably best."

He squeezed her shoulder lightly. "Just grab what you need to stay for a couple days at my place. I'll take care of everything." Huh. He liked saying that. Me, Tarzan. You, Jane. I kill bad guy. Beat chest. Tarzan howl.

Her phone rang, and she picked it up. "Hi, Reina—" She stopped, and her face got even paler. "Oh, no. I'll be right there." She slammed the phone shut. "We have to go."

And then, before he had a second to stop her, she was running for the door.

"Hey!"

But she was already gone.

What was up with this woman? Didn't she understand he was in charge here? Didn't she comprehend how important this was? It had to be done his way, or Christian was going to die.

But when he heard Trinity's footsteps thunder down the stairs of her building, he knew she wasn't thinking about his issues. And that really pissed him off.

He'd had one hundred and fifty years of his life being complicated by the witch and her progeny, and it ended now. No murderous black widow with sea foam green eyes was going to mess it up for him.

Blaine headed straight for the window he'd busted through on the way in, and grinned as he launched himself out of it.

Yeah, she'd be surprised when he was waiting for her outside.

Then she'd realize exactly who was in control.

Trinity's heart was racing as she sped down the stairs, clutching her phone.

And the EKG overkill wasn't from the exertion.

It was from the way he'd held her hand, as if she were some magical gift, some precious jewel. The way his throat had moved when he'd placed her hand on it, in the ultimate gesture of trust. She stumbled on the steps, and barely caught herself on the railing.

Didn't he understand how dangerous she was? Didn't he care what monster swirled inside her?

Her phone rang again and she quickly answered it. "Reina! How is Cherise?"

"Oh, man, you've got to hurry. She's locked herself in the conference room and she's crying her eyes out. I can smell smoke, and I know she's got one of her pitchforks ready to jam it into her heart. She said she'll talk only to you."

"Tell her I'll be there in ten minutes." Trinity shoved her phone in her purse as she leapt off the last stair. She didn't have time to talk down one of the desperate clients at Triumphant Women Jamboree, Inc., the divorced women's empowerment agency she worked at, but she didn't have time not to.

Helping these women was the only thing she did that made her feel good. It nourished the nurturing side of her she was so desperate to tap into. It gave her hope that there was something worth redeeming inside her soul. No matter how worked up she was, the widow always went to sleep the moment she walked into TWJ.

And now... dear God, now... she had to go. Blaine was unhinging her, and pulling Cherise back from the edge of utter despair would stop the bleeding in a way nothing else would. She flung open the door to the parking lot and screamed as she plowed right into a hard wall. A wall that was warm and smelled really, really good.

Blaine's arms closed around her, and she caught the faint scent of smoke. "Going somewhere?"

She looked up at him, and saw the hard lines to his face. Felt the tightness of his grip on her shoulders. The man was a solid mass of muscle and immovability that made her stomach do a little dance. Oh, crap. Her female side was totally jonesin' for some loving from him. Was there any planet on which a manly man was convenient? Because this wasn't exactly handy dandy for her right now. "It'll take ten minutes, and if I don't do it, I'm going to snap."

He narrowed his eyes. "And that's bad."

She lifted her chin. "I'm a black widow. Take a guess." The She-Beast-of-Love was stirring again. How could she not? Blaine might have killing issues, but he was so freaking tough that what woman wouldn't respond to him on a biological level? Not that biology would get him killed, but Trinity had read way too many issues of *Cosmopolitan* not to know that women turned sex into love the way they turned chocolate into a three-course meal.

Example #1: Barry.

Blaine's scowl deepened. "We don't have time for this."

"Trust me, we don't have time not to do it."

He searched her face, then he swore and released her. "I'm coming with you."

She shook her head. No man had been allowed to cross the threshold of the Jamboree since the day its doors opened five years ago. "Oh, I don't think that's a good idea."

Blaine raised his brows. "It's that, or we're going to my place. Take your pick."

"You're insufferable! Such a guy!"

He grinned, clearly pleased with her statement. "I appreciate the compliment, but that doesn't change anything. I'm not letting you out of my sight."

"You ever been around women who hate men?"

Something dark flashed in his eyes. "Oh, yeah."

"Then you'll feel right at home."

His jaw got hard, and she sensed his sudden tension. His apprehension. And she wished she didn't have to take him. For his own well-being.

Which was ridiculous.

He was a warrior, for heaven's sake.

He could handle himself.

Then she thought of the women at the Jamboree, and she wasn't so sure...

———

"Let's get it done." Blaine grabbed her arm and began to propel her down the sidewalk.

"My car is the other direction—"

"We'll take mine." He nodded ahead, and Trinity saw a large, black motorcycle parked up beside the curb.

She stopped. "I can't ride on that."

He frowned. "Why not?"

"It's… dangerous." It was the best word she could think of. She didn't take risks right now. She kept all emotions tucked deep away inside, held tight like steel netting was wrapped around her. The motorcycle… too wild. Too adventurous. Too passionate. Too everything she didn't dare to be.

"Been riding for over a century. I'm good." He strode toward it, not bothering to wait for her. "I'll keep you safe."

"No." But she was already walking toward it. She had to touch it. To feel what that kind of freedom felt like. She laid her hand on the seat. The leather was soft, but it felt tough at the same time. The chrome was gleaming. The wheels were immaculate. It was the ultimate expression of daring to take on life, of refusing to go gently, of feeling the passion and fire burn through her until she wanted to explode. Of embracing risk and danger.

It was everything she couldn't afford.

Not in this moment. Not with the spider edging so close to the line.

Right now, she needed to keep a stranglehold on her emotions. It was about self-control. It was about showing she could manage the cravings and desire burning inside her. It was about driving her Subaru below the speed limit while wearing her seatbelt.

Blaine swung his leg over the seat, straddling the huge machine like he owned its soul. Like it was a demon he controlled by his mere presence. "Just got it. Nice, huh?"

"I can't ride that."

"You're my ticket to freeing Christian." He held out his hand to her. "Trust me, I'll protect you. No chance you're getting hurt with me around."

"It's not that." She clasped her hands behind her back, against the urge to climb on there with him. She could almost feel the wind blowing through her hair, that sense of being utterly free in a way she never had been. Ever.

He turned the key, then punched the ignition button. The engine roared to life, so loud it drowned out the thoughts in her head. It thundered in her chest, made her body vibrate, reducing her to nothing but a physical, visceral reaction to the power and freedom it offered.

He didn't bother with a helmet. He didn't bother to shout above the din. He just jerked his chin at her and revved the bike with a twist of the right handlebar.

She saw the determination in his eyes. He was a man who wasn't going to lose his race for Christian's life.

He wasn't even considering it. He'd do whatever it took, and he'd succeed.

She wanted to be like that. She wanted to be so sure, so confident, so certain in who she was and what she wanted that she never doubted herself again, never feared the monster within. She wanted to wake up in the morning with that same expression that Blaine was wearing. The one that knew, without a doubt, that she could have anything and everything she wanted.

Maybe she'd been going about it the wrong way. Maybe fighting her passions had been a misguided approach. Maybe the right choice was to embrace her inner fire and let it shine.

Blaine grinned, a smug look that told her that he knew she'd changed her mind.

Even as she started toward the bike, even as she slid her leg over the seat behind Blaine, even as she wrapped her arms around his muscled waist, she knew she was using the logic as an excuse to get on and feel that fire, a choice she knew in her gut was the wrong one, the dangerous one, the choice of an addict unable to ditch the high.

Blaine let the engine idle, and it subsided to a quiet roar. He pointed to pegs poking out of the bike near her feet. "Rule number one. Your feet never, ever come off those pegs unless I tell you. Not even when I stop. Your feet get in my way, and we could crash, or you could burn your leg off."

Her heart started to race, but she put her feet on the rods. What was she doing, riding this bike? This wasn't her. But it was too tempting. She wanted to live, just once. How could a bike ride trigger her into going crazy and becoming a murderer?

By stripping her of what little self-control she had left, that's how. What if she liked the high too much? What if she wanted it again? What if—

He twisted around so he could look at her. "Second rule: You tuck up against me and let your body fall in with mine. When I lean into the corners, you relax and go with me. Got it?"

Oh, man, she so couldn't do this. Release all resistance and let the world take her? "I—"

"If you need to stop, tap my side with your left hand. Other than that, just keep your feet on the pegs and let your body move with mine and the g-forces of the bike, and you're good." He grabbed her knees and crushed her thighs against the outsides of his.

Heat began to throb through her inner legs. An awareness of his strength. Of the intimate feel of his body between her thighs.

He flipped a grin at her over his shoulder. "The name of the game is submission, Trinity."

She stiffened. Submission was a dirty word in her vocabulary. Submission meant giving in to the curse.

"Surrender yourself to the bike and to me."

"I can't surrender to anything—"

He revved the engine with a flick of his right wrist, drowning out her protest. She frantically hit him on his left side to tell him to stop, but all he did was raise one eyebrow at her. Then he ditched the kickstand and the bike began to roll.

She lunged to get a grip around his waist, hugging desperately with all her strength. What had she been thinking—

She suddenly became aware of a deep vibration echoing up from the bike, like the pulsing of a bass drum throbbing in her core, down her legs, in her belly, along her thighs where she was pressed so tightly around Blaine.

And then the bike lurched forward with a squeal of tires. She tightened her grip around his waist, and then she felt the earth move beneath her. As the bike roared down the street, the cold wind whipped at her face, yanked at her hair, and her whole body shook with the vibration of a thousand pounds of force, she felt her soul come to life in a way she never had before.

She raised her face to the sky, felt the sun fighting to warm her against the wind's coldness, felt the heat of Blaine's body between her thighs. He turned a corner and they leaned as one with the bike.

She looked down as her right knee skimmed just above the pavement. They were going so fast, the ground was nothing but a gray blur, rushing past. Another inch closer and her kneecap would turn into a Frisbee. So close to utter destruction, dancing on the edge—

He straightened the bike and they moved upright again. Away from danger. She'd threaded the edge, but she'd never really been at risk. She could feel Blaine's complete control of the machine, of the power beneath them. One wrong move and the bike could be an instrument of carnage and lost dreams. But in Blaine's grasp, it was a tool of pure, unadulterated freedom.

To be able to control death so easily? To turn it from hell into joy? Tears filled her eyes as she pressed her cheek to Blaine's back. The heat from his body pressed at her inner thighs, burning through her jeans. Her hair knifed at her cheeks, her shirt flapped ruthlessly, as if the fabric wanted to rip free from her body, to fly through the air. She hugged tighter, suddenly afraid.

Blaine tapped her wrist and held his right arm up to the sky, like he was reaching for the sun. "You can let go," he shouted over his shoulder. "Try it!"

She shook her head and held tighter.

She felt the laughter rumble in his chest, and then he leaned over the handlebars and the bike leaped forward, as if he'd unleashed a wild cat from a cage. She felt his muscles flex, felt a sudden energy pulse through his body, like sparks were jumping from his skin onto hers, and then he whipped the bike onto the highway, and let it all out.

And all she could do was hang on.

Chapter 10

BLAINE LET OUT A SMALL WHOOP AS HE EASED THE BIKE off the highway. Hellfire and damnation, he'd never get used to that. After a lifetime of chains, the feeling of that bike on the highway was pure freedom.

Kicked ass.

Trinity poked her hand around his shoulder and pointed up ahead. "Take this right," she shouted.

He glanced down at her hand. It was trembling. Fear or cold? He caught her hand and felt it. Like ice. Had it been cold on the highway? He hadn't even noticed. He realized suddenly that her whole body was shaking, and she was pressed tightly against him. Shit.

He immediately turned up his body heat and set it outwards, and he grinned when he felt her stiffen, and then snuggle tighter against him. Her thighs tightened around his hips, and her breasts were pressed up against his back. He could feel her ribs expanding with each breath she took, and she was so tightly wrapped around him that he could sense the minute the shivers began to ease.

The intimacy felt weird. Foreign. He'd never been close enough to someone that he could feel them breathe. Hadn't been touched by anyone without having to concentrate on where the next assault was coming from. Hadn't used his heat to ease someone's pain before. Hadn't even thought of it.

But he'd done it instinctively for Trinity.

As he said, weird.

Trinity let out a sigh and she sagged against him, resting her cheek against his back.

The shivers were over, and he could feel the softness of her muscles. He could tell that she'd relaxed, and he liked it. Liked knowing she was trusting him enough to let down her guard.

He slowed the bike down even further, made sure to avoid the pothole as he eased the bike gently around the corner.

"Red doorway," she shouted. "On the right."

Blaine looked up ahead, and swore when he saw what she was pointing to.

The brownstone had large windows, a broad staircase with iron railings, and snapdragon flower boxes. English ivy climbed the walls. Ceramic swan pots of geraniums flanked a red door with a stained glass archway, a window almost exactly like the one he'd made when one of his young charges had been too injured to complete his project. Failure to produce would have meant more torture, so Blaine had stayed up all night with Nigel and Jarvis, trying to figure how to turn cross-stitching and painting skills into a stained glass masterpiece that would satisfy Angelica.

This place was all girl, all flowers, all feminine, and it reminded him almost exactly of the hellhole that had ripped his masculinity from him for the last century and a half.

A woman was hurrying up the front walkway. She was wearing jeans and a skimpy tank top—

He stopped the bike dead before it registered that it wasn't Angelica.

He wasn't back at the Den.

"Blaine!" Trinity yelped and jerked back from him.

He realized he was on fire. "Shit."

He shut it down as Trinity tumbled off the bike. She landed on her butt on the brick sidewalk, then scrambled to her feet. Her shirt was on fire, and she was frantically pounding at it. "Come here." He leapt off the bike and grabbed her. He didn't ask for permission, just yanked her against him and crushed her against his body. He immediately concentrated on drawing all the fire from her body into his, drinking it in like a stack of newspapers sitting next to a spark.

Trinity went still against him, and he felt her heart hammering where she was rocked against his chest.

"Almost done," he said.

Trinity pulled back, and her cheeks were still red. "You set me on fire?"

He winced. "Yeah. Sorry about that. Wasn't intentional." What the hell? One look at an Angelica look-alike and he'd lost his shit? The chick hadn't even had the same color hair. Yeah, that was cool. What was he, a freaking kid?

Soft. Trinity made him soft. He'd been all gooey thinking about her, and it had completely messed with him. No more of that crap. It was all business from now on.

Her eyebrows went up. "You lost control?"

Yeah, that was manly to admit. "I was distracted. I—"

She grinned. "I'm so glad to know I'm not the only one."

"One who what?"

"Loses control."

He stiffened. "I'm in complete control."

She raised her eyebrows. "So you meant to set me on fire?"

"I—" Shit. Where were his comebacks now?

"Trinity! Come on!"

They both turned, and Blaine saw the woman he'd confused with Angelica waving at them from the top step. Now that his brain was functioning, he could see that petite auburn-haired gal wasn't the witch, but she had a darkness to her aura that made his tattoo start to smoke. He'd felt that sludge around him every time he'd been teetering on the edge of death.

Trinity waved. "Coming—"

He caught her arm. "She works for Death."

Trinity looked at him in surprise. "I know. That's my friend Reina."

He scowled. "You know?"

"Yes, but this is her day job. She's not killing anyone right now—"

"Yeah, she is. I can feel it."

Trinity looked back at the gal, and she paled. "Oh, God, you're right. Someone's going to die. Reina!"

She broke free of Blaine's grip and started hauling ass right toward Death's finest. Was she insane? He'd brokered a few deals with Death to save the souls of some of the kids in Angelica's care, and the last thing he needed right now was a visit from that arrogant egomaniac.

He was out of chits to bargain with if Trinity got herself embroiled in something she couldn't get out of. He broke into a run to chase her down. He needed her, and he'd do whatever it took to keep her alive.

But as Trinity disappeared into the building that looked way too much like the Den, his tattoo began to

smoke at the thought of entering it. A building filled
with women, including one of Death's assistants and the
witch's Chosen? Who knew what the hell he'd find?

He was going in ready to fight. He set his skin to
simmer, pulled a couple of blue balls out of his pocket,
and went in.

———ᴍ———

Blaine charged through the front entrance, then skidded
to a stop when five women turned to face him. They
were gathered around a closed door, and their faces went
from worried to stark shock when he entered the foyer.
Except Trinity, who simply raised one eyebrow in a
classic "I told you so" look.

Five women. In one small room. He instinctively took
a step backward and began to spin the blue balls in his
right hand. A spiral of smoke rose from his chest, and
he caught the acrid scent of his shirt beginning to burn.

A tall woman with red hair and alabaster skin spoke
first. "Well. This is an unexpected treat."

Sarcasm intended, he was sure.

Trinity waved in his direction. "Everyone, this is
Blaine Underhill. He's helping me with a personal matter. Ignore him." She cocked an unsettled look at him, as
if concerned for his safety, then turned back to the door
and knocked on it. "Cherise, it's me. Will you unlock
the door, please?"

Ignore him? Yeah, not feeling the success of that
order, as all of the other women continued to stare at
him. The tall one looked curious, three looked like they
were channeling some evil force to shoot at him, and the
Death chick was alternating between inspecting him and

looking at Trinity. She looked fascinated, furious, and rabidly worried at the same time.

Okay, yeah, so maybe he should have taken two seconds to grill Trinity on the talents of these women before walking in here. Might be helpful to know whether they were more likely to start slinging oversized killer bees at him or simply try to vilify him with the silent treatment that women were so good at.

Vilification, no problem. He could take it. But if one stinger-loaded bug appeared, he was going on the offensive.

Reina tapped Trinity's shoulder, still eyeing Blaine as if she couldn't decide whether to ask him to dance or skewer him with whatever it was Death's peeps were using to knock people off these days. "Trinity," she whispered. (Stage whisper, anyone? Not sure the people in the next state could hear.) "What are you doing with a man like him?"

A man like him? He pulled his shoulders back. Screw that. He didn't have to take that shit anymore. There was nothing wrong with him, and he knew it.

Trinity rolled her eyes at Reina. "Don't worry about him. He's a good fit for me. I'll fill you in later."

A good fit? He shot a smug grin at the other three women still eying him like he was a cat that had just dumped a dead rat on their Oriental carpet.

He got back four impassive stares.

Shit. He didn't like this. He shouldn't be here. This was a female zone, and he was well-versed on what hostile women could do to a man and his genitalia. He did a quick recon of the battlefield. Three window exits. Stairs went north. Computer room to the right. Oriental carpets. Very nice ones. Handmade. A three-foot bouquet of white roses on the hall table. A cross-stitched sampler on the wall... His gaze went back to it. "Proportions are off on the trees," he said. "Wrong shade to get the right depth—"

He realized suddenly that all the women were looking at him again, even Trinity. Why the hell had he said that aloud? He managed a casual shrug. "Understanding depth helps me to hit my target from a mile away," he muttered. "Colors help determinate how far away it is. So I kill on first shot," he added.

They continued to stare.

Hell. Were they going to come after him? He really didn't want to hurt anyone. Not a female.

A loud wail echoed from the room, and everyone turned back toward the door.

Hallelujah.

"Oh, man." Reina's eyes were black now. "Something just died in that room."

"Cherise! Open up!" Trinity swore and thudded her fist on the door. "Don't we have a key?"

"It's magically protected from the inside," a short brunette said. "I did it after that vampire tried to convert his ex during our Wednesday night We Love Our Bodies meeting. Cherise must have seen me set it and triggered it herself tonight."

Magically protected? Blaine eyed the woowoo girl, massaging his balls with a little more force. Witch? Black magic or white? He narrowed his eyes, but there was no smut on the woman. Didn't mean anything. There was no smut on Angelica either. Some poor bastard was carrying her smut, and this woman could be doing the same thing.

Women who played around with magic were not the kind of girl that gave him a hard-on.

"Okay, so you locked the door and Cherise set it." Trinity fisted her hands, and he saw her fighting back aggravation. "Did you at least put in a safety, Lacey? A back door or whatever it's called?"

Lacey shrugged. "No. Never thought I'd be on the outside of it."

"So, how do we get in?"

"We don't."

"But we have to help her!" Trinity was pale and Blaine shifted at her obvious distress. Once again, the black widow was going in after someone who needed her. She had a dad to save, a witch to kill, and a curse to defeat, and she was taking time to save someone else?

Yeah, that was aggravating. Did she really need to keep doing that? Because each time she did it, it completely screwed with his plans of being ruthless, dominating, and focused only on his goal. People who sacrificed themselves to go after others were his freaking Achilles heel. The last thing he wanted to do was get involved with a bunch of hostile women, but if he could help someone save someone else, damned if he could walk away. He sighed. "I can open it," he muttered.

But no one even acknowledged his comment.

"I might be able to mist into the room," Reina said. "Since something died, I could write it off as a business expense."

"No," Lacey, the lock-builder, said. "It's impermeable. Vampires can mist, right? So I blocked vapor."

Reina scowled. "Well, that was brilliant. How could you allow no way in? Didn't it occur to you that you might lose control of your system? I mean, it's not like you're the only one in the world who's magically inclined."

"Get off my case, Death Girl," Lacey retorted. "Getting all hostile won't help things right now."

Blaine scowled. Did none of these women appreciate a warrior offering to solve their problems? "I said I can open it."

Trinity turned back to the door and started banging on it. "Cherise! Open the door!"

Reina continued to argue with Lacey about whether it was actually possible to block mist through magic, the tall one was scowling at the door as if she could intimidate it into opening, and the other two had run off to the computer room and were frantically searching the Internet.

Fine. He folded his arms over his chest and propped up against the wall near the sampler. They wanted to run around in circles? Teach them to ignore a man's offer for help. Someday, some woman somewhere was going to realize that men had some value, but until then, they could just—

Then he saw Trinity's face as she pounded on the door. Her skin was ashen, her shoulders rigid, and the tendons in her lovely neck were strained. She bit her lip and rested her forehead against the door, her eyes glistening as a single tear rolled down her cheek. "I'm so sorry, Cherise," she whispered. "I'm so sorry I wasn't here for you."

"Bloody hell." He immediately levered himself off the wall and strode through the women. Didn't even bother to flinch when they bumped against him. He just grabbed Trinity's fist as she raised it to hit the door again. "I've got it."

She looked up at him, and something registered in her face. Intense relief. "Okay."

For an instant, all he could do was absorb the expression of raw gratitude on her face. Damn, he was so liking that look of utter capitulation in her eyes, the way she'd instantly turned the problem over to him and trusted him to take care of it. Couldn't remember any female ever looking at him like he was what she'd been searching for her whole life, and not some deviant bastard who needed to be punished. Trinity was making him feel like a hero, and he loved it.

He gently clasped her arm and dragged her away from the door. After the way Trinity had looked at him, he was so getting this right. "Everyone back," he ordered.

He shoved the blue balls back in his pocket, not knowing how close Cherise was to the other side of the door. Then he ignited his tattoo, sent the flames rushing along his skin until his whole body was on fire. A simmering blue, flicking along the surface.

Then he walked up to the door, braced his palms on it. The magical protection prickled at his palms. It was strong, powerful, but there was no pain when he touched it. It was white magic, not black. Since all his mutations were the result of black magic, he was powerful against black magic. Against white magic, the poor cousin? It was like putting out a match with a tsunami. Good luck to the match.

He heard the women murmuring behind him, and tension prickled down his back. Instinct told him to turn around, not to take his attention off them. Hah. He was so much tougher than that. Instead of doing the damaged-wimpy-male thing and turn around, he focused his fire into his palms. Heated the door until the wood was smoking, and he could feel the magical shield buzzing. He shifted the color of his flames from blue, infusing some tendrils of white to match the tenor of the magic that had been used. "*Hasta la vista*, baby." He lifted his hands off the door, then slammed his palms against it.

The door incinerated instantly, and ash floated down around them. He grinned and stepped back. "Impressive, huh?"

Trinity set her hand on his back with a small sound of relief, then she rushed past him, not waiting for the ash to settle. He watched her go, his back still burning from the way she'd touched him. She'd said nothing, but that touch… yeah… that had said all he needed.

He tossed a grin at the other women, but they shoved past him, crowding the doorway to see inside the room. His smile faded at their lack of appreciation, and then he watched Trinity race toward her target. The sight of her reaching her goal was all the reward he needed, and he folded his arms over his chest to watch. Yeah, he was responsible for this, for getting her in there. He was the man.

In the corner, below a painting of Amazon warriors, a young woman was huddled, her knees pulled to her chest. Her head was down, her eyes were closed, and her aura was a muddy mix of crimson, black, and brown. A woman in bad, bad emotional shape.

He was suddenly glad that Trinity was going to help her. She might be female, but she was clearly a victim, and he had a thing for helping those who'd been jerked around by someone else. As Trinity fell to the carpet beside her, whispering gentle words of reassurance, he was struck by a memory. Of a woman kneeling beside him. Being kind. Her hands gently rubbing his back? His mother—

And then the memory was gone.

―᠁―

"Oh, thank heavens!" Trinity's heart leapt when Cherise raised her head. "You're alive."

Cherise lifted a white linen napkin. "Mister Fancy just died."

"Mister Fancy?" Trinity looked down and saw a rainbow colored fish cradled in the ivory cloth. "Your fish?" All this was about a *fish*? Not that she didn't like scaly water-dwellers but dear Lord, she'd thought Cherise was dying.

Suddenly too exhausted to sit up, Trinity slumped against the wall next to Cherise and draped her arms over her knees. "A fish," she repeated wearily. Her dad was in danger of dying. She had a witch to kill, a hot guy to hate, and she was here on account of a fish?

"My fish." Cherise leaned her head back against the wall. "It's over. It's done. I don't know what to do."

"About what?" Trinity looked up as Reina and her boss, Elise Parsons, slipped into the conference room. Elise's auburn hair was in a tight bun, as always, and her blue eyes were worried.

Elise had opened the Jamboree five years ago after she'd left her sex-addicted husband (who was, unfortunately, addicted to sex only with females to whom he wasn't married. Females of all sorts… ahem…). After getting hammered by people who tried to convince her it was a mistake to leave the only man who was big enough to make a six foot four woman like her feel petite and girly (you know, the same helpful souls who liked to point out that if she kicked him out, the only sex she'd ever get again would involve mail-order appliances) she'd decided that women who took control of their lives needed a champion, and the Jamboree was formed.

And yes, there was a Friday night class once a month on appliances. Nothing wrong with self-love when the mood strikes.

Reina sat in a nearby chair, and Elise knelt beside Trinity, her long legs elegant in her narrow, black skirt. "Your friend did a nice job on the door, Trinity." She let the question hang in the air as to what exactly Trinity had been thinking bringing a man with her, but she didn't press it. That would be for later, when Cherise was no longer on the edge of whatever precipice she was about to leap off of.

As for Trinity's friend? That wasn't exactly how she would have described Blaine. More like an unfairly hot, arrogant jerk who was going to either save her soul or make it implode. Trinity peeked over her shoulder and saw Blaine standing in the doorway. He had an odd look on his face, as if he were confused. Like he'd just seen something he wasn't sure about. Something that had bothered him. She started to rise to her feet to go to him, to see what was wrong.

Cherise let out small a moan. "It's Damian."

"Your fiancé?" Trinity looked sharply at Cherise and sat back down. Damian was a much bigger problem than Mister Fancy. If Damian was the issue, then she was very, very glad she'd come. "I mean, *ex*-fiancé?"

Last she'd heard, Damian was in "ex" status, and they'd all been so hopeful that Cherise would be strong enough to stay away from him before he broke her.

Sometimes seeing the clients at the Jamboree continuing to go back to the men who treated them so badly almost made Trinity want to hand them her curse, just for the night, just to get them free.

Almost.

Cherise nodded. "He came over last night. He'd been out chasing foxes with his friends, and you know what he and the boys are like when they do the werewolf thing. The women, the drinking, and the farm animals."

"Feeding on raw steak before he went out didn't curb the need to eat sheep?" It had been quite interesting hearing all the women's suggestions on how to successfully date a werewolf, but loading up Damian's stomach had seemed like the best choice. Indulging his furry fantasies had evoked a resounding "No" from most of the women, though not all.

"It didn't work. He still had wool in his teeth. I couldn't make love to him. He had bone fragments and wool in his incisors, you know?"

Blaine raised his brows, and Trinity felt her cheeks heat up. It was one thing to discuss sex openly with the girls, but it felt different with Blaine listening. Especially when she could still feel his hands on her naked body when he'd plucked her away from Thor-the-Kidnapper, the way his palms had slid over her oil-slicked skin—

Ahem.

"Yeah, sheep remnants would be a major mood killer," Trinity agreed, trying to focus on the conversation. Maybe dating a werewolf would help with her murderous tendencies. She'd always had an aversion to guys with hairy backs. A guy who had hair over every body part might be perfect for her.

She glanced over at Blaine again. Sort of wondered how hairy his chest was. Would he be smooth and bare, with just warm, lush skin taut over his muscle? Or would there be that curly dark hair, weaving a path downward toward his—

"So, anyway, when I kicked him out of my bed," Cherise continued, "he got all pissed and started howling about his animalistic need for sex. You know, the whole 'guys can't live without it' and stuff? How, as a dominant male, he's naturally programmed to need to spread his seed and everything."

"Yeah." Trinity had to admit, on some levels, that it didn't sound so bad. Having a man not be able to live without her? A real relationship, with commitment, bonding, and even too much sex? What if a man like Blaine couldn't get enough of her body? Those shoulders, his biceps, that strong jaw. All day long, getting naked and sweaty? That hard-core male body wrapped around her—

Reina kicked her. "You're staring at him," she whispered. "Close your mouth."

Trinity instantly averted her gaze from the way his jeans sat on his narrow hips, and tried to concentrate on Cherise.

"So when Damian stared to tear up my favorite pillow—like that's going to make me want him—I got a rolled-up magazine and smacked his nose, like it said to do in this new *Fix the Problem Dog* book, and did it work? No! He growled at me, then he ran into my office and started eating my fish!"

Trinity suddenly understood what Cherise was saying. Cherise, the world renowned fish geneticist who had spawned seventeen new species of fish in the last eight years, had pet swimmers all over her house, but the ones in her office were a completely different story. "Your work fish? The new breeds you're developing?"

"Yes! In one stupid, hairy moment, Damian set me back a year on my research. What kind of man eats your fish when you won't sleep with him?"

"Werewolves, apparently." Reina moved off the chair to sit beside Cherise. "Men who act like dogs are one thing, but guys who actually are canines are notoriously difficult to keep indoors. They're best off chained up outside under the stars when you're not using them."

Trinity raised her brows. "Chaining him up? Isn't that a little bit harsh? I mean, he is a man sometimes."

"Oh, my sweet black widow, being chained up is one of the joyous pleasures of being in an intimate relationship." Reina leaned forward and lowered her voice. "Have you never done the handcuff thing?"

Trinity rolled her eyes. "Are you kidding? The last thing I need is a guy getting more defenseless around me."

Reina raised her brows. "What about *you* being handcuffed?"

"Me?" Something pulsed deep in her belly at the thought of being restrained during sex. So she could enjoy herself and not worry at all that she could hurt the guy? She glanced at Blaine, and his eyes were nearly black, and his jeans were getting a little tight. "I never thought of being handcuffed," she managed. "But I can see the benefits." Amen to that, sistah!

One of his eyebrows went up, and his eyes got even darker.

"Hello?" Cherise waved her hand, and Trinity jerked her gaze off Blaine.

Good heavens! What was her problem? "Sorry, Cherise." She could still feel Blaine's gaze on her, and she fought not to look at him. But her shirt was suddenly itchy, and her bra felt too tight over her breasts.

"We're talking about me right now, thank you very much." Cherise glared at Reina. "I can't believe you want me to chain Damian like he's some husky."

"I don't date werewolves, so I've never been in your situation," Reina said. "But if I did, and he started playing the pooch card as an excuse, I'd throw it back in his face and treat him like the dog he wants to be."

"It's a little late for that!" Cherise held up Mister Fancy. "I just got an offer to sell him for almost a million dollars. I was in the middle of negotiating it and then Damian ate him. Ate him!"

"Cherise." Trinity took her hand and squeezed gently. "You need to start really thinking about whether he's right for you. I mean, eating your research isn't a great thing to do, regardless of what form he was in when he did it."

Tears filled Cherise's eyes. "I know, but he's so cute when he gives me those puppy dog eyes and wags his really nice butt—"

"Cherise." Elise finally spoke up. As always, she was letting her minions handle their own clients, and Trinity appreciated that. "Dating the wrong man is just trouble. We can't all be like Trinity and kill them off when they hurt us—"

Trinity stiffened. "I didn't mean to kill Barry—"

Elise waved her off. "You're a wonderful example of taking control. We all admire you."

Trinity's gut tightened. Barry was as far from taking control as could be. He was the moment when she'd lost complete and total control.

Elise turned to Cherise. "If Trinity can be strong enough to kill the man she loved, surely you can find the strength to take out the doggie door. Then at least he'll have to shift back to human form to get inside."

Trinity shook her head. "I told you, I didn't kill Barry on purpose—"

Elise shot her a sharp glare. "Try and be helpful."

Trinity snapped her mouth shut. Yeah, Elise reminded her far too often that her greatest value at the Jamboree was to be that shining example of standing up for herself. Elise knew the truth about the curse, but she blew it off. She believed her job was to empower the women who came to them for help dealing with the vampires, werewolves, incubi, and other beastly men who were ruining their lives, and using Trinity as an example of getting out of a bad relationship was what she was going to do. If Trinity didn't like it, she could get over her holier-than-thou attitude and get on board with being a liar for the greater good.

For Trinity, the rush out of helping others was worth the guilt over lying about her past, and Elise knew that all too well.

Cherise sighed. "But I love Damian—"

"You're a city girl who waxes her entire body except for her eyebrows because you don't like hair. Not a fit for a man who sheds and has to go on twenty-mile hunts at night." Trinity set her hand on Cherise's arm. "Damian's trying to be the man he knows you want him to be, but he can't do it. He's a werewolf, not a Lhasa Apso. He needs his freedom, and if you don't let him go, he's going to keep eating your furniture, and maybe you."

Cherise leaned forward, and her eyes sparkled. "But I like that part," she whispered. "The fact that he might snap and bite me someday. I kinda like the danger."

"Well, that's easy." Reina said. "There's a lot of men who are inches away from killing you, who would fit in with fine china and an indoor lifestyle. Men who don't shed."

Cherise gave them a skeptical look. "Like who? A bad boy biker? That's so cliché."

Trinity couldn't help but slide another look toward Blaine. He was leaning against the wall, arms folded over his chest, as he studied an angel tapestry. With his dark hair, his bulk, that motorcycle, and his fire thing... he was bad boy all the way.

Yeah, she could see the appeal of guys who were a little bit dangerous...

"How about demons?" Reina suggested. "They aren't hairy."

Cherise rolled her eyes. "They smell like sulfur when they get turned on. Gross."

"Black witches?"

Blaine shifted so suddenly in the doorway that all three women turned and looked at him. He scowled. "Black witches leave something to be desired," he muttered.

"I agree." Cherise shook her head. "There's just something effeminate about a male witch. I need a man."

"How about a dead guy?" Elise suggested.

Cherise wrinkled her nose. "I get that a dead man can't cause trouble, but necrophilia isn't my thing."

"I meant vampires," Elise said. "I was at a black tie fundraiser the other day for saving the Woldsmith Cemetery, and I met at least seven vampires. All of them were completely hairless and wearing designer suits. No tails, and they were wearing only silk. No wool at all."

Cherise frowned. "I'm kind of blood-averse."

"Maybe you just haven't encountered blood in the right situation," Elise said. "There's something pretty sexy about a couple of puncture wounds on your inner thigh. You know, how he's got to lick them to seal the wound and all… and then his tongue starts to wander…"

Cherise's eyes widened. "Oh. I hadn't thought of that."

Trinity thought of being on the bike with Blaine. Of the way her thighs had wrapped around his hips… the feel of his body between her legs… the deep vibration of the engine… the way his hand clamped down on her thigh, anchoring her around him. She glanced over at him and saw he was studying her. His eyes were dark, his expression hooded. But a slow spiral of smoke was rising from his chest. Oh, wow.

"Maybe it's time to branch out," Reina said. "Vampires might rip your throat out, but they're way too classy to eat your fish or tear up your pillows."

"That does sound good." Cherise nodded and sat up. "Okay, I think it might be worth a try." She took a deep breath and gave them a trembly smile. "I can do this, right? Walk away from the werewolves?"

"I know you can." Trinity smiled, trying not to look toward Blaine, but she could feel his stare boring down at her. "You'll find the right guy. Just be patient."

"And hide the fish," Reina added.

"I will." Cherise held up her arms and hugged Trinity. "Thank you so much for coming," she whispered. "I didn't know what to do."

Trinity smiled. This was why she worked here. Because there was no feeling as good as helping women find their way to true love. She could live vicariously through them, and it felt good to help others. Yes, it made her uncomfortable to be lauded for her past, but at the same time, if it could help one woman, then that was one moment in which she could stop hating what she was and what she'd done. "Of course I'll always come. You know I will."

Cherise set her handbag in Trinity's lap. "You keep this. I was going to do what you did, but now I think I can manage without it."

Trinity took the bag and peeked inside. A gun was in there. She went cold. "Cherise—"

"I knew you would understand," Cherise said. "No one else here knows what it's like to want to kill the man you love, but I knew you'd get it." She hugged her. "Thank you for everything." She smiled. "I know I can—" She froze suddenly, looking past Trinity's shoulder. "By all that's hairy and fanged, who is *that?*"

"The fire guy?" Trinity stiffened, not liking the way Cherise was looking in Blaine's direction, as if she wanted to start dancing naked with him. "He's with me," she blurted out, then winced when she saw Reina raise her brows. Oops. That had sounded a wee bit possessive, hadn't it? "I mean—"

"No, not him." Cherise pointed. "*Him.*"

Reina looked past Trinity, and her eyes widened. "Oh, cactus balls. He's back."

"He, who?" Trinity caught the sudden scent of rotten bananas, and she whirled around in time to see Augustus charge through the doorway. Something pink flashed in his hand, and then a six-pointed star was hurtling right at her face.

She had no time to duck.

He was going to dust her.

Chapter 11

BLAINE HAD NO IDEA WHO THE STINKY ROT WAS WHO'D just busted through the front door of the chick palace, and he'd never seen a flying girlie star, but it took him less than a split second to figure out that his ticket to Christian's freedom was about to get some serious harming done to her. "Down now!"

He threw an orange fireball at the star, and it ignited the thing, and then it kept on trucking, right for Trinity. No time to try another color. He launched himself through the air, and he landed between the torpedo and Trinity just in time for the cotton candy wannabe to plow right into his chest.

The pain was instant and blinding, and it dropped him to his knees before he had a chance to recover.

"Blaine!" Trinity scrambled to her feet and raced toward him.

"Don't touch him!" Reina intercepted Trinity as she lunged for him. "That stuff might be contagious, and you can't do any good if you get dusted."

Blaine looked down and saw that his chest had turned pink. He'd never thought of pink as an instrument of pain. The witch would love this trick—

Agony ripped through his gut, and he hunched over. Screw that. He wasn't being taken down by some chick-colored weapon. Even the witch had the respect to use manly colored weapons.

"Let me go!" Trinity was screaming now, fighting to get to him, and didn't that just make him go all soft and woolly inside.

Then he saw the slump-backed assailant reach into his pocket, and a flash of pink peeked out of the edge. He was going for take two? No chance, fruity boy.

"Get behind me," he ordered.

Trinity turned to see what he was looking at, yelped when she saw the second star, then ducked behind Blaine. Again with the trusting him to take care of her problems. He could so get into that.

Blaine immediately set himself on fire and sent the flames sweeping through his body, exactly as he'd done to cleanse the schnoodemgon poison gas. He gritted his teeth against the pain, and felt his body continuing to weaken. Apparently, the cleansing fire wasn't going to be quite as successful in this situation. Note to self: pink = bad news for men.

He fought harder, drilled heat into the flames until they were white-hot, and finally the pain in his chest switched from icy cold numbness to the searing burn that indicated all his internal organs had caught fire. He felt his muscles return to life. Back in business, baby!

The invader whipped out the star, and Blaine leapt to his feet. He shot a white fireball, and then a green one, but nothing worked as he charged across the room. The bastard was still on his feet when Blaine tackled him into the wall. The plaster crumbled around them as Blaine fought the wiry scrap for control of his little pointed weapon.

Took longer than he liked, and his wrist got nicked, but he finally had the guy face down on the floor in a

KISS AT YOUR OWN RISK 153

headlock. He sat on the dude and pinned his wrists under Blaine's knees, the star sitting harmlessly on the floor next to the guy's face. "Say uncle."

Trinity peeked out from behind the table. "You got him?"

"Sure did." Blaine felt pressure building under him, and realized the guy was amassing energy of some sort. He had no clue what was going to happen when the guy erupted, and he wasn't about to risk Trinity, and it wasn't like he had time to figure out what color fire would work on him, if any. "Go get on my bike," he ordered. "We're leaving."

"No. Not yet!" Trinity ran over and knelt beside Blaine's captive.

Did the woman have no sense? Yeah, he had the guy secured right now, but something was brewing and it wasn't going to be primroses and pansies. Granted, he was so getting off on her complete faith in his ability to manage the bad guy, but he wasn't sure exactly what he was dealing with yet. "Get back."

Trinity ignored Blaine and looked right at his captive. "Why did you come after me, Augustus?"

The dude twisted his lumpy head. "I have yet to determine how you succeeded in convincing the Triumvirate to divest me of your father in return for that monster's heart—"

Trinity shook her head. "No, no. I didn't talk them into anything. They brought it up to me!"

"But," Augustus continued, "I have never given up my prey and I'm not going to start. The only way to break the contract is for you to die, so that's got to happen."

Trinity paled. "Oh, wow, that's really not what I was hoping to hear."

Blaine ground his knee into the man's kidney, but the assassin just smiled, a thin, creepy grin. "You won't make it to Sunday, Trinity Harpswell. I never lose."

"Well, if that's not just melodrama—" Blaine felt his body begin to tingle where it was pressed against his captive's. Fantastic. Black magic. Building fast. What the hell was this guy? "All right, buddy. Time to cap your ass—"

"No!" Trinity grabbed Blaine's arm as he was about to fire up some sparks. "Don't kill him."

Blaine stared at her. "Are you kidding? He's angling to kill you, and he's got some sort of powerful shit going on. I don't want to wait around for a tea party when he finishes whatever game he's preparing right now."

"No! I can't just kill people." She jumped to her feet. "We'll take care of the monster before Augustus finds me. Then it's over."

Blaine's palms began to throb where he was pinning the bastard down, and he knew without looking that thousands of microscopic pinholes were bleeding out his palms. That's how his reaction to black magic always started. "We don't want to mess with him—"

"Then let's go!" Trinity started backing toward the door. "Come on, Blaine. We don't have much time."

As if there was any chance he was leaving this guy alive. Blaine ignored her and sent a testing spark into his captive's body. The dude shuddered, and then the magic intensified. Son of a bitch. The scumbag had just tapped into the black magic roots of Blaine's fire and fed on it.

That was bad news. Even Angelica hadn't been able to feed on it. What was this dude? He didn't know, but he knew one thing: Any attempt to use fire on him would only make him stronger. Which meant that he wasn't going to be toasting this guy into oblivion anytime soon without doing some serious research on how to deal with him.

He needed to regroup with his team to find out what they were fighting here, and he needed to do it fast.

He looked at Trinity, who had paused on the threshold. "Go get on my bike. Now."

"But what about Augustus? He's going to come after us. Can you tie him up or something?"

"Tie him up?" Blaine echoed. "That's not going to hold him…" Or… maybe he could do something just as good though. If Augustus could feed off Blaine's black magic, maybe Blaine could return the favor. Deprive Augustus of his black magic by sucking it into his own body, the way he'd absorbed the fire when Trinity had gone sparkly. No guarantees that it would make Blaine stronger, like it had with Augustus, but it wasn't like he wanted to dine on the guy. He just wanted to weaken him long enough for them to take off.

Yeah, he was liking that. Absorbing some black magic into his body couldn't be worse than some of the fun he'd had with Angelica, right? "Bottoms up," he muttered, and then he placed his hands on the sumbitch's head and opened himself up to the poison he'd been fighting his whole life.

─␣─

Trinity gasped as Blaine's skin turned ashen, and then his eyes rolled back in his head. He was gripping Augustus's head, and the air around them filled with a murky, green smoke. Augustus was struggling beneath him, but Blaine was holding him still with brute strength. "Blaine?"

He shook his head once, and the muscles in his arms flexed. Augustus's body convulsed, and then he let out a loud moan, and then went limp.

Blaine released Augustus' head with a grunt, and then fell forward on his hands. His skin was gray, and his hair was smoking. "Blaine?"

"I'm good." He lurched to his feet. "Let's go."

"Augustus isn't dead. He'll be up again soon." Reina ran up. "That's such bad news if he's after you for his own personal vendetta."

"I know." Trinity caught Blaine's arm as he stumbled. "Help me get Blaine outside."

Reina grabbed the warrior's other arm and they began to help him toward the front door. He tripped again, and they had to fight to keep him on his feet. "Damn, girl, he's heavier than your dad. What's up with you picking up some well-muscled warrior as an appendage?"

"I'm fine," Blaine muttered. But his eyes were closed and his muscles were trembling.

"I'll help." Elise ran over and slung Blain's arm over her shoulder. She was so tall that she was able to support him. "What's going on, Trinity? What can I do for you?"

"Nothing. I just need to—"

"Hello?" Cherise's cheerful voice filled the room.

Trinity looked over her shoulder as Cherise sat down beside Augustus and tapped his shoulder. "Excuse me, sir. Are you okay?"

"For heaven's sake, Cherise," Trinity said. "Even a werewolf is better than Augustus."

"Did you see what he did to your guy? Very

impressive." Cherise patted his cheek. "I'm just going to make sure he wakes up okay."

"Cherise—"

"For heaven's sake, Trinity," Reina snapped. "Stop trying to save yourself by helping everyone else in the world. Leave Cherise to her own bad choices. You need to get out of here!"

Blaine pulled out of their grasp. "I can walk," he snorted, and promptly careened sidewise into the wall. "Shit."

"Stop being a hero," Trinity said. "Let's go."

"I like being a hero," he muttered.

"Of course he does," Reina said. "He's a man. They all get off on that." She eyed Trinity as they half-carried him out to the curb. "So, you going to tell me where you picked him up, and why in Death's name you'd do something so risky right now?"

"It's not risky. He's a jerk. No way I can like him." Together, the three women got Blaine out to his bike, and he managed to swing his leg over the seat.

"Screw that," Blaine muttered. "I'm awesome." He tried to grab the handlebars and missed completely.

Trinity set his hands on the grips. He grasped them and let his head fall forward, as if he were about to take a little nap. "I need him," she said. "He's going to kill the Chameleon for me."

Reina's eyebrows shot up. "In exchange for what?"

"Help with a little project."

Reina grabbed her arm. "What kind of help? This guy doesn't care about you. He—"

"I've got it covered," Trinity interrupted. "Trust my judgment."

Reina let out her breath. "Look at him, Trin. He can't even sit up, let alone keep you safe—"

Smoke began to pour from Blaine's chest, and he lifted his head. Pockets of small flames danced in his eyes. Sparks danced on his shoulders, and Trinity sensed a burning strength within him. "I'm good," he said, his voice much stronger. "Let's go."

"Oh, hello," Cherise's voice drifted out through the open door. "My name is Cherise. Would you like some coffee to help you perk up?"

Trinity exchanged nervous glances with Reina. Augustus was waking up!

"Go!" Reina backed up. "I'll hear the details later." She poked Blaine. "And you. Keep the bike upright, okay? That's my best friend you've got on there with you."

He levered a hard look at Reina. "I'll keep her safe."

Reina's eyes widened and then she grinned. "Yeah, I bet you will, won't you?"

Trinity leapt on behind Blaine and wrapped an arm around his waist. His skin was hot, burning through his clothes, as if he had a fever. She hesitated. "Are you going to set me on fire again?"

"No." The bike roared to life, and he didn't hesitate.

He just peeled out on the motorcycle, and Trinity had to hug him to keep from sliding backwards. The machine vibrated between her legs, and her hair began to whip, and then he was peeling down the street. The bike wobbled for a split second, and she caught her breath, then it lurched forward, and they were off.

To where?

And was it going to be far enough to get away from Augustus?

That was such bad news. They didn't have until Sunday anymore. They had hours. Minutes. Seconds. Until Augustus found her again.

The monster had to die. And fast. But as a shudder went through Blaine and the bike wobbled again, she knew they were in big-time trouble.

———

Angelica was utterly dismayed to see that Napoleon looked exactly the same as he had the last time she'd seen him. How did three centuries of amoral woman-izing, black magicking, and self-indulgence not give a man a saggy butt or a potbelly?

But no, he was still tall (taller, even? He looked near six and a half feet now), well-muscled, and he had all his hair. He was wearing a black suit even more expensive than her grandson's, his eyes were still that compelling blue, and he still had that perfect amount of five o'clock shadow decorating his jaw.

At the sight of the man she'd loved so deeply, for so long, something bubbled deep inside her, something she hadn't felt since that day he'd walked into her gym class, looked right at her, and said he'd come for her, in that deep, resonating voice. It was that indefinable spark that made her feel like a woman, like a cherished female, like a sexual being with more fire inside her than any living being should be able to generate.

He flashed those perfect white teeth at her. "My dear. It's so lovely to see you."

Angelica swallowed, her throat suddenly tight. She couldn't think of what to say. How to speak.

Prentiss folded his arms over his chest. "Hey, Gramps."

But Napoleon didn't take his eyes off Angelica, gazing at her as if he couldn't go another moment without drinking her into his soul. She felt her skin begin to heat up. Anyone have a fan?

"You look beautiful," he said quietly. "I've missed you."

A small squeak made its way out of her throat. He'd missed her? Was he sorry? Did he still love her? "Napoleon—"

"Cut the shit, old man." Prentiss moved in front of her, feet spread, shoulders back. His fighting stance. "Don't mess with my grandma."

Angelica blinked as her grandson cut off her view of Napoleon. By all that was sexy and bad news, what was she doing? She wasn't taking him back! She didn't care if he'd missed her! Under no circumstances was she giving him the power to turn her back into the sniveling wuss she'd worked so hard to leave behind. No. Chance.

"I've got it, Prentiss." She touched her grandson's arm and moved up beside him. A united front.

She levered a hard stare at her ex-true love, and really looked at him. At the laugh lines around his eyes. At those full lips that had kissed so many other women. At the underperforming hands that had failed to give her the ultimate pleasure those thousands of times she'd entrusted her body to him. At the violet-blue eyes that had looked right at her and rejected her. At the handsome face that had haunted her for so long. "This is my home now," she said. "You aren't invited."

Prentiss grunted with approval, and respect flashed in Napoleon's eyes.

And then the womanizing man-whore opened his big mouth. "I hate to divest you of your self-empowered notions, but this home is actually mine. The magic that holds its walls up responds to me, and nothing can keep me out."

Crap. Was that true? She'd never had the grounds inspected. Next time a man walked out on her and left her with a castle, she was so going to bring in an expert surveyor.

"Why are you here, Gramps?" Prentiss interrupted.

Napoleon finally looked at him "My boy, you are quite impressive. Details of your successes have reached me across the worlds. I never thought you would wind up controlling the fate of every soul in existence."

Prentiss drew his shoulders back, and she saw the pride flash in his eyes. "You've heard?"

"Of course I have. I keep track of you." Napoleon walked across the mats and held out his arms. "I never stopped thinking of you. I'm proud of you."

Prentiss stiffened. "No thanks—"

Napoleon grabbed his grandson in a huge hug. For a moment, Prentiss resisted, and then Angelica saw a little boy expression of complete vulnerability cross his face, and then he was hugging the man who'd played the role of his father before he'd walked out on them both.

Tears filled her eyes as she watched Prentiss embrace the icon of self-gratification who'd abandoned him. How dare Napoleon come back in here and mess with them both? But at the same time… she knew how badly Prentiss had missed his father, his grandfather, and his mother.

Prentiss suddenly pulled back out of the embrace. "Enough." His voice was hard. "What do you want from us?"

"Can't an old man come home to see his loved ones?" Napoleon spread his hands, an acorn-sized ruby ring blinking on his left pinkie finger. No wedding ring. Gee, what a surprise. So glad she'd used hers to make penis rings for some of her men years ago. Sort of a fitting use for it.

Angelica snorted at his innocent expression. "Oh, come on, Nappy." She got a silent chuckle when she saw Napoleon wince. He'd always detested that nickname, so she'd never used it, not wanting to upset him. Now? She just might feel inspired to sprinkle it liberally into their conversation. It had such a lovely ring to it.

"You don't expect us to believe you came home for a family reunion." She cocked her head and looked pointedly in the direction of his more intelligent head (the one in the nether regions, of course). "Unless your women have finally gotten tired of not having orgasms and you can't get laid anymore? Hoping to come back home and play the same game?"

Napoleon's face went carefully blank.

"Gram!" Prentiss looked horrified. "I don't want to hear about orgasms from you. That's the kind of stuff that can damage a man for life."

Angelica almost laughed at his expression. "For heaven's sake, you're Death now. Get over a little sex talk from your grandma."

"But—"

"I have orgasms." She was aware of Napoleon staring at her, so she added on. "A lot of them, actually. I'm so aware of my body that I can get a man to bring me to multiple orgasm ten times in an hour. And when I'm by myself, I can climax in under three seconds pretty much every time."

Prentiss looked like he was going to pass out.

Napoleon's eyes had gone as dark as the deepest ocean, and his right hand was clutched in a fist by his hip. His pants had gone a little tight, and he was breathing with a little more weight than he had been.

She met his gaze. "Clearly, I wasn't the problem when we were together. It was the man."

"Okay, I can't hear this. I'm out of here." Prentiss gave her a desperate look as he inched toward the door behind Napoleon. "You okay if I jet?"

She didn't take her eyes off the underperforming sex peon she'd once loved, afraid to break the sense of self she'd never felt before. She felt deliciously strong. Sensual. A woman of substance. "Yes, I'm fine." And she was. Yay, Angelica!

"Hey," Napoleon interrupted, his voice cold. "Any sexual success you have now is because of what I taught you. It wasn't my fault you were too frigid to abandon yourself to the pleasures I could give you."

Prentiss whirled toward his grandfather. "Don't you dare speak to her that way."

At Napoleon's words, Angelica felt that tug at her gut, the one that made her feel smaller, weaker, insecure. She lifted her chin against the sudden shrinking of her heart, against the little voice in her head wondering if he was right, if there really was something wrong with her as a woman. She scowled and set her hands on her hips, ignoring the sudden pounding of her heart. "You don't get to belittle me anymore," she said. "I—"

"I can treat you however I want, my love. You're mine, and you always have been." His gaze shifted to include Prentiss. "You're both mine. Family bonds never die."

Prentiss stalked across the room and slammed his fist into Napoleon's jaw. Nappy went flying back into the wall and landed on the blue mat with a startled look.

Wow. She was so wanting to do a girly cheerleading chant for her grandson right now.

Prentiss leaned over his grandfather. "You stopped being my family the day you murdered my parents." He spat the accusation then strode through the wall without another word.

Booyah for young men!

Chapter 12

PRENTISS STALKED OUT, LEAVING ANGELICA ALONE with the man who'd once had the power to make her smile simply by acknowledging her presence. Now? She was in charge of her own smiles, thank you so much. She propped herself against the weapons table as she watched Napoleon struggle to his feet, rubbing his jaw.

Did her grandson have potential or what? Sometimes there was just no substitute for a caveman-like blow to the jaw. There was something so elemental, so manly, so raw about it. A punch like that over some bastard insulting his woman would give Prentiss a great deal of wiggle room for his other faults, and holy cow, it was some kind of high to be the recipient of that kind of protection. Every girl should have a moment like that—

Wait a minute. She hadn't done a lot of hand-to-hand combat training with her boys lately. Seemed like it would benefit both the girls and the men. She immediately whipped out her Blackberry and began to type a reminder to herself.

"He's become quite the pugilist. Impressive."

She didn't even bother to look up. Maybe she'd start as soon as this afternoon. Reschedule the exploding asp torture session and bring them all to the Girl Power room for—

"Hey." Napoleon yanked her phone out of her hand. "I'm talking to you."

She frowned at him. Hello? Did the blind man not see that she was working? "I'm brainstorming." She snatched the phone back and tried to remember what she'd been working on. Ah, yes, she was going to need to do some role-playing where the guys insulted her girls and then another one punched him out. Oh, how delightful! Then she frowned. Were her girls tough enough for even pretend insults? They were such vulnerable sweet things—

The phone suddenly melted, dripping through her fingers like microwaved peanut butter. "Napoleon!" She cupped her hands, trying to catch the precious bits of data and phone before it slid through her fingers onto the floor. "Fix this, you copulating underperformer!"

"Don't dismiss me, my dear." His voice was cool, and she looked up sharply.

He strolled over to the tea set and picked up the pot of hot water. "Your aura is awfully white for someone who's been engaging in black magic for three hundred years."

She tensed, not liking his smug tone. Did he know something that he could use against her? "Yeah, well, I'm part angel." She hurried over to the stack of towels and dumped the melted goo pile onto the top. She so should have synched it last night. A whole day's worth of experiments were in that electronic device.

He set a tea bag in the Girls Kick Ass mug and then poured hot water into it. "You learned your black magic manipulation from me." He sounded thoughtful, like he was processing something.

"Actually, what you taught me was to distrust any man who dabbles in magic or women." The goop began to ooze off the side of the towel. She quickly picked up the edges like a kerchief and tied the corners together. Okay, so it shouldn't be that hard to fix a melted Blackberry, right? She would have notes… in her phone. Damn.

He dropped a sugar cube into his tea, and droplets splashed onto the lace cloth that one of her boys had hand woven two days before he'd frozen to death in the Tunnel of Frigidity. She cherished that doily, and she bet Nappy had soiled it on purpose. A complete bastion of rude and nitpicky insults.

He tossed in another cube. More splashes. "You created a smut monster to take all the backlash from your experiments, didn't you? You're so clean, it must carry every bit of filth you've ever generated."

"Of course not. I use only white magic. I'm a good girl." She grabbed a towel and hurried over to the table to wipe off the lace. Yeah, big-time lie. Just ask Charles Morgan, the manipulative real estate mogul who'd taken advantage of her vulnerability after Napoleon had walked out. After she'd realized exactly what a devious snake Charlie was, she'd gifted him with her dirty laundry for the rest of eternity. Smutty, as she affectionately called him, was well hidden from all society. Well-hidden as in unkillable and eternally shifting form, of course.

Napoleon leaned so close his lips brushed her ear. "Where's your smut monster, my love?"

She jumped at his question, accidentally banging the towel into the teapot. She lunged for the silver receptacle, barely catching it before it tipped over. Was her sudden klutziness because of his question, or the endearment? She righted the pot and set it carefully back in place before turning to face him. "I am not your love."

He didn't crack a smile. "You are, and you always will be. I'm here to take you back."

She quickly turned away, pretending to mop up the rest of the spilled hot water. Yeah, that would so not be a good thing if that was really why he was playing the prodigal son thing. As tough as she was, she wasn't entirely convinced that she could resist a full-scale assault on her independence. "You don't get to have me."

"Ah, but I do."

At the smug finality in his voice, she peeked over at him. He was wearing an extremely satisfied expression that made her grip tighten on the towel. The well-endowed warthog thought he had something all figured out, that was clear.

He met her gaze. "And you want to know why I get to have you?"

"No. Not particularly." Abandoning the tea set, she grabbed the towel with her phone goo and hurried for the door. By all that was broad-shouldered and arrogant, how was she going to get rid of him? Absolutely nothing good could come of further interaction with him. "I'm really past the days of caring about your interest in me." Wow. How haughty had that sounded? Damn, she was good.

He twirled the tea bag around in his cup as if he had all the time in the world. "I've been brought into town as an expert consultant."

"Congratulations." She reached the door and toed it open. "You know the way out—"

"There's a shape-shifting monster running around town killing otherworld beings."

Angelica paused at the door, not quite able to walk out. "And this matters to me why?" So not party time if that particular creature happened to be her own dear Smutty. She hadn't checked on him in years. Just passed him fallout through their connections and let him be. Most people kept their smut monsters chained up, but she felt that the fact he was contaminated was enough punishment. Seriously, it wasn't like she was heartless or anything. She'd given him an extra zing to make sure he was unkillable and then she'd let him go have fun.

Napoleon took a long sip of his tea, his gaze never leaving her face. "The troublemaker I've been brought in to deal with killed someone important, and now he needs to die."

Panic shot through her, then she immediately halted it. Get real, Angie. What were the odds it was Smutty? Last she'd heard, he was running around in the North Pole trying to kill Santa. "Well, that's great. Right up your alley, isn't it? World renowned black magic assassin and all that."

It was one thing to be a great hit man. It was something else to be able to kill people and leave absolutely no trace of the target. One snap of Napoleon's powerful fingers, and he could make it seem like his victim had never even existed. It made him highly sought after and very, very expensive.

And yes, she'd tracked him a bit once he'd gone off with his blow-up dolls. She'd once been naive enough to be impressed with his career, until she realized he was a brutal mercenary. No morals. Just money. Prentiss at least was fulfilling the important role of soul management. It wasn't like creation could exist without him, even if he was abusing it somewhat. Napoleon on the other hand? Money grubbing fornicating bastard.

"It is up my alley," Napoleon agreed, taking another sip. "The Triumvirate has already made arrangements to have it killed, but a few members don't expect success. They've paid me to come and assess the situation, and then to take action if the first plan doesn't work." He smiled. "You can't imagine how much they paid me just to come take a look."

She blinked at him. "Oh, so you're here to offer me spousal support? Fifty percent of your earnings? That's fantastic. And to think I thought you were a selfish bastard who took off on his own wife and left her with nothing. So sorry to have misjudged you."

Napoleon ignored her barb. "Imagine my surprise," he continued, "when I located the target in question and saw that he was loaded to the horns with my wife's smut."

Angelica felt the blood drain from her face. "That's impossible." Oh, yeah, excellent comeback. Sure to bowl him over with that one.

Napoleon walked over to the buffet and set his cup down. "I'm not sure what you did with the first waste receptacle I created for you, but there's a serious amount of tarnish on the new one."

Try three hundred years' worth. She'd cleansed her life of anything having to do with Napoleon, including taking all the smut from the homeless waif he'd rotted up and dumping it all onto Charles. The girl had become one of Angelica's first projects, to try to help rehab her from the damage Nappy had done to her emotionally, and as a woman. But Angelica had been very, very careful about how she'd managed it. She was the queen of safeguards. "Smutty can't be killed," she said. "I've made him immortal."

Napoleon appropriated a lace napkin and tapped it over his mouth. "We both know nothing is truly immortal. I'll be able to kill him. You know I will."

Angelica clutched the phone-goo-towel more tightly. Of course Napoleon could kill Smutty. It might take him some time, but there was a reason he was the best assassin in existence. He'd even usurped the vampire triplets who'd been so effective with their three-pronged assault on the mind, the body, and the spirit. "You're wrong."

Hoorah for the completely convincing denial. Not.

"Am I?" He crumpled the beautiful lace treasure and tossed it onto the floor, and then sauntered toward her. "And what do you suppose will happen if I kill your garbage disposal?"

She knew exactly what would happen. The three hundred years of backlash that had turned Smutty from a good looking, debonair fairy prince into a grotesque, humpback den of iniquity, brutality, horrible body odor, and lethal dementia would come flying back and hit her right smack in the face.

She'd be insane before she had a chance to get rid of it, and she knew from the look on Napoleon's face that he was well aware of that fact.

Smutty's death would be her own epitaph, as well as the death of all the boys and girls in her care, because the minute the spoilage took over her mind and body, it would be a kill 'em all fiesta until all that was left was blood, carnage, and hell.

Napoleon eased to halt less than a foot away, completely invading her personal space. "I want something from you, babe, and you're going to give it me. Or your smut monster dies."

She raised her chin, refusing to take a step back and relinquish her territory. To think there was a day when she'd thought manly, controlling men were hot. She folded her arms over her chest, and her heart started to pound. "What do you want from me? My true love? Because you burned that bridge a long time ago."

He trailed his finger over her cheek, exactly like he used to do. "I don't care about your love."

The words were like a sledgehammer to her gut. Of course he didn't care about her love. Why had she even let herself think it? Because despite three hundred years of self-training, she apparently still sucked at protecting her heart from him. She smacked his hand away. "Don't touch me," she snapped.

She could handle this. Negotiate the deal and get him out of her life for good. As long as she kept this all business, she could survive intact. It would be a test. She loved tests. Made her stronger. Imagine the example she'd set for her girls? In fact, she didn't even need to out-negotiate him. All she had to do was keep him at bay until she could find Smutty and hide him. She could do that, right? Yeah, right. Girl power! "I can't imagine what I have that you want."

He caught a lock of her hair and tangled his fingers in it. "It seems that my ugly duckling has blossomed. Word of your allure and sexual talents has reached me even across the globe."

"You want lessons?" Oh, wow. She brightened and pulled her hair out of his grasp. "You want to stay at the Den for a while? I could totally whip you into shape." God, she knew she'd been a good girl! The universe delivering Napoleon to her for sensitivity training? Torturing him without recourse? "That's a great idea. I've got some empty beds in the Hair and Makeup area and—"

"No." He cupped the back of her neck and yanked her close. His chest was so broad, and he was so near that she had to crane her neck to look up at him, to meet his gaze. "I don't want lessons."

She caught the scent of sulfur and burning cinnamon, and her knees began to tremble at the familiar smell of death and sweetness, of taint and spice, of man and demon. "So, what do you want?"

Then she saw the look in his eyes. The arrogance. The gleam of anticipation.

Oh, man. This was not going to be good.

"I want the one thing you wouldn't give me before."

She swallowed and braced her hands on his chest, trying to keep distance between them. "What's that?"

He fisted the back of her hair and anchored her head still. "Total and complete surrender."

She grabbed his wrist and tried to pry his hand off, but his grip was unyielding. "No chance. I'm not the woman I used to be. I have my career and—"

"I don't give a shit about your career." His gaze went to her mouth, and suddenly she knew what he wanted.

The one thing that would break her soul forever if she gave it to him. The single area where she had no defenses. The sole vulnerability that would turn her back into the sniveling, weak, desperate woman she used to be, the one she'd spent three hundred years leaving behind, the cycle of self-destruction she'd worked so hard to protect her girls and boys from getting sucked into.

All her dreams. All her hopes. All that she'd accomplished. *By all that's powerful and womanly, please let me be wrong.*

But he smiled, and she knew she was right.

"All I want, my love, is the total and complete surrender of your body." He thumbed her lower lip with his free hand. "Your body has always belonged to me, and I'm here to take it back."

Weird. Blaine had never realized that asphalt streets could actually move back and forth—

Trinity punched him in the left side. "Stop!"

Blaine halted the bike so fast that Trinity slammed into his back. "What's wrong?"

She peeled her face out of his jacket. "Oh, I don't know. Maybe the fact you're headed straight for the edge of the bridge?"

Blaine squinted and realized that the undulating asphalt was actually the Charles River. "Damn. That's confusing." It wove out of focus again.

"Are you okay?"

"Yeah. Fantastic." He sat back on the bike for a sec. He could feel all the black magic he'd taken off Augustus riding his cells, clinging to his soul. He looked down at his hand and saw a charcoal-colored gelatinous substance bleeding from his palm. Huh. That probably wasn't a good sign.

On the plus side, with this much garbage in his body, Augustus would be worshipping the carpet for a least a few hours. Bought 'em time. On the negative, he kinda felt the same as when the witch had tied him down and let a couple of hundred cranky water moccasins have their way with him.

Hadn't been his best day, and it had taken a week to recover.

Didn't have a week right now.

"All right. Let's go." He went for the handlebars and missed. Took the thing on the jaw instead. Damn things were moving all over the place.

Trinity leaned over his shoulder, and he tensed. The witch always hit him when he was down.

"What can I do to help you?" Her breath was warm on his neck.

He scowled, trying to concentrate. Had she really just offered to help? That made no sense. She was clearly trying to determine how weak he was so she could figure out where to launch her attack. "I told you. I'm fine."

"Blaine." Trinity slid off the bike and walked around to face him. She planted her hands on the rubber grips (how the hell had she grabbed those mobile suckers?) and eyed him. "You're not okay, and I need you okay. What do you need?"

"I'm a man. I need nothing."

He kinda thought she snorted, or maybe that was the sound of his brain exploding.

"For heaven's sake, Blaine! Don't be an idiot. What is up with the 'I am an island' thing?"

"Women love that shit." His eyes were playing tricks now, he was pretty sure of it. Trinity's face was getting smaller and her breasts were getting larger. Or maybe that was actually happening. That would be nice of her to do. Grow some knockers just for him. "Nice rack."

"What?"

"I said…" Shit. Couldn't remember what he'd said.

Something hard hit him in the side of his head, and he whirled around. Who'd come at him? He tried to flare up a fireball and—

"Blaine! It's me! You fell off the bike and hit your head on the pavement."

"I never fall." But he could see some gray shit stretching out endlessly next to his head. Was that really road? Damn. Okay, maybe it was time to admit that the black magic harvesting hadn't gone quite as well as he'd hoped. "Where the hell is Nigel? He should be here by now."

"Nigel?" Trinity was kneeling beside him now. "Who's Nigel?"

"He's like my personal EMT. Handy guy." He studied her face, fascinated by how it was morphing forms. "What's up with the blurry? You can do that at will?" He reached up for her face and felt her cheek. "Weird. Feels normal."

"Blaine!" She sounded a little desperate now. "Tell me how to help you. Who is Nigel? Can he heal you? How do I reach him?"

"Forget Nigel." He moved his hand down the side of her neck and ran his thumb over her collarbone. "Anyone ever tell you that your skin is softer than the petals on an orchid?"

"Blaine—" She hesitated. "No. No one's ever said that."

"Well, then you've been hanging with a bunch of no-brained dimwits." He traced the tendons in her neck. "No prickly tingly yucky stuff. Just skin. Dig it." He blinked, trying to focus on her, but she was sliding out of sight. A peach-colored blur. Like she was dissolving or something. Like she was leaving him behind…

His fist closed in her hair and he yanked her close. "You do not have my permission to leave me," he snarled.

"I'm not." She palmed his chest, trying to hold herself away from him.

"That's what all the chicks say. Screw that." He tightened his grip and pulled her closer. Needed a better hold on her hair. "Tired of people walking out. You trust 'em, they should stay."

"You're right. They should. And some do. Like me. So calm down." She palmed his hip. "Is this a phone in your pocket?"

"A phone? Are you blind?" He grabbed her hand and set it on his crotch. "That's like ten times bigger than a phone. More like a phone book, woman."

She yanked her hand free and shoved it in his pocket. "I actually meant your phone." She pulled out something silver and waved it in front of him. Maybe it was a phone. Maybe it was a harmonica. Hard to tell when she was moving it so quickly. Did he have a harmonica? Wasn't sure.

But he did know that the item in her hand used to be in his jeans. "You stealing from me?"

"For God's sake, Blaine! Of course not!" She fiddled with the object, and he hauled her down on top of him.

Her breasts hit his chest, and it felt right. Liked it. Liked her body against his. He set his hands on her hips and adjusted her to fit more closely between his thighs. "This is good."

"Your face is turning gray. That can't be a good thing." Her voice echoed at him from a great distance, like it was dancing around his head

He tried again to look at her, but her face blended into the sunset behind her. Blurs of colors. He palmed her face, watching his hand meld into her lighter skin. "Nigel would like to paint this. Can't cross-stitch it. Too amorphous." Wanted to, though. Might be able to figure out a way. He lifted her hair and watched the golden streaks move across the sky. "Pretty."

"This can't be good. You're hallucinating. Tell me you have Nigel's number in your phone."

His eyes were hurting. Too hard to see. He gave it up and closed them. Concentrated on touch. Tunneled his hand through her tresses. So silky. "Didn't think there was anything softer than the Ritz Grande embroidery floss," he mused. "Wrong."

"Hello? Is this Nigel?"

He caught the back of her neck and pulled her down. Pressed his face to her throat. She smelled like baby powder and lavender. Barely there. Just the faintest hint, like she'd spritzed herself just for him, just for this moment of intimacy—

"No, this isn't Blaine. I have his phone. I—" She stuttered as Blaine blew lightly on her neck. "Um... my name's Trinity Harpswell, and I'm with Blaine. Something's happened to him, and he kept saying you could help him, so—"

He kissed her throat.

"Stop it!" She pushed at his face, and he caught her hand. Pressed his lips to her palm. "No, not you, Nigel. Sorry. Yes. We're on the BU bridge."

Damn, her skin tasted good. The sweetness of brown sugar, with the delicacy of the lightest meringue. He caught her finger in his mouth and sucked on it. Wet and warm and so tantalizing. He wanted more. More skin. More tongue. More action. He licked the inside of her wrist.

"I—" She tried to get her hand free, and he tightened his grip on her.

"Not finished," he muttered. Or maybe he said that. Wasn't sure. Head was hurting like hell.

"I'm sorry, Nigel. I'm a little distracted. You want to know if he's hot? Like on fire?"

Fire. Huh. That sounded familiar. Pretty sure he was supposed to be doing something with flames right now. Not sure what. Take a bath in a barbecue? Something like that.

Didn't know. Just needed the girl. Felt good to be touched. Made him not think about how much his body hurt right now. He hooked his leg over her calf and trapped her. Yeah, liking that.

Trinity tried unsuccessfully to free her foot. "No. He's not currently engulfed in flames. Why?"

Blaine grabbed the back of her head and tugged her face down toward his. He missed her mouth, caught a full frontal with a cold hard piece of electronics. His phone? Weird. Why was it in her cheek?

Trinity braced her hand on his chest, her fingertips digging into his skin. "Okay, I'll try to get him to set himself on fire, but hurry up—"

Blaine yanked the phone out of her hand, tossed it aside, then fisted the back of her hair and brought her right down toward him.

"Hey—" Her mouth landed right on his, and he grinned. Bull's-eye.

Chapter 13

DEAR LORD ALMIGHTY, WAS THIS WHAT A REAL KISS was like?

Trinity had a split second to think that it probably wasn't a good idea to get intimate with a man who was potentially seconds away from a nuclear waste death after being contaminated by Augustus, and then the thought just didn't seem to matter.

Nothing did.

Nothing except the feel of his mouth. Of the way his lips were consuming hers, taking them, compelling her response (as if he had to force her!). It was the kiss of a man who had decided he wanted it, and he was taking it.

No asking for permission.

No begging for forgiveness.

Just a kiss of utter and compete confidence, like there was no chance in hell that she didn't want it as much as he did.

And you know, he was pretty much right.

She wound her hands around his neck, gripping the back of his head, trying to kiss him more deeply. How could she not? It felt so good. She was so used to being the strong one. Of worrying for the safety of the man she was with. Of running away if she was attracted to a guy. Of trying to seduce him if he grossed her out, which of course was just so anti-nature it was pathetic.

She never got cozy with the males who made her glad

to be a woman. Too risky. But right now, in this moment, she didn't really care about repercussions, control issues, or self-preservation.

She just wanted to be kissed.

Blaine ramped up his assault, and excitement danced in her belly and rode down her legs, like when she'd been on the bike and felt that vibration drive through her core. Only it wasn't the bike between her legs. It was Blaine, and only Blaine. She could feel the muscles in his stomach flexing beneath her belly, felt the rising heat as he pressed his hips into her pelvis.

His thumb brushed over the side of her breast, and she jumped. Then his hand settled over it, cupping it like he was treasuring it. She was so liking that...

The man feeling her up had taken down Augustus for her. How could she not be jiving with a little down and dirty with him? That moment when he'd tackled Augustus and she'd seen him suck that black soot right out of her assailant... never in her life had she felt more like a woman than when he'd jumped in to protect her.

In that instant, she hadn't had to be the strong one. He'd taken care of that for her, and it was the best feeling ever. When she'd watched him protecting her, it hadn't been the black widow inside her that had responded with such longing. It had been herself. The core of who she was, because this man... this warrior... he was strength that she didn't have, a raw tenacity that had eluded her in her quest to defeat the curse.

He was the personification of what she'd tried and failed to be, and she craved him on every level of her being. He was a warrior who could protect himself against her—

A dark force stirred, and she tensed. Hello, eight-legged freak, welcome to the party.

Oy. What was she doing? She couldn't afford to succumb to her base instincts like some happy-go-lucky serial killer! She was a tightly wound spring and there would be no letting go. She wrenched her mouth away from his. "I can't. We need to stop."

Blaine began to suck on her collarbone. Yeah, how good did that feel? No wonder *Cosmo* listed it as the number one erogenous zone.

No! Stop! "Blaine! We can't—"

He gripped her hair and forced her head back so he could kiss her throat. Oh, wow, total manly beast kind of thing to do, but... so hot. He was holding her so tightly, like he wasn't going to let her go until he was finished with her. And in a supremely non-girl-power way, she absolutely loved it. Which is why she had to stop! "Get off me," she managed.

"You're on top."

Was she? Weird. How had he managed that?

"You taste so good. Safe." His words were slurred, but his mouth seemed to know exactly what it was doing as it worked her lips, caressing her mouth until he could slide that tongue of his right inside...

Safe? What did that mean? She knew what it was like to go through life being scared, but how could a man like Blaine have any reason to use that word?

He began to suck on her earlobe, and some sort of somethin' somethin' shot through her body. Ah... just a second. She'd stop him in a minute and—

"Well, hot damn. The king of abstinence has finally folded. Beer's on me."

She opened her eyes to find two huge guys crouching beside her. One of them was sporting an expression that made him look like he was ready to kill the next person who crossed his path, and the other would pass for the boy-next-door in his blue jeans, white T-shirt, and curls… if not for his blackened palms and the razor sharp blades poking out from the fingers on his left hand.

Both men were grinning at her, the kind of arrogant, male look that usually made her wish she could give the black widow gift to the string of broken hearts they'd left behind.

Then Blaine's hand clamped down on her breast, his teeth sank into her earlobe, his whole body shuddered, and she looked down as his eyes rolled back in his head and a pink dust began crawling up his chest toward his head.

"Shit, woman!" The angry one yanked Trinity off Blaine and tossed her aside. "What'd you do to him?"

"Nothing!" She skidded across the pavement, wincing as the gravel scraped her palms. "It wasn't me."

"Nigel. Tell me you can heal him." Not even bothering to check if she was okay after nearly throwing her into the Charles River, the warrior pulled out a large sword and began to whip it over his head, like he was winding up to unleash some catapult across the city. The air began to crackle, and the hair on her arms stood up.

Nigel hunched over Blaine and set his palm over Blaine's heart. "He's not tapping into his fire. What the bloody hell? You got a read on this, Jarvis?"

Jarvis pointed his sword at her. "What happened?" he demanded.

"He got pinked by Oh, Shit, It's Augustus. And then Blaine sucked a whole bunch of black soot out of him. I'm not sure what it was." Trinity grabbed the railing and scrambled to her feet. "He did it to save me."

"Black magic." Nigel shuddered, but he leaned over Blaine, pressing the heel of his hand into Blaine's ribs. "Feels like I'm back in the Den. Can't say I'm digging it." His skin began to glow, and it seemed to pulse in time with the humming coming from the spinning sword. "Okay, buddy, let's get you back with us."

Trinity hugged herself as she watched the warriors work on Blaine. "Is he going to be okay?"

Nigel shrugged. "He hasn't died on me yet."

But that wasn't an answer, and she knew it. A cold dread clawed at her heart as she watched Nigel rub Blaine's chest, as Jarvis tried to generate more energy with his sword, as Blaine lay there unresponsive.

The scene was too familiar. Too haunting. Too many times she'd seen it. Kissing a man then watching helplessly as his life bled from him. "You have to save him."

"Trying," Nigel muttered. "Appreciate the advice, though."

Her throat tightened as she watched Blaine's chest fight for breath, the massive combatant strung out along the asphalt like he was dying. She inched toward him, and both warriors glared at her.

"You come one step closer," Jarvis said, "and you're toast."

Um, yeah. There was no missing the promise in his eyes. Smart guy, not to trust her. She was high risk, in a major way. What was wrong with Blaine, claiming that it felt safe to kiss her? Hello? Could she be any more dangerous?

But when he'd made that comment, she'd forgotten that he was an arrogant killer. Instead, she'd let him into her heart, touched by the pain of another soul who lived in fear. She knew what it was like to crave safety, and her heart bled for anyone who felt the same. Had she loved him for that split second? Crossed that line and hurt him without even realizing what she was doing?

But as she looked at Blaine fighting for his life, she knew in her heart that she hadn't. She didn't love him. She hadn't tried to kill him.

Not that it changed the fact he was still dying because of her. Because he'd protected her from Augustus.

Nigel leaned over Blaine. "The witch paid a visit while you were gone." His voice was etched with concern that made her heart ache. As tough as these warriors were, they cared about each other, and that was so cool. No islands here, folksies. "Christian's dying. And it's your fault because you left without him."

Jarvis cursed. "Are you insane, Nigel? He'll kick your ass for that comment when he wakes up."

"That's my hope. Nothing like pissing a guy off to get him to decide to cheat death."

But Blaine's body went still, and the two warriors exchanged grim looks.

"What about Trinity?" Jarvis eyed her. "If she touches his tattoo, he might think she's Angelica there to torture him. That'll wake him up in a hurry."

Trinity frowned. "Why would he think I'm Angelica?"

Nigel snapped his fingers at her. "Come here. Quick."

Trinity didn't hesitate. If she could keep someone else from dying, she was all over it. She bolted over to

Nigel and dropped to her knees beside Blaine. "Tell me what I can do."

Nigel ripped open Blaine's shirt. On his chest was a skull and bones tattoo, a blackened brand burned into his skin. Nigel grabbed her hand and pressed her palm down over the mark. "Is it getting hot?"

"No. It's cold." Too cold. Like a corpse. And sadly, she knew what a corpse felt like.

Nigel adjusted his grasp on her wrist, shoving her hand more firmly against Blaine. Smoke began rising from Nigel's palm, and she felt her arm begin to warm where he was holding onto her.

"She's definitely got traces of Angelica," Nigel told Jarvis. "We might be able to amp it up enough to fool him into going on the defensive."

Trinity looked down at her fingers digging into the dark hairs on Blaine's chest. This was so not how she'd envisioned finding out what his chest looked like. "I don't understand. Why do I have traces of Angelica? Isn't she the witch who tortured you guys?" She was so not liking the idea that she had a bio-chemistry akin to that of a murderous black witch. That couldn't be a good sign, could it?

Nigel didn't answer her. "Jarvis, harness more power. When I give the signal, put your sword over Trinity's heart. I'll hit her up the same time. I'm hoping we can amplify her energy level enough that it shocks him the way Angelica does."

Jarvis began to whip the sword even faster, and Trinity's skin began to smoke as Nigel's palm got hotter. She bit her lip against the growing pain. "What are we doing?"

"Jumpstarting his tattoo. A magical defibrillator, if you will." Nigel glanced at Jarvis, who nodded. Nigel looped his other arm around her neck, anchoring her against his body. "Three seconds."

Trinity's heart began to pound at the feel of being trapped against Nigel. He had one of her hands pinned to Blaine's body, the rest of her locked down. She began to tremble. She couldn't cope with not being in control. "Can you let go? I'm not going to go anywhere."

"Just a precautionary measure, sweetheart." Nigel tightened his hold on her as Jarvis moved closer. The hum from his sword was so loud she could feel it beating at her ears, throbbing in her chest.

Nigel wedged himself more tightly against her, and shoved her hand more firmly against Blaine. "This is going to hurt."

She let out a weak laugh. "Yeah, well, I can live with that." Anything to stop there from being one more death around her.

Respect flashed in his eyes, and then he nodded at Jarvis.

She looked up as Jarvis thrust his sword right toward her chest.

The sword was coming too fast, a blur, and she suddenly realized he wasn't going to stop. Oh, no! Did they think she was immortal? "Wait—"

Then the sword sank right into her heart.

Angelica was trying to kill him.

Blaine suddenly became aware of her hated life force beating at him, her claws in his chest, trying to rip out the tattoo she'd always detested. Screw that. He wasn't letting her win. He fought to open his eyes, to strike out. Couldn't do shit. What the hell?

Muscles shot. Mind fried. Time for a car wash.

He set his tattoo on fire and then sent the conflagration racing through his body. The flames cut through the inertia, his body seized, and it was his own again.

He jerked upright and opened his eyes...

Only to find himself staring at Nigel. He blinked and turned his head. Jarvis was shooting some lame ass grin at him. Just the boys? He looked up. Blue sky. No Den. "Where's Angelica?"

"Not here," Jarvis said. "We tricked you."

Painter boy grinned. "Nice recovery, Trio. Thought you were done there for a minute."

Blaine realized his body was still aching, and he sent more fire through it to heal. "What happened?"

"Apparently, some dude named Augustus dusted you. Nearly took you out." Nigel pointed over his shoulder. "More in a sec. Gotta save the girl."

Blaine followed Nigel's glance and saw Trinity on her back, blood pouring from a wound in her chest. "Shit! What did you do?" Her jumped up and jetted over to Trinity.

Her eyes flickered open when he crouched beside her. "Thought you were dead," she mumbled. "Don't scare me like that. I can't deal with that stress."

"I wasn't dead. I'm immortal, for hell's sake." He pulled her onto his lap, and scowled when he felt how cold she was. He glared at Nigel. "You had to kill her?"

"Had to spill her blood and make you think it was Angelica attacking you. It was the only way to get you out of your self-pity apathy. And you're welcome."

Nigel set his palms on Trinity's chest as a faint humming filled the air again, indicating that Nigel was sending healing energy into the wound in her heart. "I couldn't reach you. She saved your life."

Trinity's cold hand slid up to his face, and he looked down as she traced his jaw. "Yeah?"

"Did he just say I saved your life?"

Blaine snorted. "That would imply that I was dying, so no."

She turned her head. "Truth, Nigel?"

Nigel smiled and began to rub the wound in a circular motion. The sound of running water filled the air, as it always did when Nigel was healing. "You did well, my dear. Blaine is like a motivational actor: always needs the right reason to decide to live again. Today, he needed you."

She let her head fall back against Blaine's arm. "Wow." She was smiling now, and her face looked so at peace. "I've never saved anyone's life before. I like that."

Jarvis crouched beside them. "I used my sword, so Nigel should be able to heal her." Jarvis's sword was a flexible weapon, and it could cause pain, severe damage, or instant death, depending on what Jarvis intended.

Trinity's body seized and convulsed in his arms, and she let out a yelp of pain. Blaine swore and tightened his grip on her. "What the hell are you doing, Nigel?"

Nigel sat back. "All set. She's healing now. She'll be fine."

Blaine peered down at Trinity. Her eyes were closed and her body was still. "Hey. You okay?"

She didn't respond, and something tightened in his gut. "What—"

"Give her a sec. Chill out."

Jarvis wiped the blood off the end of his sword. "I was impressed. She knew what we were doing, and she was up for it. Never seen a chick sacrifice herself to save someone."

Blaine raised his brows. "You sure she knew what was up?" Hard to believe she took a sword to the chest on purpose.

Nigel and Jarvis exchanged glances. "Well, maybe not the whole extent, but she was game," Jarvis said.

Blaine felt something roil inside him at the thought of Jarvis plunging his sword into Trinity's heart. "I need her," he growled.

"And you'll get her." Nigel shoved his hair back out of his face. "So, fill us in. You found Trinity Harpswell. She a black widow?"

Blaine moved her so her head was cradled on his biceps. "She claims she is. I haven't seen it in action."

"So, what's the plan?" Jarvis stood and surveyed their surroundings. Taking first watch.

"Keep an eye out for a short guy who smells like bananas." Blaine pulled Trinity more tightly into his arms and turned up his body temperature, trying to warm her up. "You guys figure out how to get back into the Den?"

Nigel shook his head. "The portals aren't listed in her files, and we can't sense them when we're actually in the field." He nodded at Trinity. "You think she could pick them up? She's the Chosen. She might have the touch."

Shit. He'd forgotten that she was the Chosen. Had it been Trinity he'd felt attacking him, not Angelica?

Her aura was the same as the witch's? She had that kind of evil in her? He loosened his grip on her. "Yeah, she probably could."

Nigel stood up. "So, let's take her to the Common. Go in, get Angelica, and then—"

"No way." Trinity sat up suddenly, and her eyes were bright. Alive. Blaine had never quite gotten used to that moment when Nigel's healing finally kicked in. Still freaked out newcomers to the Den. "We're not taking out this witch next. My quarry first."

Nigel and Jarvis exchanged glances. "What's she talking about, Trio?" Jarvis asked.

Blaine gritted his teeth and explained the deal. When he finished, his two buddies were both staring at him in shock. "Just make her do it," Jarvis said. "We don't have time for this shit."

"Make me?" Trinity pulled out of Blaine's arms and stumbled to her knees. Blaine caught her as she started to sway. "It doesn't work like that. You can't make the black widow come to life. I'm the only one who controls her..." She frowned. "Well, maybe control is a little optimistic, but the fact is that you can't make me kill anyone. Blaine knows that. We take care of my situation first, and then yours."

Jarvis swore. "We don't have time—"

"The portal won't open for another forty-eight hours, even for Trinity." Who carried Angelica's DNA in her blood. Blaine eyed her as she rubbed her wound. He could still feel that pain in his chest that had made him think Angelica had come after him... *and it had been Trinity*. She might seem sweet, she might have saved him, but she'd triggered every defensive response that the witch could elicit. Deep inside, Trinity Harpswell was witch, and he had to remember that. No trusting. Not again. "We take care of this monster, so there's no argument when that window opens."

Jarvis scowled. "I don't like it. How do we know she'll come through?"

Trinity raised her chin. "I'll help you." But she wouldn't look any of them in the eye.

Hold on. Was she thinking of bailing on him?

Of course she was. She bled Angelica's blood. Trinity Harpswell was the enemy, end of story. Shit. He'd been a damn fool to trust her.

Screw that. No chance was he letting her derail his plans to save Christian. He was taking control. Now. He stood up and jerked her to her feet. "Follow us," he said to his team. "We're going on a monster hunt."

He was going to find that shapeshifter and take him hostage until that witch was dead. There would be no serving up of the Chameleon's heart until Angelica's soul was properly dispatched. Trinity was about to learn what it was like to take on a real warrior. There would be no reneging allowed.

He didn't wait for an answer from anyone. He just shoved Trinity on the bike, started the engine, and peeled out. Trinity grabbed for his waist, and then hunkered down against his back.

Yeah, Trinity Harpswell thought she had some kickass plan for getting out of her end of the deal?

She was going to find out exactly how wrong she was.

Chapter 14

As Blaine cruised down the road, Trinity realized she was not really feeling the love for life right now.

It wasn't so much the fact she'd nearly been killed by a sword to the heart. (Hello? Anyone want to try that twice?)

It wasn't so much the fact she'd almost gotten a guy murdered. (Been there, done that, still sucked.)

It wasn't even the fact that Augustus was stalking her. (So not happy that anything pink was going to make her run away screaming from now on.)

Okay, yeah, so those things were all wigging her out. But the big ugly was the fact that she was minutes away from intentionally using her powers to get someone killed.

Yeah, it was to save her dad.

Yeah, she'd killed before.

But this was different.

This was going to be on purpose.

Blaine eased the bike to a stop at the edge of the road and killed the engine. They were outside a small, black building with a blood red sign declaring it to be the Primrose. Blaine looked over his shoulder at her, and she could see the darkness of his expression.

Oh, fantastic. Like all she needed right now was a cranky assailant. "I already apologized for almost getting you killed. I really am sorry."

He said nothing. He just took her hand and hauled her off the bike.

"Hey—"

He didn't turn around, he just strode into the bar, dragging her after him. Jarvis and Nigel were behind him, and all three warriors were looking badass and mean.

If she wasn't being manhandled like some rag doll, she'd almost be digging the idea of walking into a bar with three hot guys. It wasn't like she'd had a lot of chances to do that, after all.

They stepped into the dim light, and she was surprised to see it was packed, even though it was still early in the evening. "See what you can find," Blaine instructed Jarvis and Nigel. "It has no common form, but it must have a black aura. See if you can pick it up."

"I'll check outside." Jarvis headed for the back door.

"I'll take the upstairs." Nigel loped toward a staircase with a sign that pointed toward pool tables, and vaulted up the steps.

"We'll check down here." Blaine didn't look at her. He just took her hand and hauled her across the room to the bar. He sat her down on a stool and took the one facing her.

Trinity yanked her hand out of his. "What's your deal?"

"You." Blaine sandwiched her knees between his. "You aren't planning on killing Angelica, are you? You're going to save your dad and then bail."

Trinity felt her cheeks heat up. Nice day, when a guy can read your face. "It's not like that. I have issues with taking lives and I don't even know her. How can I justify killing her if—"

"I don't know why you have this loyalty to her after

what she did to you. I don't get women, sometimes, I really don't."

"What?" Trinity shot a sharp look at him. "What are you talking about? What she did to me? What is up with all you guys thinking I'm like her? And while we're at it, why did my blood make you think she was attacking you? That was never made clear to me."

Something flickered across Blaine's face. "That's why you don't want to kill her. Because she created you and gave you your powers."

Trinity stared at him, something deep welling open inside her, like a fissure in her recently repaired heart. "You know who did this to me?"

He frowned. "Yeah, Angelica. She kidnapped you when you were a baby."

She stared at him, shocked at the casual way he'd just dumped the information she'd been searching for her whole life. "Are you certain? How do you know this?"

"You're in her computer. That's how I found you."

"Oh, God." Trinity clutched her chest against the sudden tightness. A lifetime of unknowing, and suddenly she had answers.

Blaine caught her arm, and she realized she'd been tilting off the chair. "You didn't know?"

"No, no. I didn't have any idea. None of us did. I just disappeared and then reappeared." She pressed her hands to her head against the frantic whirl spinning around in her mind. She felt like something had just been unlocked, a past, secrets, information, but it was moving so quickly she couldn't decipher what it was. "I—"

Blaine looked uncertain. "So, that's not why you don't want to fulfill your end of the deal?"

"No!" Trinity pulled her hands away from her face. "I just have a problem with killing!"

He blinked. "That's it?"

"That's it." She tried to catch her breath, to focus. To pull herself together. "You thought it was because I had a fondness for her?" She started to laugh, a high-pitched hysterical sound. "Do you really think I'd want to save her? That's too funny."

Blaine frowned. "Trin—"

"Why did she curse me? Did she realize what she was doing? Or was it a mistake?" She hugged herself, trying to understand, trying to get a grasp on what he'd just told her.

"Because she's a psychotic she-bitch from hell."

Trinity blinked. "No one is just evil. There's always a reason." It made her sick to think of being victimized on a whim. She'd always held out hope that maybe it had been for the greater good, that there was a reason she'd endured so much. "I mean—"

Blaine shoved his sleeve and held out his arm. A large ragged scar ran down his arm. "This is what she did to me when I was four years old, when she took me from my family for experiments. I resisted. She didn't like it."

Trinity stared at the injury, shocked at the sight of it. On a four-year-old? "But—"

"That's what she does." He leaned forward. "She steals children. She tortures them. The tough ones survive. The not-so-tough die. Only a few, like you, get to go home."

Trinity felt her throat tighten. "I—"

"And now she has the man I consider to be my

brother, and she's torturing the hell out of him unless I turn myself and the team back in. Every day I delay, he suffers. I promised him I'd get him out, and I won't let him stay behind." His eyes flashed, and she felt his intensity. Saw his loyalty.

She reached out and took his arm, and touched his scar. Her finger tingled and she pulled back.

"Black magic," Blaine said. "That's what she uses on us." He leaned forward and caught her arm. "Some people need to die, Trinity. Or they keep on hurting others. The witch is one of those, and you're the only one who can stop her. You going to let people keep dying, or you going to step up and use your powers for good, for once in your life?"

Use her powers for good? The idea floored her. She'd never even considered that her powers could be anything but evil. She'd spent a lifetime trying to save others, hoping it would clear her soul. But what if she actually used her powers to save lives?

She looked down at the scar on Blaine's arm, the damage done to a child...

And she could stop it from ever happening again. No other girls would be kidnapped and cursed like she had. No other boys would be tortured. And she was the only one who could save them.

Something began to beat in her chest, something that felt right. Something that settled her. It made sense. To end the hell by using her own powers. It was what she was meant to do. "Okay."

He squeezed her knee and nodded. "That's my girl. I'll help you. You won't be alone."

She took a breath. "Promise?"

He touched her face. "Promise. I—" He swore and spun around, searching the place.

"What?" Smoke was rising from his chest, and she could see fire simmering on the backs of his hands. "What's wrong?"

"The witch. She's here."

Blaine leapt up, Nigel came charging down the stairs, and Jarvis bolted in through the back door. All of them were armed. Blaine shook his head, and the other two stopped where they were. They began searching the crowd.

"Where is she?" Trinity was beside him. "What does she look like?"

"Blond hair, tall, stacked." His veins were burning. His skin was prickling. The black magic he was sensing had that feminine slant he associated with Angelica, and he could smell the lemongrass that always filled the room when she was present.

The air was dark, heavy with the sweat of patrons. Men. Women. Sex. Stale beer. Lights dim. Floor was sticky. The lemon was cloying to his skin, and he knew he was going to smell like a girl when he left.

But as long as he had Angelica's heart in his hands, he was down with that.

A blond head moved into the shadows, but Nigel was already there. Grabbed the girl, then shook his head at Blaine.

False alarm.

Where the hell was she? Angelica didn't hide. She put herself out there. If she was in stealth mode, it meant she was there to make sure it was done right.

What was she after? Not him. She thought she had him by the balls.

"I smell lemon," Trinity said.

Trinity. She was there for Trinity.

Blaine caught her arm and hauled her against him. "Stay close." Of course Angelica would want Trinity. She was the Chosen, and she was ripe for harvesting. "She might be after you."

"Me?" Trinity stiffened. "Why?"

"Because you carry the curse."

"Oh…" Trinity looked around. "Well, I'd really like to have a little chat with her about my curse. I have a few bones to pick with her."

"Don't we all." Blaine began to move through the crowd, trying to get a sense of where the perfume was strongest. But it was all over. Like it was moving around, faster than he could see—

A thick patch assaulted him, and he instinctively grabbed the tall blonde on his right—

She turned, and he realized his eyes had been playing tricks on him. It wasn't a woman at all. It was a tall man, dark hair, wearing a suit with a diamond in his ear. The man was all class and dignity, didn't fit the joint. Blaine's hand burned from touching him. "Who are you?"

"We need to talk," the man said. "Outside. Now."

"Yeah, we do." Blaine jerked his head toward his friends, and they all fell in behind as he followed the man toward the back door. He could see the black aura emanating from him. Tainted like the devil himself. But he smelled like lemon. Like Angelica. This man had some connection to her, and Blaine was going to find out what it was.

He set his hand on Trinity's shoulder, moving her behind him, as he shoved open the back door and stepped out into the alley.

The man turned and faced them. His stance was arrogant, and his gaze flicked over all three of the warriors, as if they were nothing more than peons.

But then his attention settled on Trinity, and he smiled. "Nice to meet you, my dear. Angelica is very proud of you."

Trinity tensed. "Who are you?"

"I am her greatest accomplishment. Let me introduce myself." The man bowed with perfect grace, but Blaine set his hand in his pocket to retrieve a blue ball.

Something was off, and he knew it.

Just couldn't figure it out.

The man raised his head and his eyes had gone coal black. "I'm the hell you wish you'd never met." He opened his mouth, and it was nothing but a bottomless pit of blackness. And then he launched himself at Trinity.

—◊—

Well, wasn't that the coolest thing ever? Trinity had a brief moment to admire the fire shield Blaine had just tossed in front of her, when the devil-man crashed into it and emitted a horrific scream of agony.

Oh, wow. That sounded like it hurt—

He burst through the wall of flames and launched a set-o-claws at her face—

Blaine knocked her out of its demonic path just before her pearly whites would have become charcoal ugly dinner. Okay, so a little close—

"Why didn't you move?" Blaine yanked her to her feet.

"I got distracted by its pain. I felt bad—"

Her assailant leapt to its feet and spun around... but it was no longer a man. It was a petite brunette with kick-ass breasts, big brown eyes, and a scared little face. "Please don't hurt me," she cried. "Please."

Blaine swore under his breath, and Jarvis halted, his sword inches from the woman's heart. "What the hell—"

The girly-man plunged a spiked fist right through Jarvis's stomach.

"Hey, he worked hard for those abs." Nigel unleashed a set of blades at the well-stacked-assailant, and the creature didn't even flinch when they slammed right into its head. Just picked them out and whipped them right back at Nigel.

Nigel caught them easily and hurled them back, faster this time, while Blaine grabbed Jarvis and hauled him out of the way. "You okay, buddy?"

"Flesh wound." Jarvis pressed a hand to the gaping donut hole in his stomach. "Give me a sec to shake it off."

Trinity watched Nigel spar with the Queen of Kings. A shapeshifting assassin couldn't be a coincidence. "You think that's the monster I'm supposed to kill?"

"Odds are high." Blaine sounded a little tense. "But I'm guessing that we just found Angelica's smut dumpster as well. Always wondered how she kept her aura so peachy clean."

"The gods must be smiling on us tonight. Can't think of anything I'd rather destroy more than her trash can." Nigel and the demon-thing were playing catch with Nigel's blades, but Trinity saw that the bad guy was getting stronger, and its skin was getting darker.

She backed up against the wall and tried to focus on the humpback death trap and get some prism action going. Not totally feeling bad about killing it right now.

Jarvis rolled to his knees. "May I request the opportunity to change my stance on taking time to kill Trinity's monster? I'm really liking the idea of Angelica getting hit with all the smut before we kill her. Nice way to go out, don't you think?"

"Agreed." Blaine looked over at Trinity. "You get a read on this?"

"Trying—"

The giant freak whirled suddenly and threw Nigel's blades right at her. She yelped and dove toward the Dumpster (yeah, like she had a chance of moving faster than demon-sped daggers. Say bye-bye, Trinity—). Blaine leapt in front of her and the blades hit his chest with a rapid thumpety-thump-thump that would have sounded a lot better as a snare drum.

Again with her protector getting himself killed? "Blaine!"

The blades jerked out of his skin and flew back into Nigel's hands, and Blaine set himself on fire and the holes in his chest sealed up instantly.

"This isn't really working here, folks," Nigel said. "Any suggestions?"

The big baddie charged her again, and Blaine dragged her out of its reach just before it made contact. Being assaulted by some deranged-killer-chick who could move faster than Trinity could see, let alone react to, was so not her vision of a happy day.

"Trinity," Blaine warned. "Tell me how to kill it."

Jarvis leapt to his feet, stomach looking much less

see-through, and he flung his sword right into its heart. But before the blade hit, the pompom girl shifted into a thousand cockroaches, and his sword split harmlessly though the crowd. "Yeah, that's a witch thing," Jarvis said. "Forgot how brilliant she is."

Trinity scrambled on top of the Dumpster as the gaggle of bugs spread out over the alley. They scrabbled toward the men, and Blaine set them on fire. Then it became flaming cockroach fiesta, and the little suckers didn't even flinch as they zipped along the ground.

"Now that's just nasty." Jarvis stomped on a pile of them, and then shook his foot when they started crawling up his leg. "I like the puppies better—" He swore and slapped his calf. "Since when do cockroaches bite?"

Trinity leapt onto a fire escape ladder from the Dumpster and scrambled partway up it. She focused on one of the bugs, tried to tap into her black widow side, but all she could see was a bug. No prism. Nothing. Crap!

She'd never tried to go widow on purpose. She just knew that it had happened on occasion, when she got really worked up. Like the time when she'd sat on Santa's lap when she was eighteen and he'd told her that the odds of her being a good enough girl to get a present was about the same as the odds of her waking up the next morning and being queen of fairy.

Granted, he was a fake Santa, but the words tapped into her core insecurities big-time. And then he'd laughed and tried to make out with her. Yeah, she'd seen that prism. Santa and his reindeer had been inches from packing it in a little early that year.

"Trinity!" Blaine was standing at the base of the ladder, and he was shooting little fireballs at the bugs. The flames were white now, and the cockroaches he hit were going ash… but then each piece of ash was turning into a new bug. Cockroach fertility treatment, apparently. "Tell me how to kill it!"

"I can't."

"What?" He shouted something at his team, and then vaulted up the ladder. "What's the deal?"

She watched the cockroaches circle Jarvis, closing in on him. "My power needs strong, hot emotion to be triggered. Love. Anger. Passion. That kind of thing. I'm grossed out and terrified, so yeah, nothing's really coming to light."

Blaine swore, and she saw that the creepy crawlies had reached the bottom of the wall and were climbing fast.

She grabbed the ladder more tightly. "I think we need to bail—"

"No chance." He hooked his elbow around the rung and swung toward her. "You want to turn your emotions on? I can do that." He grabbed the back of her neck. "Nothing hotter than sex."

"What? Hello? Did you not notice attack of the carob beetle aka *The Mummy*?" She snorted. "You've got to be kidding! There's no way I can get turned on right now."

He gave her a grim smile. "You'd be surprised at what a century and a half of seduction training can accomplish."

"That is such a guy thing! We've got a bad guy who turns into well-stacked chicks, and flesh-eating cockroaches, which, by the way, are starting to crawl up the wall toward us, and you're thinking about sex as the answer to our problems? This is why the world is in decay, because we have all these male leaders who—"

"Shut the hell up." He slammed his mouth down over hers and started to kiss her.

Chapter 15

TRINITY STARTED TO LAUGH THE MINUTE BLAINE'S LIPS touched hers. How could she even think about a little lip locking when they were hanging from ladder rungs with a dung beetle posse on their tails—

His hand clamped down over her breast, and he pinned her back against the ladder. Oh, hello. Okay, so the aggressive male thing was kind of hot, but still... creepy crawlies coming up toward—

He fisted her hair and angled her head for deeper penetration. Relentless. Thorough. And yeah... the word penetrating kept whizzing around in her head. Not sure why *that* particular word needed to be surfacing—

He grabbed her hand and slammed it down on the front of his pants. Either he'd packed a stale Twinkie in his jeans or he was not having any problem getting hot and bothered on a fire escape with deadly nasties down below.

Hmm... kinda liking this... It wasn't every day a girl had the chance to affirm her sexiness by successfully turning a man on in a completely non-intimate setting. Especially a girl who had spent every day since puberty doing her best not to turn anyone on, including herself.

But yeah, baby, hot warrior was digging her. And that got her a little bit fired up. Made her curious to see what else she could manage... She threw one hand around his neck and palmed the Hostess dessert through his jeans, giving it a friendly little massage. You know, just to work the kinks out. The ding-dong twitched in response to her exploration.

Oh, yeah. She was hot.

Blaine released her hand to its own creativity and slid his palm around over her butt and toward her inner thigh. He broke the kiss and worked his way down her collarbone. Girly gasp of pleasure when he hit that spot. Then his mouth was lower, on the swell of her breast, his other hand working its magic on the seam of her jeans, the one that went right between her legs—

Hot tamale pleasure shot through her and she gripped the front of his pants tighter. He groaned and then he was kissing her so hard, so deep. And then all she cared about was the heat of his body against hers, the hard swell of his muscles under her hands, the way he had her pinned against the ladder, the feel of her blood throbbing at the junction of her thighs—

He ripped his mouth off hers and shoved her back against the ladder. His eyes were dark, and his jaw hard. "Next time we're alone, the clothes are getting ditched."

She nodded vigorously. "Yeah, okay, sure."

He grinned, then kissed her again, so deep she was sure that they were going to lose track of whose tongue belonged to whom. Which would be fine. She was down with taking hours to figure it out—

He broke the kiss. "Do the spider thing, and do it fast, because I need to get you alone and naked as soon as humanly possible, or we're going to be hanging it all out right here on this ladder." His voice was low and all growly, and every single girly cell in her body stood up and cheered for the promise he was throwing her way.

"I always liked ladders." Which was the silliest thing ever to say, because she'd never even thought about ladders one way or another. But the thought of letting it all hang out on this one... yeah... ladder love.

He cupped the back of her head, and his grip was tight. "You hot enough now?"

She gave a vague nod. "Yeah, pretty sure."

"Then let's do it." He wrapped his arm around her waist, securing her against him in a take-charge-kind-of-way. "I've got you."

She didn't bother to thank him, or to enjoy it. She just leaned down and looked below. "Good lord, how long were we kissing?"

Cockroach hotel had gone out of business, and in its place was an eight-foot-tall T-rex/dragon/demon mutant with pink hair and a "Pirates for Peace" T-shirt. Jarvis and Nigel were hanging on the bottom rung of the ladder, engaging in some serious hand-to-hand (aka knife-sword-claw) combat. But the thing was getting bigger, and bleeding way less than the men.

Blaine threw a small blue ball down at the creature. A bank shot off Jarvis's sword sent it right down the gullet. For a split second, nothing happened, except Jarvis raised his sword and it began to glow and hum like a horde of fireflies had descended on them.

And then there was a faint noise, like an explosion had gone off somewhere in the distance. Smoke began to fan out of the creature's ears, and the three warriors tensed.

"What was that?" she asked.

"Blue ball. Took a chance using it this close to us, but nothing else is working—"

The monster opened its mouth, and Trinity could see

a blue fire raging in its throat. Then it let out a loud noise, and the scent of rotting human flesh drifted up to them (not that she'd ever had the pleasure of such olfactory treats before, but given the monster's dining tendencies and the fact that it smelled like the rat that had died in her wall and decayed last summer, she was standing behind her rotting human flesh assessment).

"All you did was make it burp?" Jarvis swore. "We're fucked, guys. And not in the good way."

They were in trouble? Big tough warriors? What kind of awful demise had all its other victims faced? The ones with no defenses? Anger began to surge inside Trinity at the thought of the hell those poor people had endured, and her vision became blanketed with spots of red. Blaine gripped her tighter, and he splayed his hand over her lower abdomen. "Yeah, that's right," he whispered. "Get pissed."

The dark alley began to brighten, and she felt the heat from Blaine's body kick up, like she was wrapped up next to a bowl of oatmeal that had been overheated in the microwave. You know, when you grabbed the bowl, burned your hand, and dropped it so it shattered and spewed oatmeal all over the floor? Yeah, that hot.

A buzzing sound filled her ears, and she smiled. It was coming.

"No more killing sweet things," she shouted down at it. "You get to go visit Reina!"

"I'm already here, girl!"

Trinity looked up to see Reina standing on the rooftop. Her friend waved cheerfully. "There's some near death going on here, so my boss sent me. Don't let it be you, sweetie."

At the sight of her best friend's smile, strength coursed through Trinity. Yeah, she could so do this. A sense of calm settled over her. A feeling of rightness. This thing did need to be stopped, regardless of her dad, and she could do it.

Rock on! Spider power, all day long.

Light began to reflect around the creature, and she concentrated harder—

The creature slashed Jarvis's arm, and he swore.

"Ignore him." Blaine's voice was low in her ear. "He's fine. Just focus on the monster. Tell me how to kill it."

Trinity fought not to notice Jarvis slipping off the ladder, Nigel jumping down beside him, dragging him back as the oversized rabid brownie closed in on them. She just concentrated on the prism glowing more brightly. The light began to refract and a form began to take shape. "I'm getting it!"

Blaine palmed her belly more tightly. "I can see the hologram."

The figure was holding a sword. One that looked familiar... She glanced down at Jarvis as he whipped his weapon over his head, churning up the energy field, creating a whirlwind to confuse the monster. Same jewels in the handle, same writing on the blade. "Jarvis's sword," she said. "That's how to do it."

Blaine nodded. "Keep going." He threw another blue ball down there, and this time Jarvis rebounded it into the creature's nose. The explosion blew green monster snot all over Jarvis and Nigel. "Come on, Trin."

Trinity focused again, and the prism became clearer. It was a woman.

Blaine swore. "That's you."

"Me?" Trinity looked closer and realized he was right. "It's never been that specific before."

The holographic Trinity moved toward the monster, and she was carrying Jarvis's sword. The holographic badass went to eat her, and the Trinity-the-prism threw herself into the monster's mouth (hello???? even holograms should have heard of self-preservation) with the sword. Then there was a roar, and the monster in the hologram convulsed, turned back into a man, and then fell to the ground. He twitched a few times for good measure, and then was still.

Trinity waited.

Blaine waited.

Trinity the savior never reappeared.

Suicide stabber mission, anyone?

"Huh." Blaine leaned his chin on her head. "Does that mean you have to be the one to hit it, and you'll die doing it?"

"I think so." Trinity nodded. "So, yeah, not really liking that option."

Blaine adjusted his grip on her. "Look again. Find another way."

"Hey!" Nigel shouted from below. He and Jarvis were pinned in the corner, covered in green snot, and the monster was looking a little too hungry. "Either kill the thing, or we're going for pizza and a beer."

"Hey, guys," Reina called down. "I'm seeing a couple dead warriors soon if you don't get out. It's not going to be the big creepy tentacle thing tonight."

Trinity looked up and saw Reina's eyes had gone gold and black, and she was looking at Nigel and Jarvis as if they were a double fudge caramel brownie with homemade ice cream on top. "She's telling the truth. Jarvis and Nigel are about to die."

"We need to regroup," Blaine yelled down. "I'm sending you guys up here. Hang tight."

Jarvis began to set his sword whirling, and he and Nigel hunkered down behind it. Blaine's chest caught fire. (Bizarre and cool at the same time. A little freaky.) Then he grabbed the fire out of his heart, tossed it around in his hand like he was prepping a snowball, then he hurled it at his two buddies.

The explosion hit beneath their feet and blew them straight into the air. The two warriors thudded down on the roof above Trinity and Blaine, behind Reina.

Blaine grabbed Trinity and then hauled ass up the ladder. He caught up with his buddies, and then they were all sprinting across the rooftops. The roar of the monster's outrage echoed through the night, and Trinity glanced over her shoulder in time to see an orange light glowing from the alley they'd just been in. Then the creature shot up into the air and landed on top of the roof.

It was a four-legged demon dog now, crouched like it was ready to launch itself at them.

"A dog again?" Jarvis muttered. "I gotta say, I'm kinda tired of the canine thing right now. I'm getting a goldfish."

Up ahead, Trinity noticed a wide gap between the buildings, and she tensed as they neared it. "I can't jump that far—"

Blaine grabbed her and hauled her across the abyss easily, while the other two warriors leapt over it like it was a puddle. Reina disappeared and reappeared on the other side in a flash of black light. "It's coming for you guys," Reina warned.

The giant mutt was leaping from building to building, like a slathering ping-pong ball with matted fur and horns. It opened its mouth and a loud roar filled the night.

"On the next jump," Nigel said, "you two go south, and Jarvis and I will draw it away."

Trinity shook her head. "It almost killed you before."

"Have a little faith, woman. We let it box us in to keep it in one place." Jarvis was grinning, looking delighted to be prey. "Now we've got the city to play in. It'll never catch us. It'll be fun to fight in the wide open. Haven't been able to do that before."

Nigel whipped out a headband and strapped it around his head. It had a lovely floral lake scene painted on it, with a black wolf peering out from behind a tree. "It'll be a kick," Nigel agreed. "We'll try some new tactics on it."

"Gap up ahead," Blaine said. "Splitting off in five."

Reina was running as hard as the rest of them, and her eyes were still black. "Sorry, Trin, but I need to stick with the guys. I've been assigned to stay with them until the death threat is over. You good?"

"Yeah, okay. I'm fine. Do what you need to do." And then they were at the edge of the roof. Trinity glanced down and saw the street far below. "Oh, man—"

Nigel and Jarvis vaulted easily across the gap, but Blaine simply wrapped his arms around her and stepped off, allowing them to plummet straight toward the asphalt.

Chapter 16

ANGELICA WAS IN FULL PANIC MODE BY THE TIME SHE skidded around the corner and finally found the entrance to the Hotel of Love and Healing. She was definitely going to have to start periodically reviewing her maps to make sure she knew how to get to all areas of her kingdom, even if she never thought she'd need to get there.

It wasn't like she was going to go visit the warriors who were recovering. She knew seeing her face wasn't going to help their healing. And yes, it bothered her that they didn't feel her love, but whatever. She wasn't doing it for them. She was doing it for her girls.

She charged up the steps, completely impressed at how well she was running in her stilettos. Her agility with the spikes might be her naturally exceptional balance and athletic ability. But it might also have something to do with the fact that she was pretty close to a complete mental implosion thanks to a visit from the certain oversexed underperformer who had deflowered her.

No telling how long he'd wait before he figured out that her trip to the bathroom to freshen up for some love-making had been a complete lie to cover up her frantic dash to get help.

She threw open the door of the Hotel, and then skidded to a stop, shielding her eyes against the suddenly blinding light. By all that was unwelcoming and soul-sucking, where was she?

She backpedaled quickly, checked the sign by the door. Hotel of Love and Healing. Right place. But where were the dank stone walls? The mind-numbing dripping water in the corner? The metal bunks without any blankets, and the overly permeating scent of mold and decay? Gone was the dungeon-like atmosphere she'd paid a fortune to an architect to design and even more to a builder to construct (it was before the days where her magic skill could have adequately created the doom, depression, and sense of hopelessness that the Hotel had to have in order to motivate the men to recover and get back to their canopy beds and flower comforters). Like utterly vamoose.

Heavy plaid curtains decorated the windows that didn't (shouldn't) exist. King-sized beds with navy quilts lined the circumference of the vast room. Beautiful mahogany desks were beside each bed, and a massive flat screen television was artfully mounted on the dark wood footboard of every bed. All the patients were wearing the bottoms only of dark and masculine pajamas, and a couple just had boxers on. And none of them were leopard print!

There was a bar at the end of the room, and one of her girls was pouring beer into a beautiful stein Angelica recognized as coming from her own kitchen. The sound of rap music was beating through the speakers, and it didn't quite mask the sound of tweeting whistles and the thud of football players tackling each other coming from the televisions. Another tweet, and then a collective groan went through the room, and one of the warriors swore. "Throw another damned interception, why don't you?"

Angelica set her hands on her hips. "What is this? I—"

"Burgers are ready!"

Angelica turned around. A commercial-sized barbe-cue grill was built into the wall and one of her girls was hoisting a tray filled with burgers that smelled abso-lutely fantastic. Angelica never bothered to eat, because magic could give her all the nourishment she needed, but hello? How good did those look? "I'll take one."

She snatched a burger off the tray. The girl holding them saw Angelica, and her face went sheet white. The music suddenly shut off, chatter stopped, and the only sound in the room was the thud of football players crash-ing into each other.

She took a big bite—Sweet Juicy Decadence! She was so starting to eat again—and then faced the room.

Ten guilty female faces and fifteen warriors had gone utterly still. Three of the men were on their feet, looking all too spry, and the others were still in their beds. But alert. Ready. Tense.

Little children caught with their hands in the cookie jar.

It reminded her of the day she'd walked into the base-ment and found Prentiss with his stack of girlie maga-zines when he was nine. His look of utter horror, and that possessiveness as he slid them behind his back and jutted his jaw out, daring her to steal them. His cheeks had been flaming red, and he hadn't been able to look her in the eye.

It had been so cute that she'd just let him keep them.

Maybe that was why he'd become such a woman-izing letch. Maybe if she'd done her job three hundred years ago, Prentiss would be wearing white and haul-ing souls up to heaven, instead of having a monopoly on all things decadent, irreverent, misogynistic, and utterly deplorable.

"This was my idea." Mari stepped forward. Her face was pale, and her voice was quavering. But her hands were fisted. "Our death rate has gone down seventy-three percent since we redecorated."

Angelica folded her arms over her chest. Dear Goddess of Sexual Stimulation and Lust, the number of things wrong with this scenario were mind-boggling. But she was really liking Mari's attitude. Her willingness to stand up and to save lives. That was what she'd come looking for tonight. "Come with me, my dear."

No one else in the room moved, and Angelica had to keep from biting her lip at the look of fear on everyone's faces. How delightful to feel like such a tyrant. So good for the ego, especially mere minutes after being reduced to a quivering ball of subservience by an overgrown lout. She beamed at them. "Thank you all. I appreciate it."

None of them reacted. Too terrified.

On a regular day, she'd feel a little bit regretful that her relationship had to be one of domination and cruelty when she loved them so much, but right now, she needed an ego boost as much as Blaine needed cross-stitching. And that was saying a lot.

"I'm staying here." Mari grasped a nearby headboard. "I'm taking care of Christian. He needs me."

"Oh, for heaven's sake!" Angelica strode across the room, nearly giggling as everyone scrambled out of her way. Let them worry. Yes, they were going to have to learn that going mutiny and making their own decisions didn't benefit them. But right now, there was an orgasm

overlord hot on her tail and she didn't have time to deal
with bad little children.

Her smile faded as she reached the bed and peered
down at Christian. His eyes were closed, hollowed into
his face like someone had sunk a hole-in-one into his eye
socket. His face was the color of old cement, and scraps
of metal were flaking off him. His skin was glittering,
as if he'd tried to shift and gotten stuck. His lips were
parted, and his chest was barely moving. And there was a
weird purplish stain beneath the skin on his stomach, as if
his blood had ditched the restraint of veins and was going
on a cross-country jaunt. She frowned. "If he dies before
the boys get back, I'll lose my leverage on Blaine."

Christian stirred, and his eyes slitted open. The corner
of his mouth curved up.

Angelica blinked. "You're *trying* to die so Blaine
doesn't give up his freedom for you?" As orgasms were
her witness, she just didn't know how she had gone
wrong here. She'd assumed Blaine's loyalty would get
him back to save Christian, but that was Blaine. He had
a thing about leaving people behind, and she'd planned
to take full advantage of it.

Christian, on the other hand? Not part of her plan!
She'd made sure Blaine had tortured Christian repeatedly. How could Christian possibly have any loyalty to
the other man?

Christian closed his eyes again, and Mari squatted
beside him and took his hand. "See? He needs me. He
needs a will to live."

Angelica sighed as she saw the shimmering in Mari's
eyes. "Oh, lordy, lordy. You've gone and fallen in love
with him, haven't you?"

"No!" Mari's denial was too quick, too panicky. "Of course not!"

"Mari." Angelica gestured at Christian. "Look at him. He's killing himself to save his friend. His boys are more important to him than staying alive for you. Don't you see? He's already making the choices that will break your heart. He's not worthy of your love yet."

"I admire Christian's loyalty." Mari sat next to him and stroked his forehead. "And of course he's mad at me. You made me betray him—"

"No." Angelica grabbed Mari's shoulders and yanked her to her feet. "You made the choice to call me when he was escaping. How many times have I told you that it disempowers you to claim you didn't have a choice! You always have a choice! We always do!"

"Not the men you torture! What choice do they have?"

Angelica gestured at the room full of beds. "They can choose to live or die. They make that decision every day."

Mari snorted. "That's not a choice."

"It is." Angelica suddenly became aware of the silence of the room. Even the football games were off now, and everyone was watching them. She swore under her breath. None of the men needed to see her talking to her girls as if they were people. She made sure never to come across as empathetic or soft. A man could sense a weakness in a female faster than a dragon could burn up a stack of newspapers on a windy day. She grabbed Mari's elbow. "Come on."

"But—"

Oh for the love of overly muscled pectorals! "Your only chance to save Christian is to come with me." Total lie, but whatever. It was all for the good of her prize girl, and if she had to lie to help her, well, then she'd make up stories until there were no truths left to tell.

And it was also to save her own kingdom, which, ultimately, saved the girls, so self-preservation was a good enough reason to fabricate as well.

She snapped her fingers at burger girl. "Christian doesn't have my permission to die, so keep him alive even if you have to torture other men to do it. Got it?" She saw Christian's body flinch, and she smiled. "Well, Chrissy, if you're going to be such a martyr for the sake of others, you're going to have to decide who you value more: dying to save Blaine, or staying alive to save all the other warriors stuck here with you." She waved her hand. "All of you, girls and boys, are hereby granted the gift of staying here until I release you. Your only job is to keep my main boy alive, whatever that takes." She rolled her eyes. "And if it takes football in addition to torture, then it takes football."

She felt like the room had suddenly gone bug-eyed.

Hello? Did they not realize that she was a flexible, loving mama who was always willing to shift her modus operandi for the good of her peeps? Sometimes she just got so tired of being considered a mindless, ruthless autocrat. "I'll be back soon, my darlings. Have fun."

She shoved Mari toward the front door, then paused to peer outside.

The yellow brick road was empty. No Napoleon yet. Excellent. She'd clearly done a great job convincing him that the new sexual dynamo she'd become needed time to get it all together. She'd told him it required forty-five minutes for the edible glitter to adhere to her nipples, and she was so sure he'd believed it.

Napoleon was a raging hormone. He'd be willing to wait quite a while for the best sex ever, which is what he had somehow deduced he was going to get from her...

Oh... wow... sex with Nappy... it had been good enough back then, but now? Knowing what she knew about her own body and the male trigger points? It would be some kind of night—

"Angelica? Your cheeks are flushed."

She cleared her throat. Yeah, sex with Nappy would be some kind of night indeed. It would be the kind that stripped her of all the independence and self-supporting ego she'd worked so hard to create. No thank you.

"Here's the deal, my love." She hurried Mari down a woodsy path lined with pink rhododendrons. "We've got a situation."

"What does this have to do with Christian?"

Oh, sweet lily of the valley, was she really going to tell the truth to one of her girls? She'd been such a beacon of independence, such a model for the girls. Would it destroy Mari forever if her mentor admitted she needed help? If she acknowledged she wasn't perfect? Angelica reached the clearing and sat Mari down on the white marble Bench of Peace and Introspection.

Mari frowned. "What's going on?"

Angelica swallowed, her throat suddenly tight. "I—" Oh, for the love of flavored condoms, spit it out! "My black magic doesn't come without a price. I've taken all your smut and mine and everyone else's and I've diverted it to a resource I call Smutty."

Mari's eyes widened. "You said it wasn't black magic!"

"No, I never actually denied it. You just heard what you wanted to hear."

"But—"

"That was a good tactic for you, my dear. There's no reason for any of us to face reality if we don't like it. Much better to see the world as we want to see it, because then we can feel strong and empowered and happy, and that's a self-fulfilling prophesy that gives us exactly what we wanted in the first place."

Mari's face was pale. "So, all this time, I've been creating smut?"

"Yes. Couldn't be avoided, but that's okay because there's this lovely gentleman who I've been loading it onto. But my ex-husband is back in town, and he's planning to kill Smutty so he can take the kingdom back."

Mari gripped the edge of the bench. "But if your smut monster gets killed, that means—"

"Yes, it means all the fallout will come back onto us." Oh, she hated to admit that. Her only goal had been to protect her girls and empower them, not turn them into Smutty juniors. "I'll get the most, but—"

"I have over a hundred years of magic." Mari looked like she was going to tip over.

Angelica caught her shoulders. "It's okay, darling. I have it under control."

Mari stared at her, and Angelica's heart sank at the look of fear and betrayal on her baby's face. "I trusted you."

"No, you didn't. You never have." Angelica sighed. "Can you really tell me that you never suspected you were using black magic? White magic could never cause the amount of damage we inflicted on those men, and you knew that in your heart."

"I—" Mari's mouth opened, and then shut. "You're right. I did know. I'm so awful—"

"No!" Angelica tightened her grip on Mari's shoulders. "It was the right choice, and denying it was self-preservation. You're a good girl, dearie, and I'm proud of you."

Mari took a deep breath. "I can't deal with this right now."

"You're absolutely right. We don't have time to get all hung up on ethical discussions." Oh, how proud was she of her little trouper! No whining by Mari. "We need to go out and find Smutty and get him to a safe place where Napoleon can't touch him."

Mari stared at her. "I mean, I can't deal with any of it. I want to go back to my room and meditate and—"

Oh, well, that wasn't quite as impressive. "Where's my warrior girl? Are you going to sit back and let some murderous philanderer give you smut? Or are you going to stand up for all that is large-breasted and estrogenous and take control of your life?" Oh, that was good! Maybe this wasn't a mistake. This would be so empowering for Mari to take her own life into her control against a man.

Mari hesitated.

Angelica could tell Mari was so close to seeing the light. To finding her strength. Just one more dig and Mari would be empowered. "If Smutty dies and you become smut girl, exactly how long do you think it will be until you're more interested in carving Christian up than saving him?"

Mari blinked. "I wouldn't—"

"You would. It's what smut does. It hops you right on that express elevator to demonhood and all sorts of nasties. Makes you cuckoo girl, and Chrissy goes bye bye."

"Oh, wow, that's not okay." Mari took a breath and stood up. "You're right, Angelica. I'm not letting some jerk cover me in smut."

Angelica clapped her hands with delight. "That's my girl! Let's go find Smutty!"

Mari nodded. "Where is he?"

"I don't know. Somewhere in Boston, I think." Angelica hurried down another path, the one that led to the portal.

Mari didn't follow, and Angelica turned around. "What?"

Her apprentice looked shocked. "You're going outside the Den?"

"Of course I am. Why?"

"You haven't left the Den in two hundred years." Mari broke into a run and caught up. "You wouldn't even go outside that time we all got tagged by that vampire and he said he'd kill us if you didn't come out and meet him."

"Well, yeah, he was pissed that I'd stolen his daughter. There was nothing to discuss." And, quite frankly, a ticked off vampire was outside her range of skills, every bit as much as un-melting her Blackberry had been. She'd made the conscious decision to specialize, which meant in the Den she was as powerful as Death on a battlefield. Out in the real world… not quite as confident. She used her powers for torture, not for offensive tactics or warfare. Who knew what the people of Boston were like? Okay, yes, so maybe she had consciously decided to avoid the outside world for the last couple of centuries. Nothing like an ex-husband and the threat of losing your empire to motivate a girl to go adventuring. "But that's why you're coming with me. You're an expert on Boston."

Mari shot a sharp look at her. "I'm coming along as the expert?"

"Of course you are." Oh, yes, it was time to elevate her most prized girl. Angelica stopped outside the portal and yanked open the weapons cabinet she'd set up for girls to arm themselves on their way out, and disarm themselves on the way back in. She grabbed several of the new daggers Prentiss had been so impressed with. "My dear, I'm so proud of you. I would trust no one else with a mission of this importance. Not only will you save yourself, but you will also save all the others, and the men in their care."

Mari drew her shoulders back and a sense of authority settled over her. "You can count on me."

"I know." Angelica put her hand on Mari's shoulder. "Someone needs to take over the Den when I retire, and I want it to be you." Which was true, in a vague sort of way. Of course, she never planned to retire or die, so it was kind of a moot point, but if she did decide to pack it in, Mari was the only one even close to talented enough to run it, even if she did still have that soft side to her.

But once Mari got the curse… oh, yes… different story.

Maybe Angelica would retire after all. A tropical beach, stocked with manly, half-naked island boys all at her disposal? Might be nice…

"Angelica!" Napoleon's voice bellowed through the forest.

Angelica squawked and whirled around. "Oh, dear Lord, here he comes."

"The jerkoff?" Mari glanced over her shoulder, her face curious. "If he's here, why don't we just kill him instead of trying to find Smutty? Wouldn't that be easier?"

Angelica grabbed another handful of weapons and began shoving them in every pocket, in her bra, and stashing them in her skirt. "He's very difficult to kill."

"So? You're very good at killing." Mari turned toward the woods as Napoleon shouted again. This time closer. She hefted a flamethrower. "It'll be a lot more efficient."

"No! We need to—"

Napoleon burst out of the woods. He was stark naked, as erect as the Tower of Pisa (and yes, still just as off-center as the famous building), and the muscles in his quads were flexing. He was breathing hard, and his eyes were dancing with delight. "Oh, my," he panted. "I didn't realize you were going to play with my predator instinct by fleeing. I am greatly enamored of that move." He let out a low growl and began to advance toward her, his body lithe and lean like a wild cat hunting his prey. "I'm going to have you for dinner," he said, a guttural growl low in his chest.

Angelica's lower belly convulsed and she caught her breath as the man of her fantasies began to stalk her. Her warriors were putty in her hands. But not Nappy. Nappy would pin her against the wall and hammer home until he was through, no matter what she wanted.

Moisture began to pool between her legs, and—

"By all that's well-endowed and tanned," Mari breathed. "I finally understand what you've been telling me, that some men are simply too dangerous to be allowed to live."

Napoleon set his hand on his boytoy and let out a small groan as he continued to close the distance between them, a slow, precise walk of a man who was enjoying every second of the anticipation until he would be inside her.

"One shoe," Napoleon demanded. "The left one. Take it off."

Angelica immediately toed off her shoe and flicked it at him. Napoleon snatched the Manolo out of mid-air, then ran the spiked heel down his chest. Scraped a circle around his nipple, leaving a raw red trail behind. "Mark me, woman," he growled.

Oh, yes, hot mama coming to you—

Mari hoisted the flamethrower and shot him.

"No!" Angelica tackled Mari and wrenched the flamethrower out of her grasp. It shot upward and set the tree on fire as the two women tumbled to the ground. Angelica whipped it around, and then aimed it at Mari's face.

The girl's eyes widened, and she went utterly still. "You're going to shoot me?"

Angelica suddenly realized what she was doing. Shooting Mari because she'd tried to hurt Nappy? Holy blue balls. She whirled around and aimed the gun back at Napoleon, who was still patting out the flames that were dancing on his skin.

Dear Lord, she couldn't bring herself to kill him. Couldn't let anyone else kill him either, apparently. Because she still loved him. By all things that were grossly unfair and highly disadvantageous, how could she still love him enough to want him alive?

"Oh, wow, that didn't even bother him, did it?" Mari was on her feet now. "What now?"

There was a feral quality to Napoleon's smile now. One that said he was ready for things to get rough. The kind of edgy sex that made a girl a little scared, but oh, so curious.

"Time to go." Angelica grabbed Mari's arm. "The portal still closes after you, right?"

"Yes, of course, but I kind of think that magical fire-guy over there isn't going to be deterred for the full three days it's supposed to be shut down."

"We'll take what we can get." Angelica yanked Mari backward, and she saw the instant that Napoleon real-ized what she was doing.

He let out a howl of outrage and leapt through the air, torpedoing toward them like an overgrown coconut launched from a catapult. Mari screamed, and then they fell through the portal. It snapped shut with a loud sizzle, and then there was an explosive boom as Napoleon face planted into the blockade.

As the mist closed around them, Angelica strained to listen, to see if Napoleon had broken the safeguard.

Then through the mist, she heard a distant roar of fury. "That was a very serious error in judgment, my love," he called out, his voice echoing through the vor-tex. "Now there's no deal. Smutty dies, and I'm still taking your body."

Mari looked over at her. "What deal?"

Oh, yeah, that was exactly what she needed. Admitting to Mari that she had to rescue Smutty be-cause she couldn't handle trading a night of sex with him in exchange for the safety of her kingdom. Not that it would actually save her empire if she did sleep with him. Nappy would take the sex, mess with her mind, and then manipulate them all.

"I could feel how much you want me," Nappy continued, his voice becoming more distant. "You won't be able to resist me, and we both know it." His deep, masculine, and entirely smug laugh echoed through the chamber.

And she knew he was right.

She didn't need the curse for her girls.

She needed it for herself.

Chapter 17

TRINITY WAS SO HAPPY TO DISCOVER THAT STEPPING off a building and free-falling toward the earth with nothing but a very non-birdlike companion to keep her safe was not high on her list of preferred activities.

A loud roar rocked the night as they plummeted toward a grisly and splattered death, and she looked up to see demon-dog sailing through the air above their heads. It landed with a thump on the opposite roof, and then disappeared from sight, its raspy breathing fading as it moved into the distance.

Either that, or it was getting fainter because they were getting closer and closer to the asphalt... "Um, Blaine?"

"Have a little faith, my dear." Blaine ignited the air beneath them, and the force of the explosion halted their freefall and shot them upwards.

Travel by explosion. Who knew fire could come in so handy? Maybe she would trade in her Subaru and get a little feisty with fire once she was a free woman...

They landed next to an exhaust vent, and Trinity quickly scanned the Boston skyline to make sure Dark and Grisly hadn't done a one-eighty to come check them out. Yeah, it needed to die, but there was no good plan on how to accomplish that right now, so for the moment, *keep on running, fur head.*

"Good to see the guys having fun," Blaine said, satisfaction evident in his tone. "It's been a long time."

Trinity followed Blaine's gaze and saw the bogey-man lurching across the rooftops after Nigel and Jarvis, who were whooping and hollering as they played chimney tag. They were keeping a two-building lead on it, and Trinity saw the men pause more than once to let their pursuer catch up.

How about that? The men really weren't in any danger now that they had space to run.

Hmm… wonder if she could outrun the curse? Get a little fit, drink some Gatorade, and hit the trails? Brilliant.

"That looks interesting." Blaine was looking over her shoulder, back in the direction of the bar where they'd first met the Beasty Boy-Girl-Bug.

She turned and saw a glowing white light rising up from the alley where her "Twin" had done the suicide stabbing mission. It was like an angelic beacon, growing larger and larger. She frowned. "It looks like one of my visions, but it can't be—"

Holographic Trinity suddenly bounded up into sight from behind the building and landed lightly on the roof. She raised Jarvis's bloody sword over her head and let out a howl of victory that Trinity could hear even though they were a good half-mile away.

"Hey! I survived!" How fantastic was it to see her perky face? Granted, it was a little creepy to see herself howling like some pre-adolescent werewolf on his first hunt, but alive was alive, and she'd take it.

Blaine nodded. "That means you can go ahead and kill the Chameleon without worrying about dying."

Trinity grimaced, her elation fading fast at Blaine's suggestion. "Yeah, well, I'm not sure I could actually make myself dive into the gullet of a smut monster—"

Blaine set his hand on her shoulder and squeezed. "Don't worry. I'll help you."

Trinity blinked. Yeah, assisting his girl with tough tasks was the role of a man, and she appreciated Blaine's willingness to help her do what it took to save her dad, but drop-kicking her down the throat of a rabid mutant wasn't exactly what fantasies were made of. "Well, I appreciate the sentiment, but there's still that whole curse problem if I kill anyone."

"Hey." Blaine rubbed her shoulder and she looked up at him. "I get that you have aversions to killing, but you should know that if that's the only way to save your dad, it's not that big of a deal." He smiled and brushed his hand over her cheek. "It wouldn't change that you have a good heart, no matter how many people you kill."

Her throat clogged at the honesty in his words. Yeah, he had weird values when it came to violence, so it wasn't as if he represented the general sentiment in society, but she could tell he really didn't think that it would make her a bad person. And that just felt so, so, good. "I really wish I could see myself as good. But—"

He placed his thumb over her lips. "Don't let other people's opinions affect your own sense of self-worth. Your view of yourself is the only one that matters, trust me." He rubbed her lower lip. "I've tortured my best friends thousands of times. Doesn't bother me. Doesn't bother them. Because we know that garbage isn't what matters." He put his hand over her heart, above the swell of her breast. "Right here is what counts."

She searched his face, and saw he lived by those words. "How do you get there? How do you just get over all the stuff you do?"

"You decide and then do it."

She rolled her eyes. "It's not that easy—"

"No. It's not easy. But it's doable."

She frowned at him, realizing that he really didn't see the big deal on becoming a death monger and not letting it bother her. Truly. He simply didn't think it made her a bad person. Her throat tightened and she stared blankly across the city, fighting the urge to fall into his arms like some blubbering girly girl, begging him to convince her she was okay—

As she watched, her look-alike suddenly rose up into the air, like a balloon that had gotten a helium enema.

Trinity set her hands on her hips, watching herself float up into the night sky. "Now, that's weird. I can't fly—"

It let out a loud shriek, then its hair turned into some tangled mass of damage, it got all shadowed and gray, then it tore across the night sky right toward Blaine.

He swore, but before he had any chance to move, the apparition raised its prismy fist, which appeared to be clutching a snowball. It plunged the white sphere right into his chest and ripped out a holographic vision of his heart. Raised it high to the sky with a loud shriek, and then a spectral Blaine tumbled off the roof, plummeted to a silent thud on the cement below.

Trinity gaped as her holographic self turned toward her. Eyes were blazing black like some coal miner's worst nightmare and there was blood dripping from her hand, where Blaine's heart still beat.

For a moment, the two stared at each other, then the image smiled, a delighted grin that could only be described as wolfishly gleeful. And then it slowly faded from view, until all that was left was a glittering hand and a beating organ.

And then even that blinked out of sight.

Hello, future self. Welcome to the world of the dementedly-insane, murderously-inclined black widow.

"Sweet Mother Mary." She was going to be sick. Pass out. Something. So, yeah, the anticipation had been killing her, but the *reality* of going eight-legged? Worse.

It was supposed to be the other way. The anticipation worse than reality and all that. Yay for bucking tradition.

"I need a minute." Her legs stared to shake, and Blaine caught her as she sank onto the tar paper roof. "Did you see that?"

His grip on her waist was firm. "Yeah. Split end hell."

She stared at him. "Split ends? Are you even a guy?"

He stiffened. "It's a sign of my security as a male that I can talk about hair."

"Hair?" She stared to laugh, a freakish sound eerily reminiscent of the hologram. "You noticed my beauty gaffs? What about the murderous look in my eye? What about the cackle of glee when I ripped your heart out? Did you happen to notice that?" Oh, wow. Stomachache.

"Well, yeah. Saw that too. Hard to miss. It was my heart, after all." He eased her down to the tarmac, supporting her as she sat.

She bent her knees and hung her head between them. "I can't be like that. I—"

"Hey." Blaine sat behind her, knees on either side of her hips, and began to rub her back. "That was only a vision. It's not reality."

She shrugged off his grip. "Listen, I appreciate the attempt to lull me into dreamville, but the truth is that my visions always get it right. It's part of the curse." She hunched over and pressed her hands to her gut. "I feel like I ate a live squid—"

Blaine yanked her so she was facing him. "Trinity. Calm down."

She shook her head and pulled away. "I've been calm! I've been meditating until my brain is so dead that I forget how to speak, and it's not helping!" She scrambled up and a black bug scurried beneath her foot a split second before her shoe came down right on top of it. "Crap!" She yanked her foot up. Nothing left but beetle guts and shell. Dead. "Do you see that? It's starting already!" She scooped the beetle off the roof. "Look at it! First the beetle, then you, and then—"

A small smile quirked the corner of Blaine's mouth. "It's a *bug*."

"Easy for you to say! If you were a bug, you'd be a little more empathetic! A life is a life, and I clearly can't even keep a beetle alive. What's next? Puppies? Guinea pigs? And then people? Everywhere I go, I'll just knock someone off. Maybe I'll develop a clubfoot so that I can take out anything without breaking a stride. Just a 'hey, good morning, check out my new Manolo Blahniks,' then whap! Stilettos in the eye sockets! And—"

Blaine fisted her hair and slammed his mouth down over hers.

What? Hello? So not kissing time! She was having a meltdown—

He kissed her deeper, harder, and his hand slid down to her butt. Caressing. And oh, my, it did feel good to be

touched. He'd seen her future self, and been an eyewit-
ness to the ruthless offing of an innocent bug, and he
still wanted to touch her?

Even her mom had given her the hairy eyeball for a
year after she'd killed Barry in cold blood while he was
wearing his candy cane pajama bottoms.

But Blaine's holding her so intimately was a visceral
statement that he thought she was okay. That there was
someone in the world who didn't think she was this
awful freak. Some of the pain in her stomach eased, and
she sagged against him.

Blaine broke the kiss but didn't release her. He just
looked down at her. "You capable of listening now?"

Now? Listening? "What?"

A low chuckle rumbled in his chest, and he had a
look of utterly male satisfaction on his face. Me-he-
man. Me-conquer-panicking-female-with-mighty-kiss.
Me-pound-chest.

If she wasn't so loving the feeling of not losing her
mind, she would definitely be offended by his attitude.
As it was, she was more in the camp of "more, more,
more" right now. If he kissed her constantly for the next
week, would her brain be so distracted that she forgot to
murder anyone?

Almost worth a try. You know, if Augustus wasn't
trying to find her and incinerate her, and if her dad
wasn't going to be roasted over a Sunday night bonfire.
You know, except for those small details.

Blaine tunneled his hand through her hair, like he was
game for the kiss-for-a-week plan. "I meant, are you no
longer bordering on a complete mental collapse?"

She thought of the holographic killer bitch and her

body tightened again. "Not so much. Give me a sec and I'll be right back there."

He was quiet for a moment, like he was thinking, before he spoke again. "You heard of Darwin?"

Well, that was a totally logical question. "Darwin who? What are you talking about?"

"The law of natural selection? Only the strongest survive?"

Oh, that Darwin. Of course that made sense. Girl freaks out, kiss her until she's at least a reasonable facsimile of mentally sane, and then bring up Darwin. "I don't—"

"Stupid beetles get stepped on."

She stiffened. "Well, I think that's a little judgmental."

"The beetle is about a thousand times faster than you. If it was smart, it wouldn't have been there."

Okay, it *sounded* like he was pretty sure he had a valid point. Just couldn't quite figure it out. "What are you saying?"

"It's a natural process. This way, we get smarter beetles who can give birth to smarter babies, who will in turn continue to make their breed stronger."

"That's so callous. I—"

"No, babe. It's not callous. It's the only way to look at it." Blaine released her (sadness!) and walked over to the edge of the roof. He clasped his hands on his head as he watched Nigel and Jarvis fade into the distance as they led the giant killer demon away from them. "I've seen over a hundred men die at the hands of the witch. Boys. Young men. Seasoned warriors. In the end, they all made the choice to die instead of live."

Trinity looked down at the squashed beetle in her palm. "I find it hard to believe that this guy chose to become pancake fodder." The poor baby needed a funeral. An epitaph. She walked over to a small storage shed on the south side and knelt by the corner.

"Yeah, well, if he didn't choose it, then he at least allowed it to happen." Blaine turned toward her. "We choose our destiny, Trinity, including bugs."

"Well, yeah, of course you'd see it that way." She peeled up a bit of tar paper and laid it on her palm. Not much of a coffin, but it would have to do. "You're this macho warrior who loves to kill, who's in total control of your life—"

"I'm in control?" He snorted. "When I was four years old, my father sold me to the witch for a pittance, and I heard him make the deal. He stood by and let the witch rip my arm off to kidnap me. And then he left me there."

Trinity stared at him. Okay, starting to feel a little like a jerk here. "Why?"

"Because I was the older brother, and my dad didn't like it."

Trinity set her victim on the tar paper, making sure each smushed body part made it from her hand to the blanket. "That makes no sense."

"Back then, the older brother was everything, and my dad wanted the younger son to be the one to get all the benefits. I was in the way."

Wow. So feeling the love for being an only child right now. "What about your mom?"

Blaine's jaw flexed. "She watched the whole thing. Sat there the night before on my bed. Told me she loved me and that I should never forget it, no matter what my dad did to me. And I believed her." He looked over the skyline, his back to Trinity. "And then she turned me over to that bitch."

Yeah, okay, that majorly sucked. "I can't imagine being betrayed by your parents." She tucked the beetle more securely in his new home. Not like she could make up for squishing him, but after Blaine's story, she was feeling the need to do some nurturing. What if her victim had a little beetle family waiting for him somewhere?

Hmm. That had really not been a helpful thought.

Blaine snorted. "Parents are overrated."

"No, no, not necessarily." Trinity couldn't bear that hardness to his voice. "My dad sacrificed his own life to keep me from murdering my old boyfriend. Right now, he's sitting there in some Ziploc baggie, happy to die if that means it will save my soul. Some parents are like that."

Blaine studied her, and a muscle ticked in his cheek. She could see the denial in his eyes.

"My parents ordered me not to kill the Chameleon," she continued. "They want me to save myself and let my dad die."

"Then do it."

"Don't you understand? The fact he's willing to die for me is why I have to save him."

"No." Blaine's interruption was harsh. Quick. "Don't prostitute yourself for anyone, Trinity. They'll let you down. In the end, the only one you can count on is yourself."

She felt his belief in his words, and she was saddened for the lessons he'd learned. "My parents would never abandon me, no matter how murderous and horrific I become. They'll always love me, and they'll always support me, and I'll always be there for them." She swallowed and voiced the truth that terrified her. "If I have to sacrifice my soul to save my dad, I will. Screaming banshee notwithstanding." The thought was so awful... but it was true. So horribly, egregiously, awfully true.

He was staring at her now, a look of envy on his face. "You're like this crazy, bright light of innocence," he said, walking toward her. "I didn't think there were people like you out there." He laid his palm on her cheek. His hand was icy cold, which was probably not a good sign for a fire guy. "But they'll let you down," he said quietly. "It's not worth it."

Okay, that was so sad he believed that. She put her hand over his. "I'm so sorry for what your parents did to you."

His jaw tightened. "I'm not." His eyes darkened, and his muscles tensed in his shoulders. "I'm glad I learned my lesson early. Made me stronger."

"But it still sucks. I mean, I know what it's like to have a terrible past you can't get away from." She realized suddenly that she was gripping the bug too tightly and quickly unclenched her fist. Great. Wrinkled coffin. She couldn't even bury her victims well! "Especially if you're dragging that hellish past into the future with you."

"It doesn't drag me down. I thrive on it. Crap happens, and you get stronger and then toss the rest in the garbage."

She frowned. "It's not that easy to let go—"

"Sure it is." He nodded at the smashed bug. "You think he's feeling regret for getting stepped on?"

"Um, no. He's dead. I don't think he's feeling anything." She pulled out of Blaine's grasp and walked over to an air vent. She set the coffin gently beside it, tucking it in so it would be protected from the wind. Just in case beloved family and friends came looking for him.

Blaine raised an eyebrow at her cemetery. "Sure he is. You know that souls don't end when the body dies. We go on, and that bug made its choice."

Well, now, that was just ridiculous. "You don't always have a choice—"

"No? If you don't believe we make choices, then why haven't you accepted the curse as your future? Handed yourself over to it already?"

She stood up and set her hands on her hips. "No! I'm not going to give up! I—"

"See? You do get it." He strode across the roof toward her. "No matter what, we always have options. You can be too weak to exercise the choice, or you can fight it." He nodded at the beetle. "Your bug made his choice, either by inactivity or on purpose. You were the tool for implementing, but heading off to neverland was his own decision."

Trinity scowled. "I see your point, but getting stepped on is different than deciding not to become a serial killer—"

"Do you know how many times I've died?"

She looked up at Blaine. "Is that a trick question?"

"Six hundred and seventy-one times. I died. And then I decided I wasn't ready, so I came back. I've got so much shit in me that Angelica foisted on me, but I'm still me." He tapped his fingers on her chest, right over her heart. "That banshee you saw in the hologram will never change the core of who you are, no matter how often she comes to visit. You're making the choice to fight for who you are, and the witch will never take over your soul as long as you fight her."

Something pulsed inside her, an acknowledgement of the truth of his words. She *was* fighting it. With every fiber of her being. "But it's not enough—"

"It has been so far, hasn't it?"

Well, he had a point. Six days left, and she was still who she was. "But I feel the monster inside me. I saw that hologram. And I killed a bug—"

"The beetle carnage was just a bug that got axed by natural selection. Nothing more. Let it go." He gave her a grim smile. A smile that told of a long, hard journey. "One day at a time, babe. Big pictures will knock you on your ass."

Let it go. Maybe he was right. If Blaine had somehow survived intact, then maybe there was hope that she wasn't the evil murderous 'ho that was inside her.

After all, a man who knew exactly what she was, who knew exactly what her future could hold, thought she was okay. Even her parents and Reina had always looked at her through death-colored glasses.

But not Blaine. This man who had no reason to believe in anything good thought her soul was pure. He saw her the way she wanted to be. Could he be right? Was there really a chance for her? He made her think there was, and right now, she'd take it. Tears filled her eyes, and she hugged him. "Thank you," she whispered into his neck.

His arms tightened around her and she closed her eyes. Absorbed the sensation of a man holding her. Not for sex. Not for ulterior motive. Just because she needed to be held, and he thought she deserved it.

Blaine Underhill might be too fond of killing, and he might make the evil girl inside her want to party, but right now the only thing he was bringing to life was the woman she wanted to be. He was saving her soul, one hug at a time. Her heart swelled with appreciation, a warm, wonderful feeling that she'd never allowed before—

Oh, no.

She was starting to like him.

Chapter 18

GETTING EMOTIONALLY INVOLVED WITH THE WITCH'S Chosen was asinine. For hell's sake, he had to kill her, right? Right?

But the way Trinity's body was pressed against him. The story she told.

No one returned for those left behind.

But she had come back for him.

No one sold their soul for family,

But she was willing to do it.

And so were her parents.

Trinity Harpswell had shown him something he didn't believe existed. Loyalty. Trust. Self-sacrifice. She and her parents could count on each other. And as torture was his best friend, he'd never believed it existed.

For the first time since he'd watched his mom turn her back as the witch dragged him away, Trinity Harpswell gave him hope.

"This is getting too risky." She pulled back suddenly, and her eyes were wide. "I really can't afford to like you. You have to stop being nice, right now."

"I'm not nice." Maybe it was the fear that had suddenly returned to her eyes. Maybe it was the image of her dad throwing himself into Augustus's way to save his own daughter. Maybe it was simply the warmth of her tone, the love in her eyes when she'd spoken of her parents.

Didn't know what the hell it was.

Didn't care.

Fact was, he was done fighting it.

She stiffened at whatever expression she read on his face. "Oh, no, don't you dare—"

He kissed her.

He kissed her hard, he kissed her deep, and he gave her no chance to breathe, or think, or to realize that this idea was as bad as trusting Mari with his best friend's life. And unlike previous tongue tango moments with Trinity, this time he had every intention of seeing it through to the very, very end.

Yeah, it could lead only to hell.

And he didn't care.

Not at the moment.

Right now, all that mattered was the way her body fit against his. The way she kissed him back. The way her hands twisted in his hair.

He teased at her mouth, and she parted for him. Yeah, baby, that's what he was wanting. He brought out his best weapon, and showed her exactly how talented he was in waltzing to tongue music. He knew how to seduce, and this black widow was going to have no chance to resist him.

Why?

Because he'd never been intimate with a woman without having to protect himself from getting impaled upon an acid-drenched ice pick or something equally fun. Yeah, it had never really bothered him, never thought about wanting it any other way, but with Trinity... it had all changed after she'd shared her inner truths.

With Trinity, he knew with absolute certainty that he would not have to watch his back. And he wanted to know what it was like. Right here. Right now. There might never be another moment when he knew he could trust a woman not to hurt him. It had to be now. And it had to be with this woman who had touched his heart in a way no one ever had.

"Blaine." Her voice was a throaty whisper and she gripped his shoulders. But her touch was gentle, and her hands slid down his biceps.

"Yeah, touch me like that." He wrapped his arms around her waist and lifted her against him, alternating with light kisses around the corner of her mouth, down her jaw, across her nose, then back to her mouth for heavy-duty penetration, exactly how he'd been trained.

Her body was secure against his, and he was so down with the feel of her against him. She was pliable and soft, her breasts against his chest. She wasn't trying to position herself to attack, wasn't keeping herself distant so she could decide when to hurt him. She was leaning into him, kissing him back every bit as passionately as he was kissing her.

He caught her lower lip and nibbled on it as he yanked her shirt out of her jeans. He splayed his hands over her lower back, over the heat of her skin, and swore. "You feel so good."

"You have to stop," she whispered into his ear, her breath tickling his skin. "I can't risk this."

He palmed the back of her head and kissed the curve of her shoulder. "No risk," he whispered. "I'm really tough to kill. Don't worry about it."

"But I'm not as offended by you as I used to be. That's not good."

He laughed and framed her face. Her blue eyes were

worried, but her cheeks were flushed with desire. "Want me to be offensive, or do you want me to stop?" He splayed his palms over her butt and pressed her up against his erection. You know, in case she wasn't sure what he wanted.

She let out a small groan and tipped her head back.

He took that as an invite and began to work his way down the front of her throat. To the swell of her breasts. He pulled her collar down, nuzzled her bra out of the way, and swept his tongue over her nipple. "I like the low neckline."

"It was a turtleneck before you stretched it out of shape."

He laughed and bit gently down on her nipple. How good did she taste? Maybe it was that there was no tingle from black magic. It was just skin. It was just woman. And below the surface was a heart that beat for love in a way he'd never believed in.

Trinity clung to him. "Make me hate you," she whispered.

Something tightened low in his gut. *She wanted him*. With a guttural growl, he yanked her shirt over her head and tossed it aside. Did the same with his, and then pulled her against him. Sweet demon poison, was this what it always felt like with a real woman? Skin to skin, from shoulder to belly, it was like nothing he'd ever felt. "You make me want to cross-stitch a dozen rainbows, and even that wouldn't do justice to how it feels to touch you."

She made a small noise of protest. "No, no." She palmed his chest, her fingers digging into his skin. "On what planet do you think that's going to offend me? Rainbows? That was so romantic."

Shit. Had he really said the rainbow thing? "I want to rip your pants off and mount you."

She went for his belt. "Hot manly talk so not turning me off. Try again."

He helped her with his pants, then ditched hers. "I'd rather be watching baseball than getting naked with you, but there's no game on right now." He used one foot to spread his clothes over the deck, and then eased her to the fabric. It wasn't the silk sheets she deserved, but it was the best he could do.

"Baseball not good," she gasped as he lowered himself on top of her. "Makes me think of men being so turned on they think of baseball to give them more lasting power."

He braced his palms on either side of her shoulders and kissed her, moving his body so his chest brushed the tips of her nipples. "Baseball wouldn't cut it for me right now." He couldn't keep his hips from moving against hers. Couldn't stop his knee from wedging between hers.

"Again, total turn-on," she gasped as she parted her legs. "A girl always wants to know she's so hot the guy can't hold himself back."

He realized suddenly he was pressing against her entrance. He instantly pulled back. What was he doing? That wasn't how he'd been taught. Had to pleasure her first. Get her hot. Foreplay. His muscles began to quiver in his back, and he tensed for the searing pain. For the punishment for nearly breaking the rules.

None came, and instead, Trinity caught his mouth and kissed him deeply. Wrapped her legs around his hips and began to pull him in.

Sweat began to trickle down his back and he yanked himself back. He knew what he was supposed to do. He ripped his mouth off hers, and began to kiss his way down her body.

"What?" Trinity grabbed his hair. "Where are you going?"

"Foreplay." He kissed the small tuft of hair at her cleft, stroked his palm across the bare skin. "Your skin is so soft." He palmed her, loving the bareness of her body. He slid down another two inches and kissed her again.

Trinity's belly clenched. "Good Lord. Foreplay and intimate compliments? Can't you take me against the wall or something? Ignore my needs? I can't even express how important it is that I not be thinking fondly of you right now."

He went rigid at the thought of taking her. Of ditching his constraints and making love to her the way he wanted, the way his passions were screaming at him to do. But then he shuddered, almost feeling the pain of the punishment for taking her too soon. "No." He kissed her again, began the swirling pattern so ingrained into his mind.

Trinity moaned and her knees clamped down on either side of his head. "You had to be good at that, didn't you? Do you have any idea how many points that gets you—"

He bit lightly and her body jerked. She was so responsive. So utterly without guile or pretense. No agenda. What would it be like to be inside her? "I want to make love to you."

"Then do it." She grabbed for his shoulders, tried to tug him up. "You've got to stop the great lover thing. It's not helping matters."

"No. I have to finish you." He moved back downward.

"No, you don't! I can't handle—"

He licked her and nearly lost it when he tasted her sweetness. Like the honeysuckle in the Garden of Delicacy that he'd tried that one time at Nigel's urging. It had been pure ecstasy, and worth the hell he'd caught when the witch had discovered his transgression. And that's what Trinity tasted like.

Her legs began to tremble, and her stomach muscles contracted. "For God's sake, Blaine, if you have any sense of self-preservation or any mercy in your body at all, you will piss me off right now."

He clamped down with his mouth and began to suck. Couldn't stop himself. This was no longer about doing things because he was supposed to do it. He was doing it because he wanted to. Because he needed to. Because he wouldn't survive if he didn't taste her. He had to feel her lose control, succumb to him—

Her whole body lurched suddenly, and then she stiffened, millions of microscopic convulsions shaking her. He gripped her thighs as she shook beneath him, as she surrendered herself to it. He stared at the look of utter rapture and disbelief on her face, and something inside him came alive. Something that made him feel like a man in a way he'd never felt before. He wanted to beat his chest. Stand up and shout. Go kick Nigel's ass.

Make her his.

Trinity's body eased. "Dear God, that was—"

He moved up her body and shoved her knees apart.

She opened her eyes and braced her hands on his hips, trying to hold him back. "You either have to offend me right now, or get off without making love to me, because I'm a girl, and when girls make love, we get all mushy and start confusing love with sex, and that's just not a good thing for me."

Hah. There was no chance he was letting her walk away. But offend her on purpose? He wasn't trained to do that. It went against everything that made him a man. Shit. *Think, Blaine, think.* "When I finish with you—" He pressed against her, and felt the first inch slide into the warm depths. Sweet Jesus. "We're going to go on a killing rampage." Had no clue if that would piss her off. Just being inside her made him want to go out and do the warrior thing. Be a man.

She groaned and parted her legs. "Yes, that's right," she moaned. "Remind me that you think killing is fun."

He slid deeper, and bowed his head at the sensation of her taking him inside her. "You're so wet." He'd heard about women being that turned on. Never experienced it. Never been good enough to make the women respond. Not like this.

"No," she whispered. "Dirty sexy talk is good. I like it." She was breathing heavily. "I need a reminder right now of why I couldn't possibly like you. Please, talk about how killing isn't a big deal to you, or something."

"It's not." Couldn't take the gradual approach anymore. "Sorry, but—" He thrust home, and then went rigid as he felt her body adjust to him. Buried to the hilt. That word would never make him think of a sword again. He'd think of being so deep inside Trinity's body that he could feel her smooth folds against his balls.

"No apologies necessary." Trinity moved her hips.

He groaned as she began to work him, setting the tempo like the other women had always done, never giving him the control. This time was different. "No." He grabbed her hips and held them still. "This is mine." He pulled out, and Trinity let out a whimper.

Then he plunged deep inside, and she gasped.

He tensed, waiting for the punishment for putting his own desires first.

"Again," she demanded. "Now."

Disbelief rocked over him. No repercussions? Slowly, he pulled out again.

Poised at the threshold.

"Hold me tighter," she whispered.

His grip responded without instruction, and this time he didn't hesitate as he drove deeper. Again, and then again. Her hips began to buck, and she fought to get free, but he didn't release her. Just locked her down and drove repeatedly, taking control, deciding when to let her move, when to be the one to move, when they both would go.

He was completely in control, and she was loving it. He didn't know which part was hotter, but all he knew was that he'd never felt this good in his life.

He pulled out again, and waited. Hovering at the entrance.

"Don't wait." She wrapped her legs around his hips. Tried to pull him in.

Her body was trembling, sweat was beading between her breasts, and he knew she was exhausted. He'd pushed them both to the edge, and no one had made him go before he was ready. Before he thought she was ready. He was setting the pace. Making the decisions. Taking the lead.

"Blaine." She opened her eyes. "If you make me wait much longer, there's going to be no problem with me hating you."

He grinned. "Can't have that."

And with that, he thrust deep, and this time, he made it count, and they went over the edge together. Not him at her mercy. Not her at his. Together. A joint effort.

And as his spirit hovered somewhere in the region of mindless, jaw-breaking ecstasy, he had the vague thought that cross-stitching was never going to satisfy him again.

Oh, yeah.

Chapter 19

BY ALL THAT WAS OUT-OF-SHAPE AND MALODOROUS, what was wrong with the women of Boston?

Angelica hadn't been sure of what she'd find upon landing in the Boston Common, but it hadn't been the sight of a bunch of flabby, overly-cologned girly-men trying to play softball, belching and drinking beer, while an assortment of perfectly attractive women cheered them on. Those poor women. Trapped by love in a cycle of subpar-male-adoration. "Dear Lord, I had no idea how large the market would be for the curse."

She was going to make millions.

Hundreds of millions.

Every human female alive would be desperate for a remedy that would liberate them from the influences of all these beer-bellied, low-intelligence, ga-ga brains, a supertonic that would free these females to find decent men. "I need to locate Trinity Harpswell." And now. No more leaving the curse to chance. She was going to make sure that final kill happened.

Imagine the freedom that kind of money would give her! She could create a new Den. One that didn't have a hard-on for Nappy. A protected reserve for Smutty.

She would finally, truly, be free. Angelica pressed her hand against the sudden tightness in her heart. "I never thought it would really happen."

"What are you talking about?" Mari grabbed

Angelica's dagger and shoved it in her bra. "You can't be visibly armed out here."

There was a distant rumble, like thunder. The air was vibrating behind them, like hot steam rising from a warrior being toasted under a UV light. "Napoleon's trying to break the safeguards. He'll be through the portal any second."

"Then let's go." Mari broke into a hard sprint, moving with crazy speed across the damp grass despite the stilettos and tight skirt. Kudos to the brilliant witch who'd trained her to be girly but badass at the same time. Oh, wait, that was her. Go, Angie!

"My car's up ahead," Mari said. "I pay a bribe to the meter maids not to ticket it so I can have easy access."

Angelica raised her brows at the shiny red number. "You can't afford a Ferrari on what I pay you."

Mari held up a key chain and the car chirped. "You don't pay me anything."

"My point exactly—"

"Angelica!" Napoleon tumbled into sight in the middle of the Common.

Sudden fear shot through Angelica. "My spell's that weak? It didn't block him for even a minute." By the hairiest five o'clock shadow, even after three hundred years, she was no match for her ex-husband? That was an ego-killer for sure.

He jumped to his feet, showing all his naked glory. "Stop," he commanded.

Three centuries of independence vanished, and Angelica halted in her tracks.

"Keep going!" Mari yanked open the car door. "He's not going to kill you if you run. He wants your body and your smut monster."

Angelica looked over at Mari, at the dear girl who was becoming so deadly. If she gave in to Napoleon, every darling in her care would suffer. She owed it to them to be strong. To take him on. She stepped away from the overpriced hotrod and raised her hand. "I don't have much, but maybe I can slow him down—"

"No." Mari knocked her arm aside. "The place is teeming with Otherworld police. No offensive black magic is allowed within one hundred yards of humans in public areas. They'll grab you."

Angelica hesitated as Napoleon began a slow, purposeful stride across the grass toward them, his manly parts jiggling around. No one seemed to notice the naked man invasion, and she realized he was glamouring to hide himself. A spell he'd probably perfected during his numerous assassin trips.

Relief soared through her. How lucky for him that nullifying a glamour spell was one of the few non-torture related skills she'd acquired to keep her girls and boys from hiding when they heard her coming. No nookie went unnoticed in her house.

She grinned. "I've got this, Mari. Trust me." Heat spiraled in her hand, black wisps filled the air, and then she flung the heart-shaped smoke bomb at him.

Napoleon didn't even bother to break stride; he just held up his palm to block it. Then she flicked her fingers at her own clothes, and they vanished (well, they appeared to vanish. He hadn't earned the right to really see her boobies).

Naked girl moment.

Nappy's eyes widened, his palm fell to his side, and her magic hit him splat in the face. His spell faded instantly, and a loud scream filled the air as people began to point at the well-endowed naked man running around the Boston Common with a boner.

Less than a second later, he was buried under a mound of jean-clad men who were all seething with magic. Angelica had figured the cops would go for a naked Nappy before they'd grab her for her spell.

The human world was funny that way.

Angelica grinned as she turned back to the car. "Point for the girls."

Mari was already in the driver's seat, her arms draped over the open window as she watched the scene. "You know, it never fails to amaze me exactly how much power we have over men. A fake breast sighting, and he forgot to block your spell?" She revved the engine as Angelica slipped inside. "Defeating men is child's play."

Angelica raised her brows as Nappy threw off the crowd and stood up, fully clothed again. "Is it?"

Mari glanced over at him. "It's not going to work a second time, is it?"

Angelica settled back in her seat as her young apprentice floored the gas pedal and the car sped away. "No, it's not."

Mari checked her rearview mirror. "How long until he catches up with us?"

"Not long enough."

"So, where to?"

Angelica pulled out two small yellow tulips, ones that had been carefully nurtured in her Garden of Delicacy, hidden by a careful spell amid a bed of thousands of other tulips. One of the precious flora in her lap had been blooming for three hundred years, one for just under three decades.

They were both still in their dirt, rooted. Waiting for the time when they were needed.

She picked up the older tulip. As multiple orgasms were her witness, she never thought she'd cut that one.

"What's that?"

"My map to my precious darlings." Angelica took out a pair of golden scissors and carefully cut the ancient flower.

She held the blossom in her palm. For a moment, nothing happened, and then the petals began to vibrate. It began to spin, slowly at first, then faster and faster, then a high-pitched ringing filled the air.

And then it stopped. Pointing to the right. "Smutty's in that direction."

Mari took a hard right through an alley. "And what's the other one for?"

"Trinity Harpswell." And then Angelica cut its stalk.

———※———

Okay, so maybe allowing Blaine to have his wonderful, amazing, and really sweet way with her hadn't been the smartest decision… but Trinity was definitely not taking it back.

She awoke to the bright light of morning to find Blaine sprawled on top of her, his face was buried in her neck, and his body was pinning her to the roof deck. The sky was gorgeous blue and cloudless, and his weight was comforting and heavy.

She sighed with contentment and trailed her nails lightly over his well-muscled back.

He jerked and stiffened.

"Sorry. Did I tickle you?" She let her fingers drift across his shoulder, and his tension immediately eased.

"No. Just startled me. Forgot where I was for a sec." He buried his face deeper in the curve of her shoulder, and his breath was warm against her skin.

How perfect was this moment? So peaceful. This was what life could be like if she survived the deadline. Nestled in the arms of a really good man, who cherished her and—

She began to feel hot.

The sun began to get brighter.

"Oh, no." She pounded on his shoulders. "Get off! Get off!"

"In a sec." He wrapped his arms around her and snuggled more tightly against her. "Still recovering."

This felt way too good. Just how she wanted to be with a man—

A blinking light began to form behind him. A prism. "Blaine! Look!"

Blaine finally lifted his head, and he swore when he saw the glittering light. "Is that for me?" But he didn't so much as shift his weight to let her get out from under him.

"I told you not to be so nice to me." The prism got brighter. It was almost the shape of a person now. Her fingernails dug into his skin. "You have to make me hate you. Right now."

"After you show me how to kill the witch," he said conversationally, still watching the emerging hologram, "I'm going to kill you."

"Oh, come on! Do you really think I'm going to buy that?" She writhed beneath him, frantically trying to get free. "I have to get out of here—"

He caught her wrists and looked directly into her eyes. "I said, I'm going to kill you when you stop being useful to me. I swear it to you." His voice was quiet. Unemotional.

She saw the utter seriousness in his expression. It was almost enough to make her believe him. But not quite. It made no sense. "Why on earth would you kill me?"

"Because you're the witch's Chosen."

"As if that means anything to me." The figure took shape behind him. It was her. Again. "Oh, come on, not another suicide mission—"

"Listen to me." Blaine framed her face with his hands and moved so he blocked her view of the soon-to-be assassin. "Angelica altered your physical being so if she's killed, her soul will leave her body and jump to yours. Second life for her. Adios to you."

She went still, too stunned to continue struggling. "Please tell me you're kidding."

He shook his head. "The only way to stop Angelica is to eliminate her escape route." He gave her a grim look. "And that's you."

She stared at him, a sinking feeling in her heart. She already knew Blaine well enough to know what he had to choose. "And you'll do it. To save Christian."

He nodded, and she saw the firm resolution in his eyes. "I made a promise to him, and I won't leave him behind to die."

She pressed the heels of her hands to her forehead, trying to regroup. "Okay, so let me get this straight. After making love to me and being so nice that I almost fell in love with you, you're going to use me, and then murder me?"

He grimaced. "Not my first choice on how it all could have played out, but yeah."

Wow. Nothing like a hot poker to a girl's heart to make the love fade fast. "You're a bastard." She hit his shoulders again, and this time it wasn't out of panic. It was anger, and it felt good. "You just lost the right to be naked with me."

The oversized lout didn't even budge. "Your twin's hitting the road."

Trinity looked past his shoulder and saw that the prism was fading. The sun was fading to a normal brightness. Her skin was cooling off. "Oh, God." She sagged back against the makeshift bed, suddenly too exhausted to fight anymore. "She's gone."

"Yeah." He trailed his fingers over her forehead, tracing the lines of her face. "See? Told you not to worry about me."

She batted his hand away, even though a part of her wanted to bask in the sensation. Wait a sec. "Did you tell me that only to stop me from going Jack the Ripper on you?"

He raised one eyebrow. "It's the truth."

But as he said it, she saw a deep regret in his eyes, and she knew that yes, it was true, but he was big-time tortured about it.

Well. How about them apples? On one level, his anguish proved he was the quality man she'd suspected, but at the same time, he was a complete bastard, you know, for the whole make-love-kill-you thing, no matter what his reason. Which meant she could let herself like him, admire him for his loyalty to his friend, but the truth would keep her affections from ever morphing into the oh-so-dangerous love. She smiled. "You're perfect."

He grinned and kissed her, and his lips were so warm and tempting that she almost forgot that she was fast developing a strong hate for him. "No," he whispered against her mouth. "I'm not. I admire you on so many levels, and making love to you is something I'll never forget as long as I live, but ending the witch's life is more important than saving yours."

"That was so sweet, and awful at the same time." Trinity pulled back and traced her index finger over his whiskered jaw. "What I meant was that you're perfect for me."

He raised one eyebrow. "Because I'm going to kill you?"

"Yes!" She hugged him. "That's just the lowest, most despicable thing a man could do to me." She pulled back, elation dancing in her heart, along with complete misery, betrayal, and devastation, of course. Because she really had almost fallen in love with him, and to have him rip that out from under her... yeah... completely sucked. "It's fantastic."

He raised the other eyebrow, and he looked more than a little wary. "Most chicks wouldn't be quite so happy about it."

"Most women aren't cursed." Trinity planted an excited kiss on him. Yes, there was this really awful element to the whole scenario, a kind of macabre disbelief that a man she was almost in love with could be so brutal, but after a lifetime of facing down the curse, the knowledge that she didn't need to worry about Blaine being Love Potion Number Five, was just... well... it was such an incredible relief. Liberating. "This is great! Why didn't you tell me this before?" She shoved him off her, and this time he granted her freedom.

"Well, I figured that admitting it straight up might make you reluctant to help me." He propped himself up on his elbow, his brows knitted in concern, as if he was waiting for her to suddenly whirl on him and chop off his head.

"You lied to me to get me to help you?" She jumped up and began pulling her jeans back on. "Priceless. That move's incredibly low." She grinned. "You don't even have to say anything else offensive for as long we're together. This whole thing is going to get you a ton of mileage." She held her arms over her head. "I can't even tell you how good this feels! No black widow! Whoohoo!"

She'd never felt so safe, so liberated in her life! "We can work together and I don't need to worry that I'm going to love you, no matter how many heart wrenching stories you tell me that make me want to hug you until all your pain goes away."

Blaine eyed her, and his face was masked. "You really were in danger of loving me?"

She felt her cheeks flood at his intense expression. Gah, so not wanting to admit love to a man who clearly didn't even like her enough to refrain from killing her. "Well, you know, as much as I can love, being as completely screwed up as I am." How embarrassing. Like it wasn't bad enough to start to fall in love with the wrong guy, but to have a glowing apparition of murder appear every time she had the thought was just too embarrassing. It was like this neon statement of "I love you" when in reality, she would so not be confessing love.

It was a total screwup to the normal evolution of a relationship in which both parties hid all their true feelings and built a relationship based on lies and superficiality and saved true confessions until the point at which they were both too entrenched in the fake relationship to run away when they actually got to know the real person.

Damn the curse for depriving her of the chance to build a relationship based on lying about true emotions!

She grabbed her bra and fastened it around her ribs. "Definitely, we kill the monster first, since I'm going to have to be on guard after the witch is dead, you know?"

Blaine narrowed his eyes, and his face became suspicious.

"What's that look for?" Trinity snorted. "After that confession, you can't possibly think we're going to kill the evil DNA splicer first, do you? No chance—"

"Is your tulip bothering you?" He sat up, his gaze fixed below her neck, and not on her breasts. "You're scratching it."

"My tulip?" Trinity realized that she was rubbing her nails across the birthmark on her collarbone. The minute she started thinking about it, it began to burn. Big-time. "Yeah, it is." She rubbed it harder. "It hurts."

Blaine jumped to his feet. He strode across the roof deck. "It's glowing. Like the sun's rising in your collarbone." His voice was urgent, his expression serious.

"It is?" Trinity tried to rub it again, but Blaine caught her hand.

He peered at her skin. "That's a homing beacon. Angelica must have triggered it so she could find you." He set his palm over it, drawing some of the heat out of it and easing the discomfort. "Your respite's over, babe. It's time for the Chosen to go home."

Trinity recalled how Blaine had been yanked away from his family, and she clutched his hand. "She's coming to kidnap me?"

"No." He scanned the skyline. "She's coming to harvest you."

"What?" She had no clue what he meant, but it didn't sound like a good thing.

Blaine jogged over to his clothes. "You're an incubator for the curse, and she's planning to harvest you when it ripens." He yanked on his jeans, moving fast. "It appears she's not leaving kill number five to chance."

"That's really not what I wanted to hear right now." Trinity ran across the roof and grabbed her shirt from the heating vent, where Blaine had apparently tossed it. Nearly twenty yards. Gotta love a man so caught in the throes of heat that he turned into a fabric launcher. "Can you burn the mark out of me?"

"I don't know." Blaine hurried over and pressed his palm to her flower. Heat seared her skin and she bit her teeth against the pain. It got more intense, then Blaine shook his head and dropped his hand. The pain eased instantly. "Can't. It's too entrenched. You'd never survive my flames."

"Try again." She grabbed his wrist and set it back on her chest. "I'd rather die by your fire than by hers."

He cupped her chin, his fingers light. He searched her gaze, and his eyes were hooded with regret. "My dear, that's exactly what you're going to get, but don't wish for it too soon."

Her chest tightened. "I won't let you kill me."

He said nothing. He just bent his head and kissed her.

The kiss was short, and its tenderness nearly brought tears to her eyes. He thumbed her cheek. "Just so you know, I—"

He stopped.

Her heart began to race at the softness of his expression. True love declaration? That would go so far to easing the pain of his treachery. "You what?"

He gritted his jaw and shook his head. "Nothing." He stepped away, grabbed her shoes, and handed them to her.

Fantastic. She'd wanted an *I'll Love You Forever, My Darling* moment, and she'd gotten footwear. Sigh.

"We need to keep moving to stay ahead of Angelica." He yanked on his boots. "Things just got serious."

"Oh, because it's been all relaxed and fun up until now." She pulled her shoes on, tugged her shirt over her head, and then a faint odor wafted toward her. "It smells like sewer."

"Not a lot of sewer on the twenty-fifth floor." Blaine finished locking down his laces. "We need to regroup with the team and figure out a plan. Now that the witch is tracking you, I don't think we've got much time."

"Great. Because I wasn't stressed enough before." The odor grew stronger, and she frowned, trying to place it. "What does that smell like?"

Blaine sniffed. "Rotten bananas." He took her arm. "So we're going to head back down to my bike and—"

"Rotten bananas?" Sweet mother Mary! "Augustus?" She whirled around, searching the night sky. "I cannot believe the number of personal challenges this week is giving me."

"Augustus? Really?" Blaine grinned, and then his smile faded. "Damn. It'll take me too long to figure out how to kill him. I'll have to save him for later." Blaine pulled her up against him. "Let's jet. Hang tight."

"Yeah, okay." She searched the sky for her stalker.

Should she be looking on the roads? "I don't even know how he travels." Heat began to build beneath their feet, and she knew Blaine was about to detonate a fireball, like he'd done before.

But this one felt way more powerful than any of the others. So not feeling the love for being accidentally incinerated right now.

"I'd guess Augustus drives a pink chariot pulled by a dozen matching horses." Energy crackled beneath them.

Trinity snorted. "Oh, come on. He probably drives a black, shrouded hearse with dead bodies tied to the bumper—" A rose-colored horse-drawn carriage rounded the corner of the top floor of the John Hancock building, and it was closing fast. The Augustus express? "Ah... looks like you were right—"

A gnarled hand shot out the window and flicked a pink star in her direction. "Oh, man—"

Blaine's sudden explosion catapulted them through the night sky like a shooting star that had just downed a couple of gallons of double espresso, torpedoing them away from Augustus. The streets of Boston were rushing past, way too far below. "Um, Blaine?"

He pulled her up against his chest. "I still need you. No chance I'm letting you die yet."

Ah, right. His personal agenda. She took a breath, knowing she could trust him to make sure she didn't plummet to a splattery death. She could rely on Blaine, not just to keep her alive, but to keep the spider girl at bay by being gentlemanly enough to periodically remind her of his contemptible plan.

He was a gift, a wonderful special treasure, and she so appreciated him. The ache in her heart that this man was planning to murder her? It hurt, yeah, but it was no match for the peace he gave her. Her honeymoon with Blaine would soon be over, so she was just going to enjoy the freedom he gave her for now, and deal with the rest when it was time.

She peeked over his shoulder and saw Augustus had fallen hopelessly behind. He pulled his beautiful copper-colored team to a halt and saluted Trinity.

He was conceding the skirmish, but not the war.

With Augustus nullified for the moment, they began to descend, and Trinity looked down to see they were nearing the bar where Blaine had left his motorcycle. The alley was still covered with crushed cockroach remnants, and there were scorch marks on the ground from the battle. The stain from Jarvis's blood when he'd gotten sucker punched was like a giant death stain on the ground.

As Blaine set them in front of the bar, next to his bike, she caught a whiff of charred bug. The whole scene was a vivid reminder of what truly mattered: saving her father's life without sacrificing her soul, and doing it while avoiding an overly ambitious witch, a pissed-off assassin, a homicidal lover, and her own curse.

Blaine slung his leg over the seat, jammed the ignition, and the bike roared to life. He jerked his head at her as he grabbed the handlebars.

She didn't hesitate. She just leapt on behind him and hunkered tightly against him as he peeled out.

They were out of time, and they still had no answers.

Chapter 20

Hello dream home!

Trinity halted in the archway of the double French doors that brooked the threshold to Blaine's condo. She hadn't spent a great deal of time wondering what being thunderstruck would feel like, but she was pretty sure she knew now.

Felt kinda like someone had taken a rainbow and slammed her upside the head with it. As if that cleared things up.

Because yeah… the open floor plan of Blaine's place exuded the passion, the energy, the unbridled emotion she craved so badly. His place was alive in exactly the way she burned for her own place to be. It was the home she wanted to wake up in every single day.

Oriental carpets with the deepest crimson reds covered the floors. Wild and bright modern art paintings of who-knew-what adorned the walls. They were so vivid, nearly leaping off the canvas.

The walls of the entry were a lemon-mustard with white trim. The kitchen was brick red with gloriously powerful black granite counters. The decadent black leather couch in the living room looked unbelievably soft, and the ivory matador sculpture-cum-floor lamp beside it gave her the chills when she looked at the triumph on the bullfighter's face. A potted palm sat at the end of the couch, its huge leaves bringing tropical serenity to the urban setting.

Ultra mod track lighting was everywhere, and the dark wood floors were glistening with rich tones. A poster-sized cross-stitched depiction of two young boys filled the wall across from the entrance, and special lighting illuminated its bright red frame. Cheeks flushed, the boys were gallivanting in a vibrantly colorful field of spring flowers, and a small black dog was running beside them, a large stick in his mouth. Their exuberance was so vivid she could almost hear them shrieking with laughter. A deer, two rabbits, and six butterflies cavorted beside them, while a pair of fish leapt joyously out of a stream in the background.

It was the story of pure childhood exhilaration, of the utter delight of the soul, of two beings so caught up in the sheer joy of being alive. It was the youth Blaine had been yanked out of. "Did you make that?"

"Yeah." Blaine didn't even look over his shoulder. He just headed right into the kitchen. "Brought it out with me."

Trinity studied the creation. He'd been running for his life, and he'd brought that with him? It was his dream. A hope he clung to. A desire that had kept him going. She knew, because she had that Passion Fire Bubble Bath that she looked at every night. She wanted to be alive. Blaine wanted his childhood. His brother.

"Christian." Blaine's voice echoed from the kitchen. "You there?"

Trinity shut the front door behind her, and then peeked into the room. "What are you doing?"

Blaine was crouched in front of the fridge. "Angelica linked us through the stainless steel before, so I should still be able to tap into the connection." He laid his palm on the door. "Christian." His voice was urgent, and she could feel the air thicken, as if he was shoveling energy into the appliance. "Come here."

The stainless steel front began to shimmer, and then a face appeared. The sunken ashen visage of a man who looked like a cross between the Grim Reaper and an ad for leprosy. Oh, dear Lord. Was that really Christian? Trinity edged closer, her throat aching for the suffering on the warrior's face. "What happened to him?"

"The witch happened to him." Blaine set his other palm on the fridge. "How are you doing, buddy?"

Christian lifted a hand, and his effort was weak as he placed it against the steel, so the two men were palm to palm. Smoke rose from Blaine's hand, and she hurried over to him. "Are you burning yourself?"

"This is Trinity." Blaine pulled her down beside him. "She's a black widow. She can kill Angelica."

Christian's gaze flicked to hers, and there was no life left in that face. He'd given up, a man whose soul was already waiting for Reina. It was the same expression she'd seen on Barry's face when he'd realized he was dying. A combination of agony, regret, and immense relief.

"Don't come back for me." Christian's voice was raspy. "She-bitch wins if you return."

"Not this time." Blaine's voice was hard and his fingers dug into the metal, making little divots. "I'll be there soon." Smoke began rising from the tattoo on his chest.

"Don't be an ass," Christian said. "The witch can't be killed—"

"A black widow can kill anything."

Christian's eyes closed, and he shuddered. "She's *Angelica's* black widow, Trio. She'll turn on you as soon as you're inside. Don't be the dumb shit I was and trust one of Angelica's girls."

Trinity sat back at the harsh betrayal in Christian's voice, and then tensed when Blaine shot a long look at her. As if remembering the woman Christian had referenced, and questioning his own judgment of her.

"I swear I would never turn you or your friend over to the woman who hurt Christian like that," she said, unable to keep her voice from breaking. And she meant it. God, did she mean it.

Blaine cupped her jaw and trailed his finger over her lips. His eyes were burning in his face, and the smoke was thickening on his chest. "I trust her."

Christian was watching them now. "You slept with her? She's messing with both your heads and—"

"No." Blaine dropped his hand from her face and turned to his friend. "We're coming for you."

"Don't bother." Christian tried to sit up, and fell back to the bed with a painful groan. "One of us has to stay free, so you can take my promise that there's no reason to come back. I'm dying, and I'm gonna let it happen—"

"No." Blaine was rigid now, his pulse hammering visibly in his throat. "If you're dead when I arrive, I'll haul your carcass out and set it up in my living room and have parties for it for the next thousand years. You might as well stay alive because I'm coming for you either way."

Trinity's throat tightened at the desperation in Blaine's voice. At his fear that Christian really was going to die before he could get there. She set her hand on his shoulder. His muscles were taut and his skin was so hot, it was almost as if he was on the verge of self-ignition.

Christian shook his head. "I won't let you sacrifice yourself for me. I'm done, Trio."

Blaine swore. "Listen up, you pansy ass. I'm not contacting you again, so if you die, I won't know about it. If you're dead when I arrive, then you can take the guilt to the grave that I'm risking my life for a corpse. I swore I'd come back for you, and I will. It's your choice about what I take back with me." Then he jerked his hand off the fridge and the connection broke.

Where Christian's face had been became a cold, inanimate kitchen appliance once again.

Blaine propped his elbow on one knee and bowed his head, as if he were praying. But who was there for a man like Blaine to pray to?

Trinity moved behind him and slipped her arms around his waist, and rested her cheek on his hunched back. He took her hand and pressed it to his face. "I know you get it." His voice was raw. "The way you and your dad sacrifice for each other."

She scooted around in front of him, and nestled between his knees. She laid her hands on either side of his face. "I do get it," she said. "I understand." And she did. Given who Blaine was, he had no choice but to go back for his friend, to do whatever it took to save him. And it was that loyalty, that courage, that made him the man she admired so much.

He rested his forehead against hers. "Once we go back in, she'll never let us get out of there, and we can't figure out how to kill her."

Trinity nodded. "So, I'm all you've got."

Blaine fisted the back of her hair and tugged. His grip was tight. Immobilizing her. Trapping her. "Can't afford to let you go."

She shook her head. "I won't break my promise. As soon as the monster's dead, I'm all yours. And then—" She left it hanging. Was he still planning to kill her?

He said nothing, and she sighed. It really complicated matters to know she had to have a plan to fend him off immediately after the witch was dead. Because it wasn't as if she had enough challenges going on in her life.

Blaine cupped her face and lowered his head to kiss her. She started to tug out of his grasp. "I don't think we should—"

"I need it." His face was wrecked, his voice haunted. "Please."

It was his emphasis on the word *need* that broke her resolve. No one ever needed her and now he needed her for all sorts of things. And honestly, if Reina was being tortured and dying, she would do anything to save her. Blaine wouldn't be the man she might love if he could walk away from his friend. Ironically enough, the trait that made her almost love him was also the one that made it impossible to love him.

But the love was what she was feeling right now, so she wrapped her arms around him and pulled him down, and gave him the kiss he'd asked for so nicely.

His kiss was gentle, almost reverent, as if he couldn't believe she was in his arms, kissing him. It felt real, raw, burdened with emotion so intense that the only way he could handle it was to share it with her.

Her heart swelled, and her skin began to heat up— *Oh, no!*

A loud crash sounded from outside the front door. Blaine jumped to his feet and sprinted toward the vestibule, a white-hot fireball blazing in his hand.

Trinity sank back on her heels, trying to catch her breath. Heavenly intervention right there. But how unfair was it that she couldn't even let herself enjoy the moment without going spider? Not even for one minute? For once, just once, she wanted to be able to appreciate a man and not have to run away screaming.

"For hell's sake," a man said. "You followed us here?"

"Of course I followed you here." Reina's voice drifted through the door. "How else would I find Trinity?"

"Reina!" Trinity leapt to her feet. Yes, so feeling the love for some female support right now.

Blaine extinguished the fireball as the door opened and Nigel strode in. His eyes were glowing and he looked excited. "Do you have any idea how incredible the architecture here is? I could paint it for years."

"You kill the Chameleon?" Blaine asked.

Trinity looked sharply at Blaine. Did he really think his team could kill the monster without her help? Because if that was true—

Nigel shook his head. "No chance. But we wore it out. Left it napping under the bridge by the swan boats. I think it'll be there for a while." He went into the kitchen and grabbed a set of brushes, a bunch of paint, and a sketchbook that he'd apparently stashed in Blaine's top drawer. "The thing will be easy to find when we figure out how to kill it." He looked at Trinity as he flipped open the sketchpad. "Or when you decide to kill it."

Trinity set her hands on her hips, bristling at his tone. "Hey, even though I'm not going to actually deliver the death blow, I'm going to make sure it dies. You can count on that."

"You're a woman." Nigel swiped a whiteboard from a cabinet, laid it flat, then began squeezing paint onto it. "Not a lot of reliability there."

Trinity sighed. These men so needed time around women who weren't trained to maim and kill.

"You're not coming inside." Jarvis stepped over the threshold, then swung around and grasped the doorframe, using his body to block Reina. "You're not invited."

Trinity started toward the door. "Let her in, Jarvis—"

Blaine caught her arm. "I trust his judgment. If he thinks she's dangerous, I'm going to defer to him."

"She's dangerous only if he tries to stop her. I'm trying to protect him from her." Trinity tried to pull free, but Blaine merely tightened his grip and propelled her back into the kitchen.

Fine. Let the men see what they were dealing with.

Reina started laughing at Jarvis. Her auburn hair was messy and disheveled, and there was blood on her jeans, but her eyes were twinkling. "You're scared of me?"

"Hah." He leaned against the doorframe and set his foot across the door. Folded his arms across his leather-clad chest. "I just don't have time for Death right now."

Amusement danced in Reina's eyes. "Well, listen, big guy, you can stop worrying. I'm not here in my official capacity. I'm here on BFF duty. Trin needs me."

Jarvis glowered at her. "The black widow has us. That's all she needs."

Reina rolled her eyes. "That's so arrogant to think a couple of macho guys are an adequate substitute for female solidarity. You're so wrong."

Nigel walked up to Jarvis. "Let her in. I want to paint

her. Never thought eyes that beautiful could carry that much guilt."

Trinity stiffened. Oh, man, that was so not a smart thing to say to Reina. "Nigel—"

The amusement vanished from Reina's face, and she glared at Nigel. "Don't you dare try your emotional artist stuff on me." She jabbed her fingers into his chest. "And I don't appreciate that you think my only value here is as a model for some creepy guy to paint nudes."

Nigel raised his brows. "Nudes? Now that's an idea—"

Reina lifted her fingers and waggled them at him.

Trinity yelped in protest. "No, don't—"

Black powder poured out of Reina's fingertips, coating Nigel in a gray cloud. He blinked, turned ash gray, then tipped over and crashed to the floor. Fantastic. Just what they needed, for Reina to piss off the men who were their only chance to save Trinity's dad without losing her soul. "Reina—"

Jarvis already had his blade at Reina's throat. "Heal him," he commanded.

"Don't—" Trinity grabbed for Jarvis's arm, but Blaine hooked his elbow around her neck and pulled her against him, so her back was trapped against his chest.

"Let them be," he said quietly. "They're working things out."

"They're going to kill each other!"

"No." Blaine pulled her back into the kitchen. "They're both warriors, and they're feeling each other out. It'll be fine as long as we let them sort through it."

Trinity scowled at him. "They're not dogs."

"No," Blaine agreed as Jarvis pressed the blade harder against Reina's throat. "But in some ways, not that different. Trust me when I say it'll all go better if we give them a minute. I have a feeling we're going to need them both before this is over."

Trinity bit her lip as she watched Reina tap the blade lightly, as if testing it. Yes, it was true Reina was a rock solid friend if she had your back, but she was also a very dangerous enemy. "Okay," Trinity whispered. "Sixty seconds, and then we're getting out the hose."

Blaine squeezed her once and kissed her hair. "You got it."

"Nigel will be fine in a minute." Reina fluttered her fingers at Jarvis, completely ignoring the weapon threatening her jugular. "Out of my way, big guy, or I'll take you down too. The sword act isn't doing it for me."

Jarvis didn't move. "Heal him or you die."

Trinity tensed. "Blaine, she's going to—"

"You have *got* to take women more seriously." Reina promptly shot a cloud of black powder at him. "See ya."

But Jarvis just gave her a smug grin and raised his blade higher. "Not that impressive, sweet lips."

Trinity leaned back against Blaine, not sure if it was a good or bad thing that the powdering hadn't worked. "Do you think we should interfere?"

"Not yet." Blaine's voice was laced with amusement. "I'm kind of enjoying this, actually. We've taken a lot of shit from Death and his peeps over the centuries. It's good for Jarvis to work this out of his system."

Reina set her hands on her hips and frowned at Jarvis. "How could that possibly not work on you?"

Jarvis shrugged, and there was a distinct smugness in his tone. "Not much does."

"That's never happened before." Reina pulled out her iPhone and began to type on it. "I need to let my boss know. He'll want to do some tests on you."

Jarvis jammed the tip of his sword into her phone, then chucked it through the plate glass window. Glass tinkled all over the floor, like a shattered icicle.

Blaine swore. "I'm going to make him pay for that," he muttered.

Reina squawked with visible alarm. "Do you have any idea how pissed my boss gets if we lose our phones?" She shoved past him and sprinted to the window. "Oh, man, oh, man, oh, man. I don't have time for a thirty-year demotion." She whirled on him. "You are a bastard," she hissed. Her eyes turned black. "I'm so short-listing you. Your life just abbreviated big-time." She leapt up onto the windowsill to jump after her phone.

Jarvis sprinted across the room, grabbed her around the waist, and yanked her back inside. "We don't have time to deal with Death right now. You're staying here."

"I don't have time for detention!" Reina tried to slam her elbow into his stomach, and he shoved her face-first to the floor and sat on her.

"Hey!" Trinity fought to get out of Blaine's grip. "Let her go—"

"No." Blaine kept her ruthlessly pinned against his chest. "They're almost finished."

"But—" Trinity looked over at Jarvis and saw that although he still had Reina pinned to the floor, he'd tucked his palm beneath her cheek to cushion it against the hard wood.

Jarvis leaned down and began speaking urgently in her ear. Reina stopped fighting and listened. After a moment, Reina nodded, and Jarvis stood up, then helped her to her feet.

Reina brushed herself off. Her cheeks were flushed. "Okay, so we're all friends now. Happy family." She didn't bother to hide the sarcasm. "Popcorn and movies at six."

Wow. Trinity was impressed. Not many people could talk Reina down. She looked curiously at Jarvis and had a sudden suspicion that there was something besides a man concealed behind all that anger and the haunting darkness in his eyes. "What is he?"

"He gets testy if you ask him. Best not to bring it up." Then he took Trinity's hand and led her into the living room to join the duo. "If you kids are finished fighting over the remote, you might want to join us in a strategy session."

"We're done." Reina shot an annoyed glare at Jarvis, who ignored her.

He walked back into the foyer and crouched beside Nigel.

"He'll be fine," Reina said. "He really will."

Jarvis shot her a hard look. "He better be."

Reina narrowed her eyes at him, then turned away and plunked herself into a leather recliner next to a potted palm. "Trinity, I have to say that seeing you as Curse Girl in that hologram changed my opinion about whether it's okay for you to cross that line. You were like some crazed murderous hag. Did you see the hair? Your complexion? And that noise..." She shook her head. "You're like a cheap horror flick, which normally would not be a big deal, except for the fact that you were the horror part of it."

Trinity sank down onto the couch and wrapped her arms around her belly, trying to ward off sudden chills. "And that's so helpful to be bringing that up. Thanks so much for it."

Blaine sat beside her and wrapped his arm around her shoulder. Instinctively, she snuggled up against him.

"No, no." Reina held up her hands in a white-flag gesture. "I'm saying that I'm on your side now. I'm going to give you all my resources to help you beat the curse."

Sudden hope flared in Trinity's chest. "Are you going to kill the Chameleon for me?" Death could take anything's soul. It was a perk of the job. Yeah, Reina was only an apprentice, but still…

But Reina was shaking her head. "Oh, no. I can't kill it. I already sort of tried when it was chasing the boys. I'm not that good."

Trinity met her friend's gaze. "And it would get you in trouble if you took a life without permission."

"Worth it for you." Reina shrugged, keeping her voice casual.

But Trinity knew what it would have cost Reina to get in trouble with her boss. "Sweetie, it's not worth it. You've invested too much, and you're so close to success."

Reina held up her hand and shook her head, silencing her. Crud. Had the men picked up on what she'd just said? Everything would be lost for Reina if anyone found out what she was really doing as Death's assistant.

Trinity shot a sharp look at the men, but Nigel was still unconscious, Jarvis was trying to help him, and

Blaine was watching his team. No one was paying attention to silly conversation between girls.

"So, what do I do?" Trinity scooted toward her friend, careful not to accidentally touch the plant. No need to give her mom a chance to find her and send kidnapper number two right now. "Any ideas?"

Blaine looked back at them. "You have insights, Reina?"

So much for Blaine not paying attention to them.

Reina's gaze flicked briefly at Blaine before focusing on Trinity. "Let your dad die."

"I can't! That's your answer?" She groaned and leaned back on the couch.

Blaine tucked her tighter against him and rubbed her upper arm.

"Yes, you can. If your dad dies, he'll go to a nice place. If you go banshee, I'm afraid it's going to be bad news for your afterlife." Reina winced. "I thought that your goodness would stay intact, but there was no purity in that hologram."

"It was an image," Blaine interrupted. "Of course it had no soul. Trinity can't be broken."

Reina gave him an impatient look. "You willing to stake her soul on that?"

Blaine squeezed Trinity's shoulder. "Yeah, I'd stake my own on it."

Trinity's throat tightened at his obvious confidence. She didn't know who to believe. Reina, who was an expert on all things soul-related, or Blaine, who saw a side to her that she wanted so desperately to believe really existed.

"Blaine. Get over here." Jarvis's voice was sharp, and Blaine immediately stood up and strode across the condo.

Reina inched forward and lowered her voice. "Okay, here's the truth," she whispered. "I didn't want to say this in front of Blaine since he's counting on the bargain you two made, but Death can harvest anything, and maybe he'd take down the smut monster for you. You know, for a deal."

Trinity peeked at the men, but they were hunched over, talking intently. Nigel was sitting up now, looking a little pale, but definitely recovering. "What kind of deal?"

"I don't know. He has an assortment of things he needs. It's worth a try. I'm not feeling great about your deal with Blaine and the guys. I don't see a way for it to work without you doing the killing."

Trinity bit her lip. "Blaine thinks if I look at the Chameleon again, I might see a different way."

"Not a lot to count on with that plan." Reina frowned. "You have poison ivy or something?"

Trinity realized she was scratching her tulip again. "The witch is tracking me through the flower." She quickly filled Reina in on everything.

By the time she finished, Reina was shaking her head. "I love you, but sweetie, you are so naive. Blaine didn't bring you back here to make plans. He's using you as bait to bring Angelica to his home turf. The witch comes, you pull the trigger, and she dies. Their need for you is over, and it's bye-bye black widow before the Chameleon is killed or your dad is free."

Trinity tensed. "He wouldn't do that."

"No?" Reina plucked a leaf from the palm tree and began to shred it. "Listen, Trin, I know you find him really compelling because he's got that whole murder thing going on like Barry did, but he's carrying a boat-load of emotional baggage. You really want to die just so he can clear his soul by saving his little buddy?"

Trinity looked over at Blaine and saw the haggard lines on his face. "It's not like that—"

"Hey." Reina shoved the palm tree out of the way so she could scoot her chair closer. "If I had to choose between some guy who rocked my world and my sister, who would I pick?"

They both knew there was only one answer to that question.

"The guy would be collateral damage to what I need to do." Reina's voice was hard. "I might feel bad, but I wouldn't even blink. Blaine's no different. And neither are you."

"I wouldn't—"

"Your dad or Christian? Your dad's life or Blaine's emotional well-being? Who wins?" Reina's voice was relentless. "Be honest."

Trinity sighed. "My dad."

"And Blaine will make the same choice. He has to. Doesn't make him bad, but it's the truth."

"Okay, I admit he's still going to try to kill me." She glanced over at Blaine and grinned as he looked up and gave her a special smile. "But he'd never betray me by bringing the witch here and killing her before we take care of the Chameleon and my dad. I know I can trust him—"

"Hey!" Reina lightly slapped her cheek. "Do *not* fall in love with him!"

Trinity scowled and rubbed her face. "I'm not."

"You better not. If you snap and kill him, then nothing

else matters." Reina set her hand on Trinity's knee and squeezed. "Tell me this, girlfriend. Do you really, truly, believe in your heart that there's no chance Blaine is setting you up as bait so he can end this now?"

"I do—" A sudden humming came from the kitchen, and all the men whirled around. The door of the fridge was vibrating so fast it was a blur. The oven door began to open and close. Then the dishwasher did the same. Knives began to fly out of the drawers, spinning around in a crazy vortex.

"This had better be a poltergeist with a hard-on for stainless steel," Reina said, sitting up.

Blaine was on his feet, flames licking at the end of his fingers. "She's coming."

Trinity's heart began to pound. "If he keeps his promise that the monster is first, then he has to take me out of here before she gets here—"

Jarvis pulled out his sword, and Nigel's palms began to blacken. Blaine strode over to the French doors that led to a patio. For a split second, he hesitated, then he yanked them open and stepped back. Inviting her in.

"You still feeling so confident, lover girl?" Reina was edging to her feet.

The warriors took a three-stance formation around the doors. The trio was ready to face the woman they couldn't defeat without Trinity's help.

"Let's go." Reina pulled her to her feet. "Never trust boys who have deadly weapons."

If she left now, would Blaine and the others even survive the encounter? "I can't leave. He'll still help me with my dad before he tries to kill me. I know he will."

"You willing to stake your father's life on that?"

"I—" Was she? Did she really know what kind of a man Blaine was? She quieted her mind and opened her heart. A comforting, pure warmth filled her chest, and she felt a sense of absolute rightness settle over her. "Yes."

"Dammit, Trinity. You are so in love."

"I'm not—"

"How bright are the lights right now?"

Trinity looked up and squinted at the sleek black track lighting. "Pretty bright."

"Skin?"

Trinity touched her arm. "Hot." *Crap.*

"You stay now, and the witch won't be the one you kill. Blaine dies. Your soul dies. And your dad dies. The only chance for all of you is to bail."

"No, I can handle this. I need to stay here for him—"

Blaine looked back at her, and he shot her a grim smile. "Don't worry, Trin. Even though Angelica's coming here now, I swear on Christian's life that we'll still save your father."

Tears filled her eyes at the raw, ragged truth in his voice. "Oh, was that the sweetest thing a man has ever said to me or what?" A light began to refract around him as he turned back toward the balcony, and Trinity leapt to her feet. "I'm so tired of the damn prisms!"

Reina shoved her back onto the couch, pinning her down by the shoulders. "Look at me, girlfriend. I'm not losing you like I did in the restaurant. I'm taking you out of here and we're going to handle this the only way that's safe." She rolled her eyes. "You know, as safe as making a deal with Death can be."

Trinity couldn't break her gaze off the glittering prism above Blaine. "You promise that once we save my dad, you'll help me free Christian?"

"Sure. As long as it won't break your soul."

"No. Even if it breaks my soul. I can't abandon Blaine after what he's been through. I *can't*." God, if she left now, she knew Blaine would think she'd walked out on him the way everyone had. No. He knew her. He believed in her. He would know she was coming back.

"Okay, yeah, okay, I promise. I can empathize with him too." Reina looked resigned, and Trinity knew she could count on her.

"Then let's do it." Before she changed her mind and made a choice that would cost them all everything they wanted.

Reina nodded. "Smart decision. I wish I could take you with me, but I can take only dead souls. Jarvis's car is outside—"

"No time. I'll call my mom." Trinity hurried over to the potted palm she'd been careful not to touch when she'd arrived. She grabbed a branch and brought it to her mouth. "Mom," she whispered. "You there?"

Reina linked her arm through Trinity's.

"Trinity!" Olivia's frantic voice crackled through the plant, like a bad cell phone connection. "Are you okay? I was so worried when my kidnapper was reported dead! Did you kill him?"

Blaine turned sharply at the sound of her mother's voice. "Everything okay, Trin?"

"Get us out of here, now!" Trinity whispered.

Blaine swore and charged her. "Don't you dare—"

"Blaine." Trinity reached out for his hands even as she began to disappear. "I swear to you, I'll be back. I'm not abandoning you—"

And then they were gone.

And she had no idea if he'd heard her.

And if he had, would his past allow him to believe her?

Chapter 21

BLAINE STARED IN DISBELIEF AS THE TICKET TO Christian's survival shot him a sympathetic smile and then blinked out of sight. "You have got to be kidding."

He sprinted across the room and passed his hand through the air where the girls had been. Nothing. Just empty space. She wasn't using a cloaking spell.

She'd actually ditched him.

Unbelievable. He'd trusted her, and she'd bailed. She'd sat there, looked his dying friend in the eyes, and sworn she wouldn't betray them. That she would save him.

And she'd been lying. Just like his mother had.

Déjà vu party at the bar, guys.

Anger surged inside him and he whirled around. Turbulent black smoke billowed from his pores, so thick he could barely see as he strode back across the room. Blaine set himself on fire, and let the flames reach up toward his beautiful ceiling. Charred marks immediately marred the crown molding. Shit. How could he let Trinity's actions affect his control like that? He immediately pulled the heat back just enough that it didn't touch anything that mattered to him. "Sprinklers," he commanded. No freaking waterfall was going to ruin his place.

Nigel unleashed a dozen tiny blades, and they lodged in all the sprinkler heads. "Disabled."

"Where is she?" Jarvis was looking at the couch where the women had been sitting. "She go to the bathroom to fix her makeup? Angelica's almost here."

"She left." Blaine felt the pain knife in his chest, and he shut it down. Trinity Harpswell no longer counted as a human being.

Jarvis swore and let his sword drop to his side. "You're kidding."

"Nope. We're going solo."

Jarvis fisted his sword and glanced out the window. "You insane? We'll be in chains in the Vessel of Pain within minutes."

"We're not on Angelica's turf. We can take her."

Nigel walked back toward the balcony. Palms smoking. Daggers out. "You slept with Trinity, didn't you?"

Blaine stood beside him and fed more power into the flames. "Yeah."

"Worth it?"

Blaine looked across the skyline and thought of Christian. "Not so much."

Jarvis strode up beside him. "Are you really thinking of taking on the Queen of Torture?"

"No." Blaine knew they couldn't kill her, and the fact he was pissed beyond reason wasn't going to affect his battle senses. "We trap her, then we go find the black widow and bring her back to finish the job." And when he found Trinity Harpswell, she was going to see exactly how ruthless he'd been taught to be.

Nigel swore. "And yeah, that's gonna be a piece of cake to immobilize a level ten black witch who pretty much controls every cell in our bodies. Hell, you won't even need me. Might as well go paint."

"Oh, come on. It'll be fun—" Blaine tensed as the patio chairs began to bend, as if someone was melting them. Son of a bitch. "I know for an absolute fact that I ordered the graphite ones, not the stainless steel—"

The chairs leapt into the air and attacked. The glider hit him square in the gut, and he swore as the rocker sliced through his shoulder. "I'm demanding my money back on these suckers."

The two side tables got into the action, and he had to set aside the dissatisfied customer complaints for later, along with the "find Trinity Harpswell and make her pay" plan. But as soon as the patio furniture was contained—

And then he heard a high-pitched yapping.

"Oh, come on," Jarvis said. "Not Lassie."

But it was the dogs. Again.

"You know, it would be really nice to have another cross-stitcher in the family. That was always a great sadness of mine, that you didn't inherit my creative gene." Trinity's mom was peering at an enormous tapestry in the gilded foyer of Death's McMansion. "You have no appreciation of how beautiful this is, do you? It must have taken years."

Trinity was pacing the lobby restlessly, waiting for Reina to return from tracking down Death. As expected, Trinity's mom was delighted at the prospect of saving her husband without sacrificing her daughter's soul. Making a deal with Death? A brilliant idea.

With great glee, she'd transported the three of them to the Castle of Extreme Opulence that Death had called home ever since he'd made his first big contract after taking over the job from the Grim Reaper. Reina had gone off in search of Death. (She'd recommended that they *not* wander around the halls just in case Death was in one of his moods, whatever that meant.)

Trinity had never been in the McMansion before, and normally she'd be sort of curious to check out the lair of the most powerful being in existence (at least from some perspectives), but now? Not so much.

She was actually feeling a little cranky. Must be that massive guilt complex at leaving Blaine behind when she'd promised to help him. She was not feeling the self-love right now, and she doubted there'd be any positive affirmations about her inner goodness coming from Blaine after today.

Which was fine, right? It wasn't like she was first in line for "girlfriend of the year" awards anyway. But still...

She felt like roadkill.

Olivia brushed her finger over the tapestry. "Does Blaine know embroidery? It would be really fun to have someone to sit with in front of the fire while you and Dad clean up after dinner. I wonder if he does his own designs."

Trinity slumped on a golden bench. "Mom, he's not going to marry me. I betrayed him big-time, in the worst way possible."

"Blaine will appreciate you leaving instead of killing him. Just explain you were saving his life." Olivia knelt and began plucking at the Oriental carpet in the foyer. "My goodness, the workmanship on this rug is extraordinary."

"Yeah, because that'll go over well with him. Nothing like insulting a man's ability to stay alive around you to interfere with his sense of manliness." Trinity jumped up. "I can't wait anymore. Let's go find Death. I have to deal with this."

Olivia looked up sharply. "I don't think running off by yourself is a good idea—"

"Reina went this way." Trinity ran down the hall toward a set of double doors. She grasped one of the lemon-sized crystal doorknobs (please tell her that wasn't a diamond), but the door opened before she could turn it.

Trinity jumped back as a beautiful woman peeked out.

"Hello. May I help you?" She had gorgeous blond hair piled artfully on top of her head, and she was wearing a necklace of so many emeralds that Trinity was surprised the woman was still vertical. Her smoky eye makeup was impeccable, and she was wearing a gorgeous black strapless dress that Trinity was pretty certain she recognized. "Isn't that the gown that was designed for Meryl Streep to wear to the Oscars? The one that disappeared from her dressing room five minutes before she was supposed to present?"

The gal smiled, revealing perfect white teeth. "You are so right. I saw it, I had to have it, and my darling got it for me."

"He's not *your* darling," a voice said from behind her.

The woman ignored the interruption. "My name is Isabella Fontine. Are you here to apply to be one of Death's HoneyPots?"

"Um, no." Was she? What if that was the deal? "What does a HoneyPot do?"

Isabella winked. "Whatever he wants us to do."

"Oh, for heaven's sake, Izzy, stop being rude and let them in." The door opened wider, and another woman walked up. She was wearing a luxurious cranberry pant-suit and a plethora of jewels as well. Sexy, but in the most classy, most beautiful way. "My name is Linnea Nogueira. I'm Death's executive VP. Won't you please come in?"

Trinity hesitated. "We don't have time to socialize. We really need to talk to Death. It's urgent."

"He'll be here in less than a minute." Linnea smiled. "I'm scheduled for his nine fifteen personal gratification session, and he's never late for his orgasms."

Well, wasn't that handy? Nothing like timing her visit with a personal gratification session. "You're sure we won't intrude?" Not sure she wanted to be around for one of those. Or maybe she did. Might be educational.

"Oh, no problem. He always makes time to meet with women." Linnea waved her hands. "I'm just waiting for my nails to dry. He prefers a French manicure when I'm going to give him a hand job in a Dolce and Gabbana suit. Versace always requires a nude finish. You know how it is."

Trinity cleared her throat. "Yeah, sure." She knew exactly how it was to try to dress to keep nice guys from noticing her. Wasn't so experienced on dressing in a way that might turn them on. Interesting thought. How hard would it be to tweak Blaine's—

No. She had to let him go, at least until she could get back there and help him. God, she hoped he was okay.

Isabella held out her hands as well, showing red fingertips. "He likes Crimson Fire for this dress." She pursed her mouth. "See how it brings out the tones of my lips? My makeup artist and I spent hours trying to find which ones went together the best. He's very discerning in his tastes." She stepped back and gestured for them to enter. "Please do come in."

"Great. We'll wait for him." Might be best to chat with him *after* the sex. Men tended to be in better moods afterward. "How long does a session take?"

"Depends on how much time he has." Linnea picked up a small hand fan and turned it toward her French manicure. "Usually about three minutes."

Olivia raised her brows. "He can satisfy you in three minutes? Can I watch?"

"Mom—"

"Oh, no," Linnea said. "It's not about us. It's about him."

Olivia snorted. "What century are you ladies from? It's always about the woman, and any man who ignores the woman's needs is just a jerk."

Linnea raised her eyebrows. "Or the richest and most powerful man in the universe."

Olivia gave a nod of acknowledgement "Well, there is that. Is he handsome?"

Isabella and Linnea exchanged knowing smiles. "Of course." Isabella winked. "You may not have come here to become one of his HoneyPots, but you won't want to leave until you are one."

"I have an MBA from Stanford and graduated number one in my class." Linnea picked up a small laptop from a nearby table. "I came here to run one of the most up and coming businesses in existence, and I've helped take it to a world dominating enterprise." She began to mouse through some files. "But I do my share to keep him happy. We all do."

"Is it your choice?" Trinity wasn't liking the direction of the conversation. Was Reina a HoneyPot as well? She'd never mentioned personal gratification sessions before. She really hoped Reina hadn't been lowered to that.

Linnea and Isabella exchanged looks again, and something silent passed between them. "Of course it's voluntary," Isabella said. "Death would never force anyone. Not an efficient use of his time."

"And apparently neither is taking time to satisfy his woman?" Olivia snorted. "You all should get some standards when it comes to orgasms, you know."

Trinity left her mom to the sex talk and strode into the office, hoping to catch Death before he dove into his PGS.

The ceiling was at least twenty feet high, and gorgeous dark mahogany beams crossed the smooth plaster above her head. Built-in carved mahogany bookshelves stretched to the crown molding, and they were packed with thousands of hardcover books. A ten-foot desk camped across one end of the gorgeous handwoven carpet. It was clearly his office, and it was beautiful.

But the most interesting thing was the beauty salon at the far end of the room. Well, if you could call it a beauty salon. It was more like what she'd imagine a spa for the Hollywood royalty would be. A dozen women in expensive dresses were working on six beauties. Nails, hair, and foot scrubs were all going on. Expensive plants and soothing music filled the room.

"He often enjoys seeing us primp for him," Linnea explained, gesturing at the bustling activity. "The salon is portable so that if he's not in the mood to see us, we can relocate in less than thirty seconds. He likes us to be perfect, so I run the salon 24/7. I require everyone to get touched up twice an hour to make sure we haven't smudged our makeup."

"Well, that's ridiculous." Olivia set her hands on her hips. "What man is worth that kind of time?"

"I am," said a deep, cultured male voice.

Trinity turned toward the door. The moment she saw the tall, well-dressed testosterone factory, she knew that coming here had been a huge mistake.

And not because of the HoneyPot risk.

It was much, much worse.

Angelica stepped out of the Ferrari just as a stainless steel deck chair crashed to the sidewalk beside her. She jumped, and then was immediately embarrassed at how edgy she was. Damn Napoleon for interfering with her calm, confident demeanor.

Mari opened the door and stepped out. She shaded her eyes and looked up. "You really trust the schnoodemgons not to hurt Trinity?"

Angelica raised Trinity's tulip, and it spun around, pointing south. "She's gone." By all that was slippery and elusive, how had the girl vacated so fast? "I knew I should never have let her back into the world." Smutty's tulip started to vibrate, and she tensed. "He's in trouble. We have to go help him."

"But what about the men?"

Angelica looked up again. She so desperately wanted to go up there and claim her boys, but Smutty took priority. "My puppies will keep them occupied until I can get back. A little suffering will benefit them anyway. Let's go." But as she got back into the car, she couldn't help but hope that the boys were up to the challenge.

She'd made some adjustments to the schnoodemgons since the escape, and she hadn't had time to test them. She wasn't sure the boys would survive them.

But that was okay, right? If they weren't strong enough to defeat a few puppies, then they weren't worthy of her girls. A loud yell made her skin prickle, and Angelica leapt out of the car. Teal-colored smoke was pouring out of the roof deck of Blaine's building, and the air was pulsing with dark energy. "Dear Patron Saint of Torture," she breathed.

Mari leaned out the window. "I've never seen smoke that color. What is it?"

"It's Blaine." Angelica pressed her hand to her heart. "He's dying."

Mari snorted. "He's always dying, and he's always fine. Unlike Christian, who's not that tough. I really want to get back. I'm worried about him—"

"This is different." Angelica took a step toward the building, suddenly afraid for her favorite warrior. He'd bled aquamarine smoke only twice before, and each time, she'd been certain it was the end. It was only when she got in his face and gloated about how happy his parents would be to know that she'd finally killed him that he'd fought back from the edge. How she'd hated pulling that card on him, but it had been for his own good. "I need to go up there—"

The tulip in her left hand began to smoke, and she realized Smutty's flower was turning brown on the edges of the petals. "Smutty's hurt."

Mari held out her hand. "My fingernails are turning gray."

Angelica realized her own cuticles had gone black. They were starting to tingle. "By all that's merciless and bloody, Napoleon must have him. The smut's leaking back already."

"Dear Lord." Mari went pale. "I'll kill Christian if I get my smut back. You know how crazy it makes people."

"I know." A loud shout of agony echoed from above, and Angelica looked up as another burst of teal-colored smoke cut across the sky. And then a dark shadow flitted into sight and perched on the edge of the roof. One of Death's harvesters. Waiting.

"I've hurt Christian enough." Mari slid back into the driver's seat. "Come on!"

Angelica couldn't wrench her gaze off the carnage taking place so far above her head. "But Blaine—"

"Call off the dogs."

"I can't." Angelica's throat felt dry. "Once I unleash them, they're on their own. They stop only when they die or their prey dies. It's up to the boys to save themselves."

"So it's going exactly right." Mari revved the engine. "Or are you going soft?"

Angelica tensed. Dear Demon in a Black Hat, who was her loyalty to? The men who still weren't worthy of her darlings, or her sweet girls who needed her protection? She looked over and saw Mari's lips had gone black as well, and her eyes were getting sunken.

There was no decision to be made.

It was her precious protégées who mattered.

"Let's go." She jumped in and grabbed hold of the door handle as Mari gunned the engine and the Ferrari took off down the street.

And when an earthsplitting scream rent the day, she refused to look back.

———∾∾∾———

On the plus side, there was nothing like pain to reinforce a man's self-image as a badass warrior.

Blaine sucked in a groan as he crawled away from the bathroom where Jarvis and Nigel were using the antique footed bathtub as a shield from the schnoodemgons. The damn things felt no pain. Didn't stop flying when they lost their wings. Didn't seem to notice when their heads got whacked. It was like each body part was a segmented being all on its own. Even the teeth were still pinching them when they got knocked out of the things' heads.

"This would make a great Halloween movie," Jarvis yelled as he decapitated a flying fang. "Crack dragons from hell. They never die, they just keep on killing."

"You making any progress, Trio? Your bathtub's getting beat to shit." Nigel's voice was strained, and Blaine knew the ninety percent severed left arm had to be hurting like hell.

Blaine swore as another dragon bodyslammed him. They'd hit him with water repeatedly, and it had an extra kick it hadn't had last time. Wasn't sure what was bleeding out of his pores right now, but it felt kind of like acid mixed with razor blades. He had no fire left. Couldn't summon even a spark. It had wiped him, and they knew it.

Sensing that Blaine was no longer a threat, the schnoodies were focusing on Jarvis and Nigel, which had given Blaine the chance to slide away. To the one thing that might save them.

He gritted his teeth against the pain, then finally reached his wall safe. He shoved his way to his knees, and the room began to spin. He braced himself against the wall, fighting against the nausea. This was even worse than when he'd been in the piranha feeding frenzy, and that had been no field trip through a bed of daisies.

Water was streaming down the wall from his palms, pooling on the wood floor. And that just pissed him off. He loved those floors. Water stains would never come out.

"Any day, Trio! Quit admiring yourself in the mirror!"

"A couple of pansies, always needing rescuing," Blaine shot back. He tried to focus on the padlock, tried to remember the combination, but his mind kept blurring. Shit. "Nigel! Knife!" He moved aside to make room for a flaming dagger to slide through the metal.

"No more left, Trio. They're all playing with the fanged birdies."

"Tell me you didn't forget the combination," Jarvis shouted. "Not impressive!"

"Shut up." Blaine shoved his hand in his pocket. Pulled out a wallet and a phone. Other pocket. Motorcycle keys. A cross-stitch needle. He started to throw it aside, then looked at it again. It was one of his reinforced ones, designed to survive even a blue ball blast, so he could find solace even in the middle of a battle. Hot damn.

Nigel shouted with pain, and Jarvis swore. Explosions came from the bathroom.

Blaine fisted the needle, focused what strength he had left into his upper body, and then slammed the weapon into the lock. The needle went right through the metal and the door sprung open. "Rock on." He tossed the needle aside, then reached inside the safe.

Three blue balls. "You guys ever see *Lethal Weapon 2*?"

"You kidding?" Jarvis yelled back. "Never looked at a condom commercial the same way again."

"Remember the bathtub scene?"

Silence. "You serious?"

"Got three blue balls and a hard-ass tub." There was a roar from outside, and Blaine looked up as a new wave of salivating butterfly-wannabes came streaming in through the window. "You guys ready?"

"What about you?" Nigel shouted. "You're too close. It'll take you out!"

"No chance." Blaine braced his palms against the wall and rested his forehead against the plaster, summoning his strength. If he died now, Trinity would go free, and that was unacceptable.

Trinity Harpswell, I'm coming for you.

A schnoodemgon launched itself at him, and Blaine let it hit him. Too numb to feel its claws rake across his throat. Barely noticed the blood pouring from the wound. "I'm engaging!" Blaine shoved himself off the wall and began to run toward the balcony. Threw the first ball into the bathroom. The second into the living room. The third went outside into the approaching swarm.

"Three seconds until detonation," he shouted as he shoved his way toward the landing. Had to get out of there. Couldn't be there when they went off. Would blow him up. Had to get airborne.

Claws went for his eyes. Teeth ripped at his flesh. Acid burned his skin. Didn't stop. Didn't care. Fought to take one more step. Getting too hard.

"Two seconds," Jarvis yelled. A loud thunk indicated that the bathtub had just been inverted over their heads. The air began to hum, and he knew Jarvis was channeling the energy into his sword. He needed to absorb enough blast with his sword or the bathtub wouldn't be able to save them. Joint effort: blade and porcelain.

Blaine went down on his knees. Palms braced on the floor. The winged cannibals cackled as they ripped apart his body. Then Trinity's face flashed into his mind. The way she'd focused those weepy green eyes on Christian and lied. The look of pity on her face just before she'd ditched him.

"One second," Nigel yelled.

Screw that. It wasn't over. He wasn't some four-year-old boy anymore. No one had the right to betray him. Not anymore.

Trinity Harpswell, you don't get to walk away from me. Strength surged into his body, and he shoved himself to his feet and broke into a run. Hauled ass across the carnage of dead horn-dogs and assorted body parts.

"Blast off!" Jarvis yelled.

Blaine was still twenty yards from safety when the blue balls detonated.

Chapter 22

THE MOMENT TRINITY LOOKED INTO DEATH'S DARK eyes, she knew she'd met him before, and that she had once loved him. She didn't know how. She didn't know when. But she knew for an absolute fact that the man before her had once held a place in her heart, and dealing with another guy she loved was the *last* thing she had time for. "Who are you?"

The master of the universe stared in disbelief, then a huge smile broke over his face. "Trinity? Little Trinity Harpswell? Is that you?" He rushed across the room and wrapped her up in a giant hug. "You look fantastic! I can't believe you found me." He kissed her forehead in what could only be described as a paternalistic gesture. "You must stay for dinner. We can catch up. What have you been up to?"

Trinity felt something building inside her. But it wasn't dark and dastardly. It was warm and fuzzy. "How do we know each other?"

Death's smile faded. "You don't remember? I used to babysit you."

Trinity glanced over at her mom, who was looking stunned. "Mom? Something you forgot to tell me?"

Olivia was gripping the edge of the doorframe so tightly her knuckles were white. "Sorry, dear, but I really think I'd remember hiring Death to change your diaper and sing lullabies to you."

"Not when you were with her." Death jerked his magnificent chin toward her mom. "When you were with my grandma."

Trinity frowned. "Your grandma? Who is she?"

"Angelica, of course. Do you remember how I changed the words to 'Mary Had A Little Lamb' for you?" He was playing with her hair now. "What was it? Oh, that's right, Trinity had a little spider, little spider, little spider—"

"Stop it." Trinity's heart was hammering now. Death was Angelica's grandson? Talk about a powerful family. "You were nice to me. You were my friend. I remember." It hadn't been romantic love. It had been the love of a child to a father. To an uncle. To a big brother. A love that had been a warmth in a scary, scary world. Not the kind to trigger the curse.

Well, that was good, almost enough to trump the weirdness of learning that Death had changed her diaper—

"You do remember!" Death beamed. "Gram didn't want you seeing what she was doing in her lab, so I babysat you while she was working. You were too important to be left with anyone else." He cupped her face. "You were the only baby I've ever known. Didn't even like babies. Still don't. Except you. My sweet Trin. When you used to fall asleep on my chest after Gram had injected you—"

"Well, this is all well and good," Olivia was suddenly standing behind her, "but Trinity has a little problem. Can you help her?"

Trinity blinked at her mom's sudden interruption. Oy, what was she doing, reminiscing about the days of being kidnapped? Her mom was right. Now wasn't the time to fill in the missing gaps about her abduction. But she would so be taking Death up on his dinner invitation when this was all over, assuming, of course, she was still alive and sane.

"Well, of course I'll help her." Death sat down on his desk and tried to pull Trinity onto his lap. "Anything for my sweet Trin Trin."

"Um, no thanks." She twisted out of his grip. Just something kind of creepy about having the lord of souls want to have you on his lap. For all she knew, he was going to whip out a pacifier or something. "Listen, my dad's in trouble."

"Elijah? What's he done? Sold one of his sculptures to the wrong guy?"

Trinity blinked. "You know my dad?"

"Sure. He—"

"About Trinity's problem," Olivia interrupted. "We're running out of time."

"Right. Keep talking." Death was still grinning at her, and there was a softness to his eyes that seemed so familiar. It felt like an oasis in a world that was spinning out of control.

"I can't find him!" Reina ran into the room, her cheeks flushed. Then she skidded to a stop, and her eyes widened. "Trin? Are you okay?"

"You know Reina?" Death's smile faded. "Reina! Why haven't you told me that you're friends with Trinity Harpswell?"

Reina's gazed darted from one to the other, clearly trying to figure out what was going on. The salon was still going strong behind her, and none of the women seemed to be paying any attention to the revelation that their demanding lover had once been a babysitter. "You're interested in Trinity?"

"Of course." Death pulled out his wallet and began to flip through it. "We go way back."

She blinked. "You do?"

"I haven't told you the story." He pulled a wallet-size photo out and held it up. Trinity recognized herself immediately, a tiny bundle cradled in the arms of a man who looked way too tender to be the same power-monger who ruled by terror. "This is my favorite picture. I keep it with me all the time."

Reina peered at it, and she raised her eyebrows in disbelief, but made no comment.

Trinity's chest tightened. "That's so sweet you kept that picture of me."

"A little creepy if you ask me," Olivia muttered. "You aren't his daughter."

"But she was my little Trin Trin." Death reached into his desk and pulled out a box. He flipped the lid. "Cigar anyone?"

"Later." Trinity declined the offer, desperately aware of Blaine fighting for his life against Angelica, of her dad waiting to die, of Augustus searching for her. "My dad was killed to save my soul, and I need to kill a big baddie to save him. But if I do it, then that's my fifth kill and the curse will take me."

Death's grip on his cigar faltered, but he recovered so swiftly that she wouldn't have noticed if she wasn't watching so closely. If she didn't know him well enough to recognize that she'd just said something that had rocked him.

He lit the cigar and took a long puff.

"Death—"

Reina shushed her with a head shake.

Trinity bit her lip and waited for him to blow six smoke rings. He watched them drift toward the ceiling, then finally turned to look at her. "I can't help you."

"But—"

"This is between you and Angelica." He took another puff. "I can't interfere."

"But what about 'Trinity had a little spider' and all that?"

"A memory I will treasure forever." Death's face softened, but then he shook his head. "But it doesn't change anything. Gram's going through a difficult time right now, and she needs my help. Saving you from kill number five would cause her undue stress, and I can't do that to her."

Trinity stiffened. Was he going to try to force that last hurdle on her?

"Oh, no, don't look so worried, my dear." Death twirled the cigar between his long fingers. "I'm not going to free you from the curse, but I'm not going to quicken your fall either. I'm staying out of it." He grinned and folded his arms across his chest. "It's a girl fight, and you know how we men like girl fights."

"Excuse me." Reina spoke up. "Just so you know, Trinity's going to get kill number five anyway, because she's fallen in love with someone, so your grandma will still get what she needs from Trinity." She glanced at Trinity, and Trinity saw Reina's belief that Trinity could still prevail, even though she wasn't sharing her confidence with Death.

"Really? You're in love?" Death looked skeptical. "Is he good enough for you? I want to meet him first.

Not just anyone is worthy of my little Trin Trin. What's his name?"

"You're not her father," Olivia snapped. "She has a dad already."

"One that's about to die, from what I gather," Death shot back. He smiled at Trinity. "I'm here for you. Whatever you need."

"She needs your help," Reīna interrupted "Doing this favor for her will be of financial benefit to you."

"Really? A deal is always possible when I'll reap financial rewards." He turned to Trinity, and he had a different expression. One that was hard, focused, and all business. "Talk, my dear."

"No one can kill the Chameleon." Reina walked forward, taking over the conversation. "The Triumvirate is desperate and would probably pay a lot of money to have you get rid of it. It would be great for the reputation. You know how corrupt governments are. Once they realize you'll hasten death for a price…" Reina shrugged. "Word gets around."

"Hmm." Death rubbed his jaw. "Tell me more. What's this creature?"

Trinity answered this time. She hurried over toward her old babysitter. "It's this serial killing shapeshifter that can morph between a man, a girl, a zillion cockroaches, and a demon dog—"

"Shit!" Death jammed out the cigar. "You were sent to kill Gram's smut receptacle?"

Okay, so it wasn't like there were enough surprises already. "You know him?"

"Of course I do." Death yanked his phone out of his pocket and dialed. "Voicemail. Gram has *got* to start carrying her phone with her more often." He sat down at his desk. "Linnea! You have one minute to find out how saving Smutty can be a financial boon to me, because I need to go help Gram keep him alive, and I need to make money off it."

"On it." Linnea ran out of the office.

Well, excellent. That had been the exact plan when they'd shown up at Death's door: Get him to declare himself as the powerful protector of the monster that she had to kill. Brilliant.

"Hey." Reina picked up a fountain pen and gripped it like a weapon. "Does anyone else smell banana bread being made?"

Trinity caught the whiff of rotten fruit and spun toward the door as Augustus stepped inside. He smiled. This time there was no Blaine to protect her.

"Stop." Isabella was suddenly in front of him, a small dagger at Augustus's throat. "No men allowed in here."

Death hadn't even bothered to look up. He was tapping an email on his phone, apparently entrusting the defenses of his inner sanctum to the well-dressed women in his employ.

Augustus bowed. "My name is Augustus. I'm here to—"

Death looked up sharply. "You're Augustus?" He inspected Augustus with great interest. "You've taken some of my clients out from under me."

Augustus gave him a toothless grin. "You're no match for me, newbie. I amuse myself watching you chase my tail. I'll always get the most lucrative contracts."

Death tucked the phone in the pocket of his jacket. "What do you want? A partnership? I work alone."

"I want Trinity Harpswell."

Death looked over at her, and she could see him contemplating the financial reward of handing her over. She began to sidle toward an orchid plant in the corner, humming "Mary Had a Little Lamb," and her mom quickly joined in. Reina did backup humming *a cappella*.

Death's face softened at the tune they'd bonded over, and he shook his head at Augustus. "Can't do it. She's not mine to sell."

"Then I shall just help myself."

Death narrowed his eyes. "No one kills in my home except me."

Augustus pulled his shoulders back. "I can kill wherever I want. You're a peon. You can't control me."

"I'm the most powerful man in creation." Death rose to his feet, towering over the hunchbacked stinky guy. "I own you. I could pluck the life right out of you in a heartbeat."

Augustus puffed his chest out, and his hand went to his pocket. "I could kill you faster."

"You don't get it," Death said. "I can't be killed, because I own death."

Trinity was almost to the plant.

"I've been killing people since before your mama came to this earth," Augustus spat. "I can kill anyone."

"Don't insult my mama." Death's face got dark, and pain flashed across his features. "She was a good woman—"

Trinity, Reina, and Olivia grabbed the orchid, and they began to fade.

The men were so involved in their standoff that neither of them noticed them leaving, until the last second when Death looked over. Respect flashed in his eyes, and he nodded.

She realized he'd intentionally distracted Augustus so she could get away.

Their babysitter bond might have let her live, but they were in a race for Smutty now, with opposite goals. She had to get back to Blaine. He was her only chance to save her father, and they had to get there before Death showed up to protect Smutty.

And she hadn't missed Death's affection for the witch. No way was he going to allow her to be murdered. Which was fantastic. If there was an enemy *not* to have when you were in the middle of a highly complicated battle revolving around offing an assorted number of beings, it was the head honcho of all things death-related.

Augustus finally noticed she was leaving, and he howled with fury. He began to race toward them. If he touched any of them before they disappeared, he would come with them. "Hurry, Mom!"

Augustus launched himself at them, and she felt the cold rush of his fingers a split second before they disappeared.

Were they too late?

Blaine had always thought the penthouse suite would be a good fit for him, but he'd never considered the benefits of a thirty-six-story freefall toward the Boston Common. Must have been his natural warrior skills that had prompted him to buy a place that came with the benefit of high winds and a suicidal straight shot down to the pavement.

His skin was raw and burned, and his clothes were on fire—unfortunately, from the blue balls and not his own sparkplug of a personality. He spread his arms and let the wind rush over him, wicking away the moisture that had extinguished his fire like a waterfall on a bad-quality match. He watched the earth rush up at him, counting the seconds until impact.

Normally, face planting at 125 miles per hour wouldn't be a problem for him. Now? As waterlogged as he was, there wasn't going to be a lot of post-impact healing going on for him. It'd be splat, and then that was pretty much it.

He took the heat from his burns, channeled it into his tattoo, and tried to ignite his pilot light. Still wet. Not good.

Not really feeling the love for his playtime in this world to end today. Had too much to do. He was aware of a few schnoodemgons chasing him. No clue how many had escaped. Or if Jared and Nigel were alive. "Come *on!*"

He kicked off his burning shoe, caught it as he fell past it, then shoved the flaming leather against his chest. The fire burned like Nigel's branding irons, and he grinned. Nothing like the direct application of blazing cowhide to get things going.

Smoke began to rise from his mark, and he ditched the shoe. Focused all the energy into his tattoo, and it suddenly caught. Steam hissed and rose from him as he burned the rest of the water out of his body.

Then he looked down and swore. Even as he ignited an explosion below him to provide a buffer, he knew it was that classic irony of too little, too late. It barely slowed him down before he hit the pavement.

———

Trinity was already in full flight mode by the time they landed outside Blaine's building, in case Augustus had hitched a ride on the palm tree and was going to come out of the fade seconds behind her.

She'd made it only twenty yards from the rhododendron they'd traveled through when Blaine crashed to the sidewalk in front of her with a horrific thud. "Blaine!"

He did a textbook tuck and roll as a massive Pterodactyl throwback came racing down toward him. Its wingspan was at least thirty feet in diameter and getting bigger by the second. Blaine came to a stop on his hands and knees, and he was dripping with blood. His body was bruised and slashed, and she could see his muscles shaking.

He looked up at the oncoming creature and threw a fireball at it. It snatched it out of the air and swallowed it, and kept coming.

Two more were right behind it.

Then five more.

He was going to die and it was her fault! And there was nothing she could do to save him! No fireballs, no gun, no nothing! She was utterly unable to help him—

A prism flared in front of the winged creature. She went still, staring in hopeful disbelief as her guilt and the terror for his life flared up into the one thing she'd feared for so long.

Blaine lifted his head, and she saw him watching it.

Come on, Trinity. You can do this! Trinity opened her heart and embraced the onslaught of emotion, the self-blame, the guilt for leaving him, the fear for his safety, the fury at the creature for stealing this honorable warrior's life. She let the emotions hammer at her, drinking in the pain and the anguish until it hurt so badly that she felt like her own soul was going to break.

The prism took the shape of a person, and a rose-colored arrow was glowing in its hand. The image hurled the fiery spear, and the weapon slammed into the left pinkie claw of the approaching beast. The spectral version of the creature promptly exploded in a cascade of colorful fireworks.

Blaine leapt to his feet and a spear made of pink fire flared in his palm. He flung it at the lead attacker that was mere yards from his face. Its teeth grazed Blaine's forehead just as the arrow made contact. It exploded nearly on top of Blaine, and the light show was dazzling.

He didn't even flinch, didn't bother to duck. He held his ground and began firing arrow after arrow at the bats-from-hell coming after it.

"Hot damn, girlfriend." Reina raced up beside her. "That's brilliant!"

"I can't believe it worked." Trinity sank to her knees in stunned relief as she watched Blaine take on the swarm of killer birdies, his aim unerringly precise. Point for being cursed by the black widow!

"Guilt is a fantastic motivator, as is trying to save the life of someone you love." Reina knelt beside her, resting her hands on her thighs as she watched the show. "Trust me, I know. Makes the reward feel awfully good, doesn't it?"

"You bet." Trinity grinned at Reina. "Makes it better to share it with you too. I know you understand."

Reina hugged her. "Oh, I do, sweetie. I really do."

"My darling." Olivia finally caught up to them. She braced her palms on her knees, trying to catch her breath. "What a wonderful use of your skill. I'm so pleased you've found a quality outlet for it."

"Nigel!" Blaine's voice rang out powerfully in the night as he continued to hammer ruthlessly at his attackers with more arrows. "Vulnerable spot is the left front claw, lateral digit."

There was no reply, but a moment later, there was a cascade of rainbow colored sparks from the top of the building. Then another and another, until it was like the Fourth of July.

Trinity sat back on her heels and raised her face to the sparks. They sizzled on her skin, and she didn't care. It just felt so good. She'd saved Blaine's life with her power. She'd done something positive with it. The pain felt wonderful, a reminder that she was alive, that her soul was still breathing.

Blaine suddenly turned toward her. His face was dark, and she saw the accusation in his expression. The hatred. The utter betrayal.

She scrambled to her feet. "Blaine! I had to go—"

Blaine threw a pink flame dagger at her, and it cut through the air, right toward her heart.

Seriously? Wasn't that a bit of an overreaction to her walking out on him? Talk about an oversensitive guy!

"Trinity!" Her mom screamed. "Watch out!"

Watch out? Was she kidding with that? Trinity threw up her hands to protect herself (yeah, pretty much the textbook definition of useless gestures), and the blade hurtled toward her chest—

Then the arrow collided mid-air, inches from her body, with a pink star.

A pink star? Trinity covered her head as the two weapons exploded in a cascade of fireworks. A second flaming pink knife sailed over her left shoulder, so close she felt it singe her hair. She spun around in time to see it bury itself in the chest of Augustus, who was digging a second star out of his pocket.

His eyes widened, and he fell to the ground, clutching his chest. "My heavens," he gasped. "How impressive of him to think of using pink fire." Then he keeled over and the scent of bananas filled the air. He coughed once, and then was still.

Reina raced over to him and crouched beside him. "He's not dead," she announced. Her eyes were still blue. "He's not even close. I'm guessing he's back up again in less than five minutes." She looked over at Trinity and her eyes widened. "Um, Trin—"

A well-muscled arm hooked around her throat and she found herself yanked back against a hard body. "And now we're even for the tip on how to kill the puppies." Hot breath seared her cheek, and the scent of burned cotton assailed her nostrils. "But we are far from even for you betraying me."

"I didn't!" She tried to wiggle out of his grasp. "Let me explain—"

"No time." He hauled her over to his bike. The seat was charred from the fireworks. "The witch is probably on her way to save her precious smut monster. We're going to find her, and you're going to take her out. Got it?"

She struggled to free herself, but his grip was un-yielding. "But what about the smut monster? We have to kill him too, or my dad dies."

"Screw your dad. You cost him his life when you walked away." He threw her onto the bike seat.

"No!" She tried to twist out of his grip, and he slammed his hand over her thigh, pinning her to the seat. She looked over at her mom and Reina, who were being amazingly unhelpful. They were chatting with each other while they were watching the scene. "Mom? A little help?"

Her mom waved. "Good luck with the Chameleon, darling. I know you can figure out a way for Blaine to kill it for you."

"Um, hello? Are you blind? You think he's going to help me?"

Blaine shouted up at the roof for his team, and his whole body shook with the effort. His muscles were trembling and there was blood seeping out of an assortment of wounds on his body. Not that it seemed to be affecting his strength. Shouldn't a man this injured be too weak to hold her captive with a single hand?

Reina inched forward. "Um, Trin, don't forget Death is probably on his way over there to protect the Chameleon and Angelica. So be careful."

Blaine jerked his head around to look at Reina. "Death's involved? Why?"

Reina set her hands on her hips. "In your haste to lump Trinity in with all the other women you've known, you neglected to ask her where she went, didn't you? Didn't even take note of the fact that she came back for you, of her own free will, did you? Might want to consider that, big guy."

"Tell me about Death." He was talking to Reina, though. Pretending Trinity didn't exist.

Jerk! She smacked the back of his head, right on a burn mark.

He ducked and blocked her hand. "What was that for?"

"You! You say I have this great heart, and then judge me without giving me a chance?" She smacked him again and grinned when he swore. It felt fantastic to stand up for herself. "You're an arrogant brute who's too caught up in his own past to realize quality when it hits him on the back of the head!" And then she hit him on the back of the head one more time, just in case he was too obtuse to pick up on her point.

Blaine caught her wrist and turned to look at her. He didn't look happy. "Don't hit me."

"Then don't be a bastard."

"Me? You left."

"I came back! You're the one person who has seen me as remotely good, and then you took it back! I'm the good person! You're the jerk!"

She stopped in surprise at her own words. Had she really just yelled that she was a good person? It had felt true when she'd said it. Maybe she was. Maybe Blaine's arrogant belief in her had finally sunk in. She grinned. How good did that feel?

Blaine shook his head in disgust. "Women."

"Women? That's all you can do? Compare me to the sluts who tortured you and left you behind—"

He whirled around. "My mother wasn't a slut."

Trinity went still at the hostility on his face, at the fury in his tone. At his defense of the woman he claimed to hate so much. Was there more forgiveness, more hope in his heart than he'd revealed? She touched his cheek. "Blaine—"

"Hey!" Nigel and Jarvis came racing out of the front door of the building. They were both limping, and Jarvis had dozens of new scars on his chest. Nigel's bandana was tattered and bloody, but both men were grinning.

"That kicked ass," Jarvis said. "Did you see how fast those gnats turned tail when we started killing them?" He pumped his fist. "Those are the witch's best creations and we decimated them—" He saw Trinity then and his face darkened. "What the hell are you doing here?"

"I saw how to kill them," Trinity said. "You're welcome for coming back and saving your butts when I didn't have to."

Jarvis snorted, but Nigel raised his brows at her. "Why'd you return?"

She met his blue gaze. "Because I thought Blaine might need me."

Jarvis glared at her, but Nigel studied her. "Interesting," was all he said, but Trinity suspected he saw far more than he was saying.

"To the bridge," Blaine said. "I suspect the witch is heading over there to get the Chameleon, and apparently Death is too. First one wins."

"On it." Jarvis and Nigel sprinted over to a Hummer parked on the side of the street.

Trinity wrapped her arms around Blaine's waist. She wasn't getting off the bike, no matter how mad he was at her. The monster had to go down, and it was up to her to do it, no matter how it had to happen. And it didn't matter if Blaine wanted the witch to die first. She was the one in charge of her powers (at least hopefully), so she would decide the order. *Please let me be strong enough to control the spider.*

Blaine revved the engine, the wheels were just starting to roll when Trinity's mom touched his arm.

He looked down at her hand, and for a second Trinity thought he wasn't going to stop. Then the bike jerked to a halt, and he let the engine idle. "What?"

Olivia squeezed his arm. "Dear boy, on the back of your bike is the most precious thing in the world to me. I owe her my life, and I beg of you to bring her back to me with her soul intact. Don't let her sacrifice herself to save her dad. She'll do it, and we aren't worth it. Make sure she saves herself." Her voice broke. "Please."

Blaine stared stonily at her, and Trinity felt her throat tighten. "Mom, it's not up to him. I can't live with anyone else dying because of me. I'll do whatever it takes to make sure Dad lives. If I die, it's because I've failed, not you."

Blaine started to let the bike roll and heartache made her mom's face crumple as she realized that Trinity really was going to do it.

Then Olivia raised her chin and got a hard look on her face. The kind she always got when she was going to lever an ugly truth on someone. Kind of like the time when she'd sat Trinity down and told her that she'd been cursed with the black widow and she was going to have to deal with it. No tears, no feeling sorry for herself, just step up and cope with it. Trinity started to shake her head. "Oh, no, Mom, this isn't the time for one of those discussions—"

"I sold you to Angelica," Olivia blurted out.

The bike slammed to an abrupt stop. "What did you say?" Dark anger laced Blaine's voice.

Trinity tightened her grip on his waist. "Mom? What are you talking about?"

"I was dying from childbirth complications, and Angelica said she would save my life if she could borrow you for six months. We agreed." Olivia met Trinity's stunned gaze, her face stoic and determined. "I was scared of dying, Dad was terrified, and we lied to ourselves about the cost of our choice."

Trinity suddenly couldn't feel her feet. Her hands. Her nose. Just numbness buzzing around in her brain. Blaine set his hand on Trinity's thigh, his palm a warm, reassuring pressure as she fought against the sudden tightness in her chest. "It's your fault I'm cursed?"

Reina let out a low whistle. "I always wondered why your parents were so forgiving of your death tendencies. I thought it was awfully progressive of them. Totally forgot to check out the guilt angle."

"It's completely our fault," Olivia agreed. "The minute Angelica left with you, we realized what a horrible thing we'd done. I was still too weak, but your father searched for you every day. Every night we laid awake praying for your safety, and then when we got you back, and you seemed fine... we were so happy."

Trinity's stomach roiled. "Until I killed Joey Martin after I lost my virginity to him." What a night that had been. He'd gotten her drunk, seduced her on the top bleachers (and it was so not romantic to be getting sexy amid old paper cups and gum, no matter how good the view of the moon and stars had been), and then she'd shoved him off the bleachers to his death. An accident, she'd thought for sure, until her parents had informed her otherwise. Discovering she'd murdered him hadn't helped the trauma of a bad deflowering. "I thought you'd worked so hard to save me because you loved me. Not because you felt guilty."

She couldn't look at her mom. Couldn't stand the scent of earth she'd always associated with her. The smell of grass was too thick. The trees too close. The vibration of the engine between her legs was too harsh, like a swarm of bugs crawling in her pants. She wanted to stumble off by herself, to think, to breathe. Her tulip suddenly hurt even more intensely. The brand of the betrayal. She dug her nails into it, desperate to claw it off, to cleanse herself, to—

Blaine grabbed her hand and pressed it against his chest. The heat from his tattoo burned her palm. His scar was a symbol of his own survival. She held tight, as if he were the only solid thing in a world that had suddenly fallen away. She breathed the oil of his bike, the leather of his new seat, felt the heat from his body fighting its way into her cells.

"It was a one-time mistake when we were too young to know better," Olivia protested. "We changed our minds the minute she disappeared with you, and we searched for you every day. We love you—"

"No." Blaine's voice was hard, and he set his other hand on Trinity's leg. Pulled her knee against his thigh. "You don't get to say that anymore."

Olivia's cheeks reddened, and she folded Trinity's free hand in both of hers. Her fingers were cold and clammy. Numbly, Trinity stared at the hands that had comforted her so many times in her life, the same ones that had willingly set her in the arms of the psychopath who had infected her.

"That's why you can't sell your soul for your father," Olivia said. "We don't deserve it."

"No. You don't." Blaine flicked Olivia's hands off Trinity. "You lose."

Trinity stared at her mom. At the woman she'd loved for so long. "I don't understand how you could do that to me," she whispered.

"Hey." Reina stepped forward and shook Trinity's shoulder. "Give your mom a break. It was one mistake and she's been paying for it her whole life." She met Trinity's gaze, and allowed her own pain to show. "I know what it's like to live with that kind of regret. It doesn't mean she doesn't love you. She does, and she's doing everything she can to fix it. Don't judge her the way Blaine blames his parents."

Trinity stared at Reina. "But you're different. You never lied to anyone about what you did."

Reina shook her head. "She loves you. Don't you dare let that go, Trinity. It's a gift and—"

"Trinity!" Tears were streaming down Olivia's cheeks. "I'm so sorry, darling, I truly am, but Reina's right. You have to know we both love you and if there was any way to change it, we would have, a million times. I tried to get the witch to curse me instead, and she wouldn't—"

"I can't hear this right now." Trinity's face felt wet, and she couldn't think. She pressed her face to Blaine's back and closed her eyes. "Blaine," she whispered. "Please take me away."

Blaine revved the engine and he peeled out, jerking

her out of the arms of the two women she loved, the only two women who had stood behind her despite the trail of dead bodies behind her.

She looked back over her shoulder as Blaine sped down the street. Reina had put her arm around Olivia's waist, and the two of them were watching.

Olivia raised her palm in one final entreaty, and then Blaine turned a corner and they were out of sight.

Chapter 23

THE LAST THING BLAINE COULD AFFORD TO FEEL RIGHT now was empathy for the woman who'd walked out on him.

But Trinity was hanging onto him like she was afraid the earth would swallow her up if she let go, and he couldn't stop thinking about her stricken expression when her mom had made that hellacious confession.

He'd had only four years with his mom before she'd betrayed him. How much deeper did the treachery dig after having built a lifetime of trust with someone?

He glanced in his rearview mirror and saw Nigel and Jarvis were on his tail. They had no time to stop and deal with this crap. But he couldn't off either the witch or her garbage man without Trinity's help. He had to be sure he could count on Trinity when the cockroach party started, and right now he wasn't sure she was capable of standing upright, let alone knocking off two unkillable opponents.

Shit.

He had to deal with this situation, didn't he?

Damn Angelica's buck-toothed snapping turtles and their penchant for male nipples for forcing him to be aware of how emotions impacted everything.

Emotions were for sissies. Not warriors.

But he flipped off Nigel and Jarvis, and then pulled the bike over to the side of the road in front of a row of brownstones. Two minutes. That's all he was giving this, and it was only to make sure the battle went the way he wanted it to go.

That was it.

He turned off the bike, as Nigel and Jarvis drove past and double-parked the Hummer just ahead. He could feel Trinity's body shaking against his, and she was gripping him so tightly he was pretty sure she was successfully tourniqueting all the bleeding wounds on the lower half of his body.

Jarvis jumped out. "What's—"

Blaine sliced the air in front of his throat with his hand.

Jarvis's eyebrows shot up, but he folded his arms over his chest and leaned against the back of the truck. Privacy? None of them had had quality alone time in a hundred and fifty years.

Nigel shoved the passenger door open and hopped out. He had a sketch pad and a charcoal crayon. He immediately sat down cross-legged on the cobblestone sidewalk, gave them a thoughtful look, and then began to draw.

Just like old times. The higher the stress, the more likely Nigel was to whip out a pencil.

Blaine shifted his shoulders, turning away from the boys. "Trinity."

She didn't respond.

Gently, he pried her arms off his waist. "Trin."

She suddenly lifted her head from his back, yanked her arms off him, swung her leg over the bike, and sprinted down the street.

Did the girl ever stop taking off on him? She was more slippery than a pig in a grease farm, or at least according to what Nigel had told him about greased up porkers. The farm kid had never quite ditched the hay-seed memories.

Blaine caught Trinity as she reached a huge oak tree that had defied all odds and managed to take root amidst a sea of cement, bricks and buildings. He caught her around the waist and swept her up as she fought him.

"I want to be alone!"

"Too bad." He sat down against the tree and plunked her down in his lap. Iron-fisted her right where he wanted her, then waited for her to realize she was trapped.

He didn't like the fact that she gave up resisting in less than five seconds. Her lack of spirit worried him. But when she sighed and collapsed against his chest, her cheek warm against his tattoo, yeah, well, not so bad.

"Tell me what it was like for you," she whispered, twisting her fingers in the front of his shirt. "The day it happened."

He wished he didn't know what she was asking. He wished he didn't remember what it was like to suck it up on his own. To want his mom to hug him, and instead to be lying in a pink bed with a flower comforter that smelled like something had died in it.

Which, he later realized, something probably had.

"Blaine." Her voice was raw, as if she'd been scream-ing for days, or swallowing recently sharpened blades. "Tell me."

He rolled his eyes, but he loosened his grip and began to rub her back. Tried not to think about the words he was saying. "I was sitting at the top of the stairs when the witch walked out of the kitchen. My dad was behind her, and I could see my mom sitting at the kitchen table. A stack of corn was on a place mat in front of her."

Trinity's hand stilled on his chest, and she raised her head to look at him. "They sold you for corn?"

"I'm assuming it was good corn. The tender kind." The bark from the tree began to dig into his back, and he shifted his position.

"Corn," she repeated. "How many ears?"

"I think it was six. Enough for two meals. Or corn-bread, maybe." He kept rubbing her back. Not sure whether he was doing it for her or for him, but it felt good, and he was going to keep it up.

"Not even a baker's dozen. I would have at least thought you'd be worth that."

He shrugged. "Not everyone appreciates my great love-making abilities."

She stiffened, and her cheeks flushed. "I wasn't talking about—"

He had to stifle a grin. "So, yeah, Angelica came out to get me, I stood up, took my carving knife, and whipped it right at her." A siren wailed in the distance and he saw flashing red lights cross at the next intersection.

Trinity raised one eyebrow. "Were you as good at throwing things back then?"

"Yeah." He tangled his fingers in her hair, watching a squirrel scurry along a wrought iron fence in front of a nearby townhouse. "My aim was dead on for her heart, but she snatched that knife out of the air, faster than I'd ever seen, then hurled it back at me." He held out his arm, where that scar still burned. "It hit right here." He pointed to the middle of his biceps, where the thick ridge was the widest. "Then it ripped down my arm, like it was alive."

Trinity laid her hand over his scar. "And your parents? What did they do?"

"My dad went back into the kitchen." Blaine watched the squirrel leap down, grab an acorn, and then scurry up a small fruit tree growing up out of the sidewalk. Nature, struggling to exist in the city. Reminded him of trying to survive in Angelica's prison.

"And your mom?"

He shrugged. "Wasn't really paying attention at that point." He caught her chin and forced her to look at him. "It didn't matter, Trinity. They sold me out, and they never looked back. That's the whole story. It sucks, but it's better to know."

Trinity searched his face. "Didn't you even look in the kitchen to see what was happening?"

"Why would I?"

"Maybe your mom was crying. Trying to save you, and your dad wouldn't let her." She hugged herself, rocking back and forth on his lap. Her face was so anguished it was making it impossible not to think more than he wanted to. Not to feel more than was smart to feel.

"No chance," he snapped, his voice harsher than he'd intended. "I gave up that fantasy long ago."

"I can't believe they wouldn't care." She picked a fallen leaf off his leg and smoothed it between her palms. "Your parents. Mine. I mean, how do you do that? Give your child away to a woman who's going to torture it?" She looked up at him. "They had to know who they were giving us to, didn't they? They knew, and they did it anyway. For corn. For…" She closed her eyes. "To save my mother's life. Do you think that's true?" There was hope in her voice, as if the reason could justify the means.

He grabbed her shoulders and forced her to stop rocking. "Trinity. Look at me."

A tear slid down her cheek, and her fist crushed the leaf she'd so carefully smoothed moments before. "What?"

His words died in his throat. His unequivocal statement that there was nothing redeemable about parents who sold their kids out. That there was no love. He knew it, he believed it, but looking into Trinity's tortured face, he couldn't bring himself to say it.

How could he take away her hope? Hope was all that had kept him alive. Hope for freedom. But for Trinity, it was hope for love. He had no right to take away anyone's dreams. Especially not when she was facing a battle for her own survival right now.

Yeah, she'd betrayed him.

But that didn't change the fact that she'd just been kicked in the teeth by the same person who'd done it to him. And it sucked. He ground his jaw. "Your mom did say she tried to find you." He expected the words to grate like granite in his mouth, a lie that smelled like his mother's perfume.

But it tasted sweet, like his first breath when he woke up from treading the edge of death. "She said she tried to change her mind right away," he added. That statement felt just as good, like he was greedy for the sentiment. Words he'd once dreamed of speaking about his parents, excuses that would allow him to forgive everything, hope he'd long ago relinquished.

She searched his face. "Do you believe my mom?"

"I—" He didn't know how to answer that question. He wrapped his arms around her, watching a doddering gray-haired couple stroll by with their equally ancient yellow lab. They were holding hands and smiling, even though they could barely navigate the uneven sidewalk.

The woman smiled down at them, and he nodded back before he realized what he was doing.

"Blaine?"

He rested his chin on Trinity's head. "Both your parents would rather have your father die than have you lose your soul." Those words touched something inside him. Death was something he understood, and he knew there was no greater statement than giving up your own life, your own soul for someone. There was no one he would die for. No one who would die for him. He thought of the way Trinity's mom's fingers had dug into his arm when she'd asked him to protect Trinity. That plea had been her absolute truth. She wanted her husband to die instead of her daughter, and it had hurt her like hell to make that choice.

Trinity played with his shirt collar, the tips of her fingers brushing so sweetly against his throat. "What are you saying?"

He nuzzled Trinity's silky hair and inhaled the sweet scent of lavender he associated with her. The smell eased the tension in his chest, allowing him to speak a truth he never would have thought he could say in this type of situation. "I think you can believe your mom. Yeah, she made a choice that was crap, but it's pretty clear that she loves you today. That they both do. You don't die for people if you don't."

She was silent for a moment, but the trembling was easing from her body. "If you were in my place, would you trust her?"

That was easy. "No."

"But you believe her for me?"

He ground his jaw and shifted uncomfortably. One

of the sidewalk bricks was digging into his hip. "Hell, Trinity, I don't know. I'm out of my depth here. All I know is that she meant it when she told me to save your soul instead of your dad's life." He shrugged. "Call it love. Call it someone's slipped her a bribe to make sure her husband gets the axe. But she meant it."

A tremulous smile curved Trinity's face, and the sight of it was like the sun had suddenly started shining down on him after a century of rain. Damn, it felt good to be responsible for that brightness.

"Thank you." She wrapped her arms around his neck and hugged him fiercely.

He held onto her, closing his eyes so he could absorb the feel of her embrace, the way she was holding onto him as if he'd given her a great gift. And maybe he had. Maybe he'd given her something that had nothing to do with violence or killing or saving her life.

It felt good. Really, really fantastic.

She pulled back and lightly brushed her mouth over his. He'd forgotten how magnificent it was to be kissed with tenderness. Less than a day, and he'd already put it out of mind. He grabbed her face and kissed her back.

"Keep it in your pants," Jarvis shouted. "We're on the clock."

Blaine broke the kiss, glancing up the street. Jarvis tapped his watch, but Nigel was still sitting cross-legged on the sidewalk, sketching.

Blaine turned his attention to Trinity, tunneling his hands through her hair, trying to squeeze every last moment out of their time together. Trying to imprint the feel of those soft tresses on his callused hands. "What do you want to do about the Chameleon?"

Not that he could afford to let her decide to walk away. He needed her help, and if Angelica was racing toward Chammie, it was all going to go down at once. He had to know whether Trinity was going to give her help voluntarily, or if he was going to have to force her.

Trinity took a breath, then nodded. "It has to die."

"It does." Perfect. He'd talked her right back to where he needed her to be. Ready to sacrifice herself so Blaine could have what he needed from her.

But he felt no relief.

He just felt like shit. Couldn't get the thought of that post-apocalyptic Trinity hologram out of his mind. He didn't want her becoming that banshee. It would mean the witch had won. "You aren't wielding the death blow," he suddenly decided. "There has to be another way."

"What way? My hologram—"

"Showed you one way. Nothing is static. If we weaken the monster, there might be another way." He gripped her shoulders and shook lightly. "You keep looking until you see that other method. Do you understand? I'm not giving you an option."

She met his gaze. "If I have to kill him myself, I'm okay with that. I accept the cost."

As she said the words, he realized he wasn't okay with it. At all.

Which was dandy timing for him.

─────

Trinity slid down the embankment toward the duck pond behind Blaine and Jarvis as Nigel followed. They were in the Boston Garden now, a bloody and burned foursome that had drawn more than a few curious looks as they'd sprinted past the softball games.

Jarvis held up his hand to tell them to stop, then he pointed.

She could see a hairy calf and a bare foot poking out from behind a pillar at the foot of the bridge. "Is that it?"

"Human form," Jarvis whispered. "It probably reverts back to its natural state when sleeping."

Trinity's heart began to pound. "I can't kill it if it's a man. I have issues with that—"

"Don't worry. It won't stay that way." Blaine was smoking as they eased closer to it. "See if you can catch a look while it's sleeping, Trinity. Most creatures are more vulnerable when they're knocked out."

"Right." Trinity set her hand on Blaine's back as they neared. They inched around the corner, and she saw their target.

It was a man, wearing torn jeans. His upper body was bare, and he was lean but muscled. Bruises covered his back, his fingernails were torn, and his hair was streaked with grime and dirt. But even in sleep, she could see his high cheekbones, his strong jaw, his elegant neck, and a gold signet ring on his pinkie finger. His hand was resting loosely around a rock, as if he was ready to hurl it if something grabbed him. His body was limp, as if he was so exhausted that he'd fallen into the kind of sleep that robbed a man of his ability to wake up, to sense the approach of danger.

"How do I kill him?" Blaine whispered.

"I don't know." She'd always felt like a murderous filthy rag, but never as much as she did right now. Sneaking up on a sleeping man to kill him. Her stomach turned. "I don't think I can do this—"

"You want your dad to die?"

"No. Of course not."

"Then there's your motivation."

She stared at the resting innocent and pictured her dad, the surprise on his face as he'd turned pink and melted away. The love in his eyes when he said good-bye. Tears thickened her throat, and she felt heat begin to build, the kind of heat she'd learned to dread.

"That's my girl." Blaine squeezed her shoulder. "You can do this."

Numbly, she watched as a prism began to take shape over the unsuspecting man, her soul screaming at her to stop. But she stood there and let it blossom.

The hologram was an androgynous being this time. No need for her to kill him. It would all work perfectly.

"You're doing it," Blaine said.

"I need his heart." Oh, man. Had she really just said that? She finally understood the choice her parents had been facing. Her mother's death, or babysitting by a nice witch for six months? So easy to convince themselves it wasn't a bad choice, so desperate to find a way to have everything they wanted. The choice between the unthinkable and the unbearable. A choice that left no one a winner. Kinda like this one.

The hologram walked over to the duck pond and scooped up a handful of dirt from the bottom.

"Mud?" Jarvis sounded shocked. "The thing that can withstand a blue ball up its nose and it can't take some dirt?"

The tulip on Trinity's neck began to burn, and she slapped at it.

The spectral assassin squatted over its prey and began

pouring sand into its ear. A sparkly dark liquid began to bubble on the glittery skin of the unsuspecting victim, oozing out of its pores.

"That's the smut," Blaine said. "Leaving his body."

The hologram stood up, walked back to the lake for another handful, and repeated the process. And again. And again.

Jarvis shook his head. "The thing's not going to sleep through a whole assembly line of sand transfer—"

A man emerged from the shadow of the bridge. "Oh, but I think it will."

Blaine and the others went immediately into battle stance, daggers, sword, and fireballs at the ready. "Identify yourself," Blaine demanded.

Their visitor was wearing a beautiful suit, and even his shoes were immaculately polished despite standing in the dirt. He exuded sex, power, and money, and she loathed him on sight. There was nothing redeemable about him at all. "The name's Napoleon, and I'm here for the same reason you are. Shall we make a party of it?"

Blaine didn't lower the weapon. "Keep talking."

Napoleon inclined his head toward the slumbering cockroach factory. "Smutty needs to die. I knocked him out, but I wasn't making a great deal of progress in hurting him." He gestured at some burn marks on the ground. "Seems to be quite good at fending off spells. I can keep him asleep. You pour the sand in his ear, or whatever it was the hologram was doing."

Trinity's tulip began to burn even more fiercely, and she stumbled back, struggling to stay upright against the sudden increase of pain. What was wrong with her?

She clawed it, trying to dig it out of her skin, but it was getting worse.

"You son of a bitch." Death suddenly appeared out of apparently nothing and he body-slammed Napoleon into the pillar. "You arrogant bastard, trying to steal Gram's smut monster."

Blaine dumped a handful of sand into the monster's ear, then sprinted back for more mud. Jarvis next. Then Nigel. Napoleon and Death fist fighting like a couple of drunken frat boys, even down to their spotless suits.

The man on the ground stirred and groaned, and he began to ooze blackness.

Pain stabbed through her from the tulip, and Trinity clutched at her mark as Chammie's eyes opened. There was nothing human in them at all. Just raw, brutal death. "Blaine! It's awake—"

Something hit her hard between the shoulders. Trinity pitched forward onto her hands, and then someone grabbed her ankles and began hauling her across the dirt. She twisted around and saw two gorgeous women manhandling her.

One of them looked up and Trinity went ice cold when she saw those emerald eyes. She had sudden, vivid recall of watching spiders crawl through her skin, of feeling venom burn through her cells, of those eyes watching her, ruthless, without mercy, without care.

They were the eyes she saw in the mirror each time she went to bed at night. "It's you," she whispered. "You're the witch. I dream of you."

The woman smiled. "Hello, my darling. It's been too long."

Trinity opened her mouth to scream and the woman

flicked a pinkie at her. Her mouth was suddenly filled with slippery balls. She gagged and spit a mouthful of grapes out onto the dirt.

"Grapes?" The other woman sounded surprised. "What happened to acid-laced needles?"

"She's one of my girls, Mari. You know I limit torturing to the bare necessity when it comes to my darlings."

Trinity spat again and more grapes tumbled out, but her mouth filled with them again before she could scream. Okay, she loved fruit, but this was so not conducive to her goal of screaming for help. She flung a handful of regurgitated grapes toward Blaine.

He glanced over and swore. He immediately dropped his fistful of sand, set himself on fire, and held up his hand to stop the other two warriors. Behind him, Napoleon and Death were covered in mud, wrestling and making a whole bunch of man-noises, the kind that were like "I'm so tough, I need to get this out of my system, but I don't want to actually hurt you."

"No." Jarvis started running for the pond again. "We take the smut heap out first. Let her play with Trinity for a few minutes—"

Blaine shook his head. "Trinity first."

Trinity first. Not the witch. Not Chammie. *Her.* Something swelled inside her as Blaine started toward her. Behind him, the half-naked mud god jumped to his feet and promptly turned into a giant serpent. Nigel and Jarvis began to engage. "Trio!"

Angelica was dragging her backwards, across the grass. The witch's skin was turning gray, her hair getting ratty. "Smutty!" The monster whirled around at Angelica's command. "Come!"

The monster morphed into a giant demon-backed dog and broke into a gallop, rocketing across the earth toward Angelica. His spiked tail was wagging furiously, and his giant tongue was lolling out of the side of his mouth.

Blaine sprinted for Trinity. She saw his determination to get to her, and tears filled her eyes. He was leaving the battle for her. He wasn't thinking. He wasn't being strategic. He was racing after her—

The witch flicked her hand, and Blaine flew backwards. He sailed through the air and crashed into the bridge supports. The cement cracked as Blaine leapt to his feet, and then the sand rose up and millions of tiny sand spiders launched themselves at him. He set them on fire, then ran right through the wall of flames, racing after her again.

He wasn't yelling at her to show him how to kill the witch. He was focused on one thing, and one thing only: rescuing her.

Something warm and fuzzy began to swell in her heart, and she stiffened. Oh, come on! Not now! Her skin began to burn, and a prism began to sparkle in the air above Blaine's head. She recoiled as a hologram flared in front of him. The specter pulled out a SuperSoaker squirt gun and shot him right in the eye.

A holographic Niagara Falls burst out of Blaine and covered the ground, and then he fell to the earth in a soggy pile of death.

The real Blaine didn't even slow down. "I believe in you, Trinity," he yelled. "Turn it on the witch. You can do it!"

Oh, wow, was that the sweetest thing ever? Even while his skin was glowing from her prism, he believed she was stronger than the curse. No one had ever done that. Her skin grew hotter, and the night grew brighter. "I'm losing—"

"No, you're not." Blaine's voice was hard, and then the earth split and a winged dragon beast leapt up out of the fissure. He slammed a fireball into its claw, and then another dragon appeared, and another, and suddenly they were all around, hitting him from all sides. Water began to ooze from a large gash in his body.

"Blaine!" she screamed, her heart filling with dread as he stumbled.

"Show us how to kill Angelica!" Jarvis's sword cut through the air and divested a winged assailant of its left appendage just as it slammed a watery claw toward Blaine's throat.

The amputated appendage careered through the air and Trinity snatched it out of the air. Water sprayed from the tip... hmm... she turned it over in her hand. Kind of like a squirt gun. It would probably work to kill him.

She heard her thoughts, and she recoiled, tried to drop the claw, but she couldn't unclench her fingers. Crap! This was not good!

Angelica stopped suddenly. "By all that's highly torturable and unlovable, you love Blaine." She sounded shocked, and absolutely delighted.

"No. I don't." But as she watched Blaine fighting for his life, bleeding from his wounds, focused on nothing but reaching her, the night glowed even brighter. She felt so hot she wanted to peel off her skin.

"Fantastic timing!" Angelica grinned as Smutty came racing up. "Good boy, darling. Go through the portal with Mari and I'll catch up." She flicked her hand and a large, rainbow-colored diamond with a teal-colored opening in the middle appeared. A portal?

She couldn't let herself be taken through it. Trinity fought harder, but the witch's grip was ruthless.

Smutty barked and trotted off happily as Mari fed him a bone and led him away. "Listen, cutie," Mari said to him. "I'm really sorry you have to suffer because of me, so what do you say we get you some cute girl poodles—"

"No!" Angelica snapped. "He gets no good treatment. He's a fornicating liar who deserves to be a smut monster. Don't ever forget it!" Then her arms tightened around Trinity's throat. "Look at Blaine," she whispered, her voice soft and compelling in Trinity's ear. "He's fighting through hell to get to you."

Trinity scrunched her eyes shut. "No. I won't."

"He's not even thinking about killing me," the witch continued. "He's the ultimate warrior, the best I've ever created, and he never screws up. Until now. Because he's so in love with you that he would rather save you than kill me. That's true love, my dear. Feel it in your heart. Here is the man for you."

"No!" Trinity shook her hand, but the stupid claw wouldn't fall out of her hand. Probably had something to do with her iron grip on it.

"Yes." The witch grabbed Trinity's chin and forced her face toward Blaine. "Look at him! Love him! Give in to the curse, Trinity. Kill number five will make you more powerful than you can ever imagine."

"No!" Trinity tried to keep her eyes shut, but they flew open of their own accord. And there was Blaine, up to his waist in some sort of muck, flanked by Jarvis and Nigel, as they fought off the flying horned nasties. As fast as they took them out, more kept coming, and she saw Blaine's jaw flexing as the water from their claws took its toll on his strength and his fire. "Blaine!"

"Feel your heart bleed for him, darling. He's dying anyway, so go ahead and allow yourself to embrace how much you love him. You love him so very much."

The truth of the witch's words resonated deep in Trinity's core, and she knew it was true. Hopelessly, completely, and wondrously true.

The moment Trinity acknowledged her love for Blaine, her hand closed around the claw to throw it. "No!" She was so tired of losing this battle! It ended now, and she didn't care if she took the wimpy way out. She crossed her fingers that Angelica's jaw was as hard as she hoped, then Trinity summoned all her curse-enhanced strength and slammed her head backwards into the witch's chin.

Pain exploded in Trinity's skull and dizziness began to spin her into a vortex of blackness. Yay for self-induced concussions! She grinned and let the darkness take her, then, as consciousness faded, she felt her arm rear back and hurl the watery claw in Blaine's direction.

The horrifying thunk of it hitting his body was the last thing she heard before she passed out.

Chapter 24

ANGELICA CRADLED THE UNCONSCIOUS TRINITY TO HER bosom as she raced down the tunnel back to the Den, following the muddy footsteps of Mari and Smutty. She jumped over the last viper pit, and the fire wall flared back up to keep anyone from following her.

The minute she was safe, her legs gave out, and she tumbled to the floor. She tightened her grip to keep Trinity from banging her head, and took the impact on her own knees instead. She hugged Trinity to her chest, unable to stop the swell of despair and desolation.

She pointed her finger, and a long black claw slid from the end. Tears tried to blur her vision as she carved Blaine's name in the rock floor. "My dear Blaine, you're my biggest regret," she whispered. "I never thought you would lose."

She bent her head against the need to cry. She hadn't cried in three hundred years, since the day she decided Nappy couldn't break her. But making that choice to sacrifice Blaine... it was the toughest decision she'd ever had to make.

She looked down at Trinity's ashen face. The sweet girl was sprawled on her back on the rock floor, her hand resting on Blaine's name. In the name of all that was painful and hellish, Angelica would never forget the horror that spilled out of Trinity the moment she'd unleashed the killing blow toward

Blaine, her scream of anguish as she killed the man of her heart.

Sweet sunlight and moonshine, never had Angelica heard a sound of such pain, even in her years and years of extraordinarily brilliant torture. Any other time, she'd be proud to be the cause of that kind of devastation.

But that sound, coming from one of her girls, to have it be pain of the soul and not of the body... she'd felt it in her own core in a way she never did when she was stringing one of the warriors up by his back hair.

What was she doing? Was this what she was fighting for? Killing her own precious Blaine? Making her own Chosen suffer?

Maybe she was wrong.

Maybe this wasn't the right way.

Maybe all her boys and girls had been right when they'd spat epithets at her. Maybe—

"Open the door."

Angelica leapt to her feet and whirled around. Napoleon was standing on the other side of the fire wall, his body a blurry image behind the silver flames. "Where's Prentiss? Did you hurt him?"

"I would never hurt my grandson." Napoleon leaned forward. "The game has gone on long enough, my dear."

Angelica's hand twitched with the need to cast a testicle-shrinking spell at him. "What do you mean?"

Napoleon moved closer, until his face was a mere inch from the searing flames. "You were a girl when I left. I didn't know how to save you from the pit of helplessness and self-hate that you were spiraling into."

"I wasn't—"

"You were. I loved you too much to let that happen,

so I did the only thing I could think of, and I left you to fight for yourself." He smiled, his teeth glittering. "I did it for you, my love, and it worked. I'm so proud of you, and I'm ready for us to resume the love affair of a lifetime." His grin widened. "And since I plan to live forever, that's one hell of a love affair."

Angelica took a step toward him. Was he telling the truth? Had he really done it out of love? She *had* been a mess back then.

"I'm so sorry you had to suffer." His voice was quiet. Soft. Tender. "I truly am. But it's over. I'm here to take care of you. To give you all you've ever dreamed of."

She swallowed. "I can dream of a lot."

"Then let me give it to you." He held up his palms in a gesture of surrender. "I've always been yours, my love. Always. You've done great work here, by the way. So impressive."

"I have?" Dear Blue Balls, it felt good to be validated. "You don't think I'm too harsh with my boys and girls?" She lifted her hand to lower the wall. Why fight it? She loved him. He loved her. That was all that mattered—

"What you did out there to those warriors? Brilliant. And that girl? The black widow? I saw what she could do with your smut monster. She's incredible. Think of how useful she could be in the assassin business. Why, we could make millions! Just look at her!"

Angelica glanced down at Trinity, who looked so small and fragile on the floor. Her sweet baby. Carrying the hopes and dreams of millions of women in her soul. Facing her own worst hell to help others. "My darling," she whispered.

"That girl is my ticket!"

"Your ticket?" Angelica frowned. "What do you mean?"

He was beaming now, hands gesticulating with excitement. "Even *I* occasionally run into targets that I have trouble figuring out how to kill. With Trinity by my side, I can be unstoppable. I'll be more powerful even than my own grandson. Think of that! More powerful than Death! I'll rule the world!"

Oh, right. Of course. She'd forgotten who she was talking to. A man who manipulated words and women with equal aplomb. He wasn't there for the love. He was there for the money he thought he could make by prostituting one of her girls.

And he was taking advantage of her love to do it. She glared at him, furious at herself for almost succumbing to his poetic words. "For all that's well-endowed in Hell and beyond, you have got to be kidding! I am not doing this so you can go be powerful." She scooped Trinity off the floor. "I do this out of love, to save my girls from men like you."

"Angelica," he warned. "Don't you dare walk out on me."

"You don't get it," she snapped. "You don't get to have me or my dreams anymore. Yes, I love you, but as soon as I harvest Trinity, you'll be the first to die."

Napoleon stiffened. "You don't mean that—"

"Oh, but I do." But even as she turned and hurried down the passageway holding Trinity so tenderly in her arms, she knew she was lying.

She would never be able to curse herself, knowing it would mean Nappy's death. She might hate him, but she loved him, and that would never change. Life was too thrilling with him in it, even if was dangerous and insane. He still made her come alive.

And someday, if she could learn to be strong enough, it would be so unbelievable to take him back in her bed and show him how much she'd learned. He was hell, but he was *her* hell, and she was too addicted to end it cleanly by empowering herself with a cocktail of black widows and prisms.

But her girls were different. They didn't love yet. They could still be saved. And it was her job to do it.

And the time was now.

───※───

It was bad enough to have a nightmare about killing her true love and becoming a murderous banshee woman.

It was much worse to wake up from the dream to find herself chained down to a hard metal slab, listening to the sounds of men screaming, and realize it was all true. "Blaine?" How great would it be if it were Blaine being tortured? Not because she wanted him knocked around, but it would mean he was still alive. "Is that you?"

But no one answered, which was a major bummer.

With a sigh, Trinity lifted her head and saw she was in what could only be classified as a museum-quality dungeon. Crumbling rock walls, the stench of mold and rot, a dampness in the air that was like a cloying weight caking her lungs. The walls were filled with steel cabinets that had locked doors, and Trinity shuddered with a faint memory of the horrible, horrible things inside those cabinets.

"This wasn't how I figured we'd meet."

Trinity turned her head to see the man from Blaine's fridge stretched out on a slab next to her. He still looked like someone who'd been tap-danced on by Death, but there was a hint of pink to his skin now, and his eyes weren't as sunken. "Christian?"

"Son of a bitch returned for me, didn't he?" Christian let out a shuddering breath. He was wearing a pair of pink boxers and pale yellow socks with butterflies on them. Nothing else to cover the purple streaks radiating beneath the surface of skin that seemed to glimmer like mica. "I can't believe it," he whispered. "He came back."

Trinity felt his disbelief, his intense relief, and guilt flooded her. This man had fought off death because he'd believed Blaine was going to save him. And thanks to her, Blaine was dead, the witch was alive, and her own father was going to die.

"Where is he?" Christian closed his eyes, and she could practically feel him willing strength back into his body. "What's the plan?"

"I—" She swallowed. How could she lie to him? But how could she take away the one thing that was keeping him alive? "He... um... he didn't tell me. He was afraid the witch would torture it out of me."

Christian shook his head. "That's so like Blaine. Always trying to protect others." He looked over at her. "He's a good man." His voice was quiet. "You betray him, and you'll have to answer to me."

Trinity pulled her gaze away to look at the ceiling. Water was leaking from it. Water just like the kind she'd used to kill Blaine. "Does any woman love you, Christian?"

He was silent.

She turned her head and saw the hardness of his jaw. "Yeah," he said. "One of the witch's females. She claims she does, at least. Not my kind of love."

Trinity knew then why Christian was on that table with her. Angelica was going to use Christian and that woman to test the curse.

Not only had she killed Blaine, but Christian was about to die because of her as well.

Nice to know that as bad as she'd feared she was, she was so much worse. It was time to do what she should have done a long time ago, before more could die. Since even a head injury wasn't enough to stop her, it was time to get some help. "Christian?"

"Yeah?"

"Could you kill me from there?"

A scrawny gray rat scurried across Christian's foot, and he didn't even flinch. "Yeah, sure."

She took a deep breath as the rat jumped onto the floor with a quiet thud. "Then do it. Now."

He raised his brows. "I don't hurt women."

"Oh, come on! This is not the time to be ethical. Trust me, you really need to kill me."

The rat scurried back up the table leg and ran onto Christian's chest. It was carrying a small piece of apple. "The witch may have forced me to do a lot of shit I didn't like," Christian said. "But lacerating the intestines of one of my buddies is different than hurting a female. There's no chance." He scanned the room. "I don't know where you are, witch," he yelled "but this is one line you'll never get me to cross."

"No, no, no! Ssh!" Trinity tried to quiet him. "This isn't about Angelica. It's about me. I need you to kill me. Now."

"No way am I killing you." Christian shook his head as the rat tried to set the fruit in his mouth. "No, buddy, that's all yours. I'm good. But thanks." The rat touched its nose to Christian's, then curled up on the warrior's stomach and began to gnaw on the apple. "If this is Blaine's plan, tell him to go to hell."

"Look, I respect your morals." And she did. She understood the need to set boundaries to believe in yourself. And she also knew when those boundaries were nothing but lies. "But you'll change your mind after I tell you my story."

And then she began to talk. And for the first time in her life, she didn't hold back. She didn't pretend she was more than she was. She didn't lie to herself about what she could accomplish.

This time, she finally admitted the truth, not just to Christian, but to herself.

She, Trinity Harpswell, was worse than Barry Baldini, serial killer.

And that was just the start.

And she was owning it all.

Son of a bitch. She'd killed him.

Blaine stared down at the water cascading out of his pores. He couldn't believe Trinity had done it. He'd never been killed before. Not really and truly. But he could feel the difference. His body temperature was on the fast-track toward arctic chill, and he was leaking like a butterfly net in the ocean. Yeah, it wasn't instant coffin-bait, but he was on his way, and fast.

No one had ever loved him enough to end his life before. "Was that the sweetest thing ever, or what? She killed me."

"You are one lucky bastard, I'll give you that." Nigel

caught him under the arms as his legs buckled. "The look on her face when she threw that claw was priceless. I'd have given my right nut to have my paints at that moment. Never seen such love."

"Did you see that too?" Blaine felt like his heart was exploding. "Didn't that expression of anguish make her look radiant? I swear she lost ten years of stress off her face with that look." He plucked the claw out of his eye and held it in his palm. "That's what she used. Right there. I need to find a baggie to preserve it. Might make it into a necklace or something."

Nigel began to drag him out of the pit, which was drying up now that the witch was gone. The schnoodemgons had stopped multiplying, and Jarvis was easily dispatching the remaining few.

"You know, I never really considered the benefits of dating a black widow," Nigel said thoughtfully. "You never have to wonder if she's telling you the truth about how she feels about you. The minute she sees that prism and kills you... you just know."

Blaine's useless legs bumped over the edge of the mud pit. "Yeah." Damn it felt good. She loved him. It was the real thing. Not the kind where you'd turn your head while you sold your loved one to the witch.

No. It was the kind where you throw a schnoodie claw right into the sweet spot of the man you love. He felt like beating his chest and roaring. Me Tarzan. Woman Love Me—

Woman who had been carted off by the witch. What was his problem? Get a taste of true love for the first time in his life and he forgets to do the manly thing and reward her for that love? "We gotta go get her."

"I hate to break it to you, Trio, but Angelica has her," Nigel said. "She's gone."

"Screw that." He turned around and searched the night. "The portal has to be here somewhere." He shoved himself out of Nigel's grasp and promptly smooshed onto his knees. "Dammit."

"I've got you." Nigel picked him up and slung him over his shoulder. He broke into a sprint. "She went this way."

Blaine swore as he bounced on Nigel's shoulder. "Put me down. I'm not a sack of corn." Nice analogy, given the moment. For some reason, the thought of corn didn't rankle him as much as it usually did. Not with a lethal schnoodie claw in his pocket. He smiled and patted his jeans.

Nigel set him down, and Blaine's legs did a smashing imitation of a wet noodle and dropped him on his rubbery ass on the grass. He could almost sense the witch's magic, but he was too watered-down to pinpoint it. He focused on his soggy tattoo, and drove all his energy into it. Not even a flicker of smoke. "This is getting really aggravating."

"Watch out," Jarvis yelled. "Incoming."

He looked up in time to see a schnoodie dive-bombing him, water claws bared. Brilliant. Another enema and he'd be dancing with Death pronto.

Nigel took it out a split second from Blaine's face, and the sparks cascaded all over Blaine, burning his skin. Energy prickled through him, and he sucked in the fire, gaining enough strength to stagger to his feet. And then, thirty feet away, he picked up the tingling of black magic. "Two o'clock," he yelled. "It's closing!"

Nigel grabbed him and threw him over his shoulder, and Blaine shouted for Jarvis, who laid out hard after them. "More sparks. Now!"

Jarvis didn't bother to ask questions. He unleashed his sword into the air. Blaine looked up to see dozens of schnoodies circling way up above them. Jarvis's blade hit them all, like a pinball on caffeine. The sparks showered down and Blaine held out his arms, maximizing body surface area. The burns seared his skin and he fed the fire into his mark as Jarvis caught up.

"The leap of faith," Nigel yelled, and then he dove, Jarvis right beside him.

Blaine's skin burned, the sky darkened, and then they were in a long, brightly colored tunnel.

Nigel dropped Blaine, and his legs were solid and strong as they landed. He didn't know how long the fire from the schnoodie funeral would sustain him, but it was enough for now.

Hot pink poison dotted the rainbow-colored walls, the air was heavy with the scent of death, and the roses lining the hall were thick and cloying with their aroma.

"Welcome back to hell," Nigel said.

Jarvis held his sword at the ready. "If we don't find the girl, we're completely screwed."

Blaine jammed his hand into a light fixture and grinned as the electrical shock burned the hair right off his arms. Smoke began to rise from his tattoo, and then it ignited. Hot damn. "Nothing like being electrocuted to wake a man up."

"Trio." Nigel's voice echoed as they sprinted down the darkened corridor. "You still need to kill Trinity, you know. With love and kindness, of course, but she still has to die. You do her no favors if you let the witch take over her body."

Blaine swore under his breath. He knew it was true. There was no way out unless Angelica was dead. Not for any of them.

Which meant the woman who loved him had to die, by his hand.

Chapter 25

"HOW ARE MY TWO FAVORITE DARLINGS?" ANGELICA rushed into the dungeon. She'd changed into clean jeans and a fitted T-shirt and redone her makeup, but her face was worried and her body language tense.

She strode over to Christian. "You're doing well, I see. Another couple of minutes and it will all be over." She sat down next to him and took his hand.

Christian narrowed his gaze, but didn't try to get away. Didn't speak. Didn't react. Just gave her a hard, impassive look. The look of a warrior who gave away nothing, a man who was looking for an out, even down to the wire.

Despite her story, her truth that Blaine wasn't coming, Christian hadn't given up hope. On the contrary, he had revived even more, and he looked pissed right now.

Angelica patted his hand. "I want you to know, my dear, that I highly admire your courage and your strength, and I'm deeply saddened to have our relationship end, but you're the only choice I have right now. I don't have time to manufacture an experiment with a man who doesn't matter." She leaned over and kissed Christian's forehead. "May love and sensitivity follow you wherever you go," she whispered.

Christian's skin turned silver and shifted into metal scales.

The witch leapt back. Her lips were blackened and

burning. "And thank you for that reminder about exactly why the world needs to be protected from men like you!" She stalked off toward the far side of the room and began to fiddle with a sparkly sphere about the size of the disco ball at the Jamming Jive, except of course that it was black. Magic cauldron?

"Christian," Trinity hissed.

He turned his head, and his face shifted back to regular skin. "Why should I trust anything you tell me?"

"But it's true! She's going to—" Trinity suddenly found her mouth full of grapes again. Okay, so not really going to be digging fruit after this.

"Quiet, my darlings." Angelica turned toward them and her hands were black and sparkly. "I don't like to be distracted."

"Sorry I'm late." Mari raced inside, still covered in the muddy clothes she'd been in earlier. "Smutty is all set in his safe house. No one will be able to find him." She lifted her chin. "And I gave him four girl poodles to keep him company. He's nice, and a man without an outlet is dangerous."

Excellent. Not only was Smutty alive, but he was so well hidden that no one would find him, and he was having his way with the girls. *Sorry, Dad*.

Irritation flashed in Angelica's eyes. "Didn't I tell you no poodles?"

Mari set her hands on her hips. "He's carrying my smut," she said. "I'm not going to make him suffer abstinence on top of that."

"He's a bastard."

"Not to me."

Well, hooray for Mari standing up for the smut

monster. That's exactly what she'd been hoping for right now. Like having Death champion Smutty's long and healthy life hadn't been enough. Add a well-stacked protector with all the same powers as the witch to the equation? Fantastic.

"Oh, for the sake of whiskers and spicy cologne, we don't have time for this." Angelica waved at a plush armchair between Trinity and Christian's beds. "Sit."

Mari got a smug look on her face, like she'd just won a battle, and she sauntered toward the chair. Then she saw Christian strapped down, and her face paled. "What's going on?"

"I'm going to give you a gift."

Mari's face brightened and she whirled toward the witch. "I knew he was worthy! You're going to let us get married?"

Christian started gagging and had to roll over to get his breath back.

"Lovely, Christian," Angelica said dryly. "After all I've taught you, that's your stereotypical, commitment-phobic male reaction? Nice."

Mari patted Christian's back. "I said I was sorry, baby," she whispered. "She promised you wouldn't get hurt. You know I love you."

Christian went scaly and she jerked her hand back just before his back turned to metal right where she was touching him.

"Oh, come on," she protested. "I truly thought telling the witch about your escape was the best thing. I swear I didn't know—"

"Enough!" Angelica walked over to the door, slid the dead bolt, and flicked her hand at it. The door turned black and began to glow, and the faint scent of lemon began to fill the room. "Christian isn't the gift. I'm giving you power to never get hurt by a man again. Never again will you reach out for a man and have the testosterone factory reject your love and turn scaly on you."

"Well…" Mari glanced at Christian. "It would be nice if he could be a little more understanding. I mean, it's not like I meant to hurt him."

Christian gave her a lethal look.

Mari turned away and looked at Angelica. "Is it going to cause him pain?"

"For heaven's sake, Mari, the fact you can even ask that question is more evidence of why you need this gift. Sit."

Mari hesitated, and for an instant, Trinity thought she was going to resist. *Just say no, Mari!*

And then she sat between them.

The chair immediately wrapped around her body, trapping her in place. Mari sucked in her breath. "What are you doing?"

"It might hurt a bit, and I just want to make sure you don't move." Angelica smiled, and her eyes were glowing with delight. "This is so brilliant, Mari. We're going to be so rich off this. Free. Independent."

Mari looked a little more interested. "How rich?"

"Monumentally rich." Angelica held up a small glass vial. "And Trinity is carrying it for us."

Trinity tensed as Angelica turned toward her. She spat out the grapes, and this time no new ones showed up. "Blaine will kill you if you hurt me."

Angelica snorted. "Blaine's dead. You killed him."

"No, he's not. I'd know it if he was." But she knew

he was. She was just talking stupid smack… but whoa… wait a minute… If he really was dead, wouldn't she be crazy murder woman? She didn't feel any different than she had before. Oh, wow! She hadn't thought of that! "Of course he's alive." She felt jubilant. "I'm not a crazy killer, which means I didn't perform my last death. He's coming, and together we're going to kill you and—"

The grapes filled her mouth again, and Trinity started frantically spitting out the little green balls.

"First of all," Angelica picked up a tulip made out of copper or something equally burnished, "you better hope no one kills me, because then I become you, and you lose your pretty little soul to me."

Trinity tensed as Mari scowled. "She's your Chosen? I thought I was!"

"Don't be ridiculous," Angelica snapped. "I need you in your own brain. If I take over your body, who becomes my right hand? Please."

Uh, oh. That sounded like she meant it. Total bummer to learn that Blaine had been telling the truth about that little story.

"And as for your very charming hope that you didn't trigger the curse with your assault of Blaine," Angelica said to Trinity, "I'm afraid I'm going to have to deflate that little bubble." She set the copper charm on Trinity's palm.

Trinity instantly threw it onto the floor, and Angelica clapped with delight as she retrieved it. "I'm so proud of your spirit, my dear. I knew you'd be strong enough to survive the curse and take it to full maturity. You were such a good choice, and I so admire your strength."

Then she slapped the tulip in Trinity's palm and forced her hand shut. "We'll make a great team."

Trinity's hand began to grow warm, and she fought to uncurl her fingers, but they were locked. Out of her control. Panic began to build in her chest. She hated that feeling of being out of control. Of not having the ability to stop herself. "Get it off me!"

"No." Angelica propped her chin up on her hands and gazed at her. "So, if you've truly triggered the curse, then this little charm is going to have a serious effect on you. If you're right, that you didn't kill Blaine, then it'll do nothing." She raised her brows. "How does it feel?

Tingling began crawling up her arm, exactly like how her skin felt when the curse was taking over her. Except it was much more intense. Almost painful. Like a thousand bugs with spiked heels dancing along her skin. "I can't feel anything," she managed. "Seems fine to me." She grinned, fighting not to show her pain. "Blaine's coming for you, and I'm going to help him take you out."

"And then I become you." Angelica shrugged. "You're a little saggy, but I can whip that body into shape in no time."

It felt like a million spiders beneath her skin, crawling right toward her heart. Up her biceps, an insidious approach.

Angelica leaned on the table and stroked Trinity's hair. "I'm going to take the curse out."

"Really?" As good as that sounded, Trinity had a bad feeling that she wasn't going to be spared quite that easily. "You're going to remove the curse? So I'll be normal again?"

Angelica laughed. "No, my dear, you'll be blessed with the curse forever. I'm just going to extract some of it, toss it in my mixer over there—" She pointed at the big black disco ball. "Do a little shake 'n' stir and then start handing it out. First to Mari, and then to the others." She smiled. "Thanks to you and your ability to survive this long, all the women of this planet are about to get a wonderful gift."

"You think they *want* to be infected?" Trinity snorted. "You're insane."

Angelica rolled her eyes. "If I had a testicle for every time someone said that to me, I'd have to buy stock in the *Nutcracker*."

The creepy crawlies hit Trinity's right shoulder and began to move over her chest. Toward her heart. She coughed, felt her body heat begin to rise, the room begin to brighten. Shit! Angelica was trying to trigger the widow on command.

You can fight this, Trinity. She had to. There was no way she could let this out into the world, to infect other women, kill men, so many innocents. She fisted her hands, willing every bit of strength she had to fight the agonizing march toward her heart. But it kept coming.

Angelica chuckled softly. "It's exactly what I thought might happen," she said. "The widow's about to come to life, and it's no longer about love. She's a little trigger happy. I'm afraid you're not going to be allowed to walk free any longer, my love. You're a danger to—"

The blackness hit Trinity in the chest and she screamed, and she knew she was lost.

—∽—

Damn water claw. Blaine was already starting to fade again when they rounded the corner and saw the wall of silver flames.

Jarvis and Nigel stopped, and Blaine splooshed to a slightly damp halt. He grinned. "I gotta say, I had no idea Angelica was that thoughtful. Leaving me presents."

Jarvis flicked his sword at it. "Take it down, Trio."

"The things I do for you guys." Blaine leapt straight into the fire and the silver flames toasted him up like a marshmallow in hot lava. His hair caught fire, his clothes melted, and his skin began to bubble.

And it felt fantastic. "This is better than when I get my new cross-stitching floss in the mail." He opened his pores and drank the fire in, so digging the feel of it making his blood boil, of it turning his cells to charcoal and his internal organs to ash. "This is what it's supposed to be like."

The fire wall began to fade, disappearing into his body. All dampness was gone, and his body felt dry and crackly. His tattoo was burning, and he knew he was good for a while. Silver flames were as hot as it got, and it felt great. Yeah, maybe he couldn't generate fire anymore, but he sure as hell could harvest it. Nothing like a feast of fire to stave off impending death.

Nigel raised his brows. "Better than a woman's body and a king-sized bed?"

Blaine thought of Trinity, and he scowled. "No chance."

"Let's go—" Jarvis was interrupted when a man burst out of the shadows and raced past them, disappearing down the tunnel before any of them had time to react. "Who the hell was that?"

Blaine would recognize that expensive cologne anywhere. "Napoleon. Angelica's ex."

"Well, damn, let's hope he's still on our side." Jarvis broke into a dead sprint, and the three of them laid out down the passageway, deeper and deeper into the lair that had nearly broken them so many times.

They hit the next corner and saw Napoleon strung up on the ceiling. He was dangling from a net of dirty athletic socks and men's underwear.

"Hey, that one's mine." Nigel leapt up and snagged a pair of boxer briefs that had a meadow scene painted on the fly. "I always wondered why my clothes disappeared whenever they got nice and ripe. You okay, man?"

Napoleon was beaming. "Is this not the most impressive booby trap ever? A thousand male undergarments so magicked even I can't get out?"

Blaine caught a stench that reminded him of the gym on a really, really hot day. "Yeah, brilliant."

"I taught her everything she knows." Napoleon took a deep breath. "I swear this stench would be enough to knock me out if I didn't have this jockstrap around my neck cutting off my air."

Jarvis raised his sword to cut it, then hesitated. "You still want to kill her?"

"Oh, no." Napoleon's grin vanished. "I don't want to harm her. I just wanted to toy with her smut monster so she came to my bed. I'm enjoying the chase. Very fun." Then his face grew darker. "You men touch one nipple on her body and I'll destroy you. I'm very good at it."

"No chance you can hurt us." Jarvis sheathed his sword. "Well, have fun hanging there."

"Yeah, let's leave him," Nigel said. "He's going to get in the way."

Napoleon studied them. "You mean to cause harm to Angelica."

"Yep." Blaine saluted him. "Have a nice day."

He and the others took off down the hall, as a thick smoke began to swirl around the black witch. "Taking bets on how long until he gets out."

"Five minutes," Jarvis said. "If that. If he taught Angelica, he'll figure out her spell pretty fast."

"Then let's haul ass—"

Someone screamed and all the hairs on Blaine's arms stood up at the bloodcurdling sound that sounded like an invasion of demon-tainted blood suckers closing down on their prey.

Nigel's blades burst out of his fingers. "That sounds much worse than schnoodies."

Blaine swore and lit out down the right hallway, right toward the horrific sound of agony, of pain, of unrelenting death. "It's not one of her inventions." He knew that sound. He'd seen it. Never in real life. Only in a hologram. The one in which Trinity had succumbed to the curse. "It's Trinity."

Only this time it was for real.

He was too late.

———

Blaine had always prided himself on his creativity. Cross-stitching, battle tactics, figuring out how to escape from the Den. He was brilliant and had vision beyond anyone he'd ever met.

But when he blew up the door to the Pit of Despair and Joy, he realized that he'd fallen way short of doing justice to the image of Trinity-the-Black-Widow. He had a split second to register that Christian was on the table and alive, Mari was wrapped up beside him, and Angelica was absent, before he looked up and saw the swamp thing that used to be the woman he'd made love to.

"Now that's not a pretty sight," Jarvis observed.

Trinity was up against the ceiling, broken chains dangling from her wrists and ankles. Her hair was gray and white, spraying out from her head at all angles, so tangled they made Nigel's muddy locks look like an ad for the Silk Protein Gloss they all used. Her eyes were black, her lips matched, and her fingers were curled in a fist that reminded him of the schnoodies' claws.

"Hot damn," he whispered, not bothering to hide his awe. It was the first time he'd seen her since he'd realized she loved him. "She's even more beautiful than I remembered." He could barely breathe, he was so overwhelmed by her sheer magnificence. "I should have brought her roses. Two dozen. Long-stemmed."

Jarvis smacked him in the head with his palm. "Get your shit together, Trio. That's no sweet girlfriend up there. That's one bat-shit-crazy-killer."

Blaine shoved Jarvis into the wall without taking his eyes off Trinity. "Hey, sweetheart," he called. "You look fantastic. Love the hair."

She saw Blaine and shrieked again. A prism flared to life in front of him and the hologram slammed a holographic icicle into his eye. It melted instantly upon contact, and his spectral image fell straight to the ground.

"She's a persistent little thing, isn't she?" Nigel said. "That's true love right there, you lucky sod."

"I know." Blaine grinned. "Hello, my dear."

A large, dripping icicle appeared in Trinity's hand and she screamed again.

Jarvis reared back with his sword, but Blaine caught his wrist. "No."

"Are you delusional? The chick's gone psychotic—"

"Trinity." Blaine walked toward her. "I believe in you. You're stronger than this."

"Come on, Trio." Jarvis shoved him back. "You're more pathetic than Christian. A little sex makes you think the girl's not going to kill you? Look at her! The girl's gone loco."

Blaine saw Trinity cringe at Jarvis's words, and he knew in that instant that Trinity was still in there somewhere. She could still feel pain. She could still be insulted. She could still shrink from the image of the monster she thought she was.

He shoved Jarvis off him and walked closer to her. She screamed and rose higher up toward the ceiling, clutching the icicle to her chest. "I know you're not going to throw it," he said. "You won't kill me, Trin, because you don't want to."

She started to shake her head frantically back and forth. "Run," she finally whispered, her voice raw. "For God's sake, Blaine. *Run*."

"No." He moved closer. "You can shift the curse to focus on Angelica. It's what we planned for and—"'

"Blaine!"

He whirled around at the sound of Angelica's voice. She had stopped in the doorway of her Closet of Creative Ideas, a small snake wriggling in her hand. Her eyes were wide and she looked shocked. "How can you possibly be alive?"

The three warriors attacked her at the same moment. Blades. Fireballs.

When the witch didn't even bother to scream and the room filled with orange smoke, he knew they were in serious trouble.

Chapter 26

BLAINE'S EYES WERE BURNING WHEN THE SMOKE cleared, and he found himself chained to the stone wall with stainless steel links. Jarvis and Nigel were in the same situation, and the room smelled like charred skin from the metal burning them. He could feel his body getting weaker, and he knew others were facing the same. Not the most offensive position they could be in.

"Well, now, this just pisses me off," Nigel said, his voice calm.

"Not much of a welcome home party," Blaine agreed. He quickly scanned the room, looking for options as Angelica raced across the room and tossed a small tulip charm into a large black ball.

Huh. He didn't have the best memories of that cauldron.

"Your girlfriend's getting feisty," Nigel commented.

Blaine looked and saw that Trinity was playing with the icicle again. "Trin—"

She looked up and he saw the desperation in her eyes. The terror of what she'd become. "You can do it," he said. "I know you can."

She shook her head, and he saw her eyes glistening with tears.

"Dammit, Trinity! I know—"

A dozen knives flashed through the air, and she was suddenly pinned against the ceiling by Nigel's blades. He'd put them through her clothes, not her skin, but

Blaine sent a fireball smacking into his buddy's face anyway. "Don't scare my girl."

"Just giving her a break. Can't you see it's not easy for her to keep from whizzing down here and poking you in the eye?" Nigel tossed the sparks out of his hair. "Have you learned nothing from Angelica? One of the key things a man has to do is know when his girl needs a little help."

Had he misjudged what she needed? Blaine looked at Trinity. Yeah, he saw relief on her beautiful features to be locked down, but he also saw absolute devastation, and he knew it was because she was so dangerous that she needed to be trapped to keep her from hurting the man she loved. "Hey, love," he said softly. "It's going to be okay, I promise—"

"Hope you made a better choice than I did."

Blaine looked over at Christian's voice, and he grinned. "Nice to see you, man. I thought you were passed out."

"Playing possum." Christian jerked at the binds. "Mari. Get us free."

Mari shook her head. "I believe Angelica. This is all for your good. For us—"

Christian glanced over at the witch, who was bent over the pot and working. Blaine knew the witch went into the zone when she was working, and she wouldn't be listening to them. "She's going to infect you so that you kill me. The curse of the black widow."

Mari's face went pale. "You're lying. You don't care about me."

"No, I don't, but I care about me. And I'm willing to take advantage of the fact that you love me to save myself."

Mari scowled. "And that's why I need her help, to deal with you."

Blaine rolled his eyes. "Nice job, man. Way to work it."

Angelica turned and she was carrying the snake in her hands. "It's time, sweetlings."

Blaine swore. "Let Trinity go, Nigel. We need her."

"No way." Jarvis was starting to swing his sword, and the air was filled with humming. "If you let Trinity go, it's over. She's bailed on you before. Don't trust her."

Blaine looked up at the woman looking down at him with murderous eyes, and he knew he couldn't do it without her. If he wanted to save Christian, to save the others, he needed help, and he needed hers. "I trust her."

"Like you trusted her before? Like Christian trusted Mari?"

Blaine glanced over at Mari, who had been released from the chair and was walking reluctantly toward the witch, her palm outstretched to be bitten by the snake. To be infected so she could kill Christian. Yeah, she looked wary and a little nervous, but she was doing it of her own free will. Shit. Was he making the same mistake Christian had made?

"Trio."

Blaine looked over at Christian. "Yeah?"

"Trinity told me the story." Christian tugged at his chains and his rat scurried off the table to hide underneath a cabinet, as he always did when things were about to get ugly. "I'd be inclined to trust her, you know, given that we have no other options. She's our best bet."

That was all Blaine needed. "Nigel. Now."

Nigel swore, but he released the knives.

Trinity screamed and came swooping down toward him, brandishing the icicle like she was about to take it to his head. Which he really hoped she wasn't. He didn't flinch. "Trinity. We need to kill the witch. Now."

She charged right for him, the icicle aimed for his heart, screaming in that really freaky way he was beginning to find so familiar and sweet. There was nothing like the piercing shriek of murder to make a guy feel loved.

"I hate it when you're wrong," Jarvis said, raising his sword toward Trinity.

"No." Blaine stilled Jarvis's hand. "I trust her. Let her come."

A voice somewhere in her mind was screaming at her to stop, but Trinity could do nothing but watch as she plunged the icicle toward Blaine's heart. She was less than five yards away and—

"I believe in you."

She jerked her gaze to Blaine's face, and she saw the truth in his eyes. He wasn't defending himself. He wasn't flinching. He was watching her with absolute confidence. Like she was a warrior he would trust with his life. "Don't," she whispered. "I can't—" But even as those words slipped out of her mouth, something inside her rebelled.

She was so tired of losing! She was sick of hating herself! She wanted to look at herself the way Blaine looked at her. She fought to slow down, to divert the icicle, but the tip kept going, she couldn't stop—

"I believe in you," he said again.

His simple words ripped right through the scream of terror driving her. That short phrase, utterly truthful, even when faced with the Son of Sam coming for him. Blaine saw good in her. Something worth loving, despite everything she was.

A man who trusted no one and nothing, trusted her.

I want to be that woman.

She grabbed the back of the icicle with her other hand and wrenched the tip to the side. It slammed harmlessly into the wall beside Blaine's shoulder and exploded. He caught her against him, a brilliant smile lighting up his face. "I knew you could do it."

"No!" She twisted out of his reach, not daring to share his jubilation. "It's not done." She could feel the fire within her, the need to kill. It wasn't over. She swung around quickly and looked at Angelica. The woman who had done so much to hurt the man she loved. "It's your turn."

She opened her heart to her love, to her fury, to her disgust at being a pawn to this abomination and she channeled it all into the vision of the woman before her. An enormous hologram flared to life over the witch's head, lighting up the whole room.

Angelica looked up as an enormous holographic warrior appeared above her head, holding a golden ring shaped like a halo. He slammed it down over her head, like a crown. A holographic image of her shrieked and began to melt.

A fiery halo immediately flared up in Blaine's hand and he hurled it across the room like a Frisbee. The witch screamed and ran for the door, and the halo landed quietly on her head just as she flung the lock and yanked the door open.

On the other side of the door was Napoleon, and she felt into his arms, her legs already melting as she groaned his name. The chains holding all the men fell away, and Mari turned and raced back toward Christian, begging his forgiveness.

An icicle formed in Trinity's hand, and she stumbled backwards as the hologram appeared above Blaine's head again. "You have to kill me," she whispered. "I'm the Chosen, and I'm cursed. Just promise me that you'll find Smutty and save my dad."

"You proved to me that you can manage the curse." Blaine tossed a fireball at the icicle and melted it. "There's got to be another option besides killing you."

But as Angelica's anguished cry of death filled the room, the tulip on Trinity's collarbone began to glow. Not a burning like before. A brilliant white light of life and rebirth.

Blaine swore and covered it with his hand, and they looked at each other, and she knew there was no other way for it to end. Which was just a tremendously huge bummer. "I really didn't think it would come to this," she told him.

He grimaced. "Me neither."

"Angelica!" Napoleon's anguished cry filled the room. "My love!"

And then the smell of rotting bananas drifted over the odor of smoke, burned flesh, and singed hair.

Trinity exchanged looks with Blaine as another icicle formed in her hands, a sudden idea in her mind. And she saw from the way Blaine was looking at her

glowing tulip that he'd just thought of the same thing.
"Will it work?"

He melted her icicle and looked over at Napoleon and
the fast-melting witch. "It might."

"If it doesn't—"

He touched her tulip, and she knew they were in a
race to win before Angelica took over her body. "It will."

But she saw the fear in his eyes, and knew he
wasn't sure.

———

Trinity whirled toward the door as Augustus raced into
the room, a pink star clutched in his hand. "You die
now," he screamed. He hurled it at her. "You are so bad
for my reputation—"

Trinity didn't flinch as Blaine intercepted it with a
pink flaming arrow. "I have an offer for you," she said.
"A better deal."

He hurled another one, and Blaine nicked it aside.
Then another. And another.

Blaine swore and she realized his fire was getting less bright with each hit. She glanced up at
him and saw water beading his forehead. Her throat
constricted, and she felt sudden fear stab her heart.
"You're really dying?"

"I'm fine," Blaine retorted. "Make the offer. Now!"

She faced Augustus again, ignoring the stars flying
at her face. "Have you heard of Napoleon? World's
greatest assassin?" She felt her tulip creeping down her
chest, and she knew Angelica's soul was moving into
her body.

"*I* own the title of World's Greatest Assassin."

Augustus threw another, and this time, the star glowed brightly before finally dying under Blaine's defenses.

She knew they were almost out of time. "What if you could knock Napoleon out of competition?"

Augustus paused mid-throw. "I'm listening."

"He's right behind you."

Augustus glanced over his shoulder. Napoleon was down on his knees, clutching a melting Angelica in his arms. He was trying to pull the halo off her head, but having no luck. She was telling him what a bastard he was, and he was declaring his love for her. "That's the big, famous man?"

Trinity coughed, and her legs started to go numb. A flash of dizziness sent her stumbling, and Blaine caught her against him. He was damp, leaking water. "You're okay," he said. "I've got you."

She tried to focus. Willed her mind to stay coherent. "Angelica is Napoleon's true love. If she dies, he'll be pissed and go on a killing rampage. You'll never keep pace. But if you dusted her and hid her in your lair, he'd spend the rest of his days trying to get her back. He'd have no time for assassinating. You'd have no competition."

Augustus stood a little taller. "Excellent idea, except for the fact she's dying. My pink stars don't reverse that process."

"I know how to save her." Trinity gasped and lost feel of her legs. Blaine scooped her up and cradled her against his chest, pressing his lips to her temple. She leaned into him, focusing on how good it felt to be held by him again, a gift she'd thought she'd forsaken when she'd walked out on him. "If you free my dad right now, I'll tell you how to save Angelica. But she'll be dead in about thirty seconds, so decide." Trinity coughed again, and her mind was getting so fuzzy. As if it was fading. She leaned her head back against Blaine's chest.

"Hang in there, babe," he whispered. "We're almost there. Stay with me."

"Trying," she mumbled. Getting difficult. The warmth from the tulip felt so good, so warm, calling her toward it.

"Done." Augustus pulled a baggie out of his pocket. "No, not that one." He pulled out another. "No, not that one."

The room began to spin and Trinity fought against the blackness trying to take over her mind. Against the vortex calling to her soul.

Blaine tightened his grip on her. "I'm not letting you go."

She bit her lip, holding his words in her heart. She wanted to stay with this man. "Hurry," she whispered.

"Ah, yes." Augustus unzipped a baggie and dumped the contents out on the floor. He threw a small red disc at the pile. A small puff, an explosion, and suddenly Elijah was lying on the cold stone. His eyes were closed, but his skin was no longer pink, and she could see his chest moving. He was alive.

"Dad!" The room blackened and Trinity was vaguely aware of falling.

"The halo," Blaine snapped. "That's what's killing her. I'll take it off and she's yours. Deal."

Trinity peeled her eyes open long enough to see the halo disappear from Angelica's head, then she felt her consciousness slip away, and she knew they were too late.

Her soul had gotten the boot.

Blaine felt his whole world shudder as Trinity collapsed in his arms. "Trinity." She started to slip out of his grip, his hands too wet to hold on. "Don't you dare leave me!"

Christian was suddenly by his side, helping him lower Trinity safely to the ground. "I've got your back, Trio."

Mari crouched beside him and ignored Christian's lethal glare. "Tell her you love her, Blaine."

"She knows." His legs gave out and he began to slump over. He fought to hold onto her, but he was too weak, too soggy. His chest hurt, he couldn't think. Just felt this overwhelming weight crushing him. The cold floor had never bothered him, but it dug into his knees. The drip of the faucet in the corner was too loud, grating at him. The scent of lavender, getting fainter and fainter as his woman left him. "Dammit, Trinity! Don't you dare!"

"For heaven's sake, have you learned nothing from being here?" Mari shouted. "Don't be a complete ass! Tell her you love her and that you'll be there forever for her. That's all a woman wants, to be loved. Tell her."

Trinity began to glow even more brightly. The iridescence began creeping up her neck, toward her head.

Napoleon howled, and Augustus growled. "She's still dying."

"Mari has a point," Christian said. "All she ever wants is for me to tell her I love her."

"And he never does. That's why I was ready to go with Angelica's plan, until, of course, I saw Trinity almost kill Blaine, and I finally understood the horror of

Angelica's vision." Mari leaned over Trinity. "Tell her now, Blaine, or Angelica's coming back."

Blaine looked down at the woman in his arms, thought of how she'd diverted that ice pick, how she'd bailed on him to save his life. He set his hand on his pocket, and felt the schnoodie claw, the one she'd used to kill him, and he knew he could trust her. "Trinity." He tried to lift her, and Christian helped him bring her against his chest. "I love you," he whispered, his voice hoarse. "By all that's good and pure in life, I love you."

He could have been poetic. Millions of poems and songs of love had been tortured into him. He knew how to woo. Knew the tune to sing. But none of them felt right. Just the three words. "I love you," he whispered.

Trinity stirred in his arms, and the glow suddenly faded.

Napoleon let out a whoop of delight, and Augustus immediately started cackling with glee.

Trinity opened her eyes and laid her hands on his cheeks. When he saw her love shining out of those green eyes of hers, he knew it was Trinity in that body. And not Trinity-the-Black-Widow. Her hair was soft and silky again (yeah, a little tangled, but sexy as hell), and her eyes were that same melt-me green that he'd been lost in that first time they'd met.

"We did it," she whispered.

Blaine couldn't think of anything to say. He just hugged her. And then his watery side took over, and she slipped out of his arms. "Shit."

She sat up quickly as he slithered down to the floor. "Blaine!"

Jarvis came running into the room carrying a flaming

barbecue grill. "I got this from the Basic Male Skills Center. Look out!"

Blaine shoved Trinity back from him as Jarvis up-ended the glowing coals onto him. His skin sizzled, and then his tattoo began to smoke, and then he set himself on fire. He took a breath of relief and sat up.

"And we have ignition." Jarvis tossed the grill aside. "Welcome back, Trio."

Trinity was staring at him with a look of horror. "I really did kill you."

"No." Blaine caught her wrist and yanked her toward him. "No more of this self-revulsion. We'll carry a box of matches around with us. I'm good."

Tears filled her eyes. "You don't blame me?"

"Hell, no." He cupped her face. "It just shows me how much you love me. Nothing less than you turning the curse on me would've convinced me that you love me. Each time I melt, it's a reminder to me that I can trust you."

An icicle suddenly flared in her hands, and he zapped it with a grin. "I love that kind of immediate feedback when I say things that make you get all warm and gooey for me."

"But I'm cursed. I can't even go out into public without worrying that I might kill a man and—"

"Not anymore." He laughed softly and kissed the tears off her cheeks. "The curse won't haunt you anymore. You love me, and you won't love anyone else. Every male in this world is safe from you—" He raised his brows. "Unless you're the type to love more than one guy at a time?"

She shook her head, fragile hope etched onto her face. "No, of course not—"

"Then it's perfect." He pulled her onto his lap. "I'm an emotionally damaged male who has trouble believing in women. Every time I melt, it'll be like an anvil to the head reminding me there's no way I can deny that you love me, and whenever you go all ice pick on me, it's giving me that positive reinforcement that you still love me."

Tears filled her eyes. "So, you're saying that you want me this way?"

"Don't you get it?" He kissed her softly. "This is the only way it would work. I'm way too messed up to be with just anyone. I need the black widow curse, baby, and I need you."

"But what if I kill you when you're asleep?"

He nodded toward the ice particles still shattered on the floor from when she'd jammed the icicle into the wall instead of his eye. "You could have killed me there. Did you?"

She looked back at them, and he saw the moment she acknowledged what she'd done. A slow smile began to spread across her face, and delight danced in her eyes. "I didn't kill you. I stopped myself."

He grinned at the wonder in her voice. "See? You're not so bad, Trinity Harpswell, are you?"

She threw her arms around his neck and hugged him fiercely. "Thank you. For believing in me. For making me believe in myself. For loving me."

"Nah." He hugged her back. How good did it feel to have the woman he loved wrapped around him? Unbelievable. "I didn't do any of it. You did it all yourself simply by being you."

She grinned and pulled back so she could look at him. "I love you, Blaine Underhill."

"And I love you, exactly the way you are." He was just starting to show her exactly what a good kisser he was when he heard Mari sigh.

"Now, that's how it's supposed to be done," Mari said wistfully. "Take lessons, Christian. Blaine's the new head of training the men after that speech."

"Screw that," Christian said. "We're out of here, and this place is over."

"No." Mari's voice was firm. "This place is just beginning, and this time, we're doing it with love, for real. People will truly be happy."

"Let 'em be, Mari." Christian's voice was quiet. "It's time to move on."

And Blaine knew it was. But this time, he wasn't hauling ass to find freedom. For the first time in his life, he was going to run toward someone, and he couldn't wait.

Blaine eased his bike to a stop outside the grand white house with the gleaming lawn.

Clay sculptures adorned the yard and there was a large buffet tucked up next to the rhododendrons. Dozens of people were milling around, admiring the art. Reina was standing next to a life-sized statue of Augustus, arguing with Nigel and Jarvis. She was being animated with her hands, Nigel was laughing, and Jarvis was swinging his sword with a little too much aggravation.

Christian was standing beside them, shoveling food into his mouth from a plate loaded from the buffet. The dude hadn't stopped eating since he'd gotten out of the Den, and he was almost back to his fighting weight already, but there was an edginess about him that Blaine didn't like. Something had happened when Christian had been inside the Den alone, and Christian wasn't talking about what it was.

Blaine felt Trinity's arms tense around his waist, and he set his hand on her thigh and squeezed. "No more fear of crowds anymore, my love."

"I know. Old habit." She kissed the back of his neck. "You ready?"

"Yeah." Blaine killed the engine, kicked the stand into place, then swung his leg over. "You see your dad?" He'd gotten to know the old man on their way back from the Den, and he liked the bugger. How could he not? The man had been willing to give his life for his daughter, and that went a long way in Blaine's book.

Yeah, he was still a little leery about the fact that they'd sent Trinity to the witch, but—

"Blaine! Trinity!" Olivia came running up. She was wearing a beautiful white dress that made her look years younger than when he'd first met her. "I'm so glad you all could come to Dad's first art showing."

Blaine stiffened as she hugged him, and he saw Trinity's mom frown.

"Sorry," he muttered.

"I'll be right back," Olivia said. "I have something for you." She turned and hurried up the massive front steps into the house.

Trinity squeezed his hand. "It's okay, Blaine. We all understand."

"I know." He still felt like a jerk for being unable to accept her mom's love. Still couldn't quite accept that her mom was different than his. Still couldn't quite trust. "At least you still try to kill me on a regular basis."

She smiled. "I can't believe you love me. I'm such a mess."

He grinned, warmth resonating in his chest. "You're perfect. I'm proud to be here with you, even if you disrupt the party by trying to kill me."

"Well, for Dad's sake, I hope I don't." Trinity tucked her arm through his and snuggled close. "I'm so glad that Dad can finally have a show. I never realized he was lying low because he was worried about getting too famous, in case we had to relocate again with a murderous daughter." She leaned her head against Blaine's shoulder. "I never thought I could be happy. It feels so incredibly wonderful to allow myself to feel the joy."

Her eyes were dancing, and he grinned, loving the freedom in her voice. She'd started wearing sexy clothes, and that had done them in. Hadn't left his place in over a week. They'd taken stock in waterproof mattresses to deal with melting icicles, and he'd installed a wood stove in the bedroom that they'd kept going 24/7. It was all good.

Trinity's mom jogged back down the stairs. She was carrying a small wooden box and had a rolled up scroll in her hand. She handed Blaine the paper. "This is for you. I thought you'd like to see it."

Blaine unfolded it and saw it was a scrawled note. Handwritten on yellowed paper. "What is it?"

"When I searching for Trinity during those long six months, I followed every story that referenced Angelica. I was going through my file last night and burning everything now that I don't have to worry about her anymore, and I found this."

Blaine looked down at the paper, and Trinity peered over his shoulder. "It's a flyer," Trinity said. "A wanted poster." She touched the yellowed edges. "It must be over a hundred years old." She fell silent as they read it together.

> Missing: A four-year-old boy. Brown hair, brown eyes, open wound on his right arm. His name is Alexander Blaine Underhill, III. Answers only to the name Blaine. Large reward for any information as to his whereabouts. Please contact Marissa Underhill or the Order of the Red Swords with information.

Blaine's throat tightened as Trinity's arm went around his waist. He swallowed, then crumbled it and tossed it aside. "Too little too late."

"The Order of the Red Swords was a deadly underground organization designed to help persecuted Otherworld beings disappear, and some say they still exist," Olivia said. "They were well known to be cutthroat, and extremely expensive. Your mother must have paid them an exorbitant amount of money to get them to help."

"We didn't have money."

Trinity's mom opened the box and began riffling through the papers. "The founder of the organization was the son of a woman who had nearly died trying to protect him from his dad, who she later killed to save the boy. The searchers had a special fondness for widows who had suffered to protect their children from their men."

Blaine stiffened. "My mom wasn't a widow, and she didn't do anything to protect me against my dad—"

Olivia set another paper in his hand. "Here's one from two years later."

His fingers starting to shake, Blaine scanned the words.

> Missing: A six-year-old boy. Brown hair, brown eyes, probably a large scar on his right arm. His name is Alexander Blaine Underhill, III. Answers only to the name Blaine. Large reward for any information as to his whereabouts. Please contact Marissa Underhill or the Order of the Red Swords with information.

"And another." She set a crinkled one in his hand.

> Missing: A seven-year-old boy. Brown hair, brown eyes, probably a large scar on his right arm. His name is Alexander Blaine Underhill, III. Answers only to the name Blaine. Large reward for any information as to his whereabouts. Please contact Marissa Underhill or the Order of the Red Swords with information.

"These are just a few of the hundreds I found." She dumped a pile in his hands. "They came out every year, every day. The oldest one I found had you listed as sixty-five years old, and the date on it was the same year as I found an obituary for Marissa Underhill." She set it in his hand. "Here."

Numbly Blaine shoved it back at Olivia. "No—"

"I'll read it." Trinity took it from his hands. "Marissa Joan Underhill died October 7, 1909, in a cave in the Upper Falls, a tunnel rumored to be a portal to the lair of Death's grandma." Trinity took Blaine's hand, and he gripped it, hanging on desperately as he listened to her quiet voice reading to him.

"Marissa Joan leaves behind a son, Wesley Maxwell, who disappeared at age twenty after following a lead as to the possible whereabouts of his missing brother, Alexander Blaine III. Mother and son dedicated their lives to finding Blaine after the suspicious death of father and husband Alexander Blaine Underhill, Jr. in 1851. Many believe young Marissa killed her husband as payback for harm done to young Blaine, but no charges were ever filed." Trinity folded the letter. "Rumors of Wesley still being alive surface periodically, though none have been confirmed," she finished.

Blaine felt his throat tighten as he stared blankly across the yard. It was difficult to breathe. His skin felt hot. His clothes felt itchy. And his scar burned like hell.

Trinity wrapped her arms around his waist and pressed her face to his chest. He crushed her against him and buried his face in her hair, letting the scent of lavender fill him. His mother had searched for him. Wes had hunted for him. For their entire lives. Just as he'd dreamed. "She killed him," he whispered hoarsely. "I know she killed my dad. He was a bastard." Suddenly, memories flooded him, of the screaming fights between his parents in the weeks leading up to Angelica's appearance. Of his mother keeping him so close every day, never letting him out of her sight. Of the tears in her eyes that night when she'd told him to always remember she loved him, no matter what his dad did.

He hadn't. He hadn't remembered at all. Not until now.

Trinity looked up at him. "You know how to trust

now," she said. "Let yourself love her. It's okay. You're safe now."

He shook his head and fisted her hair. His chest was so heavy, his throat tight, his muscles aching. "I can't—"

Trinity's mom set her hand on his shoulder. "My dear boy," she said quietly. "You have a family now. It's time to release old wounds and let us all in. We might not be able to prove our love by trying to kill you on a regular basis, but at some point, you've got to stop having that as a requirement to trusting."

Blaine fisted the papers and fought against the swell of emotion. Against an eternity of loneliness, isolation, and betrayal. He hugged Trinity tighter, needing to feel her body against his, to feel the love he knew he could believe in.

Across the lawn, Elijah caught his eye and waved at him. He gave Blaine a thumbs up and a fist pump, then spread his arms wide to indicate the spread of sculptures and all the people attending and then ended by pointing right at Trinity and her mom. "Thank you," he shouted.

Blaine saw the pride and joy in the older man's face, the intense passion for life, for his art, and for his family. A man who was willing to give it all up for a daughter he'd made a mistake with.

"Thank you, Mom, for sharing that with Blaine." Trinity released Blaine and threw her arms around Olivia and hugged her. There was pure love between them. Total forgiveness for the mistakes of the past, and true love for who they were. Trinity had forgiven. And she had love.

The two women in his life opened the hug and held their arms out to him in a silent invitation.

Yeah, it was time.

Blaine shoved the papers in his pocket, and then he walked into their embrace.

He was home.

Acknowledgments

THANK YOU TO MY TIRELESS AND BRILLIANT AGENT, Deidre Knight, for all her support and guidance. I appreciate you so much. Thank you also to my editor Deb Werksman, for her enthusiasm, guidance, and vision. Pierce Harman, for sharing his insight and passion on motorcycles. Officers Bob Paglia and David Webb of the Newton Police Department for their expertise on stun guns and tasers. Any mistakes are mine, and only mine. Thank you also to my family, without whom this book never would have been written.

About the Author

Nationally bestselling author and four-time RITA®
Award nominee **Stephanie Rowe** is the author of more
than twenty books. She resides in New England with her
family and a very large cat.

WARRIOR

BY CHERYL BROOKS

*"He came to me in the dead of winter,
his body burning with fever."*

EVEN NEAR DEATH, HIS SENSUALITY IS AMAZING…

Leo arrives on Tisana's doorstep a beaten slave from a near extinct race with feline genes. As soon as Leo recovers his strength, he'll use his extraordinary sexual talents to bewitch Tisana and make a bolt for freedom…

PRAISE FOR THE CAT STAR CHRONICLES:

"A compelling tale of danger, intrigue, and sizzling romance!"
  —Candace Havens, author of *Charmed & Deadly*

"Hot enough to start a fire. Add in a thrilling new world and my reading experience was complete."
  —*Romance Junkies*

978-1-4022-1440-0 • $6.99 U.S. / $7.99 CAN

SLAVE

BY CHERYL BROOKS

><><><><><><><><><><><><><><><><><><><><><><><><><><><><><><><

"I found him in the slave market on Orpheseus Prime, and even on such a god-forsaken planet as that one, their treatment of him seemed extreme."

><><><><><><><><><><><><><><><><><><><><><><><><><><><><><><><

Cat may be the last of a species whose sexual talents were the envy of the galaxy. Even filthy, chained, and beaten, his feline gene gives him a special aura.

Jacinth is on a rescue mission… and she needs a man she can trust with her life.

PRAISE FOR CHERYL BROOKS'S *SLAVE*:

"A sexy adventure with a hero you can't resist!"

> —Candace Havens, author of *Charmed & Deadly*

"Fascinating world customs, a bit of mystery, and the relationship between the hero and heroine make this a very sensual romance."

> —*Romantic Times*

978-1-4022-1192-8 • $6.99 U.S. / $8.99 CAN

OUTCAST

BY CHERYL BROOKS

Sold into slavery in a harem, Lynx is a favorite because his feline gene gives him remarkable sexual powers. But after ten years, Lynx is exhausted and is thrown out of the harem without a penny. Then he meets Bonnie, who's determined not to let such a beautiful and sensual young man go to waste...

"Leaves the reader eager for the next story featuring these captivating aliens." —*Romantic Times*

"One of the sweetest love stories...one of the hottest heroes ever conceived and...one of the most exciting and adventurous quests that I have ever had the pleasure of reading." —*Single Titles*

"One of the most sensually imaginative books that I've ever read... A magical story of hope, love and devotion" —*Yankee Romance Reviews*

978-1-4022-1896-5 • $6.99 U.S. / $7.99 CAN

ROGUE

BY CHERYL BROOKS

Tychar crawled toward me on his hands and knees like a tiger stalking his prey. "I, for one, am glad you came," he purred. "And I promise you, Kyra, you will never want to leave Darconia."

"Cheryl Brooks knows how to keep the heat on and the reader turning pages!"

—Sydney Croft, author of *Seduced by the Storm*

978-1-4022-1762-3 • $7.99 U.S. / $9.99 CAN

FUGITIVE

by Cheryl Brooks

"Really sexy. Sizzling kind of sexy...makes you want to melt in the process." —*Bitten by Books*

A mysterious stranger in danger...

Zetithian warrior Manx, a member of a race hunted to near extinction because of their sexual powers, has done all he can to avoid extermination. But when an uncommon woman enters his jungle lair, the animal inside of him demands he risk it all to have her.

The last thing Drusilla expected to find on vacation was a gorgeous man hiding in the jungle. But what is he running from? And why does she feel so mesmerized that she'll stop at nothing to be near him? Hypnotically attracted, their intense pleasure in each other could destroy them both.

PRAISE FOR THE CAT STAR CHRONICLES:

"Wow. The romantic chemistry is as close to perfect as you'll find." —*BookFetish.org*

"Fabulous off world adventures... Hold on ladies, hot Zetithians are on their way." —*Night Owl Romance*

"Insanely creative... I enjoy this author's voice immensely." —*The Ginger Kids Den of Iniquity*

"I think purring will be on my request list from now on." — *Romance Reader at Heart*

978-1-4022-2940-4 • $6.99 U.S. / $8.99 CAN / £3.99 UK

Hex Appeal

BY LINDA WISDOM

"Kudos to Linda Wisdom for a series that's pure magic!"

—Vicki Lewis Thompson,
New York Times bestselling author of *Wild & Hexy*

JAZZ AND NICK'S DREAM ROMANCE HAS TURNED INTO A NIGHTMARE…

FEISTY WITCH JASMINE TREMAINE AND DROP-DEAD GORGEOUS vampire cop Nikolai Gregorivich have a hot thing going, but it's tough to keep it together when nightmare visions turn their passion into bickering.

With a little help from their friends, Nick and Jazz are in a race against time to uncover whoever it is that's poisoning their dreams, and their relationship…

978-1-4022-1400-4 • $6.99 U.S. / $7.99 CAN

Wicked by Any Other Name

BY LINDA WISDOM

"Do not miss this wickedly entertaining treat."

—Annette Blair,
Sex and the Psychic Witch

STASI ROMANOV USES A LITTLE WITCH MAGIC IN HER LINGERIE shop, running a brisk side business in love charms. A disgruntled customer threatening to sue over a failed spell brings wizard attorney Trevor Barnes to town—and witches and wizards make a volatile combination. The sparks fly, almost everyone's getting singed, and the whole town seems on the verge of a witch hunt.

Can the feisty witch and the gorgeous wizard overcome their objections and settle out of court—and in the bedroom?

978-1-4022-1773-9 • $6.99 U.S. / $7.99 CAN

Hex in High Heels

BY LINDA WISDOM

Can a Witch and a Were find happiness?

Feisty witch Blair Fitzpatrick has had a crush on hunky carpenter Jake Harrison forever—he's one hot shape-shifter. But Jake's nasty mother and brother are after him to return to his pack, and Blair is trying hard not to unleash the ultimate revenge spell. When Jake's enemies try to force him away from her, Blair is pushed over the edge. No one messes with her boyfriend-to-be, even if he does shed on the furniture!

Praise for Linda Wisdom's Hex series:

"Fan-fave Wisdom… continues to delight."
—*Romantic Times*

"Highly entertaining, sexy, and imaginative."
—*Star Crossed Romance*

"It's a five star, feel-good ride!" —*Crave More Romance*

"Something fresh and new."
—*Paranormal Romance Review*

978-1-4022-1895-8 • $6.99 U.S. / $8.99 CAN

50 Ways to Hex Your Lover

BY LINDA WISDOM

"A magical page-turner...had me bewitched from the start!"

—Yasmine Galenorn,
USA Today bestselling author of *Witchling*

JAZZ CAN'T DECIDE WHETHER TO SCORCH HIM WITH A FIREBALL OR JUMP INTO BED WITH HIM

Jasmine Tremaine is a witch who can't stay out of trouble. Nikolai Gregorivich is a vampire cop on the trail of a serial killer. Their sizzling love affair has been on-again, off-again for about 300 years—mostly off, lately.

But now Nick needs Jazz's help to steer clear of a maniacal killer with supernatural powers, while they try to finally figure out their own hearts.

978-1-4022-1085-3 • $6.99 U.S. / $8.99 CAN

DESTINY *of the* WOLF

BY TERRY SPEAR

Praise for Terry Spear's *Heart of the Wolf:*

"The chemistry crackles off the page."
—*Publisher's Weekly*

"The characters are well drawn and believable,
which makes the contemporary plotline of love and life
among the lupus garou seem, well, realistic." —*Romantic Times*

"Full of action, adventure, suspense, and romance... one of
the best werewolf stories
I've read!" —*Fallen Angel Reviews*

ALL SHE WANTS IS THE TRUTH

Lelandi is determined to discover the truth about her beloved
sister's mysterious death. But everyone thinks she's making a
bid for her sister's widowed mate...

HE'S A PACK LEADER TORMENTED BY MEMORIES

Darien finds himself bewitched by Lelandi, and when someone
attempts to silence her, he realizes that protecting the beautiful
stranger may be the only way to protect his pack...and himself...

978-1-4022-1668-8 • $7.99 U.S. / $9.99 CAN

Heart of the Wolf

BY TERRY SPEAR

A *Publisher's Weekly* Best Book of the Year

"A fast-paced, sexy read with lots of twists and turns!" —Nicole North, author of *Devil in a Kilt*

"Red werewolf Bella flees her adoptive pack of gray werewolves when the alpha male Volan tries forcibly to claim her as his mate. Her real love, beta male Devlyn, is willing to fight Volan to the death to claim her. That problem pales, however, as a pack of red werewolves takes to killing human females in a crazed quest to claim Bella for their own. Bella and Devlyn must defeat the rogue wolves before Devlyn's final confrontation with Volan. The vulpine couple's chemistry crackles off the page, but the real strength of the book lies in Spear's depiction of pack power dynamics... her wolf world feels at once palpable and even plausible."
—*Publisher's Weekly*

978-1-4022-1157-7 • $6.99 U.S. / $8.99 CAN

To TEMPT the WOLF

by TERRY SPEAR

"This dark, sexy alpha hero will capture you—body, mind and soul." —Nicole North, author *Devil in a Kilt*

HE'S VOWED TO PROTECT HER—ESPECIALLY FROM HIMSELF

Tessa Anderson is obsessed with wolves, but she doesn't understand why wolves seem to be fascinated by her, and she certainly doesn't know that werewolves exist. Now she's being stalked—but is her stalker wolf or man? And who is the gorgeous stranger whose life she saved, who now swears he'll protect her?

Hunter Greymore is an Alpha without a pack, facing a deadly enemy. When he encounters Tessa, he's alone and injured, but in his attempts to shield her from harm, Hunter discovers that Tessa entices him beyond endurance—and it's only a matter of time before his wild nature can no longer be restrained.

"Terry Spear weaves paranormal, suspense, and romance together in one non-stop rollercoaster of passion and adventure."

—LOVE ROMANCE PASSION

"Enchanting romance with a unique twist!… The characters were so well developed and the writing so superior that it felt real to me, my reactions were as if I was a part of the story."

—THE ROMANCE STUDIO

"A fast-moving read with a sizzling romance and danger-filled action that keeps readers engaged to the end." —DARQUE REVIEWS

978-1-4022-1904-7 · $7.99 U.S. / $9.99 CAN / £4.99 UK

LEGEND
of the
WHITE WOLF
BY TERRY SPEAR

"A steamy, action-packed romance set within a complex
and deadly werewolf society. This delicious alpha hero
will leave you wild for more." —Nicole North, author
Devil in a Kilt

IN A WORLD OF SNOW AND ICE, THEIR PASSIONS BLAZE

Private Detective Cameron MacPherson arrives in the icy
wilderness of Maine in search of his lost partners, who
mysteriously disappeared on a hunting trip. Faith O'Malley joins
Cameron on his quest, hoping to find her father's stolen research
and discover just what he saw in that same region so many years
ago—a sight that would lead him to lose all touch with reality.
With or without Cameron, she won't be stopped. But in the wilds
of the icy world around them, they encounter a mythical creature
whose bite changes everything...

---

*"Action-packed romance and suspense-filled plot add up to pure magic.
I couldn't turn the pages fast enough. Terry Spear is a great addition
to the paranormal genre!"*
—ARMCHAIR INTERVIEWS

*"I love Ms. Spear's lupus garou society. She creates a world that makes
you believe werewolves live among us."*
—PARANORMAL ROMANCE REVIEWS

"Tantalizing, action-packed romance... with all the magic of fantasy."
—THE PEN & MUSE

978-1-4022-1905-4 • $6.99 U.S. / $8.99 CAN / £3.99 UK

Strange Neighbors

by Ashlyn Chase

HE'S LOOKING FOR PEACE, QUIET, AND A MAYBE LITTLE ROMANCE...

Hunky all-star pitcher and shapeshifter Jason Falco invests in an old Boston brownstone apartment building full of supernatural creatures, and there's never a dull moment. But when Merry McKenzie moves into the ground floor apartment, the playboy pitcher decides he might just be done playing the field...

What readers say about Ashlyn Chase

"Entertaining and humorous—a winner!"

"The humor and romance kept me entertained— a definite page turner!"

"Sexy, funny stories!"

978-1-4022-3661-7 • $6.99 U.S./$8.99 CAN/£3.99 UK

The Werewolf Upstairs

by Ashlyn Chase

She should know better...

Attorney Roz Wells is bored. She used to have such a knack for attracting the weird and unexpected, but ever since she took a job as a Boston Public defender the quirky quotient in her life has taken a serious hit. Until her sexy werewolf neighbor starts coming around...

Roz knows she should stay away from this sexy bad boy, but she can't help it that she's putty in his hands...

———∿∿∿———

What readers say about Ashlyn Chase

"Entertaining and humorous—a winner!"

*"The humor and romance kept me entertained—
a definite page turner!"*

"Sexy, funny stories!"

978-1-4022-3662-4 • $6.99 U.S./$8.99 CAN/£4.99 UK

DEMONS
ARE A
GIRL'S BEST FRIEND
BY LINDA WISDOM

A BEWITCHING WOMAN ON A MISSION...

Feisty witch Maggie enjoys her work as a paranormal law enforcement officer—that is, until she's assigned to protect a teenager with major attitude and plenty of Mayan enemies. Maggie's never going to survive this assignment without the help of a half-fire demon who makes her smolder...

Praise for Linda Wisdom

"Hot talent Wisdom does a truly wonderful job mixing passion, danger, and outrageous antics into a tasty blend that's sure to satisfy."
—RT Book Reviews

"Entertaining and sexy... Ms. Wisdom's stories have something for everyone." —Night Owl

"Wickedly captivating... wildly entertaining... full of magical zest and unrivaled witty prose."
—Suite 101

978-1-4022-5439-0 • $7.99 U.S./£4.99 UK